Sisters Destiny

By

DAVID ZALTANA

Table of Contents

CHAPTER 1
2036

Times of The Beasts

KNOCK KNOCK KNOCK KNOCK
Maybe it's Dad. Finally back home from his long vacation. "I wonder who that can be so early, oh no…" Mom said.

One look at Mom, and I knew it wasn't him.

"Who is it?"

"Orders of S.I.L.O! This home has been charged with safety negligence!"

"Girls, finish your breakfast and go upstairs."

I can already see she was about to cry, I felt it too.

"Go, Munisha. Lakia, watch your sisters, okay?"

KNOCK KNOCK KNOCK

"It's going to be okay," my older sister, Lakia insisted as she pulled me upstairs.

"Lakia, what are they going to do to Mom?"

"I'm not sure, but we're going to be okay, I promise. Finish eating. You too, Zaraiella."

"I think it's the people who came before. Mom told us to do the same thing."

"I told you already. It's going to be okay," Lakia said.

My youngest sister, Zaraiella, had no clue what was happening either. They came twice already, now I remember.

"Are you okay, Zaraiella? Always so quiet. Munisha, keep Zaraiella calm. I'm going to see what is happening".

"It's okay, Zaraiella. She'll be right back."

Her little hand in mines seemed so small, but we were only four years apart. I was turning thirteen the following month, Zaraiella eight, and Lakia seventeen. I just wish Dad would come back. Me and Lakia miss him.

"Put on some clothes. We are leaving. Mom is downstairs with those people, and they told her we must leave."

"What, why?!" I pouted.

"Munisha, just put something warm on and get Zaraiella's doll. She won't stop crying without it."

"But I don't want us to go, Lakia. Those people are bad. Lakia, Lakia?"

Lakia walked away, rolling her eyes as if I was the one that made them show up.

"Didn't you just hear your sister, Munisha?! We have to leave right now! Zaraiella, baby. Let me find you something. This just isn't right. Just not right," Mom hissed, yanking the dressers open.

"Mom. Can you at least tell us what is going on?" Lakia asked.

"Nothing Lakia, just…just get ready, please."

I knew there was something wrong. Mom never really made a frown.

"Here, a jacket for you and something for Zaraiella."

"Mom, what's happening?" I asked.

"The people who always come"

"Yea, Mom. This is the third time, and we didn't do anything bad. Why are they here?"

"Oh, Munisha, you are so smart, but you must be strong, okay? These people say we need to take something to become like everyone else. We don't want this, but our time has come. Once this is all over, we will be back, so don't worry yourself," Mom said as her teardrop fell to the floor, but a smile reassured me. Mom, do you think Ra".

"Lakia, lower your voice. You can help me grab something warm for, Zaraiella, and I will change from this robe. They want us outside in ten minutes."

"Do you need help finding something, Munsiha?" Lakia asked, throwing around our clothes from the filled drawers. "Stop worrying. We will be okay, and Mom said we have to go now."

Knowing I didn't care to put on something warm as almost all the days were nippy in Maine.

"Remember, everything is going to be fine," Lakia shrugged.

I nodded and got dressed. Why do they need to keep coming to bother us? We did nothing wrong.

Mom smiled, "Ready, you all? We're going to be back in no time."

As we walked down the stairs, the men wearing black clothes and shiny helmets stared at us. They even had long guns on their hips.

"Be sure, mam, you have paperwork with your children's blood type and birth certificate files. Also, be sure your family follows orders as well." The soldier said, though I couldn't tell who was speaking since their faces were covered.

"No father?" the first soldier asked.

"...He's not here, and he lives somewhere else now. Come, Zaraiella, Mom mom cover your head. It's breezy and colder than yesterday."

"Please fill out these files once you enter the van. This will give the management and supervisor team everything they need to know about you all."

Climbing inside the van that was almost as long as a school bus, it felt so weird. We were better off sitting on the floor from how hard the seats were. "Sit by me, Lakia. Mom and Zaraiella can be together. There are so many people in here."

"They're going to go where we are. They seem calm, right?"

"I mean, I guess," I shrugged.

"So, let's play your favorite game. I need to get my mind off things."

"Whatever, you know I always win. Mom needs to get me a phone too."

"Munisha, come sit with me."

"No Zaraiella, stay with Mom. She has her doll, so she's okay."

"Mom isn't happy at all," Lakia whispered. "The look on her face says it all."

"I know, she was just crying. We're not going to come back home, are we? The people here are not happy. I can feel it."

The weird feeling of our house moving farther and farther away from us. Home sickness. "Mom said everything will be okay. I'm not going to cry, are you?"

"I will if we get separated. I don't think we will. We are supposed to get an…insertion, I heard, and then we can come back home. That's all. When Daddy went to get his, that was the last time I heard from him."

"Lakia, whatever happened to Dad? Mom said vacation. It's been too long. Where?"

Lakia shook her shoulders as she moved the red checker piece. "If I known, I would have told you. It's been almost a year, I think. You still remember him, right"

"Of course I do, it's been only a year. He was tall and smelled like pepper."

Lakia laughed. "That's all you remember? What about…never mind. I win! Want to play again?"

"He didn't even come to see if I was okay at the hospital."

"Try not to overwhelm yourself, Munisha. Just stay positive."

Lakia, I knew she was so scared, just pretended so well.

"How are you all doing over there?" Mom asked smiling.

She always made things feel like they were okay just with that smile.

"We're fine, Mom. Munisha and I are just here."

"Well, your little sister here is knocked out. I told you she wouldn't need this doll."

Mom seemed happier, though a strange feeling started to rise.

"Zaraiella is doing what I should be doing. I was up all night doing homework, and there was no point in doing it. When you get stupid math like mine, Munisha, you will get no sleep."

BEEP…BEEP…BEEP

I grinned. "You're so scary."

"It's so loud. We have been riding for a good twenty minutes now."

"Attention, passengers, we are five minutes to our destination. Gather all belongings and documents filled. Thank you."

I took Lakia's hand, and I could tell our hearts were beating fast. "Do you think we will get a shot? I hate needles."

"Who doesn't? I had to get three when I was seven or eight, and it wasn't that bad. Mom said it started with a V. You win again, sis. What's going on with me today?"

"Maybe because you're a little scared and can't really concentrate."

The creeps had air conditioning in the van instead of the heater. I should have brought a better jacket instead of a long sleeve shirt.

* * * *

"Zaraiella, Zarariella baby, wake up. We're almost there. You're getting big, so I can't carry you all the way, okay, sweetie?"

"I dreamed, Mommy," Zaraiella murmured while rubbing her eyes.

"You always dream, baby. Now, be sure you keep your toy with you, we don't want Mr. Blue to get lost, do we?"

Mom's face still didn't change. She eyed us and then turned to look out the window.

"Munisha, look how big it is!" Lakia said.

"Wow. It looks like nothing but glass."

The huge building looked like a mirror standing a hundred feet tall. What kind of place was this?

"This is it!" Someone blurted behind us.

"Sit down in your seat!"

"Or what?"

He must have been crazy. These people had guns.

"To mind you all, I have the authorization to execute any who doesn't follow orders."

I wanted to go home.

"Mommy, look at the pretty place."

"Yes, Zaraiella. It's…beautiful."

"I will call every individual family according to the last name first. You will get up and depart this vehicle to be accompanied by S.I.L.O team supervisors…The Anderson family!"

"Your hands are getting sweaty and shaky, sis."

"Yea, I'm a little nervous," Lakia frowned as she wiped her hands on the back of a seat.

"I thought you said everything was going to be all right."

"Mom…Mom."

"Quiet, Lakia. Listen to the person speaking up front."

"But Mom, there's"

"Shoosh, stay calm and relax," Mom said with a serious face.

"What happened, Lakia?"

Lakia looked like she had just seen a ghost.

"Don't look out the window," Lakia whispered. "Why didn't you wear long pants, Munisha? Guess I am so traumatized I am just noticing that."

"Because I didn't feel like it, oh wow. A man was just pushed to the floor by one of those soldiers wearing the same black clothes."

"Didn't I tell you not to look?" Lakia semi-whispered as she continued to look to the floor.

"Why did they push him on the ground like that?"

"He probably did something stupid," Lakia said.

"This is kind of scary. We shouldn't be here."

"See, I'm not a bad person, so they wouldn't do that to me," Lakia grinned. "You better behave."

"Hmph, I'm not bad. I just like to have fun."

"Remember when you threw the rock at Mom's window, and we both were grounded for it?"

"Yea, it wasn't on purpose, though. Dad never hit me. Tsk, he should be here with us."

"I just thought of it. Why didn't you wear long pants, Munisha?" Mom asked. "I can't believe I let you come out of the house like that."

"I'm okay, Mom, I promise."

"The Lozano family!"

"Okay, girls. Stay close to me and hold hands," Moms soft voice comforted.

I should have told her the creepy driver winked at me.

"Be sure to follow directions and remember your family will be well protected."

"Yes sir," Mom says then looks at us. "No one to release anyone's hand, do I make myself clear?"

"Yes, Mom," Me and Lakia said together, looking up at the tall building.

The different lines of people made it look like we were in school.

"I bet you can't tell how tall it is, sis." Lakia said as we both looked up at the building made of glass.

I knew she didn't care about how tall it was. Now she was scaring me. "Mmm, it's probably a thousand feet tall."

"No, that's too tall. I wish we could go to the top, though. I want to see everything. We can probably see our house from up there."

"Let's sneak and go." I smiled.

"I knew you would want to do that and end up like that guy earlier. Munisha, the bad girl."

I grinned. "You're the one who said it, Lakia. Mom, when are we leaving? Will we be here all day?"

The way it seemed, there was no way we would be leaving. It didn't even look like the lines were moving.

"Munisha…I know you can see plenty of people in front of us. We will be here for a good while. Play with Lakia's phone like earlier if needs to be."

"Yea…we will probably be here until night," Lakia says looking around at all the talking and yelling.

Men and women holding signs behind the fence. They seemed very angry. "Lakia, can you see what that says?" I asked, squinting my eyes.

"What? There are already too many things going on as it is."

The people behind the fence were like the dogs that would bark at Zaraiella and me walking home from school. "The people by the fence, they are holding a sign, no…no, injections, no…shots. No, control."

"They are afraid of needles, that's all. Aren't they, Mom?"

"Stop squeezing my hand, Lakia. Your hand hurts." I said, trying to loosen them.

"Don't worry, girls, the faster we get this done, the faster we can get home."

My heart beating faster as the crowd became louder. Some even looked scared. Why did they need to make people do something like this?

"Get back in line!" A soldier commanded a man across from us.

"Look, Lakia, they're trying to leave!"

"I said get back in line!"

"You can't make us do this! It's against our rights!"

"Your rights belong to System In Lives Omniscient now. If you all don't get back in line, I will be authorized to use force."

"I don't like S.I.L.O, Lakia," I mumbled.

"I never liked them. Mom."

BLINK

Now I know they're really mad. Only if the soldier knew who threw it.

"Do not throw bottles, or you will be taken in!"

"LET THE PEOPLE HAVE A CHOICE!" Another man yelled out behind the fence.

"They're women and children in there, and you all are just going to take someone's rights away?! THIS IS INJUSTICE!"

"Sir, I will not tell you twice, go home. Back away from the fence!"

"I'm not going anywhere. Those are my people being injected with something you all probably don't have. This isn't right!"

"Stop shaking the fence, or you will be shot! Last warning!"

"Mom..."

"Lakia, it's going to be fine. Let's just get this over with. Just...think of peace."

"Hey, don't touch me! You're not a damn cop!"

"Sir, remove yourself from this area, or you will be removed by force!"

Blinck

"There goes another bottle." Lakia said, looking at me with worried eyes.

The S.I.L.O soldier pointed his gun at the man. He must have been the one who threw the bottle.

"What are you doing, Munisha? Mom said don't look at them," Lakia said.

"It's scary, sis. There are people who just got hurt."

"Yea, they're not following directions. Munisha, whatever happens, do not let go of your sister's hand. Same thing for you, Lakia."

Once we go inside, a fight might start in there.

"Munisha, look, it looks like a hospital," Lakia pointed as the door closed slowly behind a family. "It's not a dungeon like we thought."

The white inside the shiny place made it look so clean. Mom's walls didn't stand a chance.

"See, we're going to be fine like Mom said. It's like when we go to the doctor, that's all."

"Lakia, when we go back home, can you teach me how to tie your hair like yours?" I said as I pulled it.

Lakia, especially Zaraiella, had the best hair in the family. Just never told them.

"You have to grow this much first unless I cut some off and give it to you. You know that's not going to happen, right?"

"Yea but I am trying to grow"

BANG BANG BANG

"Oh my god, they're shooting. Stay close behind me, girls."

"WAAAaaaaa "

"It's okay, Zaraiella, it's okay. Calm down for mommy. Here Lakia, hold my purse."

BANG BANG

"Mom, it's getting crazy."

"Yes, Lakia, I know."

"EYYYYGHH!"

People screaming from different lines. We all just looked lost and trapped inside the gates. "Mom, people are going crazy."

"She's right Ma, where should we go?!" Lakia asked. "It's frightening."

"It's nothing we can do. Just…stay calm."

Mom nodding her head slowly with her teary eyes closed just made it so miserable. How could she be so calm from all the things going on? "Lakia, oh my gosh. Is he dead?"

"Mom, me and Munisha are frightened. We have no choice but to leave."

"We can't! Just, stay close to me."

"But, Mom." Lakia whined.

"Stay close to me and your sister, Lakia. Zaraiella, all is well."

"Lakia, that soldier just punched the man over there."

The soldiers were more than mean. Somehow it felt like they were doing anything they wanted.

"WE'RE NOT GOING IN. WE'RE NOT GOING IN!"

People yelling behind fence even made it hard to hear my family right in front of me.

"Excuse me. You just bumped into us," Mom said looking into the man eyes that were coming out of his head.

"Sorry, mam. My advice for you and your family is to run and make it out if you can. These people are trying"

"Sir, sir, please. My family is already petrified of what's going on. Please don't make it worse."

"Hmph, good luck. I'm getting out of here!"

"Listen, girls, if we get a chance to leave, then we will," Mom said. She stayed looking straight at the building.

BEEEEEEP

"ATTENTION CITIZENS, THIS PROXIMITY IS HEAVILY GUARDED WITH STAFF. STAY IN A SINGLE FILE AND FOLLOW LAW ATTENDANT ORDERS. THOSE WHO DO NOT COMPLY WILL BE PROSECUTED."

Gosh, that thing I swear almost made me deaf.

"Munisha, the gate is open. Mom, we can leave!" Lakia blurted in Mom's ear.

"Everyone…just stay calm and don't do anything stupid. Follow what they have to say."

"It's against our rights, like the guy said," Lakia murmured. "We can't do this!"

"Yes, it's against our rights," Mom continued staring at the building.

"Lakia, he has a gun, he has a gun," I mumbled with my hand on my mouth.

BANG BANG

"Oh god, they're killing nonstop! Stay close to me."

I can't see Mom. "Eygh! Lakia, where did you go? LAKIA! Mom, where are you?!"

"Run, little girl, run!" A man yelled, holding his son's hand.

"I can't. I'm looking for my family."

BEEEEEP

"ALL PERSONNEL. NO ONE IS TO LEAVE THIS DESIGNATED AREA OF THE PREMISES."

"Stay put, or we will open fire!" A soldier shouted, pointing his rifle at a group of people.

"You can't pull the trigger! There are innocent women and children here! You all are nothing but crappy bullies!"

"They're trying to keep us here!" Another man added. "This is more than just a vaccine they're giving us!"

The fence is too high. I can't climb over. "Mom, Lakia! MOOOM! Where are they?!"

Nothing I could see but people's pants and shirts. Being tall was the only way out of this mess.

"EVERYBODY RUN!"

"WAAAah. WAAGHH"

"Zaraiella, Zaraiella! Where are you? Move!"

There were so many people. "I have to find my baby sister!"

"WAAYEEH"

"Zaraiella! Zaraiella! Oh no, you're not Zaraiella!" She looked nothing like my sister but had the same scream.

"Where is your family, sweetheart?" A woman asked. "Come with us."

"No, no, I have to find my sisters. Let me go!"

BANG BANG BANG

"Oh my gosh! Lakia, Mom! Wait. Zaraiella? I SEE YOU! STOP, YOU HAVE MY SISTER! STOP! Zaraiella, I'm coming!"

I didn't know how someone took my little sister. How did Mom lose her? "Zaraiellaaa! Hey, what are you doing with my sister?! She doesn't belong with you she doesn't belong with you!"

"I'm sorry, I'm sorry. She was all alone, and my husband and I wanted to help. Come with us, and we will take care of you, okay?"

"No, my sister and I have to take care of us and find my mom and other sister.

"Let's go, Veronica, she has a family already."

BANG BANG BANG BANG

"Okay, Zaraiella, we're going to find Mom and Lakia."

"Mom and Lakia are over there," Zaraiella said with dried tears on her face.

"Yes, I know, but it's not safe to go back inside."

"Hey, you two!" A Soldier shouted, walking towards us.

"Oh no, come on Zaraiella. The bad people are coming."

"You two, STOP!"

"Don't cry, Zaraiella, we'll find Mom. Look, people ran in the forest. We can follow them." Still no sign of my other sister or Mom, but the forest could have been a good place to hide.

"It's scary here, Munisha."

"It's okay, Zaraiella. Just keep going!"

There was so much water, it looked like our neighbors dirty swimming pool. "Oh gosh, this water is cold. Here, I'll try and carry you to the other side."

I hope there weren't anything in this dirty green, brownish water.

"Where's…where's Mommy?"

"Sssshhh."

"I want Mommy!"

"Zaraiella," I said, finally being able to let her off my back. "They're coming, okay. What are you pointing at? I don't see anyone, oh, your doll. I'll go get it."

This sister of mine should have left this thing at home. It was like another person I have to watch over.

"You there! Out of the water now!"

"Okay, okay. My sister and I are alone. We just want to be safe."

"Yes, and you will come with me. You will be under the best supervision AUGH!"

"Ruuuunn! Get out of here! Their coming!" A man shouted after tackling the soldier.

"I got your doll, Zaraiella. We have to go. Now it's starting to rain."

BANG BANG BANG

All the shooting. Only movies was where I saw what just happened. "There's a tree that has a hole in it. We have to stop in there."

"There are bugs in here, Munisha."

"Yea, the icky bugs won't hurt us. Just…no spiders. Be quite okay. They won't find us in here."

CHAPTER 2

Safe Zone

I still could not believe what I had seen. Nothing has ever happened like this before. Why did those soldiers kill people? It only looked like everybody wanted to go home. That was all we wanted. I didn't even notice my watch glass was cracked. "It's been an hour, I think, Zaraiella. They made me break the watch Dad gave me."

"It's cold, Munisha."

"I know, need to find somewhere warm."

The rain only seemed to make it colder, but the sun was starting to peek through the forever overcast skies. "I think we should go now."

"Where are we going, Munisha?" Zaraiella asked, grabbing my hand.

"This is how we came, but we're not returning to the bad place. We're going home through this forest. If the place we came from is that way, then our home should be straight the other way. Trust me, Zaraiella. I know where we are going."

We could be anywhere. The animals and trees making noise. Hope there wasn't a bear near.

"Ee, eee, spider web. Get it off!"

"It's okay, Zaraiella. It's nothing on you," I grinned. I hate them too."

"I don't like it here, Munisha. Where's home?"

"It's not far. We will get there, I promise. Be careful of the mud. It's hard to walk in this stuff. When did Mom buy you those shoes? They're pretty."

"I got them for school."

"I never really notice the pretty pink laces with the glitter. Sorry, they had to get dirty. We will get them clean."

"Will Mommy and Lakia be home when we get there?"

"Um, they should be. They will be there waiting for us, and we will watch funny cartoons too."

"Okay, I can't wait."

The only thing I could think of was when I last saw them. I didn't even know if they made it out like we did. Everybody started jumping around the place like rabbits when the soldiers started shooting. I just hoped they got out like us. "Geez, Zaraiella, your splashing mud on me."

"Sorry. I'm just happy."

I hated that I had to lie to my little sister. We walked and walked; the forest was so big.

"Munisha?"

"Hmm?"

"Are we almost there? My legs hurt."

"Yes, Zaraiella. We're almost there. Can't you smell Mom's frybread?"

"Um, noooo," Zaraiella says with her tiny nose in the air.

"Don't worry. You will soon. It will be okay, Zaraiella. I won't let anything happen to my favorite sister."

"Promise?"

"Pinky promise."

I just hoped I didn't ever break it. "It's getting dark. We need to get out of here before we can't see anything."

I hate spiders, too, and without the sun, I couldn't see the webs. "Hey look, Zaraiella. It's a house over there. Maybe we can ask to call Mom to get us."

"YYaaayyee. We're going home!" Zaraiella jumped and hugged me.

"Come on. I'll race you down to it."

"Okay."

"Ready, get set, go!"

I must have ran faster than I ever had. If Mom caught me, that was another grounding coming.

"Come on, Munisha, you, you cheated!"

"I always win, you know that!" I grinned running out of breath. The mist made it feel good to run. "Whew, that was fun. Now let's knock and have, Mom come for us."

Knock knock knock

"I don't see any cars here," I said, looking around.

Only thing here was an old rusty truck with grass growing all over it.

"So, there's no one home?"

"There should be. It's going to be dark soon, and mom wouldn't be able to find us in the dark, Zaraiella."

Knock knock knock

"What's wrong?" I asked, placing my hand on Zaraiella's wet face.

"No one is here," Zaraiella mumbled.

"Oh yes there is."

KNOCK KNOCK KNOCK KNOCK

"HELLLOOOO!"

"Munisha, I just saw a light in the trees."

"Hellloooo! We need help! Why won't anyone answer?! Probably asleep."

"Munisha, I'm cold."

"Zaraiella, you're okay, okay? We're going inside. Ugh, they locked the stupid door. Let's go, Zaraiella. We'll find somewhere else. Come on!"

Walking back to the forest that looked so scary with the tall trees made it feel like we would never get help. I knew someone had to be in that old house. They just didn't want to let us in.

"What are you going to do with the rock, Munisha? Stop!"

BLING

But it always felt so good to let out some anger.

"I don't think you should have done that, Munisha."

"They won't let us."

"HEY! HEYYY! Who the hell just broke my window?!"

Oh my gosh, he has a gun.

"Hey, stop walking right now!" The old man growled as he hurried towards us. "Who threw this rock at my window? I'm taking it was you, Miss Hot Head. Are you going to fix it?"

"I'm…I'm sorry. It's just"

"Come on, speak up! I work hard for my land, then some young girl comes waaaaay to an area she doesn't know and breaks up my damn window. Hmph, I know. I assume you and your sister were wandering off alone and got lost. Huh? Answer an adult when they're speaking to you!"

"No, we, we were looking for our mom and sister."

"What happened to them? You all from around here?" The man asked as he placed his hat on his head from the drizzling rain.

"No, sir," I mumbled. "We just came from a place where everyone went crazy, and people started shooting."

"Wait, you were at a tall, shiny building, correct? S.I.L.O?"

"Yes, sir. They said we were supposed to get a shot or something there, and people didn't want it."

The man's eyes stretched as if we he just saw his soul walk away.

"Oh my God. Then you two ended up here? Did any soldiers follow you?"

"Um, not really," I replied.

"Okay, come. It's cold out here, and you two need some better clothes on. Especially you, Miss Hot Head. Your younger sister is fully clothed, but you don't even have on long pants."

"Pants, again."

"Pardon?"

"Oh, nothing."

He had all this junk outside, like big barrels next to his house. Then he wanted to cry about his ugly window. Oh, but his house was different. It had a warm and funny woody smell.

"What's you and your sister's name?" the old man asked.

"I'm Munisha and"

"Wait, she can speak for herself. One thing I hate about a person if they cannot speak or think for themselves. What is your name, pretty young lady?"

"Come on, baby sister, tell him."

"Um…Zaraiella."

"Munisha and Zaraiella, those are new for me. Sara! We have a special guest down here! Sara!"

"I heard the knocking, but I thought you were taking care of Oh my."

Just like my mom, fair skinned and Dad brown. Felt kind of at home, but I needed to use their phone.

"Hello, you two. Missy, why do you have on short pants?"

"Ha, same thing I said," the old country looking man grinned. "Miss Short Pants broke my window. Kenneth will probably have to come by in a few days, and I'll tell him to get us a replacement.

"Oh hush, it's just a window, Tim. Why are you both out here alone?"

"We will discuss this at dinner. Is it ready, hun?"

"Yes, let me just finish preparing the baked potato."

"I'll take care of that," the old countryman said. "How about you take Miss Zaraiella to clean up? I believe she can fit into most of

Janice's clothes. For you, Munisha. I will have to have Jason loan you some of his old stuff. At least for now! So you can stay warm throughout the night, but for a second, let's talk."

"About what?" I asked.

"First of all, you broke my window, and I usually would hold that person accountable and have them do the labor. You were mad, and your sister seems to be frightened about what's going on, so I'm trying to keep things at ease. We will watch over you two until we get a hold of your folks."

"Thanks," I said as I pushed my wet hair from my eyes.

"In this family, we go by faith and strength. Always keep a good mind. You will always excel in life. Oh shoot, almost forgot. Now take off your dirty sneakers and put them to the side of the door, then you can come and grab a bite to eat. I will introduce you to the other family members. They're still outside having the time of their lives in the barn."

"Your house is big, Mr."

"Oh, you may address me as Mr. Wilson and my wife, Mrs. Wilson. Now go into the bathroom and wash your hands."

Mr. Wilson had a funny smell, like old people. He looked like he was probably fifty, maybe sixty years old, but moved like he was in his twenties. Mud and dirt all over my legs, ugh it was gross out there. The way we made it through the forest made me see there was still hope. We made it here, so I knew we could make it home. "This bathroom is smaller than the one at home. Mr. Wilson must be poor. The floor even creeks. Kind of feels like I will go through it."

I can only imagine if someone were to step out the tub and fall to the first floor naked. How can these people live like this?

"That was fast; you sure washed up properly? Mr. Wilson said while he stood right next to the door. "You don't want to get infected by bacteria and turn into the leprosy woman."

"Leprosy woman? That's not real," I rolled my eyes.

"Oh, she's not? She walks at night and hates to be seen because of her horrifying face and skin. So you best not to wander off when you're not told. Give me a second to retrieve the little rascals from outside, then we talk about returning you both to your parents. Uh, hate to get back out in that light shower."

How can kids live here? Away from the city and no friends. Wow, at least my sister was given something nice.

"Munisha, look at my shirt."

"At least you have on something clean. I feel so ugh. The shirt is cute, too. I like the horse on it."

"That is a horse very similar to what we have," Mrs. Wilson said.

She seemed way nicer than her husband. "Wait, you have a horse? Can I see it before we go? Pleeeeasse!" I said, folding my hands.

"In the morning, I promise. My husband doesn't like us out when it's getting dark. Tomorrow, I will show you and your sister around before we set you both to your family."

"Jason made me spill the cow milk, Mom! It's his…"

"Janice, where's your brother?"

"Outside talking to Daddy about what he did."

"Munisha, Zaraiella, this is my daughter, Janice. Janice, Munisha and Zaraiella."

"I like your hair, Za…za, raiel, la, pretty," the little girl says as she lifts my sister hair.

"Thanks. Um…Munisha?"

"Tell me, How old are you, Zaraiella?" Mrs. Wilson asks.

"I'm eight."

"I'm twelve, and Zaraiella is actually the same age as you. Mrs. Wilson, where is your phone?"

"Looks like everyone is introducing themselves. I hope we're not late. This is my champ, Jason. Sorry son, hope you don't mind playing with girlie things now."

"Come on, Dad. Hi, I'm Jason, as you know. Ma, I'm hungry."

Jason looked at me fast, then turned his head to his Mom quickly. He wasn't my type either.

"Well, sit, and your father will say grace, and we will all feast," Mrs. Wilson said as she unloosened her apron and opened the refrigerator.

"What do you mean, say grace? Who's that?"

"No, Munisha. Not funny children. What Sara means is we bow our heads and pray over the food. Give thanks to the one who provided the meal we have to fill us. Now let's begin. Bow your heads and close your eyes. Thank you for your humble blessings to our family and our new guest to come together in front of this meal tonight. Thank you, significant and almighty most high, for preparing this meal, and may it nourish our bodies in fulfillment of our needs. Keep us and never forsake us. Let's dig in, shall we?"

"Who were you talking to?" I asked. "I never see when someone close their eyes and talk to someone or something like that."

"That is called prayer, child," Mrs. Wilson said as she sipped her tea. "In this family, we give thanks for everything we have and the life we are given. Tim and I grew closer this way. The family that prays together stays together."

"I didn't see anyone you were talking to. My friend from school is name, Grace. That is why I asked."

"She doesn't understand, Tim."

"Her family probably doesn't…you know." Mr. Wilson smirked then shrugged his shoulders. "Wait, before you take another bite of that corn, Jason. We have a problem at the table, don't we?"

"I don't have my elbows on the table this time."

"No, no, look over at Janice. She brought her doll to the table once again. Dolls don't eat baked potato or belong to the table, Janice. We will have to wait for you to put it away. Thank you kindly."

"Listen to your father, sweetie, and put it to the side," Mrs. Wilson smiled as Janice frowned. "You can play with it after you're done eating."

"We can play together after, Janice," Zaraiella smiled.

"Better be quick. Lights out after eight pm."

"Oh, come on, Tim. Let them play for the night."

"Rules haven't changed and time is time. Are you ready now, Janice? Everyone's hungry."

"Yes…sorry, Daddy."

"Now, let us resume. Hopefully, it isn't too cold."

That grumpy old man. Mom didn't care if Zaraiella ate with her doll.

"Where does your family live, Munisha?" Mr. Wilson asked while his nose was almost on his plate. "It's okay if you don't know the address. We will figure that out later on."

"She wouldn't know how to get there from here, Tim. I guarantee you she tried to find her way back home through the forest and ended up here."

"I do know how to get home. I used to walk home from school with my sister until our mom said it was bad where we lived."

"Our house has a lake by it."

"See, even my little sister probably can help us get back. She's really smart."

"Tim, what do you think?"

"I'm still brainstorming. You see, Munisha…I don't know if you will understand, we refrain from associating ourselves with the inside world. The way things have gone has become dangerous itself and for my family. We gave nature a chance to bring us the real life of civilization. You realize what people, sausage brain people, take for granted when you make a living to where life started. Our ways are peaceful and prosperous. We have no worries of S.I.L.O because we are in the middle of nowhere, and the trees of nature provide coverage."

"What are sausage brain people?" Zaraiella asked.

"Very good question, my dear, and a simple answer," Mr. Wilson sighed. "People who ultimately and unfortunately cannot think for themselves. They take in whatever and believe whatever they hear or even see. Life shows things, but you need to be able to decipher from what is just, hmph, and unjust."

"Basically, my husband says that is why we don't affiliate with authorities."

"Oh no, we don't," Mr. Wilson said, wiping his face. "We don't need sausage brain people telling us how to live. We are living our best lives so far."

Best life? Living here in the middle of nowhere. He is a bossy, crazy, smelly old man. "So, you never had anyone come here before?"

"This potato was delicious, dear. Uh, we have had a few who gotten close but never found us in this area. The forest must have brought you both here for good reason. Only person who is welcome is our good pal who comes by along with his son. We keep our land very secluded. I'm just curious if anyone followed you two here."

"No, just me and Zaraiella, I promise."

"What school did you go to, Munisha? Me and Janice never really went."

"Not true, Jason. Your father and I had you in the fourth grade."

"Then he was out," Mr. Wilson sighed. "They weren't teaching anything really. The stuff they were teaching you, we could teach ourselves to you both. That's why we do it."

"Dad, she never answered my question."

"Oh, forgive me and my wife, Munisha. Sara and I get excited and against formalities big time."

"It's called, Bright Minds of Ellsworth. Zaraiella and I were there together. Our other sister, Lakia, went to another school last year."

"Jesus, you all live in Ellsworth," Mr. Wilson sighed.

"Do not worry, Munisha. My husband and I will do everything in our power to get you both back with your family."

"Thank you, Mrs. Wilson," I murmured.

The food they made is okay, not what Mom usually made. Mac n cheese, crab salad, and chicken strips. Mac n cheese, you could give me that any day with cranberry juice or lemonade. "Do you have lemonade, Mrs. Wilson?"

"I don't believe we do, but what would you prefer to drink?"

"Anything, this taste…icky."

It was funny to Janice and Jason, but I don't like hillbilly juice at all. "What is this? It tastes like, egh."

"It's watermelon cucumber," Mrs. Wilson smiled. "Very healthy and tasty."

"You got that right, Sara. These inside kids definitely don't know what they're missing."

"Dad and Mom says we won't ever get zits if we drink that stuff. Since I'm a teenager, I'm supposed to start getting them."

That boy's hair was so curly, almost like iron curls. I would have asked him if he permed it if I did not know better.

"That's right, son. It's going to keep you strong and fit. I can promise you that along with our morning routines."

"Besides, Munisha you have beautiful skin and want to keep it up. Back in my day, I used numerous products from stores that made my face worse. As a woman, you will need to keep yourself up. Same for you two young ladies as well."

"Do you like the food, Zaraiella?" I asked.

"Hmm…ye yes."

I knew she didn't like this stuff either. We should be on our way home.

"What is your mother's name by the way?" Mr. Wilson asked as he continued to keep his head in his plate.

"Isabella," I said.

"Is she old, young?"

"Tim."

"I have to know these things to know what we're dealing with."

"Why does it…can you call her? She should have her phone. What's so funny?"

Jason and Janice with the giggling again.

"Nothing, it's just that we don't use phones here either. One, there are no telephone poles, and two, this family doesn't really use radiation equipment." Mr. Wilson folded his arms and leaned back in his wooden chair.

"So, how do you call if you need help?" I asked.

"Ahhh, she's an observer, Tim. Can't fool her."

"Yes, but she could be a little too smart as well. Look, Munisha, we have our resources and supplies. If you were to live with us, you will understand our ways more and more. Now, since everyone is done. We need to clean ourselves and head to bed. Sara, please show Munisha her belongings to wash up with her sister. We will get these two young ladies back on track tomorrow. Goodnight, you all, and pleasant dreams."

"Munisha, here is a fresh towel and rag with a lucky toothbrush I found in my room. One thing we still do around here, and my overthinking mind husband still use, is toothpaste."

The small tube of toothpaste Mrs. Wilson gave me wasn't enough for a week. "So does that mean you all make toothpaste too?"

Mrs. Wilson grins. "No, no. Tim goes out every now and then to get supplies for the home. The farthest I will go is to collect fruits or seeds from plants in the forest. Now since you're all set, hurry and shower. You don't want to get caught in the dark when the lights go out on their own."

"Thank you, Mrs. Wilson, you're really nice."

"Ha, child. I try. I'll be outside waiting to show you your room when you get out, okay?"

I hoped Mom and Lakia were okay. "Oh my gosh, this water is cold. How do you turn the hot water on?"

Knock knock

"Are you okay in there, Munisha?"

If my mom found out about this, she would probably get so upset. "The water is cold, Mrs. Wilson!"

"Oh, you have to turn the lever all the way to the left, wait till it gets warm enough, and go ahead in. That is my fault, sorry."

"It's okay, got it!"

I want to go back home and be in my own bathtub. This house had a weird feeling to it. "This soap smells so good! Mom is definitely buying this for me when I get back home."

"All clean, Munisha? Hope you weren't too cold."

"I'm okay. Are you going to take my sister and me back home tomorrow?"

"I don't know. Tim will make that decision. Jason's clothes did not fit you too bad. Looks like you're about to go for a run. Here is your room with, Zaraiella. My wondering mind husband will have you two on your way home tomorrow, I promise. Have a goodnight, you both. Lights out in…twelve minutes. Pleasant dreams."

"Thank you a lot, Mrs. Wilson, and goodnight." I said, rolling my eyes as the door shut slowly.

Nice and quiet like our old home at night. Just never heard trees whispering to each other. "Zaraiella, are you okay?"

"Yes, but I miss Mommy."

"Me too. I think where we live is kind of far from here. Mom should be driving around looking for us."

"Really?"

"I hope so. You have a face like they won't. Mrs. Wilson gave me the boy, umm, Jason, yea, Jason's clothes and now I look fat wearing this."

"It just looks big."

"For sure, I will be warm tonight. Thank goodness the bed is soft. Thought it would feel like bricks."

"The food they made tasted nasty," Zaraiella said, making a funny face like she was eating at the moment.

"The food they eat here is mainly plants and things from trees. Like the juice, Mrs. Wilson gave me was"

"EEEYGGH! MUNISHA! I CAN'T SEE I CANT SEE!!"

"It's okay, Zaraiella! They said the lights would go out. I'm right here."

"Come to me. It's scary! Where are you?!"

I could barely see a thing myself. "I'm coming. Ouch, my foot! Ugh, I can't wait to go home."

"Hurry, Munisha"

"I'm right here," I said, holding my sister and the moonlight peeking through just a little. "It's been a weird day, and I'm so tired. Geez, Zaraiella, you're holding my arm so tight."

"I hate the dark," Zaraiella mumbled.

"There was a time when I was afraid, but Lakia always told me that if you can't see what's there, it can't hurt you. Tomorrow we will be back home, and everything will be okay."

"I hope so, Munisha. I'm going to sleep so we can go faster."

It took me some time to go to sleep. My brain wondering about Mom and Lakia of course, and it wouldn't let my mind go. I wish I could go to a place in my dreams. Life would be so much easier.

* * * *

Knock knock

"Good morning, Munisha, Zaraiella." Mrs. Wilson said. "Good morning, you two. Are you up?"

"Mmmm. Morning, sorry. I slept so well, and this bed is so nice."

"Good, because I believe that bed has never been slept on. Tim and I always said this room would be for guests, and you two are the first. Now, wake your sister and come to get something to eat. Oh, and sorry, the dark scared you both. I heard the yelling, but that hardheaded man wouldn't let me come see you. Come on downstairs so you both can go."

"Zaraiella, Zaraiella, sis, Wake your goldy locs hair up." I said, pulling on my sisters' long strands.

"Mmm, mm. What did you say?" Zaraiella mumbled, rubbing her squinted eyes.

"It's time to get up. Come on, don't you want to go back to Mom and Lakia today?"

"Munisha…we're not going home."

"What? Why do you say that? Zaraiella…why would you say that?"

"Good morning!"

That boy scared me, acting like we were miles away from him. It must not have been cold to him; he didn't even have a shirt on.

"Mom said come and get breakfast. See you both downstairs."

"We're coming um…"

"Jason, my name is Jason."

"Okay, bye, we're coming," I said, turning to look at my pouty sister.

"What's wrong with her?"

"She's okay, you can leave now."

He was annoying already. "Zaraiella, I need you to tell me what is wrong with you. You woke up mad for no reason. Okay, let's go downstairs and see what they say. We're going to be okay."

Zaraiella was acting so weird. She was just okay last night. Maybe the darkness.

"Good morning again, you two. Your breakfast is on the table waiting for you."

"This…looks good, I guess. Eggs, cheese, and this is bread?"

The bread that they gave me and Zaraiella looked like a hamburger. "Can I have apple juice, and for my sister too, Mrs. Wilson?"

"You can't be choosey here, Miss Munisha. Unfortunately, no apple juice. My, why the long face, Zaraiella?"

"…Nothing."

"Is the food not pleasing to you?" Mrs. Wilson smirked.

"I was saying the same thing when I saw them upstairs. Girlie issues I guess."

"Me and my little sister just wants to go home."

"We understand, and it will be done. Be patient. My husband should be back shortly to get you both on your way."

"Where did Daddy go?" Janice asked.

"He said to me last night he was going out early in the morning and be back before breakfast. He must have gone and bought extra supplies. Don't worry, he'll be back soon."

Janice and Jason almost had the same bushy curly hair. If she had been born a boy, they would have definitely been twins.

"Dad should have taken me with him," Jason said. "He always said we would go hunting early mornings, but he has never taken me."

"Jason, your father didn't go out hunting. He went for supplies. You know your father by now, he rarely stays put."

"He's coming back now."

Mrs. Wilson grinned. "Now look who decides to speak."

"Yea, he is," Jason said, looking out the window. "How did you know that, Zaraiella? Munisha, is your sister okay? Why won't she say anything?" Jason asked, looking at my sister as if she was weird.

"I don't know. She's just upset, I guess."

"Mommy, Can I get my hair like Zaraiellas'?"

"Cut her hair off and steal it."

"That's not funny, Jason," Mrs. Wilson said. "Grow your hair naturally Janice, and never want what someone else has. We are all made differently. Long time ago, I thought like that, and one of my best friends had beautiful long curly hair, not long as yours darling. Though, I used so many hair enhancement products and I managed to damage my hair severely. Yes, it took me decades to fix it."

"Our Mom has long hair. She always said a woman's' hair is her divinity and strength. Zaraiella can keep all that hair. I'm fine with what I have," I said, pulling my strands to my shoulder.

"I feel like everyone should have their own style. Long hair is cool on girls, but for a girl, I want her to have brown eyes, and pretty lips."

"What if she has no hair," I asked, since that Jason wanted to comment about cutting off my sister's hair.

"I can kiss her head too. I can't kiss her head if it's full of hair."

"Oh, shush, Jason. You would not know what to do with a girl. You're only fifteen. I here you two pick up ride walking through the door."

"Good morning good morning."

"Good morning, Tim."

"Good morning, Dad!"

"Good morning, Mr. Wilson," I smiled.

I was too excited to leave this boring and weird place.

"Tim, what took you so long? It's almost ten o'clock."

"Ugh, we have to talk privately. Kids, no going outside unless permission is given."

"What's going on, Tim? Tim, what's wrong?"

"For the forty three years I've been living. This is getting too out hand. Sara, let us talk upstairs. Now."

CHAPTER 3
Family Retreat

Do you think Mom and Lakia are home, Munisha?

"Probably. It's hard to know now."

"We should have never left. We wouldn't be here."

"We would've ended up in the building, Zaraiella. The people did not want to go inside for a reason. It's like they were getting hurt in there. I don't know what to do."

"Let's go to sleep."

"Sleep? We slept already, and I'm not tired. I want to go back home now. Imagine staying here and eating that nasty stuff forever. I can't do it."

"Munisha…Mommy said she was sad."

"When did you hear that?" I asked with a questioning look.

"When she was taking me to school. She was talking to someone on the phone, and she cried. She said she was sick, then told me she was okay."

"Mom is sick? She looked okay to me. Probably just worried about something."

"Mommy didn't say it again, but she would cry sometimes, taking me to school."

"It's weird she didn't tell Lakia or me anything. Mom is not sick; she is probably just tired. We have to get back home. When we do, that is when I will ask her."

"We don't know our way there."

Zaraiella may have been younger than me, but she had some good judgment sometimes. "We can find it. We will find the neighborhood, and we will be back to be there for Mom."

"Munisha," Jason says. "Dad says he needs to talk to you in a few minutes. He says it's important."

"Is he taking us back home? We're ready to go home now."

"I don't know what he's going to tell you. He just said he needs to see you."

"I'll be back, Zaraiella. We're going back home."

"Dad is in that room with Mom. Hope everything is fine. See you later."

"Jason…thanks."

He was already on my list of weird people. Either he was shy or never spoken to a girl his age before.

"Ahh, Munisha, how are you feeling? Did you enjoy my wife cooking this morning? We figured we would prepare something more…common?"

"Yes, it was good. Are you taking us back home today?"

"Come and sit on the bed. Sara, can you kindly ensure the children are not doing anything they shouldn't? I'm anticipating children will be children."

"Is there something bad going on?" I asked, looking at how Mr. Wilson did not like what he was going to say to me.

"Come, sit. I won't bite. As you may know, I went out early this morning and took a trip to the city. From what I have seen, everything is under patrol right now. I haven't seen it this bad before. Strike law is in play, and when I last went to the city, you could still go in places without authorization. I would usually go inside this small store to get my supplies, but they had S.I.L.O soldiers standing right in front of the store. The patrols will not let you in, and you will be prosecuted if they find out you have not been given what they are mandating everyone to have. My family does not believe in that, and I sure won't let us take it. It's against our rights as human beings."

"I don't understand."

"Munisha, I also seen S.I.L.O facility from afar. There seems to be a fire coming from the building. It also looks like many fugitives have left the building, and something serious happened there. When you and…Zaraiella left, did either one of you see your mom go inside or your older sister?"

"No, we had to run from there because a soldier started to chase us."

"How did you both get away just like that?" Mr. Wilson asked as he placed his hand under his chin. "Tell me the truth. I need to know."

"We weren't the only ones to leave. There were a lot of people who left with us too."

"Well, again, as I was about to say, where did they go? Okay, Munisha, you seem like a smart, strong hearted young lady. You led your sister here, and I believe you are telling the truth. In this world, that is what this family is brought up by. While I was out there"

"I told Jason and Janice to come back in, they just were on the porch."

"Thank you, Sara. I must watch them but our leader here, Munisha will help us. I was about to tell her the, actual things I've seen."

"No, Tim. She doesn't need to hear that." Mrs. Wilson shook her head.

"She will understand. The look in her eyes tells me she seeks knowledge, understanding, and most of all truth."

"Can we just go home, please?"

I didn't want to hear all about this other stuff.

"I'm sorry, Munisha. I am afraid at this time, unfortunately, we can't get into the city."

"What?! Why not?! We don't want to stay here forever!"

"I know, I know, calm down. When I was out there, I saw many deceased people, some in casual clothing and some in white gowns.

Now, I am not saying your family was in the mix, but it's very unlikely that they're home. I'm sorry."

All of that didn't mean I can't go home. It's not where I live anyways. "Mr. Wilson, I don't live where this all happened. I live in Ellsworth."

"Ellsworth?!" Mr. and Mrs. Wilson both said together. "Lord have mercy, Sara. She did say that at dinner last night."

"I don't know, Tim. It is always something."

As they looked at each other, I already felt like nothing was going to happen now. "What? You can't take us home?"

"There is still hope, Munisha," Mr. Wilson said. "Don't worry because we will find your family."

"They're not gone. I just know their home," I said as I felt my eyes getting wet.

"Then they are, and when the time is right, we will send you both on your way," Mrs. Wilson comforted, rubbing my back.

"Thanks, Munisha. You may go back to your room now. What a world we live in."

All of that just to find out we weren't going anywhere.

"Munisha, what happened?" Zaraiella asked.

"No nothing, they just wanted to talk to me."

"Are we going back home now?"

"I, I don't know."

"Why are you talking funny?"

"Oh my gosh, Zaraiella! Leave me alone, okay?!"

"Sorry."

Maybe I shouldn't have yelled. This wasn't her fault. "I'm sorry for being mad. It's just so much. When I was in the room, they said bad things happened where we were. Mr. Wilson said he saw it, and he couldn't take us back right now. You were right, but how did you know?"

Zaraiella looked down as she played with her hands. "Where is Mommy and Lakia?"

"Zaraiella, you can tell me. I don't know why you're keeping it a secret."

"Someone told me," Zaraiella mumbled.

"Someone told you? Who was that?"

"I…I don't know, someone."

"Okay, that's creepy. I know you want to go home bad, Zaraiella, but you don't have to lie."

"Munisha, I'm not storying. He did."

"It was a guy, then? I just want us to go home, and from what Mr. Wilson said, we're not going home at all. Not now, for sure."

"We have to stay here forever?" Zaraiella asked.

"I'm not!"

This was the worse day of my life.

"Hey." Jason said, peeking his little curly head in our door. "You two want to play uno with me and Janice?"

"Uno? What's that?" I asked.

"It's a card game. Come oncome on. You two will like it."

"It's okay, Munsiha. I want to stay here."

"Well, if you two want to come down and try and play, you're welcome to."

"I have a lot going on, maybe, need to go and do something. Do n't feel bad. We will go home soon, I promise."

Just thinking about it, will, Zaraiella be my only sister now? Lakia would always come to talk to me if I were alone or sad. She was my best friend. "Now, they're both gone."

"Munisha, I knew you would come on down to get this whoopin'." Jason said as he slammed cards on the table.

"We can start over, Jason. I don't care. All my brother does it cheat."

"Yea, just take the L my friend. Hey, you okay? You look like a sad chicken."

"It's messed up, aannnd, I don't think we are going home today."

"How come? What did Dad tell you?" Jason asked.

"He said a lot. Like, where we came from, a lot of people are dead."

"What! Dad said he saw dead people?"

"I knew that's what he meant. I just listened."

"I told you, Janice, that's why he didn't want us going outside."

"You and, Zare…"

"Zaraiella," I grinned. "I know my sister's name is hard to say."

"You both can stay. It's nice here."

"Thanks, Janice, but we have our own home. Me and Zaraiella have to go back to school and be with our mom and another sister. We can't stay here."

"Ask Dad again if he can take you," Jason said.

"How come Mr. Wilson doesn't have a car?"

"We have a truck," Jason said, stacking the cards. "It just doesn't work. Dad said horses are better for our world."

"Where is the car?"

"It's out in the front, right by the tree."

"Yea, that's junk."

Janice giggled. "It's ugly."

"Oh, shut up, Janice. That's your dad's truck too. Let's just play cards."

"You will have to teach me how to play."

"You never played uno before, Munisha? Jason always wins. He cheats every time or something."

"How do I cheat? This game is made by luck. It's like dominoes."

After Jason showed me how to play, the game seemed fun, but it was nothing like how Lakia and I played connect four or checkers. She used to beat me too all the time, but I got better and won some.

"I win again!"

"I told you, Munisha, Jason cheats and wins."

"Trust me. If we had checkers or connect four here, I would be the winner."

"I don't think we have those; we have scramble," Janice said as she wiped the dusty box.

"Never heard of that. It was fun, guys; I'm going back upstairs."

I cannot be stuck here with boring people. That smelly old man need to take us home.

"How are you feeling, Munisha? My apologies for letting Tim give you all of that at once. He"

"It's okay. I'm glad he told me. I was wondering, can you take me and my sister home?"

Mrs. Wilson grinned. "Child, I wish I could, unfortunately can't. Not that I would not want to, it's just that my husband is very strict on ways. I respect his wishes just like I would like him to honor and respect mine."

"I like that. It sounds fair."

"Munisha, I was curious, because you only spoke of your mother and older sister. Where is your father?"

"I, I don't know. My mom told us that he had gone somewhere, but he hasn't come back yet. I miss him too but I miss Mom more."

"I am sorry. Never let anything hold you down, though. Things will get better, hun."

"I'm going upstairs to talk to, Zaraiella, then go to sleep. I just want to wake up from this bad dream."

"Okay, you are a strong one, Munisha. You have a spirit of vitality, in other words, great energy. This will be resolved soon."

If they wouldn't take us back, then I will definitely have to find a way for us to get home. Why was this girl just sitting in here daydreaming? "Zaraiella, so you've been sitting here this whole time?"

"It's nothing else to do."

"Yea, I know, it's boring. These people don't even have a tv."

"Maybe we can buy one," Zaraiella said as if she had no care in the world.

"We can…never mind."

I wanted to use our own big seventy inch, not bring one here.

"Was uno fun? I think my class was playing it one time. I like checkers."

"Me too. They had scramble; it looks boring. I like real competition when I play with someone. Tic Tac Toe is better than all of those they had. I am tired, Zaraiella. I'm just going to sleep for this boring day."

Playing that boring uno made me tired. Maybe I'll sleep, wake up at home, and break free from the nightmare.

"Hey, hey, Munsiha."

"What, Zaraiella? I'm still trying to sleep."

"It's snowing outside. Let's go and do something."

"Mr. Wilson doesn't want us to go. I'm so, boooored."

"Can we please ask him if we can go?"

"No! Just go to sleep or just ask him yourself. You know what, be right back."

Zaraiella is right. We can't stay here bored like this.

Knock Knock Knock.

"Mr. Wilson, it's Munisha."

Knock knock knock.

"Mr. Wilson? I guess no one is here."

The floor wooden floor was freezing even with Jason's socks on, and the stairs makes noise every time I go up and down them.

"Mrs. Wilson? Have you seen, Mr. Wilson?"

"Everyone is outside, and when I went to your room, you both were sleeping. I didn't want to wake you."

"Oh no, you could have woken us up and told us. Me and, Zaraiella are so bored. We would have definitely woke up."

"Well then, go get your sister wait! No running in the house, please. You two have fun. I'm going to finish up dinner."

"Zaraiella, Zaraiella."

This girl sometimes seemed like she can be playing dead with me, then wakes up like she was not hearing me before. "Let's go! They're outside and they didn't even tell us."

"I can't wait! I'm going to build a snowman!"

"Munisha. I almost forgot," Mrs. Wilson said, throwing me a huge sweater. "You need a jacket since it's cold out there, that used to be Jason's so it may be a little big but fit you nicely."

"Thanks, Mrs. Wilson. Guess I do not have any choice but to wear anything else but boy clothes."

"Make sure you zip your jacket up, Zaraiella," Mrs. Wilson said.

At home, we would always play in the snow, and Mom would let us do whatever we wanted outside. "Eygh! What the? Oh! I'ma' get you!"

"Don't let me beat you in a snowball fight, too, Munisha."

"You are going to get it! Eygh!" Those snowballs felt like a cold, wet shirt that he balled up.

"Zaraiella! I'm your sister, hit him! He's the enemy, don't you run! I'll get you back, don't worry!"

The snowball fight made me think of other things. Getting Jason a good few hits made me feel a little better about them. It felt so weird to not have Lakia, playing and being on my team. Zaraiella would have been running away like how she was doing now, but we would always get her sooner or later.

"Okay, Munisha, you won this one. I don't know how your aim is so good."

"You're maybe the best in uno, but I'm the snowball queen. Where is your, Dad?"

"In the stable. He said he was getting our supplies for tomorrow."

"Supplies, for what?"

"I don't know; right when you two came, he went with Janice in there. Janice likes playing with the cows instead of having real fun. If you want to see them, the farmhouse is in the back on the other side."

"Ouu, cows, let's go pet it and horses, Munisha," Zaraiella says as she bounces around.

"I forgot you are the same age as Janice; I don't want to pet any cows. I would rather ride the horse."

It's weird how no one found this place. We did not even notice they had a place where they kept animals. "Oh my gosh, it's beautiful. What kind of horse is this?"

"I like cows," Zaraiella says as she walks towards Janice. "What is it with you and cows? I never knew you liked them like that."

"They seem nice, I always see them on the milk carton, and I always wanted to pet one. Why don't they put sweaters on the horses?"

"Horses don't wear sweaters, Zaraiella. Only humans do."

"They could get sick just like Mrs. Wilson wanted you to wear a jacket."

"Oh boy. Hey, Mr. Wilson!"

"Hey? Hay is for horses, young lady," Mr. Wilson said as he walked past me smelling like work.

"Jason told us you both were in here," I said.

"Yes, mam. Everyone is so bored, so I am searching for the good ol rods. We are going to have some fun tomorrow. Janice, go check over where Betsy is. If you can find the last two reels, you will get honors of less chores tomorrow."

"Can I ride one of the horses before we leave, Mr. Wilson? Betsy, right? I like her color." I said as I stared at the beautiful soft brown fur.

"No can do, we will be doing a lot tomorrow, and I have plenty of work to do; but my wife convinced me to loosen up a little."

"I found these things, Daddy." Janice said, holding a bunch of junk.

"That a girl. I knew they were somewhere in here. Hmm, the rods must be in the house. Now, let us all head back in, and we're going to have a great night tomorrow."

"Aren't those things people use to go fishing with?"

"That is affirmative, Munisha, and we're going to have a good time with them. Have you done it or at least tried it?"

"Nope, people always said it's boring."

"Never let someone dictate what you should try. You may come to enjoy it. Are you up to it?"

I rolled my eyes. "Tsk…No."

It's a guy thing. Can't this man see what I really want?

"Welp, you're out of luck, young lady. This is one of the activities for the itinerary for tomorrow. Just to get your mind off of things you know. You both had a rough day yesterday, so I am doing things a little differently from my regular schedule."

Oh my gosh, this family has to be the most boring in the world. No tv, no fun games, then he will take us to do something even more boring. Me and, Zaraiella are leaving tonight.

"Supper is ready, you all!" Mrs. Wilson yelled from the screen door.

Then she yells supper like old people would. I was trying to be nice but they we're just, ugh. "I really don't feel like eating what they have, Zaraiella."

"Me too. Mommy would have given me my favorite."

"What is that?" I asked as if I didn't already know. I believed all our favorite food was the same. "Macncheese? Yea, I would try to eat it all, greedy me."

"Lakia would eat some too."

"Yea, but she mainly eats that nasty potato salad. I would never eat cold food. She said she wanted to go; vevegan, I think it's called since Mom started doing it."

"Never say never. That is what Mommy said."

"Excuse me, young ladies," Mr. Wilson said, with his gray beard touching the side of our door.

He could be the boogeyman for Halloween if he wanted to, with his big head and little eyes.

"Sara has dinner ready. Come on, or you both will be hungry for the night. Plus, we are getting up early."

"Is it okay if we just stay here? We don't want to go fishing."

"I want to go."

"Really, Zaraiella?" I frowned, with my eyes rolling to the back of my head.

"Good, Zaraiella, very good. She's the one who's going to miss out. Besides, dinner again is ready."

"Just come with us, Munisha."

"No thanks, sis."

"Just come. We never tried it."

Zaraiella might have thought just because I was wearing boy clothes and looked like a hillbilly and that I was hypnotized into being one too. "No, Zaraiella, we're leaving tonight."

"Leaving? How?"

"When everyone is asleep, we will leave this place and go to the forest. Mrs. Wilson gave me enough clothes to stay warm, so I'll be okay, and you should too."

"We don't even have our own clothes."

"Exactly, we have to leave. I don't want to wear boy clothes forever. He smells like the things that are like white balls. The stuff Mom puts outside for the neighbor cats."

"Oh…I don't know"

"We will stay up and then leave tonight, Zaraiella. Trust me. It will be okay."

I had enough of the farm life. I wanted to go home.

"We thought you two didn't want a full belly this evening," Mr. Wilson grinned, bending his elbow and head in the plate again.

"Na, we were just talking girl talk," I smirked.

"Girl talk or no talk at all. Empty stomachs are the worse. The kitchen closes after everyone is done eating."

"Yes, sir," I said, continued smirking.

The food Mrs. Wilson had on the table smelled good. These people even ate like hillbillies.

"Tonight, you two, we have fish, squash, and potatoes," Mrs. Wilson said.

"It smells good, looks good."

I knew these people weren't drinking what I thought they were drinking. "Milk? Milk for dinner."

"Yes, mam, just got it fresh from the cattle this mornin'," Mr. Wilson said. "Janice made it fresh so it should be superb. Now let us say grace once more and then feast. All that searching around for gear started up an appetite."

These people really gave us milk to drink. Zaraiella already had a mustache from it, but she didn't look like she wanted the squash. When we get back home, everything will be back to normal. I wondered if we could find someone with a car to take us. What if we were caught by the S.I.L.O people?

"Eat up, child. You're staring into space," Mrs. Wilson grinned.

"She's not hungry Ma," Jason said. "Munisha, if you don't want your potatoes, give them to me."

"Now, Jason, you have enough on your plate. We don't go by greed in this home."

"Sorry, Dad. Look, even, Zaraiella doesn't like what her food. We sure don't waste food around here."

"You got it, son."

"It's not a problem; I mean, he can have that. I'll keep the fish." I said as I passed the rock looking mash potato.

"For someone who doesn't want to participate in fishing sure wants only to eat the thing that will fill them up tonight." Mr. Wilson grinned.

"You all are going fishing, Tim?"

"Yup. However, miss too good to fish, wants to just stay in the room, bored."

"Well, maybe that's not her thing. How is the fish, you two?"

I liked her better than Mr. Wilson. She was understanding, at least.

"It's good."

"Zaraiella likes fish. I like it fried. Sure is better than that other stuff."

"She just doesn't like your cooking, Sara."

"It's not that, me and Zaraiella just want to go home. It makes it hard to eat."

"We're working on that, but we must be patient and stay safe. The world is changing out there drastically, so we can't just do whatever we want."

We ate a little more. We wanted the food we usually eat; I don't ever think I will get used to this.

"Tonight, you all. We will turn in at usual times and be sure to lock your doors."

"Why, Dad? We never lock our door."

"At times like this, you may want to do as I ask son. S.I.L.O is becoming a big deal and we don't need any more random strollers coming to pay us a nicely visit. It's best to keep everything locked down tight and secured. Well, goodnight to you all. I'll see you early in the a.m. Be sure to lock your door too, Munisha."

"Do you still want that rematch in uno, Munisha?" Jason asked as he started to lean back in his chair.

"Nope, you'll just cheat again."

"You cheat in uno, Jason?" Mrs. Wilson asked. "I should go get the cards right now so I can observe what's going on."

"Ma, she only says that because Janice said it."

"Jason does cheat, he keeps winning," Janice said.

"Yea, that means I'm just good."

Nobody wanted to play that boring game this late. The lights were going to shut off soon anyways.

"You all can play. Zaraiella, let's go to bed."

"Have a goodnight you two and don't forget to lock up. I'll bring you a few more clothes, also."

* * * *

"Good thing we slept earlier; we shouldn't be tired when we go out there."

"Are you sure, Munisha? What if we get lost again?"

"We won't, trust me, okay?"

I wondered if there was something we could use to see out there. These drawers were empty, and this stupid lamp was in the way. "That's it! I can get a flashlight from somewhere. Hurry up, Zaraiella, I have to pee."

"Hey, Jason. Do you have a flashlight I can use?"

"No, Dad has one out in the shed. Why? You scared of the dark?"

"No, I mean yea. The room gets really dark, you know."

"Here, I can't help it when I see someone scared of the dark. Janice was like that for a while. Dad gave me this, so make sure you give it back in the morning and don't use it all night long."

"Don't worry," I said, crossing my fingers. "I'll give it back. Thanks!"

The darkness had a strange feeling tonight. The light never lies.

"Don't forget our rematch too, not just uno but our snowball beef."

"Okay, mister uno."

Me and, Zaraiella were going home. I couldn't wait.

"You're finally out of the bathroom. Look, I got a flashlight. I'll used the restroom then we are going home."

"Munisha, I don't feel like we should go," Zaraiella mumbled as she laid against the cold wall under her covers.

"What's wrong now?"

"It's not. We just shouldn't go, okay?"

"Zaraiella, just trust me, stop being so scary. Do you want to go home or not? Thought so."

The forest from the window did look scary. It looked like a whole bunch of black leaves standing up. "We're leaving when the generator turns everything off. So, you will have to be quiet when we go downstairs. Don't be scared. We're going to be okay."

"It's too dark outside, Munisha. I can't see anyeyyghh."

"Zaraiella, Zaraiella, I have the flashlight, look. We leave now."

"Munisha, we should just stay."

"Come on. We don't belong here. Mom would cry if she doesn't see us again. You already said she's sad, so we must make her happy. Now be careful going down these stairs, it makes noise."

"Munisha, the boogeyman," Zaraiella whispered.

"Oh my gosh, only Lakia told you that, she tried to scare me with that before. Sssshhh, we can't get caught."

Only if the boogeyman would pull my leg from the side of the stairs and then pull me into the dark. There was no such thing. "Okay, once we go outside, we run to the forest. Let's race there."

The flashlight, I just noticed wasn't so bright for out here. I hoped it wouldn't die.

"Munisha, what's that? Something just went in that room."

Zaraiella and her scary self was just imagining anything tonight. "What? I don't see anything," I whispered. "It's your imagination, sis."

"I just saw it; something just went in that room back there."

She was scared and seeing things, we made it to the door, and nothing or any boogeyman was going to stop us now. "Oh gosh, it's cold out here. Okay, you ready?"

"…Yea."

"Run!" I said, looking back at that lame and alone house.

"Munisha, the snow, it's hard to run!"

"Hurry up. The boogey man is going to get you!" I grinned.

"Eyyyghh! That's not funny."

"Okay, we made it. Gosh, it's super dark out here."

The tall trees looked like they were just standing there looking down at us. Who knew what lived in them.

"How do you know which way to go?" Zaraiella asked as we both looked up and around.

"I think we are going to find someone driving. We can ask them to take us to the Ellsworth. We will get home faster then."

The forest was so dark, and it looked like there were no streets anywhere. "So, what are you going to tell Mom when we get back?"

"Tell her everything and how you made us get lost."

"How we both got lost and went to that boring house, how we had to eat that nasty food. I feel bad for Jason and Janice."

"Me too. Their parents don't do anything fun."

"Exactly, don't even have tv. I'm telling Mom to get me some new shoes. Tsk, these are destroyed."

"You can probably clean it." Zaraiella said as she looked at how dirty they were.

"I don't know, it was just so, ugh. Mom was supposed to show me how to cook this year, too, I wasn't up for it, but since I tasted what those people had, I want my own cooked food now."

"What was that?"

Zaraiella again with this imaginary friend of hers. For some reason, she kept seeing things, but it was all in her imagination.

"It's the booogey maaaan."

"Stop it, Munsiha."

I grinned. "Let's hurry up and get out of here. I know you hate the dark, and this flashlight sucks."

"Lakia should have come for us," Zaraiella mumbled.

"She wouldn't know where we are. She's home most likely trying to figure out where we are. One thing I need to tell Mom. She needs to give me my own phone. Lakia has her own and we could have called her by now."

"We could have told, Mr. Wilson to call"

"Didn't you hear them say they didn't have a phone? They don't have anything, barely a shower. Gosh, something smells bad out here. Like a dead animal, ugh. Make sure we don't step in anything."

Didn't mean to be so mean. They really did not have much. I don't know how people can live like that. Out here away from everyone. "It's just so cold out here. I think I see a street, Zaraiella. It is!"

"Munisha, there's no one out here."

"…I know. Tsk, someone will drive by, and we'll tell them to take us home."

The street was so quiet and didn't look like anyone was anywhere. Could it be this way or the other way?

"Munisha, look, the bushes moved over there."

"What? Oh, I see it..."

I couldn't make out what was in there. Wind doesn't make bushes move like that.

"What are we going to do?"

"Just walk this way. Don't look. It won't bother us."

"Munisha, it sounds like an animal," Zaraiella whispered. "Munisha."

"Zaraiella, just come on!"

"It's getting closer. Eyyyghhh!"

"Zaraiella, wait!"

That girl really just ran in the bushes where animals hunt. She was going to get us both killed.

"It's coming! It's coming!"

"You just ran back into the forest. Whatever it is, it's in here!"

"It's that man! It's him. I saw him, Munisha."

"Zaraiella, nobody is"

"HEY! YOU TWO LITTLE BAD ASSES! What are you two doing out here?! Trying to get yourselves killed?!"

"Mr. Wilson?" I said as my voice cracked. "We umm, we"

"My wife told me to fetch after you two, and I had a feeling you would lead your sister out here in the dark. You oughta' be ashamed of yourself. Left my front door open when trouble could have walked right on inside my house.”

“We just…want to go home,” I mumbled.

“Jesus!” Mr. Wilson says putting his hands on his head. “Do you two know how far you are? Then in the dark? You couldn’t find your way in broad daylight. So, you tried to do it in the dark. What were…what am I thinking? You’re just a kid. You know what, if you want to go, go. You will find your way if you don’t need assistance. Go ahead now!”

“Come on Zaraiella…Zaraiella?”

“Munisha, we don’t know where to go. Let’s just stay with them.”

“Zaraiella.”

“Please, Munisha, please…”

CHAPTER 4

Faith

I can't believe you convinced me to come back here, I said as I laid my back on the feathery pillow.

"You didn't know how to get us home. We could get lost again. He came back for us and said he will take us back home soon."

"What if he doesn't? What if he tries to keep us here? Not everyone is good, Zaraiella, just so you know."

"Munisha…I, tsk. Never mind."

"It's because you know I'm right."

Throughout the night, I just couldn't sleep. Even in this dark room, I just could not stop thinking about Mom and Lakia. When would Mr. Wilson take us home? Would Mom and Lakia even be there? It was enough to make me throw another rock at a window.

"Zaraiella, Zaraiella. Goodnight then."

She was mad at the wrong person. The S.I.L.O people could come here and we don't even know.

"Hm, sunlight? I guess we are not going fishing anymore. Zaraiella, are you up?"

"Yup." Zaraiella said, lying down facing the ceiling.

"What's wrong with you? Okay, tsk. I'm sorry for last night. You know why I was upset, so you can't blame me for it."

"It's okay, Munisha. It's my fault."

"You're fault?"

What was wrong with this girl?

"Yup."

KnockKnockKnock

"It's Mr. Wilson. Are you both up? We have a long day ahead of us."

"I'll open it, but it's not your fault."

"Good morning, early birds," Mr. Wilson said, smiling. "You two ready for the adventure?"

"I decided we'll both go, Mr. Wilson. Zaraiella changed my mind."

"She did? Well, we have a change of plan as well. I have come to the conclusion that I will take you both home today. I want to get on with this to get back to what I need to do here at home and with my family. My pal Kenneth is coming today, so I will just ask him for a ride once he drops off my window which I should have you and your folks reimburse me for."

"Really?" I said folding my hands together. "Oh my gosh. Thank you, we would really like that. You heard that, Zaraiella? We're leaving to go home today."

"Hm hm."

"She's acting weird again today."

"I see. I'll be ready in about an hour. Sara will make you something, and we will be on our way. Hopefully, this guy comes. I need to get back here since I have so much work to do."

"Okay. We are ready whenever. Zaraiella…what is wrong with you? Your acting weird every morning now?"

"Can you, I just…I'm not mad, Munisha."

"I hope not, and I told you I was sorry for last night already. Let's go eat something."

"Yea, let's just go. Munisha, what if I told you Jason has a crush on you?"

"I don't think he does; I know he's a big mouth. If he does, too bad, my crush is in school, and I can't wait to get back."

"Good morning, you two. I hear you both have a long day but also an exciting one," Mrs. Wilson says, smiling at us. No matter what, that lady always had a smile on her face.

"Yes! We can't wait to go back; we miss home," I said.

"Child, I know, ever since you two been here, that's all I heard. Our place isn't that bad, is it?"

"No, it's just that we're not used to the…farm life. I have never seen a house with no tv, not even music, and it's so quiet."

"That is how we like it, all of the city living. Me and Tim decided that the best thing to do was to leave the environment where society is falling apart. We are free out in this quiet place. One day child, you will see exactly what we're asserting."

The only thing he could have been right about was how people are. Mom said too, that the world was getting bad. Maybe we could just move to a better place. It couldn't have been bad everywhere.

"How are you doing, Miss Zaraiella?"

"I'm okay, just a little sleepy," Zaraiella says, rubbing her little eyes with long hairs on them. "Seems like you're not a morning bird. What made you think you can find your way home in the dark anyways last night?" Mrs. Wilson asks with that same smile.

"I felt like we could find our way, and plus, the S.I.L.O people couldn't find us in the dark."

"Munisha, that was very, how can I say it more pleasantly? It was a"

"Stupid idea that could have gotten you both killed," Mr. Wilson said, passing by.

"Tim…they are children. You got the horse ready that fast?"

"Oh, yea, I was taking care of her last night for our fishing trip. Munisha, you are a leader. I see that in you already, but you need a little more wisdom; brains and wisdom are two different things."

"I'm smart. I make only A's and B's."

"Like I just said, brains, as in arithmetic's, book smart, are not contributions to wisdom. You may be intelligent in your studies, but your discerning lacks. It will come in time but always think ahead. I don't think this guy is coming at this time. He should have been here by now. Welp, I guess we can take the horse and at least get a move on to the city."

"You weren't always like this, Tim Wilson. Why are you so anxious? They don't need to be rushed."

"Sure wasn't. When I met Sara in college, I was still doing what the others did. Friends always were bad influences, but I became a person with wisdom, common sense. Don't let others dictate your decisions when they are just."

"Crazy man. What is he even talking about?" Mrs. Wilson asked as she shook her head, smirking at me.

"Hmm, I shouldn't be. You're right, baby. It's just that I want to get these two home and get back here my family. However, we have to keep our heads low and can't be rushing it since patrols are infiltrating everywhere. The city is so different from how we both lived in it."

"I packed you all something quick to eat," Mrs. Wilson said. "You have two sandwiches Mister, I know it will be a trip."

The bag felt like it was barely anything in it.

Please be careful out there, Tim. Children, Munisha, Zaraiella. Follow what my husband says, please. Everything will be okay, just be good."

"That's right. Thanks again, babe. Give me a kiss."

"Where are Janice and Jason? I just noticed we hadn't seen them all morning," Zaraiella said.

"They have already been up. Jason is out plowing along with Janice in the farmhouse milking. You can both say goodbye before we head on today's mission. I'm going to prepare the horse."

"He's really going to do this. Tim! Oh my gosh."

"Thank you, Mrs. Wilson, for everything," I said, hugging her. "I will miss you."

"You're most certainly welcome. You don't have to thank me for that. Be good, you too, Zaraiella. My daughter wants your hair so, be careful. Be sure you take care of it and of course yourselves."

"We will," I said. "Thanks! Can I ride the horse by myself before we leave, Mr. Wilson?"

"Unfortunately, we're on a tight schedule," Mr. Wilson said, flicking his watch. "Kenneth must have got caught up with something. Hmph, you are welcome to come back with an appointment for me to teach you how to ride. Don't frown. You are the one who insisted on leaving us so quickly. You weren't even thinking about riding a horse last night. JASON! OVER HERE! Zaraiella, you can go get Janice out of the barn. We have to get a move on."

"Yea, Dad. What's up?"

Jason looked and smelled like he'd been on the farm. Sweating but it was cold. A weirdo he is.

"Munisha and Zaraiella are getting their wish early. We've decided that we will get them home today."

"I kept wondering why we weren't going fishing anymore. I thought because of S.I.L.O."

"The busy bees were out last night, and they almost got lost. Sara told me to go and retrieve them, but our friend here, Munisha, uses optimism a little too the extreme."

"No wonder you asked..."

"Asked what?" Mr. Wilson said.

"She asked me to play...have a snowball fight."

"After the generators timed out? You know better than that, Jason."

"Yea, I apologize."

At least I knew he wasn't a snitch. Those type of people never made it in this world. Lakia always told me that.

"It's been fun, Munisha, I wish you could have stayed. We never finished our rematches but be safe. I'm going back to work, Dad." Jason said, then just turned his back.

"It's been fun too, Jason. No more cheating, okay?"

"No promises!" Jason smiled tapping my arm.

"He can cheat all he wants in those card games. But he can't cheat with that dirt and shovel," Mr. Wilson said.

"Zaraiella, Janice, I thought you two got lost."

"No, Janice was letting me milk the cow. The thingies feel funny."

"They're called udders, Zaraiella. Make sure you clean your hands, too; I don't want lactose on me while we ride."

"Our cows are clean, Munisha, and it's been a time and a half. I'll get the ol Betsy out, and then we can head out."

"Bye, Janice. Thanks for showing me how to milk a cow."

"You're welcome. I wish you could have stayed," Janice said as she wrapped around little sister.

"We will come back. I still have to get horse riding practice from your Dad."

"Just stay so we can all be happy," Janice said.

"Remember I told you that we have to go back. Our Mom and sister wouldn't like if we stayed here."

"What if you stay, Zaraiella?"

"I can't, but we will still be friends."

"Best friends." Janice said as she gave a tighter hug.

They really grew to each other fast. "Aww, you two are going to make me cry."

"You two ready? We have to get a move on. You climb up first, Munisha."

"This is so cool."

It felt amazing being sat up on the horse. Only if I can make Betsy go right now.

"Munisha, scoot up a bit," Mr. Wilson said, pushing my backside further on the horse.

"I'm not as young as I used to be. Alright, Zaraiella, your next doll."

"Mr. Wilson, aren't we too heavy for her?" I asked.

"Not at all. We keep our horses strong and healthy. I have seen a horse at the city farm carnival that looked so unnourished and brittle. It's a shame. Janice, go on inside and tell your mother we are gone. Don't know what that woman is doing in there. Love you, see you soon! Alright now, Jason! This is going to be a mission; I pray for strength."

I already know this was going to long ride too. "Which way do we go, Mr. Wilson?"

"We head southeast so we can cut through the forest and move to the edge of the city. We are looking at a at least…hmm, two hour ride."

"WHAAAATT?" I shouted. "Two hours? What do you mean two hours?"

Mr. Wilson laughs. "That is my usual route time if I ever go to Ellsworth. The way you two were going last night was going to end up on the deep part of the forest and head northwest or probably right back into S.I.L.O. I don't know what you and your sister thinking last night, Munisha."

"I learned my lesson. I won't ever try and go out without directions again, gosh."

"Good. Now, here are you first lessons. You want to yank the halter a little to make her go a little faster. You can say, yaw, geedy up, or come on, girl. Just don't do it too hard, or she may just start flying."

"This is pretty easy."

I just wished I was by myself so I could make her go faster. This trip is going to take forever.

"You seem like you've done this before."

"Nope, me and, Zaraiella was at school one day, and they just showed us a horse, never even let us ride it."

"How are your grades? That's right, you told me you're practically an A* student. What about you, miss, so quiet back there?"

"Um, I make A's."

"Really? Or are you saying that because of your sister?"

"Zaraiella makes good grades. We both never had bad report cards."

"That's excellent. If you keep it up, you'll become a doctor, lawyer, engineer one day."

"I don't want to be any of those."

I had never really thought about it. Mom's job was always boring to me, so I definitely didn't want that.

"Why not? They're all good careers. They always said if you're not pertaining to become any of those, you are nothing."

"Mr. Wilson. None of those are something I want to be."

"I want to be someone who takes care of animals," Zaraiella said.

"A veterinarian? They're alright, but you want something that keeps you from going back into the workforce when you retire unless you save, of course. What about you, Munisha? I can tell you are probably going to be a mayor or even the president."

"Naa, those are boring. I want to either be a police officer or, if I get lucky, a sports player like volleyball or something."

"You don't have to be lucky to be anything. Things come to those who are patient and willing to work their behind for it, also remaining focused on what they truly want. I, myself said I wanted to become a fighter pilot since I was in the Air Force. Turned out I had given up on what I really wanted. Things don't happen overnight though, or by luck. If I had stayed consistent and focused, I probably would have become a commercial pilot at least."

"You still can," I said.

"Not really. If I could turn back time to you and your little sister's age, I would plan with the knowledge I know now. Never would have joined the army in the first place. Hmph, life in today's world does not work as it used to when I was young. But hey! I have no complaints. Just blessed to have my family, and that is something grand. My wife and I started to build that farm when she didn't even know she was pregnant with Jason. Took us awhile but once we were finished, our family moved in. Away from the sausage brain society."

"How did you both build it?" I asked. "You didn't have people come help?"

"We did. My brother helped us out. That man would always drink and say the silliest darn things. He could work drunk and be as if he was sober."

"Mrs. Wilson, you and your brother, it seems hard to believe only you three people did it. That's like me, Zaraiella, and our older sister building a car."

"Teamwork makes the dream work," Mr. Wilson said, patting my shoulders. "Now, through this area, we're going to go through this small swamp, your feet and legs may get a little wet. It's not a long way to the city from here."

"Are there alligators in here, Mr. Wilson?" Zaraiella asked.

"Of course, there are, Zaraiella," Mr. Wilson chuckled.

"Oh crap! Then why would you tell me to go this way? It could be one right by us!"

"Calm down, calm down. I ride with gators all the time."

"You just said that they're in here," I said, looking all around.

"I did. Gators are everywhere, but I do come across some every now and then. When I do, I just tell them good morning, good evening and keep it pushing. If you mind your own business, they will do the same."

The swamp looked a bit peaceful; A nice place to get homework done. "Does anyone else come to see you besides your friend?"

"Oh no. Me and Kenneth knew each other before I moved out here. He stayed in the city since he was already chipped. Him and his son. Lost his wife during a car accident. So he and his boy, Mark come by every once in a while. Should have come this morning, I don't know what happened. If he does come out, Sara knows what to tell em'."

"Wow, that kinda sucks," I said. "Jason and Janice…I feel bad for them."

"So, you two are coming back to visit?" Mr. Wilson laughs.

"We might. I don't want to get lost again. If Mom lets me borrow her car, I will. By the way, why don't you use a car? It looks like you only use a horse to get around. I saw the truck that has plants growing through it."

I really wished it worked because it's been a long time and my bum was beginning to hurt.

"Cars are toxic for our world. The combustion from the engine is so deadly it creates problems with our global warming and our air. The farthest we will go at my home is our generator we rely on for many things. Refrigeration, cooking, and of course, our lighting source. You both witnessed how we have a timer that shuts off the generator at a certain time at night, and it's nothing compared to the juice used in the city. Our ways, I can honestly say are pure and efficient for our world."

"How does the shower work if you live out here by yourself?" I asked.

"Very good question. You've seen those blue barrels we have on the side of the house. Our water source comes from there. Even hooked up with a homemade water heater, so you wouldn't yell the wood to the ground with that cold water. Water is all around us, and we must understand, The Creator, Himself, gives everything we need. Just like this forest. Rainwater, we mainly use that to keep fresh clean water in our home. If you look inside, we have certain rocks that aid the water to be even safe to drink. We just need to manage it properly, so we don't run out. It's something I learned along from my brother to put together when I first moved out here. I don't necessarily need things from the inside world. Once you know basic strategies in survival, you become more of the survivor and not the sausage"

"Brain people," I grinned and shook my head.

"That's right. You must learn to think for yourself in this world, or they will think for you. When you have the strength, I can think for myself mindset, now you're a true threat."

"You all really like living like that?" I asked as I turned my head back.

"Absolutely, it's something we adapted to."

"Thank goodness we didn't," I said.

"We're not so bad," Mr. Wilson laughed.

As much as he sounded so bossy at home, he sounded very nice when he was away. It was like he was pretending to be someone else with us.

"Finally, Ellsworth. Haven't been here in some time. If I wasn't residing in Bangor, I would have had a place here. Can you smell the toxicity?"

"I don't care about that. We're almost home, Zaraiella!" I yelled with my hands in the air. "Never will I do this again on a horse."

"Never say never child. Let's get you both home. You two savages didn't care about the pitch dark at all. Hmph and talking smacks about horseback riding. This town isn't big at all, so where to now captain Munisha?"

"Our house isn't over here in this town part. If you take me by my school, I'll know how to get home from there."

"Munisha, we can go to the store Mommy always goes to. It's by our house."

"No, it's not. It's farther than that."

"No, it's not," Zaraiella argued.

If it weren't for me to walk her home, she would be lost every time.

"Alright, you two. We don't have all day to decide which is the best way. We will have to head the way which fits best. Everybody off, and I'll secure the horse over here. Wish Kenneth would have come by, but it's all well."

"Do we have to leave her?" I asked. "What if someone comes and steals her?"

"Let's just pray nobody does. I'll surely appreciate it if your folks give me a ride back to this area. I know it wouldn't be too much to ask. You make sure you know the way to you all home. Be a good girl now, Betsy, you hear?"

Leaving the horse wasn't a good idea at all, I thought. I felt bad for Mr. Wilson since he will have to travel all the way back home. "The school is called Bright Minds Elementary and Middle. We could have the school buses help us out if it was school today."

"Don't be so anxious, Munisha, we will find it. I think I know where it is. Jason had a game there when he played his little basketball. Is the gym blue and gold?"

"Yes, not so big either," I said.

"That's it! I know exactly where that is, and you are certain you know your way from there?"

"I should. I mean, it's not that far from the school."

"Do you have any clue, Zaraiella? She's just looking around, so observant."

"Let's take a pickup ride once we get there," I said.

"That is an awesome idea, Munisha. Sadly, I'm assuming neither of us has a cellular device. You can't take one unless you have that. I wish there were still Pick Ups around, sadly, this is the year of two thousand thirtysix. You must have your wrist out and ready to make the payment."

"This is crazy, Mr. Wilson. You need a cell phone! I'm just a teenager, so I don't have one."

"No, thank you, so the government can have more ways of tracking me down? That's for you city folks. Oh, man!"

"What's wrong? I was right?"

"No, Munisha. We rarely use radios, my wife and I got some a while back just in case."

"We'll be fine," I said. "We're almost home."

"My, you have some beautiful daughters," an old lady smiled.

We should ask her for a ride.

"What? I, I mean, thank you, mam. Yes, they're beautiful, aren't they? They will make you run up a tree if you get to know them long enough."

"They're beautiful, a blessing from the sky. Nothing is better than two beautiful sisters."

"Thank you, mam. We have to get going though. Take care."

"Mr. Wilson, ask her," I said, yanking his shirt.

"No, Munisha, no."

"Hey, Miss. Can you give us a ride home?"

"Pardon me?"

"Our car"

"Yes, what she means, mam. Our vehicle broke down, but we're fine."

"Oh my, well, I would not mind giving you all a ride. My car is just over there."

"Oh thank you, mam. We really appreciate it," Mr. Wilson said, then frowning at me. "In this inside world, Munisha, there are a lot of offbeat things that happen to people. It's such a quiet place but sometimes too quiet. The last thing we need is for authorities to ask us for identification. Do you both have any IDs on you?"

"I do. I lost it I know. I don't know about Zaraiella's own."

"I believe she's supposed to have one too. Besides that, please follow my lead. We do not want to get shambled with any authorities out here."

I grinned. "Calm down, you grumpy old man. She doesn't seem like a, sausage brain person."

"Hmph, we shall see. I like your energy, Munisha. Let me ask you. Do you all have the chip?"

"Chip, what chip?"

"I like chips!" Zaraiella says.

"No, not what you eat. I'm assuming no, so that's good."

"Oh, I know what you're talking about," I nodded. "It's like something they have in people and use it for different stuff."

"Yea, even the government can track you with it."

"So that means they can catch bad people easier then?"

"Here it is, you all," the woman said, as the door opened for her.

Her car was so shiny and definitely more expensive than Mom's.

"Just tell me where to go, I assume it is not too far."

"No, mam, we are just trying to get to this address. I will put it here on the GPS for you."

Mr. Wilson didn't even look like he could use GPS. "Her car is better than yours…daaaad," I smiled.

"These children. Your name, Ms?"

"Just call me, Heather."

"I am Tim, Munisha, and miss quiet, Zaraiella. We truly appreciate you."

"No, problem. My blessings will come for helping out a family in need."

This lady could drive a little faster. Oh my gosh, it's a thirty speed limit area, and she's going fifteen. We might as well get out and walk.

"Now, back to what I was saying earlier. Right, now what happens if you don't even show up for jury duty? You will be found the exact day and then prosecuted. This world has flipped big time."

"I think it's good because they can find bad people, and people who do things like rob a bank or kill someone will be found much easier," I said.

"Very true, but what about their personal privacy? It's basically like you're on a leash or a puppet on a string. I'm telling you these things right now, Munisha, since you're not a dumb person. In the future, you can make your decisions. You too, Zaraiella."

Mr. Wilson was a good person. Jason and Janice would live well with someone like him.

"Hm, I'm surprised to see that S.I.L.O aren't everywhere like the last time I saw them on the west side of town. How do you like living out here, Ms. Heather?"

"Ha, it is what it is. The way how life has changed so much, it is best to stay positive. When I was those girls' age, I had no clue what the world was really coming to."

"I see. Got to stay positive as you said. I hope we are not pulling you out of your route."

"No, dear, I will be fine."

"We are almost there, according to the map. Can't wait to get my vehicle back up and running."

"What seemed to be the problem with it?"

She sat up all the way to the steering wheel like she couldn't even see the road.

"Seems like she just ran out of gas on us. You know they are trying to remove the pumps out here permanently. Once we get to this destination, we can get one of my buddies to take me back and get her on the road in no time."

"I hope you all will."

"How is Zaraiella doing, Munisha?" Mr. Wilson asked

"She's asleep, Mr., I mean, dad. I'm tired too."

Is she trying to tell me something or just whispering in her sleep?

"Yea, Ms. Heather. This car is like having a couch on the inside. Must of have paid a pretty penny for it."

"Something like that, retirement fund did this for me about five years ago. Now down this road, isn't it?"

"Yes, mam. Thank you so much. I'll be sure to bring you some credits next time I see you."

"Sis, we're almost there. Wake up, ugh, you're really sleeping sis?"

I couldn't wait to just get home and see Mom's face. My heart was beating with so much excitement.

"Come on, young ladies. Thanks once again!"

"When we get home, Mr. Wilson, will you miss us?" I asked, smiling.

"You both are some good kids; just you rascals broke my window. You all had some trouble so it's a pardon. By the way, where is your father? I never heard either of you mention him."

"He is somewhere. Mom said vacation, but we hope we all can see him again. We will again, Zaraiella, so don't look down."

"See, that makes you a leader, Munisha. You know when to keep your head up and continue to be optimistic."

"I get that from my teacher at school a lot. Our dad, I can't really remember what he did, like work."

"Aw, so it been that long."

Now that I thought of it, the last time I saw him was when Mom was talking to him outside, and it was snowing. I think they were yelling at each other then got in his car and left. Mom looked at me pretending like she was okay, but I felt she wasn't. Wherever Dad is, I hope he is okay and S.I.L.O didn't take him.

"Since the school is a few blocks away. Do you know your way home from here?"

"A little. That's why I said let's get close to the school."

"Munisha, me and Mommy go this way out when she takes us to school, and then she goes straight down."

"You sure, Zaraiella? We can get lost very easily. These streets are like a mouse maze."

"Hold on, you both said that the neighborhood is by a lake, correct?"

"Yea, it's behind it."

"I have an idea of where it is, and you enter with a code before you get in?"

"Yes, Mommy presses a button on her keychain, and the gate opens up."

"I know exactly where that is. Believe it or not, I had some family that stayed there. Not sure if they're still there, but I know where your people are. Those houses I remember I nice and, sort of secluded. It should be about twenty minutes from here."

"Really?! Thank god! I can use a good bath. We're almost there, Zaraiella, we're almost there! Okay, okay, you're choking me."

Finally, couldn't wait to get back into my regular life. I had a test that I needed to study for. Mom swore she would take me to get my first manicure if I passed. "Wait a minute, I just thought of it. Where's your bunny?" I asked.

"I forgot it."

Zaraiella sounded so happy as though she never had it to begin with.

"No, how did you forget? Mom isn't going to buy you one anytime soon. You know that, right?"

"It's okay, Munisha. We're going home anyways. I'm happy."

"Looks like someone has grown up a little faster. Have you two been to the carnival this year?" Mr. Wilson asked. "I see that they have it set up, but it looks like it hasn't been running."

"It was open three years ago. Remember, Zaraiella, we went on the tall slide? She asked the guy at the top if she flew off it and then he just pushed her down."

"I remember. Then you came right behind me and hit me in my back."

"Yea, you wouldn't go down. I told you to stop being such a scaredy cat."

"The last time I've been to the carnival was when me and Sara went. We both didn't do rides like that, but we had an amazing time. Playing the games and eating elephant ears and not to mention that ridiculous size turkey leg. Mhmm, all three of us could feast on that at the same time."

"It would be cool if they open it back up," I said. "Things are just so different and boring now."

"Nine times out of ten that it won't, things have become too catastrophic and it's only getting worse. That year when everything started to fall apart was when Sara and I just returned from a trip. There was a complete black out. Yes, that is what they called it. You two weren't born yet. The nation fell under the, EMP shutdown, and people didn't know what to do. Hmph, me and my wife, as I remember like it was yesterday. We thought out that plan thoroughly and got the hell out of dodge."

"E, M, P? Never heard of it," I said.

"See, if I'm not mistaken it was about, fifteen, twenty years ago. They didn't tell you all in school about it or anything? Wow, well, all I can say from that point in time, all hell broke loose. Imagine as I know you kids love ya'll electronics, that was not able to charge, tv not working and most of all, no power. Jesus, it was hell. They said it was from a powergrid failure, but come on, nationwide? Only the sausage brains believed it. THE DAMN PEOPLE IN POWER DID THIS…forgive me. I'm getting hyped up for nothing You have to do this and that just to make a living now. It's like you sometimes have to keep your nostalgic moments to keep your happiness."

From everything he said, and yelling for no reason, I didn't know what he was talking about, only at the end. I'm guessing Mr. Wilson was saying keep my best memories. There wasn't a lot but Mom and Lakia. Hoping they will be there once we get home.

"Looks like we finally made it, you two. The community looks deserted."

"It's always quiet," I said. "Mom said she wanted to move here because it's like that."

"Hmph, I wouldn't trade peace for anything. As you both saw, our land is nowhere near noisy. The most we get are those goddarn raccoons running up and down the roof. There's no guard here? I guess we just walk right on through."

"Usually, the gate is open early in the day," I said.

"Right. The lake is beautiful. What does your mother do to live in such an area?"

"Mom is a doctor. She does the thing when you put people to sleep. That's what she told me," I said as I looked all around.

Why was my neighborhood so quiet?

"Anesthesiologist? If so, very good professional job. Why don't you two follow in her footsteps? It's a job I believe you make excellent credits without doing much."

"Naaa, that's boring."

"Mommy said to us we should do what we want," Zaraiella said.

"True, just make the right decisions, and you'll be alright."

"That's our house right there!" I said as I pointed and began to run. "The one with the red car! Let's go, Zaraiella! We made it we made it!"

"Mommmyyy!"

I knew we would make it back.

"Mom…Mom, WE'RE HOME!" I shouted.

Knock Knock Knock

"MOMMYYY!"

"You two know ya'll can make some ruckus."

"MOM, LAKIA!"

KNOCK KNOCK KNOCK

My knuckles hurt. "Hold on. I have a spare key Mom leaves for me in the back."

They must have gone out. Just hope the key is in the plant pot.

I still don't see anyone, even in the backyard. Just those cats that like to play and poop in our yard. "Back. Now let us go inside. You will like it here, Mr. Wilson," I said, opening up the door to the quiet feeling.

"You know what's strange. I haven't seen a soul in sight," Mr. Wilson said.

"Quinsa online."

"JESUS! The damn thing is in the wall?!"

"Good evening, Munisha."

I grinned. "You old man. It's just a blue face. Mom, we're home! Lakia! Quinsa, did Mom ever come home yet?"

"No, Munisha. Ms. Lozano seems to be out on errands. Left at, yesterday, approximately, eight twenty five, a.m. Perhaps I make a call?"

"Mommy, Mommyyyy!" Zaraiella moaned.

"It's going to be okay, sis. I'll try and call them. That's why you need a phone, Mr. Wilsooooonn," I said, picking up the phone.

"Hmph. Is it ringing?"

"Yea, no oh hello?! Mom, it's me, Munisha. Me and Zaraiella are here at home and…"

"What's wrong?" Mr. Wilson asks.

"She answered but hung up."

"Make call again?" Quinsa asked.

"Do it. Please Mom, let me hear your voice," I whispered.

At least I know she picked up. "Mom. Now it went to voicemail. Her phone is dead, I think."

"Probably so. Do you know your older sister's number?"

"I did, but she changed numbers. Quinsa, do you have Lakia's number?"

"Unfortunately, Munisha, I do not contain Lakia's wireless phone. Should I send a distress call to authorities?"

"No!" Mr. Wilson shouts. "We will figure this out. Anything upstairs, Zaraiella?!"

"No, I checked all the rooms."

"Quinsa said she didn't see anyone, Mr. Wilson," I said, throw ing myself to the sofa. I can't believe this."

"Does your mom have two cars?"

"No, just the one outside. She's probably with Lakia and other people, looking for us. They…I don't know. Where are you, Mom?"

CHAPTER 5

Aspirations

It was getting dark, and there was still no sign of them. Why were they taking so long to come back? "Mom usually doesn't let people in our house with shoes on. You need new shoes Mr. Wilson."

"First of all, missy. I am blessed to have shoes on my feet. Second, you and your sister just walked right on in without removing yours, so how would I know?"

All I can do is smile. I did forget.

"Come to think of it also, you little rascals came inside my house the same way. I bet your sister must be sleeping well, it's so quiet in here, just like home. You didn't even bother to turn the tv on."

"I'm grounded from watching. Mom said something about my attention."

"Short attention span. I can believe that, you're always moving around. Jason isn't even as active as you, and he played sports. So you played tennis before?"

"Yes and I loved it. It's hard but it's fun. I had a problem at school with it."

"What happened?" Mr. Wilson says, folding his arms together. "Don't tell me you started to hit someone with the racket."

"No…I uh…ran into the bleachers trying to hit the ball."

"Damn, excuse me. Really?"

"It knocked me out and I didn't wake up after the next day. It felt weird. Like my doctor told me, a foggy feeling. Like my head was spinning a little. That is why I can't watch tv. They said that word, epi…epilepsy. Said I can get that if I am not careful with phones, computers or any type of screen in my face."

Mr. Wilson nods his head. "Hmm, you hit your head so hard it caused a concussion. Thank God you didn't have anything more severe."

"Tsk, I just want to play again. I'm not allowed to play any rough sports until my doctor says I can. It happened around the beginning of the year. Hopefully in January I will be okay to play again. That is what I want. I want to become a Tennis player. Play in school then become famous and rich playing."

"Then go for it once you go back. Always put your future first. It will thank you later. Just remember, God, well, for you, obeying your parents, school, and then sports. Losing that alignment will cause a disfunction through the years to come."

Mr. Wilson talk too much. Dad never talked as much as he did. "If it gets too late, will you leave us here alone?"

"At this point, I'm not sure. The real question is, will you two be alright by yourselves? My conscious wouldn't let me leave you both anyways. I'll just have to wait till morning."

"We'll be okay. Thanks a lot! Helping us was so nice, but our family will get back. They're just looking for us, and they should be back by night."

"I pray so. If they do arrive by then, I will still have to wait till morning to head back. Curfew, I believe is still in effect at eleven p.m."

"Okay, I'm going to go and sleep with, Zaraiella. You can make something to eat if you want and if Mom comes. Just tell her you're with us. She might freak out."

"Thank you for your generous hospitality, Munisha. Hopefully, Mom doesn't shoot," Mr. Wilson grinned.

For some reason, something was telling me that, Mom and, Lakia were in that building. She said that we would leave the same day, so they couldn't be still in there. "Zaraiella, are you sleeping?"

Poor sister just looks so sad sitting in her bed. Wish I could make her happy.

"Not really. I'm thinking about Mommy."

"I know, I know."

"Why didn't they come back yet? They know we called."

"It's weird. They are somewhere though. I think they are probably looking for us, and they don't know we're home. Mr. Wilson said he would stay with us for the night, so we won't be alone."

"That means Mommy isn't coming back. She's not coming back!" Zaraiella mumbled, then teared up.

"Zaraiella, stop it! They are. Why won't you just believe that they are?"

"Because they're not. Why did this happen?"

"Stop that crying. You need to stop because it makes me cry."

One thing I hated was when she cried. That energy jumped right on me. I hated it more than Mr. Wilson's nasty food. "Let's just get some sleep, okay?"

Maybe they would come back soon.

"Wait, I didn't do anything. I didn't do anything. EYGH!"

"Munisha, Munisha, you're dreaming."

"Mhmm, wow, that was really weird. It felt so real. S.I.L.O…they came and took us. Can't really remember what happened."

"Maybe it will come true," Zaraiella frowned.

"Na, it's just a dream. Did he ever come up?"

"I don't think so. He was asleep downstairs when I went to get something to drink."

"Everyone is tired. He helped us so much. I hope Mom gets back soon so she can take him back."

"Munisha…what if they don't come back?"

"I told you they will. Why do you keep saying that like you don't want them to or something?" I said, rolling my eyes.

"Because"

"Because what?!"

"Do you believe me when I tell you…things?"

"I don't get you, Zaraiella. We'll just wait for them."

She just sounded so bad minded. Ever since we went to that farm, she had been acting strange. "It's going to be alright, and we are going to see them again," I said, rubbing my sister's back.

"Mr. Wilson, Mr. Wilson. Geez, your knocked out. Mr. Wilson wake up."

"Huh, what?"

"I said you are sleeping well. You must have been dreaming something good. Me, mines was a nightmare kinda'."

"Dream? Hmph, those rarely come. When I was about your age, dreams would come to me, then by the time I woke up. They were gone."

"I dreamed S.I.L.O took me. It felt so real and those types are the ones I hate the most."

"I hear you. It is still a little early. Once ten o'clock hit, I need to have my mind made up."

"You're going to leave then?" I asked.

"Not sure, most likely Sara is worried to death. She will shove those radios down my throat and a pan to my head when she sees me."

"To be honest with you, Mr. Wilson, you need to get a phone. I have never seen an adult without one. For your birthday, I'll tell Mom to get you one."

"Ha, yea it's going to be my first in a long time. Make sure she puts it in your name and kindly pay the bills. I'll mail you and her some funds whenever I get a chance."

"Then the phone would be mines if I'm doing everything."

"How right you are," Mr. Wilson smiled. "How's Zaraiella doing? Still asleep?"

"She's up; but she keeps being so bad mind."

"How so?"

"I keep telling her they're coming back, but she tells me they're not."

"Well, maybe she's just a little worried. Never give up hope though."

"Exactly! Our mom would tell us that if you keep saying something, it will come true."

"That's sure is true itself. Example of that is if you are broke and keep telling yourself that you will stay broke, then you ultimately will. You will keep yourself in poverty just for keeping a negative mindset. Whatever you do in this lifetime, Munisha, you have to stay positive. No matter how bad the sausage brain people tear up this country, let alone the world."

I wanted to be positive, but sometimes it didn't look like it was going to be that way. Just like what Mr. Wilson said. There have been times when things look like it never would be good again, just like right now. He's right, I can't give up hope.

"You two, I'm assuming haven't eaten yet." Mr. Wilson says getting up stretching.

"Na, I am getting a little hungry. We have everything in the refrigerator. Did you make anything to eat?"

"Nothing really. You know it's not polite and quite rude if you just barge into someone else's fridge."

"I told you, you can make something. It's my house."

"You did say that. However, you are not the legal homeowner, second, I was taught not to do many things while being a guest in someone's home. Considering I would rather the host or hostess of the house to prepare whatever they have, that would be just fine."

"So that means, I'm the host?"

"Hostess, that's right. What will chef Munisha serve this evening?"

"Ha, I can't cook. Mom taught me how to make my favorite food."

"Don't tell me, baked cookies. Some type of sweets, I'll pass."

"Nope, neither," I grinned. "It's mac n cheese."

I knew Mr. Wilson's face would turn into a toad.

"Really? Aaah, what the heck. Work your magic."

"I hope there's still more. We eat it almost every week."

"My kids would never, all of the cholesterol from the butter, uh no. If you don't have enough, I'll be fine. I'll just take a fruit or something."

"We have apples and bananas."

"Both would be marvelous, chef Munisha. Gracias!"

Mom would kill me if she finds out I'm cooking without someone watching. Especially when I tried to make hotdogs that day and it caught on fire, then I sprayed it with air freshener. She never tried to trust me again with the stove. "Mac n cheese, mac n cheese. There you are. This should be enough for all of us."

All I know is, he better like it.

"Crap, turn this down before it boils over!"

"How's it coming along so far? Woo we, this is a fine kitchen. You were not lying when you said your mom is a doctor. You all even have the stove exhaust hood. Sara and I tried making one of these, but it's a bit complex for the house, but it's sure convenient."

"It's cool. Mom makes us clean if we get in trouble or on Sundays. So that is why it's so clean."

"Speaking of clean, I see you have a bit of cheese by your foot." Mr. Wilson chuckles. "Oh lord, you're making the kids macaroni. Hmph, I should have known."

"What's wrong with it? It's good!"

"Me and Sara last bought that for Jason when he was four. I don't mind."

"Good, because then you'll stay hungry like you told me at your place. It's almost done. Call Zaraiella and tell her I made our favorite food."

"She's quite a loner, I see. She doesn't come out and talk much."

"No, she's been like that ever since. Shoot, I don't know. Since she was born, I guess."

If Mom was here right now, she would have told her to come down and talk. Zaraiella was picked on at school for being so quiet. Someone tried bullying me before, but it never worked. Lakia, our oldest sister, would always come and help me with this other girl I remember. That's why I hated when Lakia had to leave our school.

"And this is mother? I am assuming. Wow."

"Yea, that's us. The family picture."

"Your older sister looks somewhat like you. Your mother is Dominican?"

"No, Indian, Native American. Lakia told me the name of the Indian group or whatever. It starts with a, N. Na…Na, va, ho. Yea, Navajo, that's it."

"Oh, I don't know much about the tribes. It does explain why Zaraiella's hair is so long. I mean your hair is nice too"

"Yea, I know. She has the longest. I'm okay with my own. You sure are staring hard at our picture, Mr."

Mr. Wilson chuckles. "It is because the family looks so beautiful. I wanted my family to take a family portrait like this. Perhaps one day.

I saw those pictures in the living room with you all. Your mother sure loved the camera."

"Yea, she always talks about making memories and keeping them around to show us who are family is and guests like you who come. All of us have baby pictures of around one year old which I love, and of course I am the cutest," I said, twisting in front of the stove. "Zaraiella, which is weird. I don't think her firstborn picture is out there. Mom must keep them in her room."

"You cooked when Mommy isn't here. She's going to be mad," Zaraiella says stretching her eyes.

"Tsk. She can't get mad; we haven't eaten anything."

"But she said that nobody can cook when she isn't here, only, Lakia."

"I'm here. I'll let her know that Munisha is a very responsible young lady. Munisha just has to make a deal to be nicer to her baby sister."

"I am. Zaraiella always wants to cry and tell. That's why other kids will bully her in school."

"It's nothing wrong with telling, as long as it's just. Don't mind your sister, Zaraiella. Always be truthful and speak up, it will take you a long way. May even save a life."

"Ha, to keep you beat up and made fun of," I said.

"You know Janice and Jason was doing everything in school. They never were troubled kids. Only Jason would decline in some of his arithmetic's."

"He's dumb?" I asked, stirring fast.

"Oh no, my champ is sharp as a razor. Smart in other words, since you did not seem to catch the, sharp part."

"No, just hungry. This takes too long."

"Good, because I don't want anything uncooked. Anyways, it's just that, you young people want to grow up so fast. Then when the time comes to growing up, you don't want to. Just like how you want to stir that pot like you are running out of time in the world. You cannot rush life, or the flavor will be horrible."

Mr. Wilson must didn't know I did not really care.

"So, my boy Jason wants to chase after girls instead of his studies. We indeed stay in a remote area outside of town, but I told him to get his lessons first, and everything will just follow along behind it."

"Girls, heh, boys my age are dumb. I know some that like me at school."

"Do you pay them any mind?" Mr. Wilson said with a smile.

"Nope, my crush is in a higher grade than me. He seems to like girls only in his grade."

"Keep your studies and then find a nice guy. The right one will always come. This is mine?"

"Yup. It looks so good, doesn't it?" I smiled.

"I'll just pray over it, that's all."

So rude. I didn't make poison. Talking about praying over it. "Here, Zaraiella. Let's eat on the couch and see what's on tv."

"I know your mom doesn't let you eat outside the kitchen. You eat at the table."

"We won't make a mess," I said.

"Thanks, Munisha," Zaraiella says.

"Ugh, cooking is hard."

"Cooking is hard, ha, chef Munsha. You have a long way to go. You see, mac n cheese loves you so much, it followed you on the carpet."

"Crap. It's nothing. Get it later."

"Why didn't you make chicken nuggets, Munisha?" Zaraiella asked.

"Mom keeps them in the deep freezer, don't feel like going through all of that she has in there. There's never anything on."

"Find a good movie to watch."

"Like what, Mr. Wilson?" I asked.

"Put on a good western."

"Western?" I grinned. "Only old people watch that. Dad used to watch that crap."

"You mean, entertainment? Cowboy, rodeotype movies. All that foolishness you all watch nowadays, ha."

"Uh, no. Let's watch this, Love Beyond Limits. This looks good, doesn't it, Zaraiella."

"Better not be any foolishness of nudity."

I grinned. "Lighten up, Mr. Wilson."

It's dark, and they still haven't shown up. What if, Zaraiella is right?

"That sure wasn't bad, chef Munisha. Not bad at all. I have not thought about it much but I've noticed that neither Janice nor Jason knows how to cook. Well, at least make something as simple."

"Mom wanted me to learn as soon as possible, she said, because if it's only me, Lakia, and Zaraiella at home. We will have to make something."

"Mommy sometimes work very late. It will be night when she comes home."

"That's how it be with those types of careers."

"And that's why I told you I don't want to be any of those. You don't have free time to do anything."

"Welp, as I said before. You must work hard to get yourself free from this world. It's the reason"

Knock Knock Knock.

"That must be them! I told you they would be back, Zaraiella."

"No running in the house! The hell, this isn't my kingdom."

Knock Knock Knock

"Hold on, Mom!"

"Don't open that door without seeing who it is, girls!"

I can't believe it. They made it back home. I should have bet Zaraiella on something since she didn't believe me. "Mom, you're…"

"Hello, um, young girls. Is your mum home?"

I was just so happy. "No, she's not."

"I came by earlier, and no one was here. Tell her the car wash man came by when she gets here, will ya? I can be here early tomorrow morning"

"Who are you?" Mr. Wilson says, squeezing between me and Zaraiella.

"Good evening, Mister. I'm the local car wash man for the area. I was just stopping by again to see if Ms. Isabella was here. Usually do her car every other weekend."

"She's not here," Mr. Wilson says.

"Yes, her daughters already told me. Pardon me, sir, but who are you?"

"He's our dad," I said. "He came from a long vacation and came back yesterday,"

"Yea, I've been in the service and on release for a little. Good to be with family before the holidays."

"That's magnificent sir, it's an honor to meet someone serving. I'll be going, be sure to ask your mum for me, girls, and good to meet you Misterr...."

"Tim."

"Tim. Cheerio!"

"He sure is persistent to keep coming back like that. Have to make those funds. Try giving your mom a call again, Munisha. We need to begin to make some decisions."

"I'll try. Qunisa, Call Mom one more time for me. Speaker it."

My heart is starting to feel funny again. I hate this feeling. Things should be okay, no matter how I think it will turn out.

"Hello, this is Isabella Lozano speaking. I am"

"Quinsa, hang up. Tsk. Straight to voicemail. Ahhh!"

"Now, don't get all bent up about it, Munisha," Mr. Wilson said. "You say you don't know your other sister's number?"

"Nope. It's getting to the point. I'm like whatever."

"Now now. Don't give up hope. There could be some mishaps and delay. That's the reason why they haven't arrived yet."

"And the car wash man never seen them either," Zaraiella said.

"Well, we need to decide before morning what we are doing. As you know, I cannot stay here. So, my plan is for you two to just come back with me and we leave a letter. The good side to this is that we can leave early, right when curfew is over, and we head on out with all the things you need. It's just to stay prudent for the time being."

"It's just not fair, Mr. Wilson!" I said as I threw myself on the couch once again.

"I told you, Munisha."

"Oh my gosh! Shut up, Zaraiella!"

"Hey, don't yell at your sister, it's not her fault. Just know by morning, we head out. My horse is probably gone; but there's nothing I can do about that now."

"I'm so sorry, Mr. Wilson." I frowned.

"No need to be. Doing what is right is the most important. We leave before sunrise."

My brain was all over the place. There is no way we can just stay here. What if the S.I.L.O people come and take us? This is why Lakia should have been here. She always knew what to do. If I we were to go with Mr. Wilson, he most likely will turn us into hillbillies.

"You all don't have any other family? Not even nearby?"

"We don't have family around. Nobody I know," I said.

I am not really in the mood to be talking, and everybody keeps saying things like I know what to do.

"We can go to the neighbor next door, Munisha."

"Not that old lady, Zaraiella. She's crazy and mean."

"All that doesn't matter as long as you both are safe. It is just that I can't leave you both out here by yourselves. Again, you two will need to know what you want. It is a decision that affects what happens in the future. Schools are not open for two more days. It's like a gamble. Last alternative is to turn you over to authorities."

"Authorities? You mean the police?"

"We didn't do anything," Zaraiella said.

"He's saying were going to be watched by the police. We would just go with you. The police may send us to S.I.L.O too. That place is bad, and they took our mom and sister."

"I know, I know, calm down, Munisha."

"Then we will just stay here until they come back. We'll be safe, right Zaraiella?"

"Negative." Mr. Wilson said. "You two are kids. This area may be quiet and seems safe. Unfortunately, I am the one responsible for you both. It's my duty that I took upon myself to make sure everything goes well, and you all are safe."

"I don't know," I said as I just laid my head back on Mom's couch. "What am I supposed to do?"

"Better know something by tomorrow morning. At least something in mind."

"Let's go, Zaraiella."

"Where?"

"To bed. Mom and Lakia are going to be back in the morning. Goodnight, Mr. Wilson."

"You both have a goodnight. Remember what I said, you hear?"

"He would actually take us to the police. There is no way I'm going to the neighbor's house either. That's like being in detention there."

"Munisha, what are we going to do?"

"Don't really know yet."

"What if they don't come back? I know you don't like me saying stuff like that," Zaraiella says softly.

"I'm not mad about what you said. It's just that you should think good, think positive. The problem is for sure we can't just stay here."

"We have to go to the lady next door who watches us."

"Then that's going to be the most boring time ever. She will make us sit in one spot with that plastic and tell us to do nothing. Definitely not going there. Think about this. She may send us off to S.I.L.O. She's crazy."

"Then we just go back with, Mr. Wilson, I don't know."

"He doesn't want us back there. He brought us way over here, I don't think he will bring us back with him."

"We could go back and ride horses. You can, I'll be feeding the other animals."

"That's why you want to go back there. You want to play farm girl. Mom and Lakia are somewhere, and you want to play with stupid animals? I'm going to take my bath and go to bed."

Only thing she is right about is that Mr. Wilson would be the best way. How are we supposed to go to school? All our friends, teachers, will be looking for us. Maybe, Mom and Lakia are in S.I.L.O. They never been released. Maybe tomorrow. Hopefully.

"Good morning! Munisha, Zaraiella. This sofa knows it's comfy, didn't have to lay across it or recline in it."

"Mom bought it last year," I said.

"Very nice, very nice. So, what will it be? Hm? It's going to beee?" Mr. Wilson said staring into my eyes.

"We're going to stay here. We're old enough to stay home and take care of ourselves."

"Now we both know my friend that is not going to happen."

"We can't come back with you and"

"I never said that you two can't. It's that you both know our way of living is not how you two were raised. I have good news and bad news to share by the way."

"Did you hear from Mommy?" Zaraiella asked.

"What happened, Mr. Wilson?"

"The snow is letting up, and I can get back without freezing. Most likely my horse should be okay. The bad news…last night before I drifted off, turned to the news. S.I.L.O is making things a bit difficult for the city, for the country. What are they up to? Is my question."

"They came here and took us from our home," I said.

"I'm sure of it; but now they're locking down the city. Meaning that there will be no one coming in or out. This is a small place, so they can do something like that. That issue at the building, it's most likely why they're taking drastic measures like this."

"Mr. Wilson, then we should go with him, Munisha. We can just try and come back."

Look at my sister. She thinks she knows what is best.

"This isn't good, I don't know what we should really do."

"Did your neighbors ever go and get the insertion?" Mr. Wilson asks with eyes glued to the window.

"We don't know, why?" I asked.

"There's a S.I.L.O van next door. Looks like they're about to go for a ride themselves. Wait, one of oh crap! One is walking this way."

"If they already came to this house, why would they check it again?"

I thought Mr. Wilson wouldn't be so scary, but this now shows that everyone is afraid of S.I.L.O.

Knock Knock Knock

"Don't make a sound you two," Mr. Wilson whispered.

"Let's go upstairs, Zaraiella."

"Why are they here, are they taking us again?"

"No Zaraiella, calm down," Mr. Wilson said.

If they tried to take us, I swear I would fight them and run. They won't take my little sister either.

"Munisha, look out the window. They're taking her."

"That can only mean they are going house to house; why?"

"Munisha, Zaraiella, where is your mother's room? We have to get out of here and fast."

"What are you going to do?" I asked. "What are you doing in there?!"

"Where does your mother usually keep her keys?"

"In the kitchen, they're on the counter. You are going to take her car? You can't do that."

"Oh yes we can. These people are pulling civilians out of their own homes. What the hell is going on?"

"Mr. Wilson, you can't just take our mom's car. What if she comes back?"

"Hmph, trust me, I don't want it."

"Mr. Wilson, three S.I.L.O vans are outside now," Zaraiella said coming into the room.

"They're doing all this for martial law. There you are! Okay we wait till they move out, and then we leave."

"You can't just take our mom's car!"

"Keep your voice down. I know this doesn't look right to you; you have to trust me. There is no way we can make it out of here without it. Think of this as lucky shot. We have to get out of here. Even better, I'll leave a note telling whoever enters this home that Tim Wilson, Munisha and Zaraiella are borrowing the car. We'll return it along with you two safely."

"I guess, that's okay." I said.

"You both need to gather your belongings; I know you have book bags. Grab things that you both need like clothing or medication."

"My princess vitamins, Mr. Wilson?" Zaraiella said.

"If you need it, grab it. Go upstairs you two. We'll leave when we're all clear."

"Shouldn't we just stay and wait a little longer? Maybe we could wait one more day."

I thought to myself. I should bring something just in case we are stuck there a little longer.

"You two almost ready?! We're in the clear!"

"We didn't bathe or eat yet," I said.

"Don't worry, at my place you can take care of that. You won't be staying there forever."

Look what I found, I forgot I had this. Who knows how bad this was going to get? I may need to cut someone later on.

"Where did you get that from, Munisha?"

"Lakia gave me this when I started walking home alone."

"Let's move you two!" Mr. Wilson shouts.

I really wanted to stay. What if Mom came right when we left? "Quinsa, let Mom know that we came and went with, Mr. Wilson. Thanks!"

"Hope you two have everything? This is just temporary, so keep that in mind."

I wish they would just come back. I know S.I.L.O have them for sure. Why won't they let them go?

"You two brought chips and juice. Heh, that's you all youngins' health."

"We don't really like your food," I frowned.

"That is fine, Munisha. Let's go, and let's be quick. Lock the door behind you."

"Come back to us, I hope you are safe, Mom, and Lakia."

"Munisha, come on!"

Mr. Wilson doesn't know honking the horn in the neighborhood is like waking up all the dogs.

"Sit in the back with me, Munisha!"

That strange feeling looking at my house again and leaving. I hate it. "Better bring my mom's car back."

"Hmph, yes, your majesty."

The foggy neighborhood made me think how that night we left Mr. Wilson and tried to find our way back home. What was I thinking? Then she would have been scared, saying a monster would have been in the mist.

"Sweet ride you two mom has, not going to lie. The heated seat is amazing. I even feel safer with the dream catcher swinging in front of me. Hope she doesn't, as you say, freak out too bad when she sees the car isn't there. That, Quinsa, will tell her everything."

Of course, Mom will freak out. Who wouldn't when they come home, and they don't see their stuff? "Look, a S.I.L.O van, Mr. Wilson."

"Yea, there everywhere. It's only seven o' clock and they are going to people homes. My thought on it, why would they be taking people if the building had an accident? Unless there are two."

"The place is huge. They probably take will them to another spot in there."

"Yea, it's huge! Remember Munisha, there was a tall building behind it too!"

"I wonder what they do in there," I said.

"Experiments. Rumors went around that they were experimenting on people for the, cure. Those basically who are made to be superior in this world I should say. Humans that will make civilization much easier for everyone but that doesn't seem to be working so well. I know it's something like that. I heard some when they are being experimented on, they will have changes in their DNA. Crap! Tsk, how can I forget?"

"What's wrong?" I asked.

"My horse, she's still out here. I'll have to get her on foot or have Sara take me to her. Dammit."

"You just swore."

"Shoosh, Zaraiella, sorry about your horse again."

"No, no need to be."

CHAPTER 6

Affinity

ou two don't have to be quiet back there. Everything is going to be alright. You all mom should know that her two babies are going to be in good hands. How old is your mom anyways?

"She told us that ladies shouldn't ever tell their age." I said, quietly.

"Ha, I haven't heard that old saying in a long time. I know her name is Isabell."

"It's Isabella," Zaraiella said.

"Isabella, Isabella. That's right. Lakia, correct? Any chance you have a picture of either of them to take with you."

"I didn't get one. What about you, Zaraiella?"

"I forgot."

"Told you two to take everything you need."

"Yea we did. We got clothes. Zaraiella tried to take all her toys." It would be crazy if we just left, and they came back in the morning to see if anything has changed. "What if she's there? Are you going to take me and Zaraiella with you?"

"The way I move, you two won't be up at that time. We've passed so many S.I.L.O vehicles. Something is going on. I want to go back, see what's going on, and then send you both back if your mother is there. If they're really going to lock the city down on Monday, my family will have some changes to make. I don't think they will."

How they did Mom and my sister, they already caused changes. It doesn't make sense to bring people to a place to make them get something they don't want. Then like earlier, forcing people when they don't want to do something. "Why is all this bad stuff happening, Mr. Wilson?"

"Control, control in this world. Manipulation, power and wealth mandates lives. Then we have those, sausagebrain people as I always say. Just too many of those type of sheep. Also, if you are not living in a luxury million dollar home, then your out of gas somewhat."

"That's why I'm going to be rich when I grow up," I said. "Nobody is controlling me."

"Dream big, Munisha, dream big."

The thing is, what if I fail because I haven't been to school? This is bad. I can't stay in the same grade, I'll be laughed at.

"Why…why is it taking so long to get back, Mr. Wilson?"

"It's because of the forest, Zaraiella," I said.

"That's right. We have to go all the way around the trees. That's why Betsy was the best alternative. In my opinion, horses always have the better advantage when it comes to travel."

Mr. Wilson must be crazy thinking that the horse is still there. If it is, then I hope it's alive. I know there are bears and other things out here. "You don't seem worried about her."

"Believe me, I am. Especially since she's my partner in crime when I go out. No need to work myself up about it when I don't know the state she's in. I'm going to stay positive and know she's doing fine."

"Look, Munisha, a deer!"

"Oh yea, you have to be careful with those hoppers. They will jump right in front of you while driving then next thing you know you're in a tree. The ridiculous thing is when you get out and see it look at you then it just says, sorry, and hops away.

"Let me guess, you hit a lot of them before, huh?" I asked.

"When I used to be behind the wheel, I say about two or three. I have thrown those Bambi's right in the back. Good eaten right there."

"Eww, oh my gosh," Zaraiella moaned. "Why, why would eat a deer? Why?"

"Yes, mam. What's wrong with that? I'll tell you right now that it's better than them, chicken nasty nuggets you all like."

"That's because you didn't add the honey barbecue sauce on it," I smirked.

"One day you will try deer, and you're going to be like. Wow, Mr. Wilson was right, and it's actually real meat. Deer meat even has a lot of ways you can prepare it. Add it in soups, and mixed in potatoes and veggies. Mm, mm, good. That mac n cheese done wore off a long time ago. I can use some real food at the moment. The real foods are what you need in your body. Living foods, unless you want to get some grays early like me."

I can only stare and wonder what he's talking about. I'm a teenager. Other than that, Zaraiella could be the only family I have now. Just hope they're back tomorrow. Where could they be for them to be away from home that long? Something is just so weird and not right.

"This small trail here is our little private road. No one can find us unless they so happen to get lost like you two did."

"How did you find it? Like come to the area," I said.

"There's plenty of land to build a home. Sara and I chose this area. When my truck gave out, it did its duty to leave a trail."

The forest is so big, anyone can get lost out here. Even if you knew where you were going.

"How's your memory?"

"Very good, at least for me. I don't know about my little sister."

"Then you shouldn't have issues finding our place if you two get lost."

"Are there bears?" Zaraiella asked.

"That's a good question, all things. I had them on my plate, fox, squirrels and even some good ol' opossum meat."

"Ugh, yuck," I frowned. "You all eat everything."

"Yes mam, fresh natural nature giving food. If you two are lucky enough, you will also be introduced to it. Aww, home sweet home. Already know, Sara is shaking in her socks. We will have to tell her that we need to get Betsy later on, most definitely before this lockdown. Oh looky here who wants to follow behind us in."

I started to think it was S.I.L.O but of course an old raggedy truck would come to this place. "I just can't believe we came back here."

"It's not that bad, Munisha," Zaraiella said.

"Yea, until we're stuck here."

"We won't. Mr. Wilson said we'll be back home, and Mommy will either come for us or he bring us back."

"We stole Mom's car. She's going to be so pissed. We might even get grounded for a year. Lock the doors, Mr. Wilson."

"Almost forgot, these new cars are something else now. How you doing man?! What took ya? I expected you yesterday."

The short blonde hair man and his son, who looks to be around Zaraiella's age, looks like nice people.

"Well. Unfortunately got tied up at the market. My truck is acting up, all type of things. New guest, I'm assuming?"

"Yea man," Mr. Wilson scratches his head. "These two right here has a…y'know. I just took them home, but no one was there."

"I see. My son, Mark. Say hello."

He must don't know how to talk. "Yea, um…hi. Mr. Wilson, so we can try again tomorrow, and see? Maybe they will be back. Me and Zaraiella want to go home."

Mr. Wilson grins. "Persistent she is. Go on inside and let me take care of business and figure things out."

"Forget it, Mr. Wilson," I said. "Before someone steals my Mom's car."

Mr. Wilson was so old, he didn't even know about key bracelets.

"So, all you have to do is wave your hand on the handle?" Kenneth asks.

"Mom's bracelet is used to make the car do different things. Open the car and locks it without the key. With the ring connected to it, it can start it but Mom has it. Her phone can open it too."

"Yea…all of that. Tim, all this new technology keeps the system tracking your every move."

"That's exactly why I need to get rid of it before someone comes looking for it. It's the last thing I need around here."

"No problem. I can give you a ride back into town. Just come get this glass you asked for. These things are getting a little too expensive."

Living out here where no one is, is the worse. If something happened to you, no one would know.

"Time to hear the noise. Sara, Sara baby!"

Mrs. Wilson sighed. "It didn't work out well I see. Hello Kenneth, Mark."

"Howdy. Tim, me, and Mark has something to do, so we need to hurry on and get back in town if you don't mind."

"Aw man, you know I don't like putting stress on people. You've done enough by bringing this glass that Miss Hot Head owed me. Sara can take me back, and I'll get my horse. She's not far."

"You sure, Tim? I don't mind, you know I just don't want issues with curfew."

"I understand. Plus, you have some ways back to Lewiston. Better yet, better plan. I will keep the car here for a week or so. Once she gets back, their mom will notice it's missing, and they will track it here. Their wall maid will pick it up along with these two and that will be that."

"Tim, I think we should"

"No, no. I know what to do baby. Just need to make this quick. Kenneth," Mr. Wilson says grabbing and shaking hands hard. "Thanks for all your help. Take care of your boy out there. I'll see you in town in a week or so."

"Alrighty. I wish you to be safe out here. Good luck getting those girls back."

All I can do is feel the anger, and my heartbeat grows faster. We we're supposed to be home. I should have asked for the Kenneth guy to take us back, but his son acts so weird and quiet, almost like Zaraiella. What am I going to do?

"Dad, finally your back." Jason says, coming from upstairs. What happened? Why didn't you all go home?"

"Long story, champ. Where's Janice?"

"She is outside with the clothes. We were all kind of worried, but we all thought you were coming back late last night or early this morning."

Mr. Wilson sighed. "It's been a mission, Jason. Are you all good? Sara? Everything well with the farm?"

"Everything is just fine, I have work to do," Mrs. Wilson says as she puts her head down and walks away.

She even felt bad for us.

"Still wondering why they're back. What happened?"

"Geez, the cheater sounds like he doesn't want us back," I smirked.

"Miss you too, Munisha. Your best friend is outside, Zaraiella. Go see her. It's good to see you again, friend. Who's car?"

"Hmph, we borrowed it," Mr. Wilson said.

"It's nice! You finally thought about getting another car, Dad. About time."

"Hmph, you know better than that. It's their Mom's own. You know what, let get everyone inside. Munisha, I'll help you take these things upstairs. Then meet us back in the living room."

This place made me feel we should have just gone to the mean old neighbor's house. We could have gone there and then left to go back home. We should have just waited. I hate people sometimes.

"Hey, Munisha! Good to see you again," Janice said. She seemed happier to see my sister though.

"At least you have your best friend, Zaraiella. I'm stuck here pretty much by myself."

"Why did you both come back?" Janice asked.

"Our, mom wasn't home. Tsk, this is soooo baaaaad."

"It's alright. Mr. Wilson will take us back one day. Show me some of your dolls, Janice."

"You two have fun. I'm going downstairs."

"Was just coming to get you." Jason said. "Dad says that Zaraiella and Janice can stay. Just need you."

"Your dad must really want me. He always calls me for something like I'm an adult."

"You're funny. You're the leader, remember? Anyways, what actually happened?"

"A lot of things, it's been very weird. I don't know what's going on."

"Understandable. Dad always said to us about living in the city, it is actually really bad there now, it used to be so quiet and nice."

"Munisha and the boyfriend," Mrs. Wilson grinned.

"Oh gosh, no way! Sorry, Jason."

"Let's all sit down and talk," Mr. Wilson said. "Sara, kindly warm up something. Haven't eaten anything all morning. We will chat right when you are done. How are you feeling, Munisha?"

"I don't know, things are not good."

"Definitely don't you worry. Everything will work out for it's own good," Mr. Wilson comforted.

"What if I don't see them again?" I frowned.

"The problem is, Munisha, is that I can't promise you anything. The city is even not safe to go to at the moment."

"What's going on in the city now, Tim?"

"The city is, well first, let us begin with how that we made it to their home and then no one was home. We waited, and there still was no sign of the family."

"My goodness, mercy," Mrs. Wilson covered her mouth. "I'm sorry, Munisha,"

"Now, about the city."

"Dad, sorry. Not trying to cut you; but what happened to, Betsy?"

"She's out there near the town outskirts. I'll need you to drive me in a few minutes to get her, Sara."

"Mr. Wilson." Zaraiella said, walking down the stairs slowly with, Janice.

"Oh, now you two want to join us. We're all growing and learning. As I was saying. The city is going under lockdown in a few days."

"What? Tim, why?"

"Not to see my observation from what I've seen at the S.I.L.O building here comes what is called martial law. It's in effect and to the point where no one can do anything to a certain point. Something severely went wrong, and there is something they are not telling people."

"It's probably because they killed so many people at the facility."

"Very good possibility, Jason," Mr. Wilson rubbed his chin.

"How is me and, Zaraiella going to go back to school?"

Zaraiella face looked like we weren't going back now. I was starting to get so mad. Why did this happen?

"If they are locking down the city, then most likely, schools won't be open. People are not even supposed to be on the streets. Didn't the city go under this before, Tim?"

"It started on and off and began happening more often about five, six years ago."

"I remember. Zaraiella, that's when Mom said we couldn't go anywhere, not outside to play, to the movies, nowhere. I don't even remember if we could go to the store."

"That's what happens when the city goes under this particular law," Mr. Wilson says. "Good thing is, we are under no jurisdiction around here. It's unethical the way how they do manage society. Sara let's make way. Need to head out and get my other favorite girl. I want to get rid of that car, but hopefully, if we can't get them back, their parents will come."

"You're going to just drive my mom's car around?" I asked.

"That is the plan, missy. Sara, let's make it!"

"You all be good. I heard about you and Jason have that rematch. This would rather see who the real winner of uno is."

Mrs. Wilson doesn't know that this boy would try and play me day and night with that stupid game.

"That's right. How about it, Munisha?"

"Um, okay," I shrugged. "Guess it can take my mind off of it a little."

"Can me and, Zaraiella go out and play with the cow?"

"Most definitely not, you two can play in the house," Mrs. Wilson said. "You have dolls, Janice. Go ahead and introduce them to, Zaraiella. Your father and I will be back. Much love, and no going outside."

"Soooo, what happened when you all went?" Jason asked, stacking the cards.

"We told you already. No one was there. I don't think they're coming back."

"Oh, don't think like that. When Dad goes over there, I think your mom and sister will be home. Besides that! Let us get this match started!"

It's hard to concentrate on this kind of boring game. I just don't want to think about what has been going on. I want to go home. I swear this boy was cheating. There is no way he kept getting good cards.

"Uno! I win. I always win."

"Really?" I grinned. "Be right back."

He says he always win. "We'll see about that. I brought something just for this. You two having fun with dolls? Oh my gosh, what happened to her hair, Zaraiella?"

Instead of them playing with dolls, it looks like they were shaving them.

"Janice did that. I'm trying to learn how to braid. Janice is showing me."

"Oh gosh," I shook my head. "Please don't let her play in your hair, sis."

"I thought you said you didn't bring any games, Munisha."

"You know I had to. That boy thinks he can keep winning, and I'll show him he's not the best at everything."

He better not say he doesn't know how to play.

"You ready to get this whoopin', Mister, I always win?" I smiled.

"Checkers?" Jason frowned. "You would bring that from home just to get back at me. Let's do it then."

"Do you know how to play? Because if I, I mean when I win. I don't want you to act like you didn't know what you were doing."

"Checkers egh, haven't played in a while; but I should remember. What do I get if I beat you in your own game?"

"I will. I'll think about it."

"Fine, but if I do win, we go for a walk," Jason says, rubbing his hands together.

"For a walk? But your dad said"

"I know what he said, and we won't get in trouble."

"Okay, deal. I'm still thinking of my deal so don't be surprised," I said, placing the pieces.

"Just make sure you don't cheat in this too. Put the chips on the side if you get jumped."

"Come on, Munisha."

Jason isn't doing too bad. He took my king, and now we almost have the same amount of chips.

"Getting nervous friend?" Jason smiled.

"Nope, not at all. Just because you took my king doesn't change anything. I have you right where I want you, actually."

"Go ahead, take it."

"No, your turn, Munisha. Looks like I'm still the king of games."

"Hm, really? Back jump, Mr. King of games. I win," I laughed.

"Wo wo wo. Back jump? Where did that come from? You can do that?"

"Yea, I thought you knew how to play Mr., I'm so good at everything. You have to know how to move the pieces the right way in this game curly head."

"I do, but you never back jumped me until now."

"Exactly, and I came right when I needed it to."

"That's cheating. You know you can build a bad reputation for that."

"Uhuh, just like you."

Jason is not the only one with surprises. "Since I win. Let me see. I want you toooo. I want you to take me to the forest," I smiled.

"To the forest?"

"Yea let's go before they get back. You said we won't get in trouble, and we won't."

"Fine, still want my rematch by the way."

Something is telling me to go to just walk around outside. Even though I barely won, I could not think straight at all. Worrying like this will only make me get sad. Need to free my mind.

"Close the door slowly. Zaraiella will come with your little sister and will follow us. She's always following me."

"Just like Dad said, you're a leader so she's following you for a good reason. Wish it would be snowing. I'm going to miss it," Jason said, looking to the sky. "You know, it never really suppose to snow around this time of fall."

"Yea...why didn't your dad get another truck or something? In books and movies, they always have a wagon or some other thing to drive."

"Dad doesn't like too many things that use gas. Then electronics for sure."

"He told me; but it's easier to get around like that. Like how he took my mom's car. He can go anywhere; the horses only can go from here to there."

"True; but guess what. Horses can never run out of gas. They get tired, their loyal and guess what else. Never get tracked! We thought living out here would be the most boring thing ever. Janice and I got used to it, and now we like it."

"Yea; but what about your friends? You don't miss talking to other people? It's only you and her."

"Not really. Dad keeps me company and Mom has a sense of humor sometimes. Janice, I do bully her in uno, she never gives up playing. You can say that I have my family to keep me company. Dad wants me to focus on building, growing my own foods, and learning crafting like woodwork. Then I'll be able to build my own home one day like they did."

This boy was a true hillbilly. "Good luck finding a friend or girlfriend out here. You won't be able to find one if you're here all the time. Now maybe if someone like that guy and his son come by, they could bring someone you might like. It might work."

"You're right. I just focus on what I have to do first if the girl of my dreams comes along, then that's that. Dad said this one thing about having a woman. If I build a house and she can't hammer a nail with me, she isn't the one for me."

"I don't know. I never had a boyfriend before. Never thought about stuff like that. I understand you though. Means that boyfriend and girlfriend should work together."

"Hm, hm," Jason smirked.

He seemed like a nice guy. I just can't talk to him forever. "So where are we going?"

"You said you wanted to walk, so we're just going to walk."

It was peaceful out here. Birds chirping and small animals making noises as we walked past. I wouldn't actually mind living in a place where nature is. Animals to me were always creatures that helped each other. Even the tiniest bugs like ants will help the other lift something to the ant bed. Only time I see anyone helping someone else is when their close friends. I guess family should just help family.

"Thinking about what you said. Maybe I will find someone that way. I definitely won't find anyone out here."

"Umm, duhh! You just realize that? I have a question. How does your dad even talk to that guy? He doesn't have a phone."

"Well, Dad goes to some store in Bangor, where we all used to live. He leaves notes with the clerk and when Mr. Kenneth comes, he swings by if he needs to. He lives far from us but Mark told me he does some type of estate business here. That is why he comes by every now and then, only Dad knows. Now his son is boring. He's kind of young anyways but it's cool. We just play ball then I am left to be by myself."

"Wow, I feel bad for you. That sucks."

Jason grins. "Tell me about it."

"What was that?" I said, squinting my eyes pass the tress.

"What did you see?"

"Something just flew behind that tree."

"Oh, it could've been anything. Me and Janice saw a bat one time while we were out fishing with Dad."

"I bet it was so boring, wasn't it? Only guys like standing with a stick and worm, waiting for an innocent fish to come and take it."

"No, not at all. I enjoy it because it's"

"Boring?"

"Was going to say, peaceful. Never really like all a lot of wild things. Even at school, big events like that pep rally, I hated those."

"You played basketball, so you were going to be in it anyways. We were supposed to have one Friday coming, and now this stupid lockdown is going to start," I frowned, kicking a rock.

"Like I said, I hated it. The loud music, people jumping all over. It made me want to not play because I just don't like crowds and people staring at you."

"Aww, curly hair is a scary cat. You look like the type."

"You know, if Mom and Dad had stayed in the Bangor, I probably wouldn't even be going to prom. I don't know. Maybe I would. It's a onetime thing."

"Never thought about that. I'll be honest with you; I love it here. It takes my brain off of what's going on," I said, looking up at the tall trees.

"It should, it's so many things out here to do. I definitely can't wait when Dad teaches me how to shoot. He said he's going to get me out here soon and see if I can hit a raccoon or something."

Now that wasn't right. Using animals for target practice. They should only kill it if they need to. Pretty sure they wouldn't like it if the animals shot at them.

"Look, is that what you were talking about?" Jason asked, pointing behind my head.

The trees sure made this place look a little creepy. What if a tree limb grabbed you and took you up there with them? "Yea, what is that? Wait, that's a squirrel."

"Yup, they can fly. Bet you haven't seen any in your neighborhood."

"Sure haven't. That's pretty cool."

"The nature is mainly here in the forest. Come on, let's catch it!"

"No! Leave it alone. He is just doing his own little thing while we do ours. Awww, it's so cute too…and you want to catch it, then probably barbecue it."

"They taste good too you know," Jason said, kissing his fingers smiling at me.

"Oh my gosh. Don't make me puke."

"Squirrel stew. One day we will try it together."

I grinned. "You are by yourself; I won't be here. I will be home eating good food, not a poor squirrel. I can't imagine you all killing it, then fry it, bake it, or whatever."

"Mom and Dad do it all the time. How do you think we eat? Girls are always grossed out by something they don't understand."

"Just let me know how your future wife will be when she finds out you're into eating squirrels."

"And guess what, she's going to love me and love it too."

I can tell, me and Jason would never have the same mindset. "Wow! This is so beautiful! Look at the water, I can see myself so clearly."

"This stream literally goes all the way to the ocean," Jason says as he looks at me through our lake reflection.

"Really? I have to walk to the end then."

"I thought about walking to the end actually. Maybe when Dad and I go fishing again."

"Let's go. Let's walk in it."

"Are you crazy?!" Jason frowned. "That water is cold. I mean, you can go in there if you want."

"You're right, but since I won the bet, I dare you to put your feet in."

"Nice try, Munisha. You got your bet by wanting to come out here."

"It was actually your idea. You said you wanted, and I just chose to. My bet that I won lets me dare you to walk in. If you don't, then you're a scary little boy, and I'll never play you again in anything."

"You will have to choose a different dare. I am not about to get my feet wet, and it's cold. It's"

"Scary boy scary boy. My little sister would do it if she was here," I pouted.

"That's supposed to persuade me to jump in? Won't work my friend."

"Ha, you're just scared. Let's go back before they come back."

"Yea, oh shoot!"

"Ha, how's the water? That is what happens when you don't keep promises," I giggled.

"Aghhh. Crap! Look what you made me do!"

"You did that yourself, Jason. Are you okay?"

"I'm already in for a cold. Need to get these wet clothes off."

"Oh, you'll be alright. Don't be such a crybaby. If you had just put your feet in and do the dare like I told you, you wouldn't have fell."

"I hope you're happy, Munisha. Let's get out of here. Crap, the water was so cold!"

Maybe I was a little mean. That water did have have the steamy stream. "You know, Jason. I feel like things happen because it is supposed to."

"Why do you say that?"

"It's just something I feel. I even feel that I will not see my mom and Lakia again. Things just happen because it is supposed to, you think?"

"I don't know what you're talking about, all I know is these cold, wet clothes need to come off."

"Oh hush. That was supposed to happen. You didn't have to be all wet and cold if you just did what I told you. Ha, you might as well get half naked," I chuckled.

"You know…you are something else, Munisha," Jason says as he tries to squeeze water from his shirt. "Your name, no lie sounds like ammunition."

"Aww, I know, your mad. It's cute. I justhey, did you see that?"

Jason sighed. "What, another flying squirrel?"

"No, it was someone. It looked like it was a woman."

"What? Tsk, I don't see anyone, is this another one of your tricks? Make sure I"

"No, really. It was a woman or someone behind the tree. She was wearing like some long clothes. I am not crazy."

"Hmph, maybe it was someone lost. People do get lost in these woods. As long as they don't come and bother us. Crap, I don't have my knife."

Jason doesn't know a girl always comes prepared.

"Woo, nice. Where did you get that from?"

"My older sister gave it to me," I smirked. "I like knives for some weird reason."

"Don't play with it, opening and closing it like that."

"Trust me, I know what I'm doing."

"That reminds me, Janice took mine to cut her patients hair. Let Mom or Dad find out."

Mom would kill me if she knew I had a knife. Then especially if I tried to teach, Zaraiella how to use one. "They're still not back yet. Mom would have tripped out that my clothes are so wet."

"Now it's time to put it to the test. Let's race to the farm. Me and, Zaraiella did it."

"You are always moving; you never get tired or what?" Jason said.

"Come on, it was fun. Don't be such a loser."

"If I win, I dare you to wash and dry my clothes," Jason says as he takes off his shirt.

He does have an interesting body. "If I win, you must walk me to the ocean."

"You, you are so, never mind. Just be careful with that kn"

"Go!"

"Wait, that's not fair!"

"Oh shoot! Okay wet boy," I chuckled.

Jason talks too much so I will always use that against him. I definitely wasn't expecting him to catch up like that.

"What makes you think you were going to beat me? An exstar basketball player."

"I'll give it to you this time," I smirked.

"That's right, I wasn't going to let some girl beat me that easily. I should nickname you Tricky from this point on."

"Now where the hell have you two been?!"

"He looks upset. We're in trouble," I whispered.

"Dad, didn't know…didn't know you were back already."

CHAPTER 7

Tribulations

If only we had just walked around the farm. This old man would not shut up.

"What do you mean you two just went out?! I told everyone to stay indoors!" Mr. Wilson said.

"We didn't get hurt. It's not a big deal," Jason said while drying off with a towel.

"Not a big deal? It will be a big deal when you two get taken and never see life again. Ahh, I see. You are trying to impress Miss Pocahontas here. You better wise up, champ!"

"We're okay, Dad. My apologies."

"Uh, huh. Please do not let me catch you being disobedient at a level like that. What has gotten into Sara to make her take this long?"

"I don't know how you got here before her," I said.

"We went to the horse location, and thank God, Betsy was there safe and sound. I figured we would keep the car so we can check on your folks again sometime soon," Mr. Wilson folded his arms. "Told that wife of mine to come straight back here."

"Maybe she's lost. Like Munisha told you, you need a phone, and Mom too."

"Hmph. You will learn someday champ."

At least I am not the only one who knew better.

"Dad, you can't stay stuck in your old ways. Things are changing, aren't they? So that means we have to too."

"Enough, Jason!" Mr. Wilson said.

"Mr. Wilson."

"Yes, Munisha? I already know you're ready to give your twocents."

"I'm sorry, it wasn't…Jason's fault. I told him, let's go out since I beat him in a game."

"The master of uno has been finally beaten?" Mr. Wilson asked.

"No way, she brought checkers from her house."

"Checkers, uh oh. No one wants to see me in checkers now. I remember trying to find that game at store and it wasn't there. Thank you for being honest with me, Munisha. That's a brave thing to do as in telling the truth."

"Yea, thanks a lot, Munisha," Jason says, frowning then smirking.

"Yes, thank her. You would have had a nice behind whoopin' later." Mr. Wilson says.

"Man, Dad, I still get beatings?"

"As long as you stay in this house, you will. Speaking of the devil, I thought she did manage to get lost for a second. She pulled right on up when I said whoopin. Maybe she will offer it to you instead of me."

Mr. Wilson didn't seem like the type of dad to hit his kids, neither did, Mrs. Wilson. Mom would never, as I know it's illegal to hurt your children.

"Sara, what took ya?"

"How do you lock this from the outside?" Mrs. Wilson asked.

They all seem like they haven't been to civilization in a very long time. "Oh, you can do it with the bracelet too. Coming!"

"Yea, Sara, these new cars," Mr. Wilson says, wiping his finger on the side. "That's why I don't necessitate myself with them."

"That's it?" Mrs. Wilson asked. "You have to put this on with the key fob when you lock it?"

"Mom's phone and ring could to but we have neither."

"You didn't tell me about a ring." Jason said. "Yea, that's sick. When I get my own place, I'm going to buy one of these."

"That's it son, speak it into existence. Now again, what took you, Sara?"

"You know, since I was in town. I had to stop by the store and grab a few things."

"Like what? We have enough things here already, especially in the fridge."

"You'll see, Tim. It's a surprise."

"The real question is, how much did you trade? A radio?" Mr. Wilson frowned. "Now why do we need a radio, Sara?"

"You said S.I.L.O is out there making things so atrocious, so I thought it was best to know what's happening. Also new walkietalkies and a few groceries of course."

"Good Lord, Sara. We have walkietalkies already."

"Those cheap things. The store clerk said these will go miles. When you go out to Bangor, I can keep in contact with you."

"Meaning you traded something valuable on walkietalkies we don't even need," Mr. Wilson says with his hand on his head.

"They're cool, Dad. The old ones we have don't work that good anyways."

"Forty five mile range. You spent a pretty penny on this. Okay, I can see the walkietalkies; but the radio, we don't need it," Mr. Wilson said.

"So, how can we know what's going on out there, Tim?"

"It's because these two radio frequencies you bought already has a built in AM/FM installed," Mr. Wilson said.

"Well…we can still use it when we want to listen to music or something."

"We don't need all that, Sara. Hmph, since you got it, we'll put it to use."

"Of course! We should use them when we get lost, or if me, and Zaraiella get lost," I said.

"Don't tell me that means you're trying to wander off again. If you do, you're on your own next time because I am not going back out there to get you all in that darkness."

Adults always say that. I know he would still come. "No, we're not leaving. If we go off into the forest, we won't get lost with them."

"She's right, Dad. We could go out there and don't have to worry about finding our way back. You did say you wanted me to learn to hunt on my own one day."

"And when you're ready for that," Mr. Wilson said. "Nobody is going out to the forest. I hope I'm making myself clear."

"Yes, sir."

It does give me thoughts of going back alone with, Zaraiella. I knew where to go this time for sure. Just too far and too many animals.

"No going out in the forest missy."

"No Mr. Wilson, I won't. I'm going to nap outside."

"Suit yourself, it's cold out there."

"It's not really that bad out here. I like the cold sometimes anyways."

It is nice and cool out here. He said the house doesn't have heater or air conditioning. I feel that horrible feeling under my heart again. Where is my Mom and sister? I wish I can call them. "Wish I knew how to drive this thing."

I wonder if I drive, will S.I.L.O come after me? "Zaraiella? I never even noticed Mom had a picture of her near the cup holder. She looks a little different from her other pictures even though I have never seen her being this age, especially inside the house. Just don't remember, I guess. She always had a lot of hair. What else does Mom keep in here? Hand sanitizer, booklet, perfume. Aw wow, the keychain I bought her last year for her birthday. No wonder I never seen her wearing it, she keeps everything in here. "Wish she left her music player in here too."

Knock Knock

"What the, what does he want?"

"Open the door!"

"What do you want, Jason?"

"Just wanted to see what my friend's mom car is like. It's nice in here. Smells like perfume. I want my car to smell like cologne. Wow, the roof, it's cool. The glass makes it look like two different skies. What's wrong with you?"

"Nothing, just here thinking," I said, leaning my head back on the soft seat.

"Thinking about getting that rematch in checkers? Or is it uno, madam Cheater?"

"Nope, I don't feel like it right now. All you do is play games, huh?"

Jason smiled. "I know you want to go home. You will, trust me."

"It's not only that. Thinking about the city, what Mr. Wilson said is kind of scary. What did Mr. Wilson say to you? It's shutting down or something, isn't it?"

"I don't know. Dad says things, he could be wrong."

"He said he saw something on tv at our house, saying they will shut it down."

"Yea, they could be wrong too. If you push the start button, will it turn on?"

"No, I don't have the ring. The bracelet only lets me open the door or lock it. I need Mom's ring with the bracelet or the key fob to start it. See, it says requires key fob or key ring."

"Now that's cool."

"What? The key?"

"No, no. A girl who knows about cars. I like girls like that."

I didn't know if he was trying to make me smile, but it was working. "Yea, some are pretty. Our neighbor has one that the doors slide forward. Tsk, if I knew how to drive, trust me, me and Zaraiella would be gone."

"Driving is easy. You know Dad taught me when I was eight, I think. His truck was running of course. You just put your foot on the break, put the car in drive, and then hit the gas. One time I almost had hit the house."

I shook my head. "You can't drive then."

"It was a mistake. I bet I could drive this thing if you had the keys."

"Yea right. I wouldn't let you drive my mom's car. Next thing you know you have it rammed into one of the trees. Here comes your dad. He's going to tell us to get out, watch."

"Hey, you two. Hope you two aren't doing anything we all will regret later."

Jason grinned. "Come on, Dad. Let me have some privacy."

"Hmph. Sara has dinner ready. You all come on in, it's cold out here. Don't know how ya'll do it."

"Even better, nasty dinner is ready," I mumbled.

"Mom had bought something different when she went out. I'm hungry so I'll see you inside. And Munisha," Jason says, looking at me with his light brown eyes and placing his hand on mine. "Everything will be okay. Come on."

Jason was very nice for that. His hand made me feel a little better even though I'm not sure I want to stay in this place.

"Munisha, look! I braided her hair!"

"It looks good, Zaraiella. Now you have to finish all of her hair. You will have to teach me how to braid, Janice."

"It's not hard, it's three different things you do when you twist hair."

"What do we have to eat, Mrs. Wilson?" I asked.

"Chicken and spaghetti."

"Really? Oh, thank god!" I said, throwing my hands in the air.

"I told you, Munisha. No need to keep pouting."

"Don't get too comfortable, you all," Mr. Wilson says. "This is a treat we have this evening. No one is getting fat around here with only protein and carbs. Sara baby, you did great with this by the way."

"It's not going to hurt anyone, Tim. Everybody seemed to have it a little rough the past few days."

The spaghetti smelt so good and taste like how our mom makes it. She didn't put the green stuff on it like how they have it. I was afraid they were going to give me some opossum or raccoon.

"Tomorrow, you all, early in the morning you know I will be checking to see about, Munisha and Zaraiella family. If I am not back by sunrise, do not come looking for me or start worrying. Especially for you two wanderers. Please do not let me find you all out there. I am not obligated to punish someone else's children. However, other things will be accepted."

"What are you going to do, Tim? Make them clean?"

I wish he would make us do that. Then we will know exactly why he would want to keep us here. To make us clean this hillbilly farm.

"No, that's not a punishment. That's a chore," Mr. Wilson smiled as he kept his head in his plate.

"I won't go anywhere, Mr. Wilson. Only if Jason tries to make me play uno again. Hate that game."

"She beat me in checkers, almost had her though."

"See Jason, told you uno is just your game. Tim will play checkers all day if he could."

"I told them, that's my alltime favorite. Oh, it's been a time and a half," Mr. Wilson yawned while patting is belly. "You all have a goodnight."

"Don't worry, you two. I'm sure Tim will return with good news in the morning."

What if he doesn't? What if they still haven't come back? That only means we will be stuck here. I will try to be positive, it's just so hard. One more night here, then we will be back, and in my own bed. Not the these hard wooden floors. When winter ends, and summer comes, this place will be boring and hot.

"It's morning, and he still isn't back yet."

There is no sign of him, and it's almost sunrise.

"Stop worrying so much, Munisha. He is coming back," Zaraiella said, fiddling with her friend's doll.

"He said he will be back by sunrise. That means when the sun is up, Zaraiella."

"At least we don't have to work. Mrs. Wilson said I can't play with Janice until she's done with her chores."

"You want to play; I want to go home. I want to see Mom and Lakia."

"It's nothing we can do. We have to wait, Munisha. Just wait."

"Let's go outside," I said, pulling my body from the bed.

"We didn't eat yet."

"I'm not in the mood."

As Mom used to say all the time, her blood is beginning to boil. Now I knew what it meant.

"What are we going to do? We can't do anything outside since Jason and Janice have chores."

"We will do something."

I can't help it. I just have a funny feeling that they are there. Maybe Mr. Wilson is there talking with them, and they are coming after Mom feeds him.

"It's not ready yet you two," Mrs. Wilson says right before we can enter the kitchen.

"We're just going outside. Zaraiella and me are going to look around."

"Hmm. Alright, now remember not to go wandering beyond the our land."

"We won't," I smiled.

"Also remember not to bother with, Jason or Janice. Their work is crucial this morning, and they need to be finished before Tim gets back."

This was so horrible. "We're going to end up like them, Zaraiella."

"Janice! Heeyy!"

"Mrs. Wilson just said don't bother them. She's going to make us go back inside."

Zaraiella pouts. "I'm just saying hi."

"Maybe you could go help her with the milking. You like it too, don't you?"

"Yes; but Mrs. Wilson said I can't," Zaraiella frowns.

"It's up to you. You're helping, so I don't see anything wrong with that."

"Are you sure, Munisha? I don't want to get everyone in trouble."

"You won't. Go ahead."

Baby sis is so funny sometimes. I love her so much. I will be alone if she were to disappear. "I wonder what's in here. Hack hack. It's so dusty, what the?"

Mr. Wilson must like to collect big knives. I had never seen things like these before. "I wonder what this is called. Usually, ghosts carry these on their back in movies. Then swing it!"

Bling

"Eygh!"

I know what this is, what they use to catch big animals with on their foot. "Geez, this thing is heavy."

Mr. Wilson must have brought all of these things from another place. It's old and dusty.

"Hey! What are you doing in here, Munisha?"

He scared the heck out of me. "Oh, I was just looking around. I didn't touch anything."

"You didn't? Why is this scythe on the floor? You want to kill somebody?"

"Only people who took my mom and sister," I smirked.

"Wow, I was just joking you know."

"Why does he have all these things in here?"

"Never really knew. Dad always liked weapons. I forgot to tell you, Dad trains me on how to fight. He used to be in martial arts long time ago. Did it while he was in the army or whatever."

"That's cool, I wanted to take martial arts classes; but my overprotective mom didn't want me to. My older sister was in it, so it made me want to go and do it too."

"Well, if you stay here, Dad can show you some things. He's teaching me how to do this."

"Spin a stick? That's what us girls do in cheerleading. I think they're called batons."

"Yea, I can use this to kick some behind, believe me," Jason says, spinning the pole, making a breeze.

"Ooh, tough guy. Ha, if you tried to hit someone with that thing, they would probably take it from you and hit you with it. Does he teach you how to fight with your hands?"

"Of course, that's the first thing he taught me."

"I definitely want to learn one day."

It's good to know how to defend yourself. Never know when you need it. "Your Dad has a lot of things. You should be…why are you looking at me like that?"

"Oh," Jason grins. "I don't know."

"You two love birds in my sawmill now?! Get outta' there!"

"Dad, um, she was just looking around."

"Yea yea yea. Miss Pocahontas here leads you into temptation I see. Out!"

"Mr. Wilson, were they there? Please tell me they were."

"Hmph, Munisha, something is going on," Mr. Wilson says as he tries to clamp his lock with a frown.

"What? Were they there or not?"

"…Munisha."

"Just tell me, tell me!"

"Calm down," Mr. Wilson said. "Just"

"I can't. I can't, I hate them so much! I hate them!"

"I'm sorry, Munisha," Jason said.

"Get off me, Jason! I hate those people. I…I. Why did they have to take them?"

"Tim! I told you not to tell her so soon. Now she's all upset."

"I didn't say a word. I feel just as bad. Dammit!"

Mrs. Wilson tries to smile with her arms open. "It's okay honey, it's okay. It's okay."

"No, it's not! They killed them. They…they, took my Mom, and Lakia and killed them. Why?!"

"Go upstairs and ease your mind," Mr. Wilson says. "You need some rest, and we will speak on it together soon."

I am breaking down. There is no way they are alive now; they never came back.

"Munisha, you have to be strong," Mrs. Wilson said, hugging me tightly.

Seeing my Mom, and her last words to me before we left home was just that. "I…I can't. I just know that's what happened."

"You will have to calm down. Zaraiella, your little sister will be distraught. Please, Munisha, here, wipe your face. Go upstairs and run a bath or I can do it for you and try to relax."

"No…sniff. I'll go. I'll do it."

This was going to happen just like I already knew it would. I didn't want to believe it; but it hurt so much. What are we going to do now? We can't be stuck here in this place. We need to go home. The floor creeks every time you walk in. This isn't my life, and no bath can make me feel better. "Don't even feel like bathing. Feels like, I just want to…"

"Munisha, are you okay in there? Munisha?!"

Knock Knock Knock

"Munisha, is everything alright? What is going on in there? Sweety, open the door, please."

Knock Knock Knock Knock

"Oh, God! TIM!"

"Munisha, open the door! How long has she been in there, Sara?!"

"A good hour."

"Alright, you won't open it?!"

BING

"Munisha! Oh Christ. What have you done?! Sara, get me bandages with towels immediately!"

"Oh God! There's so much blood!"

"Munisha, can you hear me? Munisha. She's unconscious. What the, where did you get this knife from?"

"Dad…damn."

"I have the towels! Tim, this is bad."

"She's going to be alright, Sara."

"I'm…I'm sorry."

"Don't speak, Munisha, don't speak. Just rest."

"You need my help, Dad?"

"Just help me open this door. Sorry your sister has to see you like this. Damn it child!"

I feel it in my chest, I feel it in my heart. I just wanted them back, I love them, and there is nothing to heal the spot.

"Agh."

"Munisha, are you okay? Mrs. Wilson, Mrs. Wilson! She woke up!"

"I'm…sorry, Zaraiella. I'm okay, just…agh."

"I heard them say you were bleeding bad."

"Good to see your up," Mrs. Wilson says walking fast to me. "What were you thinking, Munisha? No, really."

"I don't know, just…very upset."

"So, you go and take a switchblade. Don't even know where you got it from; but you stabbed yourself pretty good. Child, I am very disappointed in you."

"I just…want them back."

Mrs. Wilson frowns. "That's not how you solve things. What I mean, I know your pain. However, there is so much to life sweety. Just because something isn't going right doesn't mean you should end it."

"I understand, and I'm so sorry. Sorry too, Zaraiella. Agh. Tsk, where is, Mr. Wilson?"

"He's outside. I thought you were just crying in the bathroom; but once I didn't hear you for a minute, I ran and got him."

"It felt so weird. Promise…I won't do it again"

"Surely you won't," Mrs. Wilson frowned, placing her hands on her hips. "I had to stitch your chest up, so take it easy please. You'll be fine, though you will definitely have a scar on that beautiful, golden tan skin. Shame on you, Munisha. Please don't ever do this again."

I didn't know what to say. Something just felt like it came inside of me and made me do it.

"Now, I still have some tidying up to do. You two can talk but keep it short. Not too long, okay, Zaraiella."

"Agh, this thing hurts," I said, trying to lift up out of bed.

"They said you passed out. I was so scared, Munisha. The bucket that I was carrying turned over when I came to you. They might be mad at me"

"That's okay. Before I passed out, I heard them talking. I thought I died."

"Why did you do it? Why did you hurt yourself?" Zaraiella murmured, looking at me with her big watery eyes.

"Something made me do it. It's nothing, Zaraiella."

"Munisha, I'm not stupid."

"I didn't say you were. I'm okay and, oof, that's what matters."

"You did it because we won't see them again."

"Let me rest, Zaraiella. We will talk later. I'm sorry."

"I'll let you sleep. Love you, Munisha."

Couldn't believe I stabbed myself. Soon, Mr. Wilson probably doesn't want us here now. I've caused so many problems. It's not my fault.

"Heard you were awake. Dang, Munisha. What would make you want to do something like this?"

I rolled my eyes. "It was a mistake, Jason."

"Dad didn't say it was. You deliberately wanted to end it in the restroom. Glad you're okay though, here."

"What's this?"

Probably some nasty medicine to make me feel better.

"Taste it. You'll love it."

"Lemonade, oh yea, this is good. You made it?"

"Mom did. I believe this is the best tasting lemonade in the world. I don't know how she does it; but it's amazing."

"Are they mad at me?"

"Mad, why would you think that?"

"Kinda', caused a lot of problems. Broke the window, tried to run away, and Mr. Wilson got mad about that. Now this."

"Don't worry about it. They're not mad. I'll say they're concerned about you. Dad is actually worried about something else too," Jason said as he sat next to me. "He told us something happened in the city. S.I.L.O is messing up everything he said."

"I know that already."

"That, he also said they're shutting down the city and making places close early. Dad goes to this place in Bangor to exchange things we have here for temporary credits or just trades. As soon as he left, he said S.I.L.O came inside the place, forced people out, and made the store close shop. I think it's the same place where he drops off letters to Mr. Kenneth."

"This is so bad. Why are they doing this?"

"I have an idea; but you will have to promise me not to tell anyone, not even your little sister."

"Promise. I'm not a person who tells people things. I might forget anyways."

"Good. He told me this; but not to tell anyone. I trust you and feel like you can keep this a secret. When he was coming back, something was running around on the streets. S.I.L.O was shooting at it, and it didn't do anything. He even said people were running, some taking pictures of it and crowding the streets everywhere."

"Wow, that's what he told you?"

"Ha, you don't believe it do you?" Jason chuckled.

"It's a lot of things happening so I don't know. My mom and sister are gone. My sister has weird things she sees and tells me about them. For some reason, she tells me something, and I don't want to listen or even believe it. Then next thing you know, it comes true. Don't tell her I told you that."

"As long as you keep your promise, I will too."

"Your dad is telling you that…a monster is out there? Of course, I would have believed it if he had a phone. Ha, and with a camera."

"Dad hates technology, especially new stuff. He will never get a cell phone. He took mines away long time ago when Mom did get me one. When we moved here, he stomped on it and tossed it somewhere saying, no son of mine will be a sausage brain."

I grinned. "Ouch, this, hurts. Why did he break it? Is he crazy?"

"He said, the internet is dangerous. When people have cell phones or any type of internet, they see things, look up things, and believe what ever they see or hear. Basically saying, people who can't think for themselves, the cyber world hacked mines in this matrix . That's what made everything so crazy."

"Oh, okay. I want more lemonade friend," I said, pulling my lips from the sweet taste.

"Guess it's that good. There's more downstairs."

"I'll go, I can still walk."

"Wait, you should rest. Stay put for once."

"Agh. It still does hurt a little. Thanks for helping me up."

"Don't mention it. What are friends for?"

Jason telling me that there is something out there gives me hope. Mom, and Lakia probably ran away from, whatever it was. They ran out of the city, still looking for us like we're looking for them.

"Munisha! What are you doing out of bed?" Mrs. Wilson asked. "You're supposed to be resting. Why did you come down here?"

"She never stays put, Sara. May have to chain her to the bed."

"I wanted some more lemonade. It is so good. Can I have some more, please? The radio is working. What are you listening to, Mr. Wilson?"

"Not now, Munisha," Mr. Wilson says with his ear to the radio. "I am working with this radio here. You could have just had Jason bring you more."

"I can do things myself; I don't need anyone. Where's, Zaraiella?"

"In the kitchen playing with, Janice," Mr. Wilson said. "Now kindly…my apologies. How are you feeling?"

"I'm, just sore. I'm sorry again for what I did."

"You're fine. Ssshh, Munisha," Mr. Wilson said as he listened in on the radio.

"And we are here live in Bangor. The S.I.L.O building seems to be still under uhh, investigation. The hole on the side as you can see is blown through. Hours ago, smoke was escaping along with reports of fugitives that have escaped this building. There is a great possibility that a riot led to this outbreak from the inside."

"What happened?" I asked.

"An issue happened again at the S.I.L.O building. A huge outbreak this time. There is something big happening. People are becoming less afraid. It's inevitable that this was going to happen now that these people have gotten out. Some are innocence, yet some convicts in there. They are the major issues."

"They're going to run for their lives, and hopefully they catch them," Jason said.

"No, Jason. As I said, some are innocence. This is a problem because now there will be a riot on the streets. Yesterday, I witnessed it myself at first hand."

"So, they will shut down the city like you said? Now we can never go home."

"To be honest with you, Munisha," Mr. Wilson said turning off the radio. "The inside world isn't where you want to be right now."

"Dad, let's go out for training. Or you're not feeling like it today?"

"No, no, nothing has changed. Today is training day."

Jason just looked like a little kid who just got what he wanted. "Let me join, I want to learn how to fight."

"Missy, you're in no condition. You get yourself some breakfast and rest. Let's hit it champ!"

After breakfast, I'm still going to learn. It was nothing else to do around here.

"Thanks, Mrs.Wilson for the lemonade. It was excellent. Please make more of it."

"You are very welcome, dear. How was the toast and eggs?"

"Very good, and better than the other stuff."

"See, I asked you, so you know what to look forward to. Look forward to the great things in life. Even if it's just the toast and eggs."

"Are you okay, Munisha?" Janice asked, with her sad face. "Zaraiella told me what happened."

"No, don't cry. I'm…alright. I'm going out with, Jason, and Mr. Wilson. Thanks again!"

"My husband just told you to rest today. You need to be taking it easy, not playing rough!"

"I'll be fine," I smiled.

I told them I was okay. It felt good out here. The sun feels fantastic.

"Munisha!" Mr. Wilson grinned as he shook his head. "What did I say to you before I left the house?"

"I'm okay, Mr. Wilson, I promise. At least let me watch."

"Dad, trust me, Munisha's an animal."

"I believe you; she won't stay put even if I placed barbed wire around her tied to a chair."

"Yea, I don't have to train today. Just let me see what you guys do. I always wanted to learn this stuff," I said, looking at them hitting each other with long wooden poles.

"Alright, but you sit or stand right there and observe. Don't need those stitches to break."

Jason chuckled. "She might break them just by standing there."

"Hmph, probably. Now, forward and then behind the back."

I hate this. If I didn't do what I did yesterday, I would've been training today.

"Dad, do you hear that?" Jason says, looking up.

"Sounds like a helicopter. Look, over there!"

"Oh shoot, never seen those before," Jason points.

"Those are the new Osprey choppers I bet, I should have known from the sound. It's going down now for sure."

CHAPTER 8

New Ways

Got you again, Munisha. This is too easy.

"Whatever. Let's do this again, sis. You are not beating me in checkers three times in a row. I'm telling you that right now."

"Looks like the queen of checkers isn't the queen no more," Jason said smiling.

"Shut up, Jason and just watch."

"It's my turn!"

"Yea, Munisha," Zaraiella says. "Let Janice play. I already gave you a rematch."

"Let's be fair, M. I mean, queen, M."

"Quiet, Jason for once, please. I will get you back soon, Zaraiella."

"The reason why you lost is because you get angry too easy," Zaraiella said, placing the checkers pieces back on the board.

"Let's go outside and practice. I need to get that figure eight spin right."

Something was wrong with me today. I lost to my sister twice, and she had three kings the last game. No one has ever done that to me before.

"You know, Zaraiella is right. You do get mad, and it seems that it messes with your thinking."

"I don't get mad. When you normally win in something all the time you get a little frustrated if you lose. Especially more than once."

"That will happen in anything. Back then in basketball, I remember we played against schools and won a lot and lost to some. One time this team we played. We had like sixteen points on the board, then you looked at the visitor score, it showed the forty. I threw that basketball out of bounds from a rebound. There was no hope."

"Look at the sore loser. I would've been mad too, so I don't blame you."

"Exactly! You can't get mad because, you will win some and definitely lose some. This is your staff."

"Mine has the purple tie on it."

"I don't know why you put that on there. They are the exact same thing."

"Nope, this one is better because it's mine. Yours is ugly," I grinned.

"Uh huh. Didn't know a stick was supposed to look pretty. Now, you remember how to do it?"

He knows I've been working on this for a while but not just a pro yet. "A little. This way…isn't it?"

"Two hands, spin side to side."

"You're breathing right on my neck. I think I have it now."

"That's right, now spin on each side and go faster and faster."

It's been a good few years now. I should almost be to the point I have this mastered now.

"Whew, this was tiring."

"See, you got it."

"Kind of, I can do it with one hand side to side."

"It's been three years since you started. I believe you have it now," Jason said.

"I don't know how Mr. Wilson does it so fast. He looks like a fan when he spins his."

"Dad has been doing it forever. He knows how to do every technique with it."

"When I first saw your dad, he just looked like a farmer. You know, he wore those suspenders when he came outside after I broke his window."

"The funny thing is, since you two stayed here, I really thought he was going to make you fix it," Jason grinned. "Why are you going so slow?"

"This thing is hard. I hate to say; but I'm not on your level yet."

"You will be soon my apprentice. Go ahead, M, go faster. Faster, faster, faster!"

"Agh, dammit, I mean darn it."

"That's it, Munisha. Feel the pain." Mr. Wilson said, walking towards us. "That's the only way for you to learn. It's a bit warm out here, isn't it? Did you both finish your chores?"

"I did, I don't know about, Jason."

"You know me, Dad. I don't start anything I don't finish."

"Good, very good. Let me see that staff, champ!"

He looks like an old skeleton about to show us something.

"When spinning, use every muscle from the chest, biceps, triceps, shoulders. Also, make sure your breathing nice and slow doing this, control. Breath in, inhale, exhale. Know that you're in control of the staff and are one with it."

"Dad, how the hell are you doing that?"

"I love it when he does this, it's just a nice breeze."

"This is the way you do; however, you will always start slow and go faster. No need to rush to the end. Haste and life does not mix. Let me get out of here, need to get a few things."

"Let me go with you this time, Dad."

"Not yet, it's dangerous out there, and S.I.L.O aren't playing anymore. They are everywhere. Stay here and protect the house and, of course the women."

I looked at Jason up and down. "You…protect us? Mr. Wilson is so funny."

"Funny, what's funny about what he said? I am the only man here and you all need some security."

"There's no one coming around here. Only person that came around is that woman I swear I saw that time."

"That's the problem, M. That means someone else will find this place. If you did see someone, that means S.I.L.O can probably find this place."

"I thought about that too," I frowned.

"Then again, Dad. I know he has thought about it; ultimately, it's nothing we can do."

"If they ever come, me and Zaraiella are out of here. I'm already thinking of us moving out. Maybe a year or two from now."

"Where will you go? You heard him, those people are everywhere, and once you're in the system, you are definitely not getting out."

"There has to be a place where we can go to. When Mrs. Wilson is teaching us about the world, she tells us there are places outside of here, maybe not in this country but where you can live and not be bothered by S.I.L.O. You can still have a life not ruled by some crazy government. You have to live in a forest or desert to live decent. Kind of like this."

"Sorry to burst your bubble, M. This whole world is ruled by one government. There is no more of that different jurisdiction and political lifestyle differences."

"Look at you trying to sound all smart."

Jason frowned. "…Dad told me this stuff would happen a long time ago. Life just will never be the same anymore. It sucks really."

"Whew, my risk is tired."

"Mines too, no pain no gain though. Mom is going to want us to go and do math work in a little."

"Ugh, I forgot we didn't get to do it this morning. I hate math. I don't know why I need to learn everything all the way up to that trigonometry stuff. That type of math is ridiculous. Don't you need it if you build houses?"

"Probably, there are many things you can do with it. Dad and Mom built this place along with my uncle and none of them are architects. It shows you it's useful."

"Right…somebody knew what they were doing."

Being fifteen and three years from becoming an adult is a little scary. Not once have we had a birthday here like how Mom threw us parties. It just does not feel like things are nice anymore. I should be happy turning eighteen. Once I am old enough, we will have to decide to move out of this jungle and have a life.

"Munisha, it's your turn."

"I'm practicing, Zaraiella. You can play with Janice more."

"I beat her fives time," Zaraiella smiled.

"Darn," Jason says. "Not my little sister."

"Well, come out here and practice with us, you need to learn this."

"I tried this already, Munisha. It's not for me since I can't spin it."

"Help her out, Jason," I said.

Zaraiella beating, Janice that many times, she's better than I was when I first started playing. We didn't really have time for games anymore, we have to get out of here one day. There is no way I'm living on this farm for another three years.

"I can't do it."

"Sis, pick the stick back up. Don't be so weak. You got this."

"Her hands are kind of small, M. She can't rotate it that good," Jason says, trying to help Zaraiella out.

"Nonsense, here. Just turn, turn, turn. Now, try it by yourself. You got this, sis."

"Told you I can't do it!"

"Yes you can! Pick it back up," I frowned.

Zaraiella just wanted to play and have fun. Just play with hair and stay in the house all the time. I told her already, the world is evil.

"I'm going back inside."

"Okay. When you come back, you will do it again. That little sister of mine. She needs to learn how to fight to protect herself. The world isn't all these butterflies and sunshine, she probably thinks. What are you looking at?"

"I like what you did."

"Just trying to make her learn, she needs this."

"That, and you still believed in her when she dropped it."

"Of course, that's my sister, little sister at that. I'm still working on this spin; but I'll get it soon enough."

"What about your handstands?"

"Oh!" I grinned. "Watch and learn loser."

"See, I can't do that to save my life."

"It's not, so hard. I told you, I was going to be in gymnastics. Now this stupid S.I.L.O messed up everything."

I gained so much energy from hand standing. Feeling the blood and aura go to my head was soothing.

"That is sad. You would've been something."

"Sssh, you hear that?" I said. "Betsy, she's making noise."

"Dad said we can't go into the barn without permission."

"I'm going to see what's wrong with her."

She never made noise like that before. I don't know how he could just not go and see what's wrong. "Betsy, Betsy what's wrong girl? Oh, this stupid chicken flew in here. It's okay girl."

"You never listen to anything I say. You're going to get us grounded again and we'll have to do chores all day!"

"Oh, shut up. This crazy chicken jumped in her stable. You okay, Betsy? Such a good horse. Mr. Scary over there didn't want me to come to help you."

"Scary?" Jason grimaced.

"Yes, you are. Tsk, I'm bored. Let's go before your, daddy comes."

"You're bored? Let's go for a ride then."

"What?" I said, stopping before exiting the barn.

"You said I'm scared. Let's take a ride. Better yet, to the outdoor mall then."

I did not know what I implanted in this boy head, but he may been on to something. "We can't go to a mall. We don't have credits."

"There is a strip mall that is not far from here. Maybe fifteen minutes and we will have some fun. You want new clothes anyways, right?"

"I don't have credits, Jason. Besides that, what about S.I.L.O?"

"They're in the city heavy, not so much outside. How do you think Dad and Mom get things for us?"

"Wow, okay…I'm in."

"Tomorrow morning, we go, no chores, and Mom, and Dad won't be looking for us since they always sit in the house meditating on their relax Sunday."

I really needed new clothes, at least the ones that I liked. Mr. Wilson and Mrs. Wilson has no taste at all. Making me wear t-shirts and overalls at time as if I belong on this farm.

"No, Munisha, why would you want to get in trouble?" Zaraiella says.

I knew she would be too timid to come. "We won't. The place, Jason said is only fifteen minutes away. We will be gone for an hour. Mr. and Mrs. Wilson won't notice."

"I don't like it. I'll just stay here."

"Suit yourself. Me, and Jason are going to have fun there. There is a whole bunch of stores there and he even said there are new clothes we can get. You won't get any new clothes and see all the pretty stuff, sis."

"Dresses?" Zaraiella says, looking back up at me. "I haven't had one in a long time."

"You're right, it might be there. Look, you can pick your favorite colors, isn't it pink? You can have that with pretty glitter all over it."

"How do you know that?"

It was sometimes hard fooling, Zaraiella. Since the years passed by, she has grown a bigger brain more than anything. "It's a clothing store, Zaraiella. Everything is in there. Why do you think I'm so excited to go? I need to get rid of this crap."

"I don't know, Munisha; but how would you buy clothes? We don't have any credits."

"We have bookbags though," I smirked.

"No, Munisha, no!".

"You know we need new things. Then how about when we have to move out on our own?"

"Stealing is bad, you will go to jail for it. Don't you know that?"

"If we need it, we need it. Sis," I said putting my hand on her back with her hair that has grown drastically below her hips. "If you don't want to go with us, I can't promise I'll bring you back anything. My bookbag isn't that big."

"That's okay. I like my clothes anyways."

Mr. and Mrs. Wilson never gave us anything we like to wear from the stores. It was all just plain t shirts and ill favored pants. That little sis of mine just doesn't care. Maybe if we were out in society, she would be more in interested in her looks. "What are you writing anyways?"

"Poetry."

"Poetry? I didn't know you were into that. That's nice."

"Mrs. Wilson writes it, and I wanted to learn too."

"That's good, I just hope you will come out and staff with us sometimes. You will need it one day."

Zaraiella wasn't a dumb person for sure. I wish we could be back in school. Everything has fallen apart.

"Have a good time, Munisha. Just be safe when you go."

"Nothing is going to happen to me, sis. I'll always be alright."

She rather stay here and write then start to stare off into space and claim she sees that ghost. "Oh well"

Now the only thing we have to figure out, how are we actually going to sneak out of here. Who knows what that man will do to us if he finds out we're trying to leave without permission.

"M, we really doing this?"

"Oh gosh, come on, Jason. Don't tell me your punking out. This was your plan and now you don't want to go through with it?"

"It's not that, trust me," Jason says as he scratches his curly hair.

"Then what? We ate already, we did everything. Let's go."

Jason sighs. "I don't have the keys..."

"You were thinking of driving there with my mom's car? You must be out of your mind."

"We sure wasn't walking, and Dad would probably kill me if we took Betsy."

"You're right. Where are the keys?"

"In their room of course. The plan has to be canceled since they're in there with it."

"Tsk," I frowned. "Okay, this is what we can do. You tell them to look outside for something, maybe something you saw in the forest. I'll go in the room and get them."

"If we get caught, you're doing my chores."

"We can do this. I'm going to talk to Zaraiella and I'll be listening when they come out. You look so scared right now."

"Going now, M."

Maybe we shouldn't go, or just do it next week. That boy might tell them to look at a fly on the wall and get us in trouble for the dumbest trick in the book. "You all love hair, braiding must be your favorite, Janice. In the future, I will stop by your hair salon."

"We should start one one day, huh, Zaraiella?" Janice asked.

She already had the face like she was going to snitch.

"Um…yea"

"Is she okay? She has been acting weird all morning."

"You should know her by now. My sister is just a straaaange person."

"Maybe it's because I don't want to get in trouble. Tsk, strange."

Her attitude has changed definitely throughout these years as well.

"Why are you getting in trouble? What happened, Zaraiella?"

"I don't know," Zaraiella frowned.

"You know what, last chance, Zaraiella."

"I told you no already."

"What are you talking about?" Janice asked.

"Me and your brother are going to go have fun. We are going to ride there and come right back. Want to come?" I said, smiling as Zaraiella would only give me that side eye.

"Sure, it sounds fun."

"Don't do it, Janice."

"Come on little sis. Everybody wants to go and it's going to be fun. You don't want to miss out."

"Yea, let's go, Zaraiella," Janice says, pulling on Zaraiella's arm. "We can go look around. It's not like we're going to go and do something bad."

"Well, you two figure it out. Be right back."

Looks like Jason has them occupied. "Now where are those keysoh on the dresser. Together as they should be. Too easy."

If they were to stay here, I already know one of them will probably say something. "Last chance, coming or what?

"Me, and Zaraiella will stay. She doesn't want to go," Janice frowned.

"Okay, bye, sis."

That girl needs to stop being so afraid of everything. "Hey there, Mr. Wilson…Mrs. Wilson."

"What did you do?" Mr. Wilson asked.

"What do you mean? I am just, going outside. I um, yea."

"I didn't ask you any of that. I asked what did you do? Jason is acting unusual; he sends us outside saying he saw an old lady in the forest with a black coat. Now he's seeing witches."

"I told you, Tim. It could've been someone and they ran."

Mr. Wilson shook his head. Hope not. I don't have time for pranks. Why are you carrying your bookbag?"

"I'm just um, going outside…."

"Okaaay," Mr. Wilson said, with one eyebrow up and other down. "You kids get stranger by the hour."

"Phew, that was close."

He would be standing by the car like an idiot. "Let's get out of here before they notice something odd."

"Wait, not yet," Jason says, looking up at the house.

"Why? You're always so scared. Stop being so scary like my sister."

"We can't leave just yet because they saw that…I was acting strange, they said. They might just come outside to see what we're up to."

"They told me you said something about what I saw in the forest. Now if you didn't believe that long time ago when I said it, why would you tell them you saw her? Mr. Wilson thinks I'm making you go crazy and it's making him crazy. Let's just go, come on."

"Hmph," Jason grins. "You know, M, we could get in big trouble for this. Wait, they're coming too?"

"Oh gosh, they probably told on us."

Jason leans back in the seat. "Gigs up. Welp we tri"

"Wait."

Only my sister I bet. We will never have any fun with her knowing anything. "What are you two doing? You told them, didn't you, Zaraiella?"

"No we're coming," Janice says. "Open the door!"

"Thought you two didn't want to go," I said, as they hopped in.

"I told Zaraiella where we're going and it will be more fun than being home all day."

"Thank god someone tells you something, sis. I didn't want you to miss out."

"Oh crap!" Jason shouts.

"Wait, Jason, wait. Have you driven a car before? Not when you almost hit your house."

Jason chuckles, "Dad used to let me drive forward on his lap, when I was…five? If I remember right."

"Oh my gosh," I sighed. "You all put on your seatbelt."

It feels so good to be away and seeing the road. I can't remember the last time I've seen outside from the farm land. The trees mainly cover our view. Mr. Wilson said that everywhere is pretty much under the army or how he says, martial law.

"We can get in so much trouble for this."

"What's wrong now, Jason?"

"I'm driving a car and with no license. I look…young."

"Here, wear my hat," I said, pulling down on his curly hair.

"What is this supposed to do? Make me look like an adult?"

"Yea, you look like you can be my older brother or sister. Your curly perm is getting in the way a little. Kinda' makes you look like a girl."

"Then take this"

I grinned. "No no. It looks good on you."

"You know this car is almost out of gas, right? Can you imagine if we were to get stuck out here? We're good as done."

"S.I.L.O will take us, then we won't go home. Tsk, Munisha."

"Don't say that Zaraiella," I said. "We are going to have fun. Something different for a change.

In back of my mind, she does have her ways of being right at times. Now that will be on my mind the whole time. "How far are we? You said fifteen minutes."

"It's right down the street, M. Chill will you?"

It feels so empty. "I'm surprised there is no one out here. Absolutely not one person."

"Dad said there won't be since this new law is in effect. Only a few probably are out. We passed only six cars I think."

"Jason, there it is right there!" Janice says, pointing.

"I see it, Janice, and wo."

No wonder. Everything appeared to be ran through and just left alone. "Everything is taped off."

"Exactly! Hey, we tried. Let's go back now."

"No!" I said as I held the steering wheel. "Let's stop and look around. So scary."

The parking lot looked as if there was a killing spree. Just yellow tape blowing everywhere and stores with broken glass.

"There barely isn't a place to park with all this tape, M."

"Park on the side so no one doesn't see the car. Don't need someone taking mom's car."

"I think we should go back, Munisha," Zaraiella says.

"Listen to your sister this time, M."

"Why would we do all what we did to just go back? Just park here, we're going out to look around."

This place doesn't look like it was open for weeks, really. Trash and quarantine, keep out tape everywhere. I guess they just made this place shut down.

"Make sure you lock it, Jason. Before we never go back for real," I said.

"You're a piece of work, M. Let's hurry up, look around and go."

I just can't believe they would just leave this here like this. I don't understand. I know the area is small, but someone should be around to protect their store, at least.

"You all look. Someone broke the glass to the toy store. Jason, Daddy brought us in here one time,"

"You still remember. This is bad. They robbed the place already, even action figures."

All I saw was a great opportunity. "Or they just shut down, and people can get what they want. Ouuu the clothing store. Bingo!"

I never got all lavish before and today is the day I will get everything I want.

"Why did they close the store, Jason?" Janice asked.

"Don't know. Dad probably knows about this or NO MUNISHA!"

BLING

"What is with you and breaking windows," Jason asks. "Lucky the alarm didn't go off."

"Some of them are already broken. Who cares," I said, stepping foot over the glass and into the vacant but lavish store.

"I wonder what happened. And what are you going to do in there, M? Try on everything?"

"That and take some of course. Didn't I tell you I need new clothes? Come on, Zaraiella. Be careful of the glass. The lights don't work. Everything is free so I don't care."

This place was heaven! All I saw was nice things just for me. The cute shirts and pants sets will be the first things that go inside my bag. Oh, this is too good.

"Looking at your face, I can tell you're going to have a good time in here," Jason says.

"These are so pretty!" Janice says holding a pair of obnox iously sized high heels.

"Help yourself, Janice. I know I am. What about you sis? Don't tell me you should have gotten something once we leave. Like these shoes."

"Maaan, Dad did say women love to shop. I'm going to look in the other stores and see if I can get in."

"Do your thing. This is paradise and us girls love it!"

It was about time I can pick my own things. Shirts, pants, coats, and jackets. "I'm taking everything I can carry. Trying on these clothes makes me remember I haven't stepped foot in a dressing room in awhile. "Oh my gosh, this outfit is the cutest."

"Look at these shoes, Munisha. I love these!" Janice says while holding up more heels she probably couldn't even walk in.

"You know you can't wear heels, Janice. Better try them on and see if you can walk in them first."

"Look at what I found; you think it will work?"

"There you go. I knew there was something you would like to confiscate. A camera, really?"

Zaraiella frowned. "I can't open it."

"What do want with that anyways, Zaraiella? You want to take pictures of the animals when we get back?"

"Ugh, these things are hard to walk in. A little help would be nice."

She looks like a deer in six inch heels.

"Eygh!"

I grinned. "Are you okay? I told you, you will have to get used to those. I don't think you can take them back. Mr. Wilson sees you with those on, you're going to be…ha, more than grounded forever. Aghh, geez, that's bright."

This girl wants to snap photos like she never seen a camera before. "Oh, you got it to work. Okay, Zaraiella, okay, my eyes! I never really been a picture person, you know that."

"Take a picture of me, Zaraiella, before I fall again."

"You two have fun. I'm going to bag up. Might as well take some of there bags."

I am still a little curious on why this all happened, and no one is here. Maybe it could be some type of quarantine zone. Mr. Wilson said there was one every other week. "Oh wow."

"What's wrong, Munisha?" Zaraiella asked.

"It's them…S.I.L.O."

"Are they coming?"

"Zaraiella, get away from the window!" I semi whispered.

Just when Jason told me it wasn't a good idea. "Okay, good. Oh my gosh, I thought we were done shopping," I grinned.

Zaraiella eyes were so big. I knew she was scared out of her mind, but even my heart was hitting my chest hard.

"Let's hurry up. I need more!"

This should have been enough for me to last a few years. These pairs of shoes. I'm not a boot person but these sneakers I got are so cute with this purple and gold outfit. I should get myself some tennis shoes for running in. "Looks like someone paid two hundred credits just a few days ago. Bags and shoes of course. By the date, this literally just happened. Oh well, we won't be coming back here."

"Here, Munisha, let's take a few before we leave," Zaraiella said.

I never seen her so energetic as this. "Okay, okay."

"You smile funny, like open your eyes," Zaraiella says as she stretches her face while I stay centered face.

"Ha, I told you already. Pictures never been my thing."

"These are nice, we can go now."

"Did you get everything you want, Janice?" I asked. "I don't know if we can come back here."

"I did, I just put them in a book bag."

"I didn't know they had book bags! I am crazy over bags; too bad they don't have purses in here. Oh shoot, spoke too soon. Now I can get more things."

"Alright, alright! You ladies aren't finished yet? What in the world! Where do ya'll think you're going with all this stuff?" Jason said, shaking his head.

He doesn't know we will do this forever if we could. "We shopped, that's what girls do," I said. "This outfit is this cutest isn't?"

"M, you look like you just came out of a fashion show. If they see that when we get back, they'll say something. You all have everything? Pretty much the whole store looks like."

"We do," I smirked. "And we're taking it all. Let's go."

"We've been here for about an hour and thirty minutes. You better hope were not caught, M."

"We'll be fine. Be sure to take extra battery packs, Zaraiella. You might lose one. Ouuu, I like this shirt too, so cute."

"M…never mind. See you all to the car."

CHAPTER 9

Face Your Agitation

Water is calm. Water is kind, water helps me see the beautiful sunshine. Even when it's dark, it will still shine. "Not bad, sis. You have a nice voice. Maybe you will be a poet one day. I can just see you on stage as a spoken mentor in front of many people."

"I think I would get scared up there. Every play in school I was nervous. Never liked it."

"You'll get over it. In my opinion, everybody goes through that."

"I miss school," Zaraiella mumbles as she puts her pen to the paper.

"Me too. There's no way we can go back. Unless we go into a foster home. We're better off here now, don't you think?"

Zaraiella shrugs. "I guess so."

"When we get older and ready to move out, there's a place waiting for us."

"Are you almost done? Let's go play checkers or uno. I'm done with poetry for now."

"I definitely don't want to play uno. Checkers, yes. Whenever I get done with this algebra, sis. Then, I'm going to train with Mr. Wilson and, Jason. When are you going to practice with us?"

"I…I don't really want to."

"Why not, it will make you stronger," I said as I placed my pencil to my lip, figuring out the equation.

"It's dangerous. You are all hitting each other with sticks."

"In this world, Zaraiella. You either protect yourself or die, really. I'm just telling you this, so you know I just want you to protect yourself. Those S.I.L.O people that destroyed everything and the hell they brought to us, taking Mom and, Lakia. Those people deserve to die, and I must be ready when one comes my way, even if I have to learn how to shoot a gun. I'm sorry, this is going overboard."

My thoughts on S.I.L.O automatically forced a heavy heart on me. I hated them with my living guts, and I promised our mother that I will get them back, some way, somehow. If not, help someone to cancel out S.I.LO. One day, it will happen. Someone will do something about the chaos they made.

"Life is beautiful. Life is nice. Only way to be happy is to love it twice. No, I don't like that. Maybe…"

"What are you taking a picture of, sis?"

My sister was so weird at times. "Anyways, I'm done. I'll let you do your thing with that. What are you still staring at? Zaraiellaaa, helloooo?"

"It's….it's nothing."

"You keep staring at the door again. Like someone is right there."

"I'm okay, sorry. I was thinking about something," Zaraiella says, hiding her camera under her notepad.

"Right. Well, see you! Come outside when you're done at least."

Being in this house is almost becoming like a prison. Only thing to do is sit in there and stare your eyes at the wall until they start to bleed.

"You ready my friend?"

"Always ready, brother!"

"Brother?"

"Yea, brother. You know I only have sisters. So, you being my only brother would be cool."

"I feel honored, M. Or shall I say, sister?"

I smirked. "Either or. Jason…I'm kind of tired of this."

"Of what? I thought you love bo staffing."

"It's cool. What I meant was. Tsk…there's no one in the world living like this. Living outside the city like we are. Basically hidning."

"Hmph, you just don't know, M. There are people living just like us."

"Like who, Jason. Kenneth? Don't even try it, because he completely goes into the city for, Mr. Wilson without ducking and dodging S.I.L.O. So tell me who."

"M…there is a whole world we don't know about out there. If Dad and Mom thought of doing this, someone is doing the exact same thing. Maybe not around here of course, though they live in a secluded area. Many people don't like S.I.L.O."

"Hmph, I'll believe it when I see it."

"Dad has a surprise for us. He has something much more thrilling than us staffing I think."

"Hmm, wonder what that could be."

It could only be fishing which I just walked off and sat alone when we last went. "You know I stepped in some crap with my nice shoes last week. It seemed like that stuff was never going to come out. It would've been smart to get some cute boots instead of having to wear those hillbilly ones. Mr. Wilson, what is the surprise?"

"Geez, M. Not yet," Jason smirked.

"What? I wanted to know so I could brace myself."

"It's easy, miss Pocahontas. The surprise is, Munisha versus Jason."

"What?!" I frowned looking Jason up and down with his smile in return.

"Whoever wins from the first hit will spar with me and receive a reward."

"Tsk. That's not fair, Mr. Wilson. Jason, he's a guy and been doing this longer than I have."

Mr. Wilson sighs. "Gender matters in strength? There are women out there who can take on all of us in staff sparring. I've watched you for years, and you've only have become better. Don't ever underestimate yourself. What do you say, Jason?"

"I'm all for it. Ready when you are sister."

Me and Jason practicing on each other? Mr. Wilson knew there was no way I could do this. He just looks like he is going to cheat, just like in uno.

"Ready, Munisha? You can do this, let go of that uncertainty and fear," Mr. Wilson says as he folds his arms.

"Uhh, let's do this then. Better not hit me hard you idiot," I said, whispering pass Jason's shoulder.

"Ready, bow to one another. Begin! Remember, Munisha. Let go of that uncertainty. Don't hold anything back, champ."

"You almost got me, M. Don't stop."

"Nice job champ."

"Whew, shit!" Jason grins. "Come on, M. Stop playing and hit me!"

This boy doesn't know he's been doing this longer than I have. Seems like he's trying to take my leg off. "Agh. Tsk, Mr. Wilson"

"Jason, two, Munisha, zero! Come on, daughter. If Jason is calling you sister, then that makes you my daughter. I won't tolerate failure! Let's get it, Munisha!" Mr. Wilson claps.

"Ahh!"

"Nice block, daughter! Show him!"

"Come on, Mr. Wilson! Jason is too fast!"

"Focus. Don't worry about anything else," Mr. Wilson says with a straight focused face.

"Oh shoot, that was a lucky shot, M."

"I should have swatted you in the face instead of the shoulder."

"There you go, daughter. Jason two, Munisha one."

I feel like he's letting me get points now. I wish Zaraiella was out here.

"You're spinning that stick like you're going to do something again."

"Uh, huh," I smirked.

I was somewhat getting the hang of this.

"Woo, you're getting there, I'll give you that little sister. Don't get, agh! What the hell?! How did you?"

"She's coming back, champ. Superb block and blow to the chest, Munisha. Jason two, and Pocahontas, two! Game point!"

"I'm about to get beat by a girl," Jason mumbles with uncertainty glued to his face.

He did not look so cocky now. "I wasn't going to give up that easily, you know me."

"There you go, Munisha! There you go! Who's going to take the win?"

"That was a close one, M. Mommy must have given you lots of milk to give you this type of strength."

I know he just didn't say that. "IDIOT!"

"Oh shit! Aw crap, she got me. M, chill, you wonyou won."

"Let me go, Jason, I am serious."

Why would he bring up my Mom?

"Darn, you went all in, Munisha. Your swings are amazing, but you need a little bit more work on your parries. Very good very good, I applaud you both."

"Now, what was the surprise, Dad?"

"We're going out hunting, to learn, actually. I needed to observe what was in my new daughter. Be right back. Going to get the gear. Hang tight and rest for a while."

"You alright, M? You did great," Jason said.

"Yea, yea…I'm okay."

"You look like you just stepped in horse crap again."

"I'm okay. Don't worry about it," I said, throwing my staff next to Betsy's stable.

"Is it because I said something about your mom? Only reason I said that is because I wanted you to go harder. Sorry about that."

"You know, someone…or Lakia used to say things similar to get me to act right."

"It makes you more aggressive, good but you have to control it. You'll lose like you did in checkers. It causes you to not think straight."

"So, you let me win?" I frowned.

"Not exactly. At first I was thinking it, but then you started to go hard, catching me off guard."

I was so surprised too. All that matter was that I won.

"You all ready?" Mr. Wilson says with his gear that always looked weird to me, especially the handle.

"We're just going to go out and do a little scoping out with the rifle. You two already are kind of banged up, I'm assuming. However, today, is a good day."

"I'm good, Dad. A little sore on the shoulder. M got me good there."

"What about you, Munisha?" Mr. Wilson asked.

"I feel great. Tsk, Jason can't hurt me."

"That's the spirit and what I want to hear. You two did superb, and I'm very much proud."

Going out into the quiet woods sounded good and fun to hunt. Now that Mom is on my mind. It makes me not want to do anything, really. Should have told Mr. Wilson that my leg hurt a little but that gives Jason the pleasure of winning over me.

"What are we hunting, Dad?"

"Whatever we come across. There are plenty of things out here that we may stumble on."

"You won't be bored with this, M. It isn't like fishing."

"I grew to be like it's whatever," I rolled my eyes. "Whenever that, how do you call? Bird nest happens on my reel, I give up then and ever since I hated fishing."

"That's because ya'll youngins' don't want to do what I say. The line isn't tight, and then there's too much slack on the line to the fish."

"Have you ever thought about getting a crossbow, Dad?"

"Crossbow? What for?" Mr. Wilson frowned.

"Hunting, of course. They don't make any noise and they're extremely accurate."

"Maybe if I came across one. Those things you need to always keep clean and greased at least periodically or they will jam up on you. This here, I can clean once a month or every other one and she still fires as new. Believe it or not. This rifle almost one hundred years old. Ninteen seventy eight Steyr AUG, I believe."

"Geez, that's old?" I said. "Why do you keep all these old things around?"

"Because, one, classic never dies, and two, you take care of what you have, and it most certainly will take care of you. Why I love this baby, it has select fire. I can go from semiauto to, rip to shreds auto. Mwah!"

I just believe Mr. Wilson just like to keep old things around. Old hat, old clothes, old gun. Good thing he doesn't have that old smell all the time.

"There you go! One of those flying squirrels, Dad."

"Great. Who wants to go first?"

"Ladies first?" Jason asks, smirking at me.

"It's fine. You can go. Why do we have to shoot a poor squirrel anyways? Only guys."

"To put food on the table, miss Pocahontas. Aim and breathe in and out, champ."

BANG

"Shit, I mean shoot," I said, closing my ears. "That thing is loud!"

"Nice try champ, close, but no cigar."

"Man. I must have gone too slow."

"Rememer to hold your breath, then fire. Most important, focus. Focus is everything."

"Tim, Tim, are you there?"

"Oh boy, don't tell me she's so scared of the gunfire when she saw me with the rifle in my hand. Yes, baby, we're okay. What's up?"

"Just checking in on you and making sure these radios still work."

"They work great, baby. We're out here training. I'll get back to you on our way back. Much love. If that lady hears a pin drop, she jumps out of her shoes."

"Hmph, mommies' boy," I chuckled.

"Shut up, M!"

I could only imagine if the animals shot back at us. These animals have families, it's kind of like how S.I.L.O did ours. I believe we should respect animals and everyone. "Oh my gosh, not those huge webs again! They're everywhere this time! I'm not going under those trees. You both can go keep practicing. See you all back at the house."

"Not so fast, Munisha," Mr. Wilson said. "Why are you afraid? They're only webs."

"Yes, that means there are millions of spiders. Not me, nope!"

"Take a closer look. Do you see any spiders? Jason used to be creeped out about them too."

"I don't see any spiders, but that still doesn't mean they're not up there."

"These webs are not from spiders; they are from caterpillars," Mr. Wilson said. "Spiders won't even make webs this large."

"Caterpillars? Mr. Wilson, really?"

"Yup, now, if you're scared of those, then you can go back."

"M, I know you're better than this. You're not scared of no baby butterflies, are you?"

"I adore the sights of them," Mr. Wilson says as he pulls a thread from the tree. "These amazing insects only make these when fall comes around, hence why they are called fall webworms. Nature and its beauty are something so divine. That is why we must treat all life as precious."

When we walked through this forest to go fishing, I would see them but not so many. It looked like a nightmare stretching across from tree to tree. I wondered how it was even possible for something so small to make a nest so large.

"Munisha, take a shot there at that rabbit! Hurry before it gets away. It hopped behind that log there."

"Oh come on, man! Not a rabbit, Mr. Wilson."

"Don't mind that. It's food for us, not just us killing it for a sport."

"I, Mr. Wilson, don't interact with things like that. It's unnecessary."

"Uhuh," Mr. Wilson says getting behind me. "Now, hold your left hand on the grip and keep the stock which I like to call, thee butt of the gun, between your shoulder and chest."

"I don't…I don't want to shoot it, when I come out here with you two, I usually just watch. Mr. Wilson," I said, trying to aim but also refusing. "You just said all life is precious."

"I know what I said. That is why it will help us to nourish our bodies."

Holding this thing I know makes me look somewhat awkward.

"Hold it straight now. Hurry up before it runs."

"I heard you before, Mr. Wilson."

"Put your finger on the trigg"

BANG

"Oops."

Mr. Wilson frowns. "How did you manage to fire so quickly?"

"M is how you call it, trigger happy?"

"Certainly, we have some work to do," Mr. Wilson says, rubbing his head.

"Tim, Tim you there?"

"Oh no. Yes, Sara. We're alive. Are you going to call whenever you hear gunfire? Over."

"You know it. I'm not going to pretend I'm not jittering when you all are out there. It's dangerous!"

"We're okay, baby. One last shot, and we'll be heading back in, over."

"Good, because it's getting dark soon. I want the children in."

"We'll be there, also, you forgot to say, over, over."

"Just get back, OVER, here with the children, Tim!"

"Mom sure doesn't like us out here."

"I try not to do things without her knowing but I try to be honest with your mother and keep the peace. Let's get back to it, shall we?"

"I see another one of those rabbits. Probably the same one Miss hesitant Pocahontas missed. Your go, Jason."

"That's M's rabbit. Give it another shot. Remember to focus."

"Hmph, no, you can go. I'll observe."

"Make it happen champ. Aim, breath in and out, then fire when ready."

"This rabbit won't stop hopping all over the place," Jason said, as he aims and shakes.

"That's fine. Wait till he stalls. You got this champ."

BANG

"Darn it!"

I just could not accept it. So cruel to nature. "I think you hit him. It flipped like twice. Poor thing."

"Yea, you hit em' alright, Jason. Sadly, it seems like you gave him a flesh wound. Try to kill it. I mean, be sure to kill it because the animal won't be running around in agony. It's disgusting. These creatures are for us to eat, not to play tag."

"I will, Dad. It's starting to get dark, so let's get back."

"You two did great. Superb training today and not so bad with the shooting practice. We'll try again soon enough. Only wish you could have gotten another try, Pocahontas."

"No, I'm good for the day."

"Yea, M. You probably could have hit it better than I did."

"Another day. I just hope I don't run into those webs at night. You can't see a thing, especially that. Gosh, that's so creepy thinking about it. When we first came to you, we didn't see any of that stuff in the trees. If we did, we would've gone another way and probably got caught."

"They were out here, just didn't manage to see them," Mr. Wilson says. "Also, during winter, they are pretty much on chill mode. To mind you, worms make them. Your phobia creates the delusion that it can hurt you when they're just silk threads on trees. Who knows, your clothes Miss Pocahontas probably is woven together with that stuff. I'm surprised my wife bought you something as such."

Jason just kept his nose pointed the other direction like he was oblivious to his father words.

"Yea, um, Mr. Wilson, what is a phobia? I heard my Mom say something like that before."

"It's basically when you're afraid of stupid things."

"Incorrect, Jason. A phobia is when you have what you just explained you have a fear of. For example, I had a phobia which is called agoraphobia. I didn't care for crowds. Ever since I was a child, I've been that way until I faced it and killed it in my young adulthood. What you have, is called arachnophobia. When you walk into a web, you may just lose it because you think there is a spider on you."

I sure would, ugh. That happened to me a few times, and it was so embarrassing. "Mr. Wilson, Zaraiella…she, she sees things. Is that like a phobia?"

"She sees things, still?" Mr. Wilson asks, raising his eyebrows. "Hmph, she should have passed that stage in life by now."

"She has an imaginary friend, Dad," Jason chuckles.

"No, she tells me something tells her things. Some days, I'll catch her staring at something, and nothing is there. What? I'm not lying. She tells me this and you know from the years passed."

"Hmm, to be honest, never sounded like a phobia to me," Mr. Wilson sighs. "That always sounded like when someone has something called schizophrenia. Hate to call it that, but that is the only diagnosis I can manage to put together."

"That sounds bad. I feel sorry for your sister if she has that for real."

"Mom long time ago, I heard her saying something to our doctor that it could be a phobia that she has. As you said, she is scared of something, but it could be just that long word you said."

"Hmm, well," Mr. Wilson says rubbing his gray beard. "Hopefully, that isn't the case, and she does have a little imaginary friend."

Zaraiella did not make it seem like it was just some, imaginary friend. She gazes at it, and her eyes followed whatever it was. Maybe it was the schizophrenia.

"What are we going to do when we get back, M? I know you're scared of me in uno."

"Never scared, brother. We need new games to play. I'm tired of that checkers too. How about you get us a portable gaming system, Mr. Wilson? It can't do that much harm."

Mr. Wilson sighs. "Now, you know how I feel about any electronic devices. Your Mom car is still around and I'm just surprised my subconscious let me keep that thing near my home. No, and no. You and Jason have games and are blessed to have those to keep you occupied. By the way, through out the years you've been here, you never spared with me in checkers, Munisha."

"That's something I'll pay to see. You know, Dad. Zariella beat her in the game like five times in a row."

"Aww, she's a brainer then. A girl who is what, twelve years old and can do that? She'll be a natural on the chest team."

"Too bad we can't go back to the city or school," I said.

"You two made your choices. Offered you both a fair warning to stay and going back. It is in your judgment to return with your sister even now, but I can promise you that it will not be a smooth road. A lot has changed, and it hasn't been pretty with S.I.L.O and those sausage brain folks."

"We understand, we decided what was best since Mom and my older sister haven't returned. I guess that was what we really relied on, and nothing else was important."

"I know you've been thinking of what you both will do once you're old enough to go out on your own. Have any perceptive thoughts?"

"At the moment, Mr. Wilson, not at all. Only thing I thought of once is when Mrs. Wilson told us about going to another place. That turned out to be a bummer since the whole world is trembling as you all said it has."

"Yes, yes. Nevertheless, Munisha, you can't give up hope like I will keep saying it like a broken record."

"Dad, look! A weasel!"

"That's a fisher cat, son. Haven't really seen those in a while. Here you go, Munisha. Take your shot, nice and steady."

"I thought we were going back, maybe next time. It smells weird out here too."

"Come on, M. Last one, I want to see my sister become a sharpshooter."

I frowned. "You two like to shoot poor innocent animals."

They said they were done. Then next thing you know, we see another animal, they will want to go on and shoot it.

BANG

"You didn't even try, M. You won't be smiling when you need to shoot something for a life or death situation."

"That's fine. Let's go back Mr. Wilson before your wife calls again."

"Can't wait for her to make me some carrot stew," Mr. Wilson says, rubbing his hand on his stomach.

"You know, Mr. Wilson. I really don't care for that yet. Maybe more of the spinach she makes. When we had to alter our diets, it made my stomach hurt. It takes time for people to adapt to a healthy lifestyle."

"Aahh, ya'll youngins don't know anything about that."

"Yea, Dad, I'll pass on that one."

"Me too. Yuck!"

"When you grow up and need glasses, you two."

"Wait you here that?" I asked, looking side to side and behind me.

"Not one of your tricks again, M."

"No, something is moving in the trees," I said, looking around. "I heard it."

"It's the wind. Let's go. I can already sense Sara is going to pick up the radio and call any second now. I'm surprised she"

"EYGH, MR. WILSON, WATCH OUT!"

"OH CRAP! DAD!"

"Jason, help him!"

"Get off of him, get off of him!"

"Rocks aren't going to do anything boy! Shoot it!"

"I can't, I might hit him!"

Dark red staining his shirt and the creature wasn't letting go.

BANG BANG BANG BANG BANG

"Dad! Dad, are you alright?!"

"Agh!"

"Mr. Wilson…I didn't mean, he was hurting you."

"It's, agh, it's alright. My arm, he got me pretty good though. It's just a bite. Tsk…he drew blood, but I'll be fine. Thanks, Munisha. Agh, you could have blown my head off, but that lucky shot to his head did it."

"It didn't shoot like that earlier. I just"

"When he jumped on me, I must have hit the full auto. No big gie child."

"She didn't want to shoot all day but had the best shot than all of us," Jason said, smirking at me.

"Let's just go," I said, holding my heart from beating out of my chest. "You're arm…"

"Yea, tsk. Mom is going to spazz out."

Jason himself must be out of his mind. That thing had Mr. Wilson almost like a rag doll. I had no choice but to shoot it or it would have taken his arm off completely.

"Tim, Tim Wilson! what in the world is taken you all? I heard more shots, is everything alright?"

"We're…hmph, we're fine baby. Be there in a second, over."

"You know she was going to call," Jason chuckled. "Sorry."

Jason laughed too much. What if that thing grabbed his face?

"Sara is going to kill me. Hmph, I'm leaking pretty bad."

CHAPTER 10

Discern Your Feelings

We didn't know, Sara! Mistakes happen!

"Shush, looks like you should mind my saying, sir, Tim."

"A few stitches aren't going to kill me, baby. That was a little cat that thought he could get the best of me. I wouldn't be here right now if it were an adult."

"Yea, Mom. It was probably about Janice or, Zaraiella's height."

"That's enough to hunt or even kill someone, Jason. It's final, and my thoughts are not changing about you all going out there like that."

"Welp, you better pray the food and supplies walk to the front door," Mr. Wilson chuckles. "Ouch!"

"Thank you again, Munisha for saving my husband's life. As I told you, men are veeery hard headed."

"You all saved ours. It was the least I can do."

"So humble, I love that about you," Mrs. Wilson said, smirking.

Mom never called me that before. I was always told I'm basically outgoing, but sometimes I can be a bit too much. Lakia said once that I only cared about myself, which made me mad. Who watches out for Zaraiella if she wasn't? It's only that me, myself, am always trying to get somewhere in life.

"There, all done," Mrs. Wilson says as she finishes up wrapping up that bloody arm.

"You really needed to wrap my whole upper arm, Sara? Now I can hardly do my work."

"Again, you should have listened when I told you to come on back, and you should've never gotten bit. Dinner is ready, when you all are. Munisha, kindly get your sister and Janice. They're still in your room."

"Sorry, this happened, Mr. Wilson."

"It's alright. Thanks again, and you too, Jason."

Jason tried throwing rocks. I can't lie; I did throw one, but once I saw how bad that cat was swinging his arm back and forth, the gun was my only alternative. That rifle nearly knocked me to the ground with the rapid fire. I don't think I will be hunting again, along with those nightmares in the trees.

"Sister, your back!" Zaraiella says, then getting up and hugging me.

"We've been back and…your hair, It's pretty, I like it."

"I did some of it, then let Zaraiella braid the rest."

"You have a skill Janice, you really do. Your mom said it's time for dinner."

"Where did you all go?" Janice asked.

"We went out practicing. Your dad was teaching us how to shoot his special little rifle. Oh my gosh, Zaraiella, I wish I had brought along your camera. That spot in the forest that has all of these webs are worse. Mr. Wilson says it from caterpillars."

"Oh, I know what does are," Janice says. "They make those huge webs when it's around the end of the year. Daddy took me to see them, and it is a little scary. They're just webs though."

"Just webs? It's a nightmare. It was something I ever expected to see."

"That would have made me run," Zaraiella says.

"It's not that bad. When you see it, you will know what I mean. Plus, it's only webs."

"That makes it even worse. Anyways, they want you all to come on downstairs. By the way, Janice. Your dad is fine, so don't worry about his arm, okay?"

"What happened?" Janice asks, swifty turning around.

"You'll see when you go downstairs."

"Munisha…"

"Yes, sis. Oh no, I am not up for any pictures right now."

"No, just…look through them."

She may even be a photographer someday. Pictures and video of the room, her making weird faces, us. The tree outside, then I guess, Mrs. Wilson's, rocking chair? "Okay sis, very nice."

"You don't see anything?"

"MUNISHA, ZARAIELLA, DINNER IS READY! COME ON DOWN!"

"Never mind, Munisha," Zaraiella mumbled, then smiled. "Let's go."

I had to remember that I was out in the woods, basically the jungle. Anything can happen out there. Mr. Wilson should tell Jason to be more of a man. Just hope it's not double the chores for us now since he's a little disabled.

* * * *

"You know what I like about the morning, Zaraiella? It's never hot. I think that's why, Mr. Wilson never works past midday. These stupid leaves are everywhere. We have a long way to go," I said as the millions of leaves seemed to multiply each time I bagged more.

"Mommy never made us pick up leaves."

"We were younger, also, we didn't have a tree like this one either. We just had a simple palm tree in the front. It rarely dropped anything. Over here, we'll be raking leaves forever if we stay."

"It's not that bad. I rather do this instead of when Mommy made us make us scrub the walls and floors."

"Doesn't this hurt your hands and make your arms tired?"

"No, not really."

"To each their own. I prefer cleaning the inside, and these gloves aren't that much of help."

"I hope his arm feels better. Mrs. Wilson wrapped it up a lot," Zaraiella said.

"He'll be okay. I'm glad it wasn't any worse than what it was. That is why they tell us not to go out there alone. He is a prime example."

"Ew! What is that up there?"

"It looks like some type of nest; those aren't bees either. HEY, JASON! There is something on the roof here!" I said, pointing at the gray paste.

"It makes me itchy. Why does it look like that?"

"It's a nest, Zaraiella."

"What are you girls bothering now?" Jason grimaced. "Wo! That's a wasp nest. I'm surprised we didn't see it there earlier. Dad will take care of it. It's harmless for now, just don't go bothering it."

"He can't do anything with that cast on. Come on, Jason. Be a man and knock it down."

"You must don't know about wasps. If those things sting you, it won't be pretty. I'll wait for, Dad. Not such a good idea to bother it. Tsk, I have work to do. Don't bother it, M, I know you."

"It looks like someone took glue and smeared it all over the wall," Zaraiella says, squinting her eyes.

If she is creeped out by a nest, then she will most likely be horrified but those webs.

"No, glue is whiter than that. You're right...It does look a little nasty."

"Leave it alone, Munisha. Jason said don't touch it!"

"I just want to see what happens if I poke it with the rake. Yea, it feels…hard."

"Let's rake up the"

"RUN ZARAIELLA, RUUNN!"

"EYYGHH!"

I didn't think those things would fly all over the place. There must was thousands.

"Oh my gosh, why did you do that, Munisha?! Why?!"

"I didn't do anything. Geez, I'm tired," I said, grinning and panting. "Hi, Mrs. Wilson."

"Why were you yelling so hard? I came running thinking someone was here unexpectedly. Finished with your chores? No, I still see leaves. In the meantime, I have lemonade for you all."

"Mrs. Wilson," I tried catching my breath. "We just had to run for our lives."

"I see. You're breathing is heavy, what happened?"

Chores were done for the day since those things are out there. "There was a nest and"

"You bothered it. I told, Tim to get rid of that thing a week ago. He will do everything, but what I tell him. You two didn't get stung I hope," Mrs. Wilson said, raising her eyebrow.

"Don't think so. You, Zaraiella? Why do all these bugs have to live around here?"

"That is definitely a rhetorical question," Mrs. Wilson chuckled.

"Bugs aren't my thing, especially spiders."

"This is what you deal with when you live in the wonders of nature. My husband helped me pass that phase long before Jason was born.

"Well, it will take more time for me."

"You can say that. How was the lemonade, Zaraiella? You swallowed it down pretty fast."

"Good. I'm going back to finish now."

"That young sister of yours, Munisha has a true spirit. Something as an old soul, I can already tell."

"Zaraiella, yea she's different. I hope she learns to protect herself one day. The world, like I told her before is getting bad. Already bad but getting worse every day."

"You're not wrong for that, be sure you keep her close. Long ago, my own sister, who was much older than me, watched out for me as if she was my own mother. Our mother and father, weren't known so we didn't rely on them, only on each other."

"I've learned through the years if that's what you have left, you will have to cherish it more than anything. I can't lose another sister, or I'll be alone."

"Oh, young blossom," Mrs. Wilson says as she holds my chin up. "You're never alone, even when think you are. Go back outside and help your old soul sister finish up. Tim will have a fit if the leaves aren't raked and bagged, and were just here chit chatting. You all should be done before noon."

"But those things are out there. I might get stung."

Mrs. Wilson grins. "Well, have yourself present for when your smaller sister needs you. Remember the words you just said to me."

Thank goodness for someone like Mrs. Wilson. It always felt like I was alone even though I live with five others. Though, there was always that empty space. I just wish one day, while out, some way, somehow, I bump into, Lakia and at least be reunited. Mom would sure be happy us sisters have each other again.

"You bothered it, didn't you, M?" Jason said, with a huge smirk as he was about to laugh.

"You must wanted me to get stung you jerk."

"No, no. You're lucky neither of you were stung. Those things feel like fire when they do."

He looked so much more muscular today in his undershirt. "I was thinking…one day, you promised me to take me to the ocean."

"You still remember that? That's far, M."

"Keep your word, Jason, you promised," I pouted.

"Maybe one day. Hmph, you two need any help?"

"Yeess, help uus!" Zaraiella moans. "Munisha takes too long; I'm tired!"

She was too cute to be working like a man.

"You heard your sister. Looks like you two pretty much just started."

"Thanks to you all tree; every time I rake some, more falls to the ground right in front of me."

"Welp, let's knock it out the park then."

It was a lot, and it didn't seem like it would be done anytime soon, especially not by noon. I could imagine getting my nails done, which I had never gotten before, and then having to rake. It would suck for those who have to do chores like we do and break a nail. I could really use a pedicure before they get like Jason's.

"Finally," I said, lifting my hands to the sun. "We're finished!"

Zaraiella doesn't even want to celebrate. I am more tired than she is, but I guess she is heading for a bath.

"Not going to lie, Jason, Mr. Wilson or somebody needs to cut one of these trees down."

"The trees are our oxygen, don't you know? Also, if we didn't have as many, S.I.L.O would probably find us. That's at least what I think."

"I guess that's true; there haven't really been so many helicopters flying around. I thought they would have found this place by now."

"Whatever got loose that Dad was talking about years back, probably was killed or captured. I wish I was there to see what it was."

"Me too, then we most likely would have been the first it came after. Seems like things enjoy attacking us. Whatever it was, it no doubt had something to do with my mom and sister going missing."

"You think so? S.I.L.O had something to do with it for sure. I think they are still alive, somewhere. Think about it, you last saw them at the facility, and then they never showed back home. You told me that day someone picked up the phone but no one answered. Remember Dad said they are using people for experiments? They are alive, just…I don't know. They're not here."

"Yes, still…what would S.I.L.O do with them? We went there to get some insertion and were told we could go back home. Whatever it was, it most likely broke out soon after it killed people, including my family."

"Hmm," Jason said, scratching his head. "We will never know. So it is best to try and not to contemplate so much. It will hinder you for the rest of your life. You don't know what happened, so you're guessing a game that will never finish. Let's head in and chill. I'm tired myself."

He was right. Every day it is like my mind wonders and wonders on what happened, and I will never really have a definite answer. Me and my sister will never know unless we meet one of them again. I don't think that nightmare will ever fade away.

"Aw, I see you are ready for the next round, M. Let's get it!" Jasons says.

I don't know who would think of playing when we got through working. Especially me, my hands are almost numb. "I didn't put this here. Zaraiella must have set up the board."

"Tim was the one who set up the board. He said that he would be ready to play you shortly after he finished resting, Munisha."

"Whew we!" Jason says, rubbing his hands together. "Dad is going to take your head off in this."

"We'll see about that."

"Go see if he's up, Munisha," Mrs. Wilson said. "I would be flabbergasted if he lost."

"Flabber, what? I'll go get him. Going to make him pay for making us pick up all those crazy leaves."

My hands still felt like spaghetti from all the work. Raking for about three hours was a little too much. "Mr. Wilson?"

Knock Knock

"Are you awake, Mr. Wilson?" I said, peeking behind the door and then walking towards the bundled up old man. "Mr. Wilson, can you hear me? Mr. Wilson…Mr. you're shaking."

"I, I…help me."

"Oh no! Just hold on, okay? Mrs. Wilson! Jason!"

"What is it, dear? No running in here please."

"Mr. Wilson, he's shaking and sweating badly, somethings wrong with him!"

"What?" Mrs. Wilson says getting up from the table. "Oh, God, no!"

"What happened, M?" Jason asks.

"Just come up and look."

What could be wrong? He was just fine this morning, now all of a sudden in agony.

"Tim, honey. Tim, what's wrong?"

"My head…it's…it's pounding."

"I don't know," Mrs. Wilson says rubbing her hand on his balded hair line. "You're burning up. It has to be a high fever."

"Dad, what can we do? Tell us," Jason said.

"Go…go get help."

"We can't take you to the hospital. Oh, God, it must be the bite," Mrs. Wilson says while trying to wipe the dripping sweat from Mr. Wilson's head.

"Mom, what do we do?"

"We have to go and bring him back, something fast. Munisha, we have to take your mother's car and find a local health store."

"That's fine! Let's go now then! Come on!"

"Tim, you just hold on. Love you."

I thought he was freezing but it is regular temperature here, about seventy degrees Fahrenheit. "It's going to be all right, Mrs. Wilson. He's strong."

"Janice, Zaraiella," Mrs. Wilson says as she opens the door.

Of course those girls were doing hair.

"You all stay here, we're running off to go get supplies. Daddy is feeling a little sick, so I need you two to stay here and watch over him. Do not go in Tim's room. I mean that."

Janice gets up swiftly. "Sick? We have medicine here, Mommy, don't we?"

"We certainly do, Tim needs to get some special medicine. We will be right back."

"Be right back, Zaraiella. Um, much love," I said.

"What kind of animal was it again, Munisha?" Mrs. Wilson asked.

"Some big cat, can't remember what Mr. Wilson said it was."

"Fisher cat, that's what I remember him saying," Jason said. "It was more aggressive I think."

"So it was infected?" I said as we rushed outside to the car.

"Absolutely, I don't want to say, seems as though that animal must have had something serious, like rabies. Tim, why don't that man just listen to me?"

"Ma, only opossums and raccoons has that."

"No, any mammal out in the woods can carry it. Jason, out! I'm driving!"

"Ma, the car won't start. Think it's out of gas."

"Oh gosh, at a time like this, it's empty. Jason, out. You must don't hear well today."

"This car doesn't only take gas. It can take electricity too, Mrs. Wilson."

"Great, where is the charger for it?"

I hated to say. "Home. I guess we never thought about getting it."

"Okay, okay," Mr. Wilsons sighed deeply, placing her hands over her face. "Umm…where does Tim keep the gas cans? Check around!"

"Come on, M. There in the shed. Crap, it's locked. Let's check in the barn."

I knew I should have told Mr. Wilson to get the cable, just in case. It never crossed my mind even when we went to the mall that day and Jason told us that the car was almost out of gas. Who knows, Mr. Wilson hardly refilled them since he takes Betsy ninety nine, point nine percent of the time.

"It's nothing in here, Jason."

"I found some. Doesn't even look like it's at least it's five gallons. This is what Dad uses for the generator."

"What are we going to do now?"

"Tsk…I don't know. Mom will have to aid it."

"It's okay, Betsy, seems like she even knows too."

She had those looks in her eyes. Maybe we could use her.

"Did you all find anything in here?"

"Nothing; Dad only keeps a little. I haven't seen him resupply any for some time, and Kenneth hasn't been here in a while either."

"Oh God, no," Mrs. Wilson says covers her mouth with tears.

"Mrs. Wilson, we'll figure it out. We can take the horse."

"The problem with the horse is, I don't know my way through the woods. We definitely can't go through the woods with it. I'll go and do what I can."

"It'll be okay Ma. Crap! We should have never gone hunting."

"Yea, look. He probably has just a minor infection. Hopefully, whatever it really is, it's not a big deal. Mrs. Wilson thinks it's rabies. I thought that as soon as I saw him shivering the way he was. Let's take the horse and go get the stuff ourselves."

"You heard, Mom. Then again, you don't even know your way through the forest."

"We can still try, if you're not going to, I will."

There had to be a way to get some medicine from some place without showing verification. My mind just told me to just sneak and take what I can. We can't lose, Mr. Wilson. "Hey, move, Jason. I'm going with or without you."

"Let's just wait till morning. The sky is showing it's going to rain."

"Come on girl. It's something wrong with him."

"M, please," Jason said, holding on to Betsy's bit. "Just listen to me for once! Then again, we don't even know our way like that."

"We'll find I mean, I'll find it," I said, yanking the rope.

"No."

"Move, Jason, I'm serious this time! I'll run you over! Let go!"

"Why are you so, damn stubborn?! Mom is trying to do the best she can, have faith on that."

"Jason, if you're not going to help your own father, I don't know what to say about you."

"Enough mind games, I'm not falling for it, we'll just stay here then," Jason says, releasing Betsy's face.

I could not comprehend the fact people won't do what is right. Your own father needs help, and you can't help him because you're afraid of something? I couldn't lose someone else. He does not understand the feeling. "But we will get this done, won't we girl? All we have to do is get to a local convenient store, ask what to treat rabies with, and I'm sure we'll be able to get something."

Darkness falling, along with the drizzle of rain. If it pours, there are plenty of places where we can take shelter in the city. Maybe a little awkward, a girl with a horse sitting under a bus stop. We'll figure something out. Oh boy, not thunder. "Now which way was it? I am not trying to turn into Canadian bacon out here."

How the clouds are heading towards me looks like God didn't want me going. I don't know if it's Him or just my imagination. I will have to do this regardless. "Crap! You scared me!"

"M?! What the hell is wrong with you?!"

I sighed. "Are you finally going to man up?"

"Ha, ha, whatever! You're lost, aren't you? I told you to not come out here. Move back. We're going back."

"Jason no, we're not! The city must be this way. I know where North is from the house, Bangor is ahead."

"Okay, still you're not going to make it there. This is the way deeper into the forest, you would have to go all the way around the lake the way you're going. It's gators and all type of animals out here. You seen what happened to Dad. Are you mad?!"

"Let's go, Jason. Your dad needs help. What if Mrs. Wilson can't do anything for him?"

"One thing Dad always taught us was not to do things before thinking. This is it right here!"

"Stop your crying, Jason and let's do what we need to do. It's your Dad! Like oh my gosh."

Why does it look like a dog is just staring at me?

BOOM

"EYGH!"

That lightning was so close, I could have sworn we were struck by it.

"Sheesh, you all right, M. The horse! You see, now we're both stranded out here! Dammit, Munisha!"

It's getting bad out here. Maybe I should have just stayed. "You're always complaining."

"Because this is stupid! We barely know where we are! Thunder scared the horse off, and we're stuck on foot! What is it not to complain about?! Let's," Jason grins, shaking his head. "Let's just go back. I can even see and smell the rain coming this way."

Maybe I overreacted, just a little. I didn't want to lose the horse. "I'm sorry."

"Sorry?" Jason chuckles. "Ever since I've known you, that word never crossed my ears."

"It's not like I didn't think, you do know I have already lost people. The feeling of losing someone else is the last thing I need."

"That's understanding. Trust me, I know how you feel, M, I really do."

"How is that? Mommas' boy."

"Hmph, you need to chillout with that. Mommas' boy. Our family use to have a German Shepherd. He was mine ever since a puppy, and we grew up together. Mom had Janice, but she was too young for me to interact with. Apollo would never leave my side and was great at fetch."

"Aw, don't cry."

"I just get a little tearyeyed, sad how we lost him. Now the drizzles are really coming. Anyways, there was this squirrel I believe he was chasing, and we told him to stop. Next thing you know, he gets in a fight with a bobcat. Would you believe that Apollo tore that bobcat to shreds? We started to call him Hercules after."

"I have never seen a bobcat before, so in my mind, I'm thinking it's a oversized cat, that's all. Something like what attacked...what happened to Apollo though? The bobcat must have scratched him up and he bled to death."

"No, not really. Hercules now, had one bad scratch under his chest, he seemed fine. He looked okay to us. By the fifth day I believe, we looked around for him, it took us hours to find him and when we did. Hercules was dead under Dad's truck. That killed me at that time. He was more than a friend; he was family."

"Sorry about that, we never had a pet at my place. My mom hated cats, dogs, anything that crawled on its four legs."

"Wow, babies too?"

"No, you idiot, your something else," I smiled. "Jason, nevertheless, you're a cool guy and all. Geez, if we get struck by thunder, just know that I apologize. A fat rain drop just hit me right in my eye."

"Watch out for squirrel piss. No, not funny? All I can say is, thanks a lot, M. I forgive you. I don't know if Dad will."

The forest was so quiet, even though the rain should have made it sound livelier. Jason probably hated me now.

"Gosh we need that horse," Jason says. "Thank goodness it's not night time with this weather or we would've been stuck for sure. This rain isn't holding up either."

"When we get back, Jason, I'll play you in uno to help you feel better, deal?"

Jason grinned. "When we get back, I'm heading straight for the shower or check Dad first of course. I didn't rest at all today, plus the clothes are still on the line if Janice or Zaraiella didn't take them down."

"Forget that, I'm more worried about your dad. When I saw him shaking like that, it automatically made me think he was going into shock and be dead in seconds."

"Dad will be all right; he always comes through. Come on, M. This rain is rough!"

The bullet raindrops were hitting me so hard on my head. Those girls who love to do hair would have had a fit. That's why I like mine nice, not too long and wavy. "Where do we go now? I lost track of where we are."

"Um, um…wait. I just heard, Betsy."

"Follow it, we can at least find her and get out of this faster. Sorry again, Jason."

Jason grins. "You're good, M. You don't have to keep telling me that. Where are you, girl?! I could've sworn I heard her this way."

"Jason!" I said, pointing. "I see a light. Is that a house?"

"Now that's something I've never seen before in this forest."

"Let's go, we need some cover for now."

Thank goodness, the way how we were going, we was never getting back home in this maze.

"This place doesn't look too cool, M."

"What do you mean? It's an old house, what do you think? It's a ghost in there?"

Knock Knock Knock

"Hello? We need help! Keep a look out for Betsy Jason. You already look scared out of your mind."

The door was sure enough old but locked tight.

"This place, it just feels funny," Jason says. "It looks like a house that elves stay in, you know out of old storybooks."

Knock Knock Knock

"It's kind of like when I first saw your farm at night, be nice. Someone's opening it…"

"Yeaas? Children. How may I help you?"

Oh gosh, she looks scary just from the crack of the door. "Yea, um, me and my guy friend got stranded out here in the rain."

"Our horse got scared from thunder hitting a tree, and then it took off. We need some shelter until it slacks. Mam, can we come in?"

"…One second."

"That lady looks over a thousand years old. Jesus, M."

She had softest voice I have ever heard. She took forever to open the door.

"Come in children."

"Thank you, ugh, nice place you have here," I said, looking around.

This lady's place did appear from out of a fairy tale. A bit creepy but still cozy with her small fireplace.

"What in the world..."

"Shush, Jason."

"Are any of you hurt?"

"No, mam. That smell, what is that?" I said, covering my nose.

"Chitlins deary. Would you and your friend enjoy to have a taste?"

"No, no thanks, he probably does."

"No mam, no I wouldn't," Jason said, frowning as he continued to observe melancholy atmosphere.

"What are your names, children?"

"I'm Munisha, and this is my scary friend, Jason."

"She is just a wild animal. That is why we are trapped out here in the first place."

"I assumed he was your brother. What possessed you two to go out into the Black Forest? You can easily get lost."

"We were on our way to get his dad some medicine," I said.

"Is that so? What is his ailment?"

"He, um, he got bit by an animal, and it seems that it got infected," Jason said. "We think it could possibly be, rabies?"

"Rabies?" the old woman says as she turns to us. "There is a good chance it is. How long ago was the incident?"

"Yesterday, then earlier, we saw him shaking bad, and I'm guessing he had a severe fever. Geez Jason. Look at this stuff," I whispered.

"Wait here, children. I believe I have something to aid the condition."

"That stuff she is making reeks. Can't talk about about you all food anymore. Mrs. Wilson has her beat for sure."

"Now look whose being rude."

"That stuff reeks. There's no hiding that."

It had to be the worst smell I have ever witnessed. The stitch was like multiple people used the restroom, and not one person cared to flush it. No wonder it took her long to open the door. Who needed five locks to live in the middle of nowhere?

"I'm no genius but chitlins?" Jason grimaced, lifting the pot hood. "I think that stuff is actually pig intestines."

"What?! Yuck…Tsk, if I keep breathing it in, I think I will have to just go back outside."

"What's wrong M? Good eating. You have a web on you. Don't worry, I got it. From all of that, you forgot all about the huge webs."

"I didn't even notice, running in the rain and worried how I'm going to get chewed up for losing, Betsy."

"Yea, I don't know how Mom will take that, alone, Dad," Jason said, slowly walking around.

"These books here are so dusty, I know she doesn't read them. What's worse is that she doesn't have a phone either."

"After all these years, she's been here. Neither me nor Dad ever noticed this place."

"It is a bit in a secluded area. The trees cover it up pretty well along with the bushes all over the place. Just like us pretty much."

"She has an old record player. She doesn't look like the type to listen to music. Maybe the old, old country music from two thousand years ago."

"Stop it, Jason. Look at this glass case full of dolls. That all black one looks a little creepy. White eyes and no mouth, must have been something she found in a thrift store."

"Speaking of creepy. You wouldn't believe it, M. Betsy…she's outside. How is that possible?"

How could that be? She ran off miles from us seems like. Her window was so dusty too. "That is," I said as we both looked out the window. "She's just standing there as if she's waiting for us."

"She must have heard us or something. Or smell the food."

"I'm going down there and tell her that our horse is waiting for us. The other good thing is she may have something to give."

"She said not to go down there, M. Let's just wait a little longer or leave better yet. She could be a looney, a psycho."

"Then when Betsy leaves again, you're going to blame yourself, not me. Go get her if want. Be right back scary boy."

"M, M!"

Looking down at the creaking stairs, this place must be over one hundred years old. From the outside, it did not look like it had a basement. "Um, hello? Our horse came back. Hello, Ms? Hello?"

This place, ugh, I didn't know what smells worse, Up there or down here. "She keeps chickens. No wonder the smell is weird. Books everywhere; this one look pretty and…different."

I had never seen something so intricate and unique. Black powdered glitter. Zaraiella would love this, the colors were so beautiful. Capturing my eyes, "Forces Of Nature. What kind of book is this?"

The star had a cool color and must be over a hundred years old too. "Let's see, a person killing chickens, a pig's head, looks stupid but okay. A skeleton, how the body works look like on this page. Healings of the flesh. Destruction of the flesh. Creation of Black Talc Powder. This must be the stuff scattered on these books. Interestingshoot, she's coming."

"I'm back, Jason. She has so many things down there, it's like a dungeon."

"Why is all that glitter on you? Playing with arts and crafts down there?"

"I'm not joking, it's looks like a whole bunch of"

"Here you go children. This, you shall apply it to the wound generously. If the person is not progressing well from the first application, try again in three days."

"Thanks, Ms," Jason said.

I hope it wasn't anything weird or toxic. Could be hair grease in a jar.

"We should really be getting out of here. Thank you for helping us and my father especially."

"Before you both go, why won't you stay for supper? I am always lonesome; it would be appreciated if you were to stay awhile. Just for a little while."

"No thanks, no chitlins for us. Let's go, Jason."

"No, I insist," the old woman says, slowly walking towards us as we stepped backwards. "Please stay, won't you? Just for some time."

Thank goodness she didn't lock all what it looked like three key holes and one chain at the top.

"Hurry up and get on, M!"

"I don't want to break the jar, calm down. Alright, let's go."

"Come back, come back!" the old woman yelled from her uncanny porch.

The hairs from my head felt like they just stood up.

"Jesus, that lady looked crazy! You're a brave one for going down there."

"I'm always the brave one. I don't know what's wrong with you sometimes. Let's just hope this works for your dad."

"Copy that."

Looking back at the poor old lady, it's sad to see someone so alone. She probably have been there half her life and she hasn't been around anyone for years. Just like us.

CHAPTER 11

Contented

Does it feel weird, Mrs. Wilson? The look on your face says it's probably gross.

"It's fine. I am praying this substance works. I had no idea you two would have gone out and brought something back. I unfortunately ran out of ideas. Thank you both so much."

"Jason is the one to thank mostly. He believed we could do it."

"I"

"Good job, Jason. You both are leaders."

"Mhmm, mhmm."

"It's okay, Tim. Everything is going to be alright. This substance seems to burn the wound. The woman you said you got it from, where did you say she was located?"

"Somewhere out there. Jason kept saying she looked like a creepy witch basically, and being so rude even though she was trying to help us."

"She had a hunch back along with that creepy slow voice. How am I supposed to define her?"

"I just pray this stuff works," Mrs. Wilson says as she continues to massage that arm for almost twenty minutes. "You all better get cleaned up. I have a feeling there are mud tracks throughout the house. I will bake a cake for this lady whenever I can get to a store. Her generosity is so greatly appreciated. My goodness, rest easy, Tim. Everything will be alright."

"I think I know where she is, right by the lake and swamp. Her house was small, so it's possible you could miss it. Feel better, Mr. Wilson."

Some odd feeling, it made me feel uncomfortable leaving her out there, and alone. Helping us when she didn't have to. I'll go back one day and thank her again. I had about thirty minutes before lights out. The rain still hasn't let up. So peaceful, so quiet. "If you're out there, Lakia, I wish you a goodnight along with Mom. Wo, you were standing here the whole time? Sometimes you are creepier than that lady."

Jason chuckled. "You were having a full conversation with yourself, weren't you?"

"I was just wishing my family a goodnight."

"And I'm sure they are saying goodnight to you right back," Jason smirked.

"You have that look in your eye, you okay, crazy boy?"

Jason grins. "I can't look at you? Hmph, goodnight, M. Sweet dreams."

He just came to look at me and then leave. I don't know what has gotten into him. Maybe Mr. Wilson was right. I've made the boy a lunatic.

"Zaraiella, you're still writing? That pen never leaves your hand?"

"Just practicing. How is Mr. Wilson? Is he feeling better?" Zaraiella asked, with her eyes glued to the paper.

"The medicine we went out and got, hopefully it works. He should be fine."

"I thought he was going to die."

"What, why would you say that? You have to think positive, Zaraiella."

"People die, he didn't look like he was okay at all. Me and Janice tried talking to him, he didn't say anything. I prayed. Maybe God will heal him."

"No, I don't think so, we went out to someone that gave us that medicine. I'm surprised you never wanted to cut some of your hair. Drying it, is hell," I said, grabbing a clean towel.

"Janice wants to do my hair in another style tomorrow actually."

"What, why? The locs you have now are gorgeous. Tell her to braid yarn or something. Gosh, I don't think I have ever worn this nighty set before. It would be crazy for S.I.L.O to come and arrest me for stealing clothes."

"I love the pink with the glitter, it's cute on your pants."

"That's what drew my attention to it, I told you, Zaraiella, your sis has taste. I'm not a fan of pink, purple is everything."

"Mr. or Mrs. Wilson never asked how you got them?"

"Not exactly, they probably think it came from our house. They probably didn't notice what Janice took either. I'll just tell them I took my older sister's clothes if they ask me. It's a hundred times better than wearing those, things they try to get us and plain white t-shirts. Imagine having to steal some bra's, which is so low. Then if you were to get fat, you would have to get bigger clothes. Tsk, I don't know what to do sometimes."

"You better stop eating before your butt gets too big."

"What? Really sis. You think that's funny, don't you? How if I tickle you like this, oh yea, beg for me to stop!"

"Stop big butt! Okay okay!"

She will wish those words never came out. "Remember, we're sisters, so you'll join the club as you get older."

"No, sorry," Zaraiella said, wiping her eyes from the laughter.

Guess I've been tearing up those French toast and dumplings. Need to slow down before I'm the fattest in this house. "Tomorrow, Zaraiella, I want you to try again with the staff. I know you can do it. I want you to be able to protect yourself from anything out there. It's so important. At least learn that for self-defense."

"I'll try, Munisha," Zaraiella mumbled.

"Good. Because I am not so fond of learning to shoot guns. It literally knocked me down. I wish I had your talent in poetry. The only talent I think I have is in sports. Neither of these will keep us alive. Understand where I'm coming from?" I said as I placed my hand on hers.

"…I, I guess so."

It would have been nice for us to learn to fight and still going to school. Neither of us would be bothered by anyone. "And there goes the lights. I wish he would put the timer on for a later setting. Good night sis."

Zaraiella chuckled. "Nighty night big butt."

"Alright, Zaraiella."

I really need to go on a diet now. It was Mrs. Wilson's food and I have to do something because Miss smart mouth wants to be a toothpick.

"I am so tired of raking these leaves, can't wait for winter."

"You could just ask to do other chores, Munisha," Zaraiella says as her rake swung back and forth.

"You're right. Mr. Wilson doesn't seem to want us doing the easy work. Then he's going to make us pick up snow just thinking of it. I need to lose some weight so this will help me anyways."

"This is easy, it's leaves."

"Not like how your friend Janice gets to milk and pick greens. Jason, he's a little rough with shoveling dirt and he most likely doesn't mind."

"Exactly, so we don't have it that hard."

Only thing was, I just felt my arms, not my body. I want to go back into the city and step into a gym. "Have you thought about ever leaving here sooner?"

"No, why?" Zaraiella said, continuing to rake. "It's safe here."

"Yes, for now. I think we should just move out, maybe next year. Mr. Wilson doesn't look like he could…you know, take care of us as much as he used to."

"He's getting old."

"Right, and he has his own family he has to take care of. Last night, I was looking at this stuff from the old woman's house. The things she had in her place proved she wasn't from here. When I go back to her, I'm asking where we can go to get out of this mess."

"I don't want to lie to you, Munisha. I don't want to go."

"You're just saying that now. Once you see more out there, you will wish you moved sooner."

"Breakfast is ready you all!" Mrs. Wilson shouts.

"Thank god! I'm ready for something good today. Not too much food since I'm about to start my diet."

Hoping she made some spinach frittata. That toast isn't what I need right now. "Whew, Jason. Looks like you fell in some mud," I frowned.

"That rain from yesterday flooded the garden out. Next thing you know, I slipped right in it."

"You be sure to wash up good, Jason. No sitting at the table with that grime," Mrs. Wilson says with her hands on her hips.

"I know to wash up, Ma. Breakfast was supposed to be ready earlier anyways."

"Oh shoot, someone has a temper," I grinned.

"That's just him Munisha. My son gets moody when his chores are doing him in."

"Toast again? Oh god no."

"What's wrong?" Mrs. Wilson grimaces. "You love toast with butter."

"I do, but"

"Munisha says she's getting fat," Zaraiella says, sipping her juice.

"Getting fat, where?"

"Yes…I am."

"Munisha, you're not fat. Is she, Mommy?"

"I have a…pudge," I whispered. "It's what I eat and I barely do any real cardio. Tsk, I walk a lot, so I don't understand."

Mrs. Wilson sighs. "You children need to let nature take in."

"She said my butt is big. That is what Zaraiella said. Food isn't my best friend for…down there."

"Child, there is nothing wrong with your size. You still fit into your clothing, correct?"

"Yes, I just don't want to be…big."

"Trust me, Munisha. Your body is growing as a woman's body should. Back in my days. Perhaps you can say in school. Men loved my curves. That's how I got men to do what I wanted."

"They liked girls with big butts?" Zaraiella laughed.

Mrs. Wilson sighed with a smile. "You children are something else. People like what they like. You are beautiful Munisha, and I would not lie to you. I always believe to love yourself no matter what. Reminiscing, I even remember I was ashamed of my size and just one day, a guy offered me flowers. I believe everyone, no matter big, small, or medium, someone will find you."

"How can anyone find us if we are here in the middle of the jungle?" I asked.

"You know, Munisha," Janice said, chewing on her toast. "I saw Jason starring at you."

"Really? I don't think so."

"I see him do it too. When you're raking with Zaraiella he's staring way from his end to yours. I would say he's not just looking at your work," Mrs. Wilson smirked.

"He's funny. If I ever catch him staring, I'm going to give him a good punch to the face."

"So know this, you three young ladies. Love yourself, no matter how you feel. You all are beautiful. Remember to respect yourselves, and respect others. That is the true essence of beauty. I hear big foot upstairs coming. Now this is us, as in ladies talk. No one converse beyond this circle."

She was right. Working on my confidence is a must. I just need to keep myself in shape and definitely my waistline down. Zaraiella won't get the best of me.

"Finally!" Jason said, throwing himself on to the chair beside me. "I'm hungry as hell."

"Young man, you will watch your tone. Your father may not be at the table but I am still in charge around here."

"Is Daddy ok? Did the stuff work?"

"His body is relaxing now," Mrs. Wilson says. "The shivering is gone along with the fever. That ointment really did magic. It's quite hard to believe. Thank you both again so much."

"I peeped in his room to see him before doing chores. He looked a lot better from yesterday. That lady is the real lifesaver. No thanks to, Jason."

"M…please. Let me eat my food."

"What was her name?" Mrs. Wilson asked.

"That's funny you ask, I never even asked her. Guess we were in a panic. The rain and lightning had us worked up too."

"If you do go back, please thank her. I would go myself. However, Tim is in need for a good substantial amount time. Whenever he's better, that would be the first thing on my to do list."

He does stare at me a lot. My peripheral vision tells me all things. "Are we still training today?"

Jason grins. "If you want, I thought you would still be tired from yesterday. Told ya, Ma. M is like that animal that got Dad. Won't stop moving."

"All that means she'll never be fat," Mrs. Wilson says, smirking at me.

"I will see you outside, Jason."

Maybe I was just overthinking it. I can't be fat if I can handstand.

"That girl still hasn't come outside yet."

"Who, Zaraiella?" Jason asked, spinning his staff.

"She's supposed to be out here practicing with us. She promised me she would."

"Maybe she just isn't interested, M. Let er' be. You shouldn't be trying to force anybody anyways."

"She needs to be out here. Like I said before, it's for her own protection. I really need to clean my shoes; I wish I took the stuff that protects your shoes from dirt. It just falls right off. As soon as you come out here, the dirt is ready to jump on them."

"That's your fault. No one told you to get a whole bunch of things you should wear if you were going to a party or something. Just wear your boots. I wouldn't wear my nice things out here."

"The funny thing is, there is no way for me to show it off."

"That is why my eyes were looking at you all at the store like, huh? Confiscating all you can get to just wear it in the house," Jason grins.

"You know when us women see nice things, we just have to have it. We don't care if we don't even get to wear it sometimes. We just want it. You didn't get anything at all?"

"Of course I did."

"Let me guess. You took a watch or a chain."

"Nope, I got this."

"Ooohh."

The sun glimmered on the metal and looked sharp as a razor. "I like it. You should have gotten me one too. Almost as sharp as mines. I wonder what he did with my blade."

"There was armory store by it. They took a lot of things in there, and this knife was left there just for me. It's actually one of the best. I couldn't let Dad see it, would have wondered where I got it from."

We both love knives, one thing we had in common. "Speaking of him, did you go check up on him before coming to breakfast?"

"Yes, twice and before breakfast. He looks better, thank God."

"Why can't I handstand as much as I used to?"

"You're not focused sister. Concentrate!"

"It's…not that. It's…my ass getting too big! Uhhh, I can't believe this. What are you laughing at, chicken legs?"

"You're hilarious! That's what Mom and you all were talking about? I heard bits and pieces."

"No one told you to be eavesdropping on us. Tsk, but yea, as much as I didn't really care for a lot of the stuff we eat; it's been putting weight on me."

"You look the same to me, fine, actually."

"Aww. You're sweet, brother."

"Someone's blushiiiing," Jason chuckled. "You look good though, really."

"I'm still going to lose weight. Zaraiella last night was ridiculing me about my size. I think I saw her take a picture of me while I was getting dressed. Probably have twenty pictures of me in my pajamas and my butt all over."

"M look, you're beautiful just the way you are. Don't worry about anything. One thing about me is that I believe in confidence. If you don't believe in yourself, there is nothing you can do and no one can help ya either."

"Your Mom preached that to you. Sounds just like her."

"She did, but mostly Dad. In basketball, if you don't have that confidence, you might as well just sit on the bench."

"It's strange how you love basketball but never play by yourself, only when Mark comes. I know you probably suck at it now."

"You want some of this? Is that what your saying?"

"Last time I threw a basketball was probably when I was six. I like sports but that particular one is not my thing."

"One day, I will get you to play. You may have a better chance than this, that's for sure."

"One day, hmph, I…oh my gosh! Look who finally decided to come outside."

"I'm not practicing, Jason. I just came to watch Zaraiella fight."

"Hopefully, Munisha doesn't hurt me," Zaraiella says with a nervous frown.

"Of course, sis. I'm just going to make you be able to fight a little. Watch and observe us. Me and Jason first, then you'll try. Go easy brother," I said whispering in his ear.

Jason and I have gotten so good over the years. I wondered about being able to fight more with my hands since I can't carry a staff everywhere. "Your turn sis. Remember to focus. Don't worry about anyone judging you, okay?"

"Okay…um, I'm sorry for talking about your butt," Zaraiella grinned. "Janice, fatty pants."

"See. That is why I am teaching you this. If someone bothers you, I will sit and watch. I wish you would laugh…chicken legs."

"Hey, I'm innocent here."

Zaraiella didn't do bad as I thought, she is still so young, and Jason is right about her not being interested in this type of stuff.

"Is that it, Munisha? This always makes my hands tired."

"It made me want to try too, Zaraiella," Janice said, picking up Zaraiella's staff and giving it to her.

"Then practice with us next time, Janice. M won't be your trainer unless you want her to be."

"That's okay. Munisha is a little rough."

"No I'm not. Anyways, we will try again tomorrow. Zaraiella, your staff spins was a…B* minus. You will get there, so don't worry about it."

"Those girls are going to be best friends forever. They're like, glued to one another," Jason said.

"I see that too, Zaraiella has always been friendly. Her making enemies is highly doubtful. We might be friends forever, Jason."

"Don't make me blush, M."

Yea, I already sensed in a way he likes me but now it was all obvious. Though, I only like him as my big brother. "We won't be living here too much longer; but you two are welcome to come along."

"We're not going anywhere. Most likely me, and Janice will take over the house once our parents move on. I never really thought of moving away. This place has made me appreciate life more. Like this tree here."

"The one that makes us work all the time."

"This tree shows us that life is all about being content," Jason said, leaning against the hard wood.

"Why do you say that?"

"You say that it gives you work yet we're up under here not complaining about shade."

"I like that, I need to start calling you the wizard."

"Hmph, I'm no wizard. You will just learn to appreciate life when you really stay happy with what you have."

"So, you will be able to appreciate things when they come to you."

"See, you got it. Just remember, M. Life has it's ups and downs. I think that's how it's supposed to work."

"I hear you. It is nice here; I don't believe I ever relaxed and felt the breeze."

"Feels good, don't it? Breeze travel all throughout the forest and comes straight here. The weird thing is, I've never seen a whole bunch insects around this tree. There may be a few; but never so many where we couldn't sit here."

"It wouldn't really matter to me, as long as there are no spiders. My only issue with the"

"There's one right there. You're calling me scared, you're scared of something so small, and you're over five feet tall."

"I don't care. They're so ugly. You jerk! You should have killed it!"

Nothing creepier looking than something with a whole bunch of limbs and eyes staring at you.

"I don't believe it…Dad. Dad, you're alright!"

"He's walking! It's a miracle. He looks like nothing ever happened."

"Thank goodness, what are you doing out here, old man?"

"Coming out here showing out the miracle," Mr. Wilson says as he twist his body and flexing his arms. "I feel…amazing, and I don't know how."

"Did Mom see you?"

"She wouldn't let you out here if she saw you," I said.

"She saw me. The waterworks came as soon as I came down the stairs. The ones who I must thank the most are you two. She told me what you both did, that surprised me. Then miraculously, the ointment did the impossible. I couldn't be more proud, grateful, and highly honored to be your father, Jason. And of course, you too, Munisha, my new daughter. You two did great."

"No, problem, Mr. Wilson. My mind could only think of doing something when I saw you. Me and, Jason had a time in the forest. You wouldn't believe it either."

"Where did you get the medicine from?"

"A lady who lives in the forest. We never seen that area before, Dad. As long as we have been out there or even you, we never came across it."

"That is unusual," Mr. Wilson said, rubbing his chin. "I've been through every inch of this land, or so I thought. It's immense, I'll tell you that."

"We should celebrate some way, don't you think, Jason?"

"Have Mom bake a cake like she said she wanted to and bring some to the lady."

"Now you know, we don't have things such as that here. Sara could put us something on that's gratifying for us."

"The bite doesn't even look like it…even happened," I said as I observed Mr. Wilson's arm. "There are a few small dots, but that's it. It's amazing, she just went down there, fixed something up, and you're healed."

"About, seventy percent, Munisha. My head is still a bit foggy. It sure is breezy out here."

"Tim! On the radio, there is a tropical storm being issued out!"

"No wonder everything is blowing around out here. Do me a favor, you all. Go close the barn up and be sure it's sealed tight. I will check around to be sure there is no cracked airways around the house. Every time these winds come like this, they tend to get in and could break doors off the hinges if there strong enough."

"As long as I've been here, we never had any severe storms, Jason. Except for that hurricane that came by but went out to the ocean."

"It's rare for storms to come around here. The worst we get is snow, but down south, they get everything, hurricanes, twisters, all type of stuff. We're lucky we just get snow, and it passes on, and rarely blizzards."

"Zaraiella at times tells me she has these nightmares of tornadoes. Her and some other person in the dream would see them and go outside where they see three destroying everything around her. Hey, that is what she said."

"Well…that does sound like a nightmare. You were with her in this dream?"

"She told me no. The person she said looked older because I asked her. I don't know where she gets all these ideas and visions from, hope it doesn't mean anything."

"Looks like she's just terrified of em'. That's all," Jason said, shrugging his shoulders.

"Who isn't? I've never seen one before, but I would never want to see one. In school, they once showed us pictures of how they destroyed homes. How can, God make things like that and let it hurt people?"

"Well, it's a part of mother nature. It's like how we have those crazy mosquitoes that like to play around your ear at night while you're trying to sleep. The way I see it, everything has a purpose, know what I mean?"

"And tornadoes have a purpose?" I said, rolling my eyes. "To hurt and destroy people's homes? Give me a break. It's just sad how things are, how we have to live, what S.I.L.O has done. It shouldn't have to be this way."

"I didn't say it was something that towards humanity, M. I am saying because it could mean something to her, in her mind. You get me?"

"Hmm, nope!"

Jason chuckles. "Who knows, maybe one day, you will go out there and be governor of a city. You have that spirit of finding out what is wrong and doing something about it."

"Your dad always joked with me about that. If I were to change how things are, I couldn't."

"Why not? You seem like you want to be in charge all the time."

"My world, it's not like it can just come true. I know there is hate and despair everywhere. Wars in places that we don't even know about. If everybody just do what is right, wouldn't life be much easier?"

"Hm, you sound like a president there, M," Jason lightly clapped.

"I'm just telling you how I wish the world would be. So it can be easier for us."

"It would be paradise; it would be. Just unlikely people will do the right thing. As you said, too much stupid stuff and hate. Sausage brain people too. It's all good friend. That should be it out here. Hope those crazy chickens don't fly in the stable."

The sky was so pitch black; it appeared similar to the darkness of the night. They were not lying about a storm coming. The worst that could happen is the tree falling on the house. We would definitely have to leave then. I can only imagine the bugs, spiders coming inside after.

"You all secured everything properly? I trust that you did."

"Yea Dad, you should be resting, you were just in bed and now moving like nothing happened."

"Told you son, my body feels great," Mr. Wilson says, as he stretches. "Maybe it was just a minor infection and my body along with the ointment, suppressed the pain then eliminated it out of my system."

"No more going out unless you all need to, Mr. Tim Wilson. You had us all terrified."

"Forgive me for that, baby. You know I'm always going to be alright."

"Here comes the rain. How long is this going to last? Seems like forever, it's white," I said, looking out at the bombarding mist devouring the trees.

"With these types of storms Munisha, they never last for an hour. Remember Sara when Jason was about eight years old. There was a storm that came while we were working on the house. The rain would not let up."

"Your brother nearly killed himself trying to manage the nail gun."

Mr. Wilson grins. "That's right. I recall that. The old drunk almost shot himself in the head with it."

"Where do you think Uncle Eric can be?" Jason asked.

"In Jail or dead. He was very…let's just say, self-destructive. I wouldn't be surprised if he joined a gang or something similar to that."

BOOM

"Damn!"

"Language, Munisha, language," Mr. Wilson frowned.

"Sorry, that was loud. Hope it doesn't hit that tree right next to us."

Thinking to myself as the storm roared above. If we just had to get out of this house, where could we possibly go?

"Look who decided to join us down here, the hair salon girls," Mr. Wilson said.

"I knew they would eventually come down with all that's going on outside.

"Mommy, that sounded like it hit the house."

"What is so funny, Tim?"

"All I heard were little feet hauling tail upstairs."

"I love your new do, Zaraiella. Did my daughter do it?"

"Yes, I did some too."

"That's my princess!" Mrs. Wilson said. "You already know where she picked up that talent from. You all have talents, and you must use them."

Even if we did, we could not use it being so isolated. I didn't truly have any gifts.

CHAPTER 12

Goes Around, Comes Around

Looks like some tree limbs fell, nothing too bad. Hope it didn't push my woodwork all over the place.

"You didn't tell us to put it in, Dad. M and I would have done it."

"It's alright, just glad none of those trees came in on us. That's the last thing we need around here. Where are you going so fast, missy?"

"It's over, right?" I asked, getting up. "Wow, We are definitely not going out there for a while. It's like a river."

"You do know it rained four hours nonstop; you're going to mess up those pretty shoes you have on there. Hmm, where did you get those from?" Mr. Wilson asked, placing his hand on his chin.

"You know what, Tim? I was thinking the same thing."

"I ugh, found them."

"Where?" Mr. Wilson immediately responded. "Don't tell me around here."

"They were…in a bag. Somebody left them in the forest when me and Jason was out looking for something to help you. That's when we found it."

"Hmph, that's hard to believe. They just threw out shoes that look as though they cost over two hundred credits."

"Maybe somebody stole them Dad, and they tried to hide it out there. Then they would have come back looking for it."

"Yea, that's most likely what happened, Mr. Wilson," I said.

"Tim, we don't have any meat for tonight."

"Truly? We must have left the catch out there that day."

Thank God she got me off the hook. "I don't even think we were bringing anything back. After that animal bit you, no one was thinking of bringing back food."

"That's fine, we have our greens," Mrs. Wilson said.

"That is unfortunate. I guess so, Sara. We'll all have to have that then. Hey, fruits and vegetables are enough anyways."

"You think we could go catch some bass real quick then, Dad? The fish should be biting since the storm passed by."

"You're right. However, I'm not going out there. The mud is soft, it will be as if you're walking in grits."

"Well, I can't just eat corn and greens anyways. We can go, Jason, whenever you're ready," I said.

"You two are certainly not going out there by yourselves."

"But Ma"

"No, and no sir, whichever one you like," Mrs. Wilson folded her arms. "God forbid a weak tree limb falls on either you."

"Sara, baby. Hmph, I believe they can do it."

"Tim..."

"They went out and brought me back what I needed. They're old enough and inch by inch becoming wise. In my opinion, to go and hunt for their own food."

"So, we can take the gun, Dad?"

"It's a no! Tim Wilson, my son, is not carrying a rifle out there, especially without any supervision."

"Okay, okay, you two go out in the shed, bring me the rods, and I will be sure you are ready and safe. I trust you both. Today you will prove that you can do this. You are not getting any younger. That's what it is."

It felt amazing out here with the breeze. I wondered how the old woman was doing with all the windy weather. Hopefully, a tree didn't fall on her miniature home.

"I see you decided to put those boots on," Jason grinned.

"I thought we were busted. Oh my gosh."

"You were going to get busted for sure. I knew he would eventually pay attention to what you are wearing and say something about it. The look on his face tells me he knows what we did."

"You think so? Your story seemed like it worked."

"Could have told him that you found them at the old lady place. Dad may be a little old; but he's cool. One of our little secrets was when a kid told my teacher and my Dad I smoked."

"What! That was a little awkward. You're just now bringing that up? Please tell me why you did that. Crazy boy."

"I smoked a juice straw."

"A juice straw? How? I bet you looked like a complete idiot. Ha, trying to be a bad boy."

"Yea, no kidding. My dumb friends that I use to hang with after school did a lot of the weird things. We never did something that could put us in jail; but we did light a skyrocket on the back of a mail truck before."

"That was stupid. I would have chased you all down. I can't get the fact you took a straw and smoked it. How did you even do that? It's nothing but a tube."

"Right, and that taste of it was horrible. I still remember it sort of. Never will I smoke and I advise you not to. Here, take this one. Webs are all over the one I usually use."

"I'm not scared of webs, just the ugly spiders that make them. We should take the machete, just in case."

"Dad isn't going to let you. You heard em'."

"So, what are we supposed to use to protect ourselves? Fishing rods?" I frowned.

"Hey, these things hurt. It's just like a staff."

"Looks like you all are set," Mr. Wilson said, coming inside the barn.

"Dad, we need some sort of protection, don't you think?"

"You can speak up son, your mother isn't king of the castle you know."

"Be right back you all," I said.

I had a better plan for today. This way, Zaraiella can learn a little bit more than just doing hair all day. If she's getting it done now, it will just have to wait for another time.

"Best friends? You two came back up here after all of that thunder. Are you doing each other's hair again?"

"I was about to start," Zaraiella says while sitting on the bed.

"Good, that means she can wait. We're going out and Mr. Wilson said he needs you to come with us."

"Why, where are we going?"

"There's no food, didn't you hear from earlier. He said he needs you to come along, come on, get up."

"No, I don't want to go."

"He will be pissed if you don't come on," I frowned. "You don't need to be in here all day, Zaraiella. Come and be with us, for me for a change."

"Why does he need me to go? I never go when you all go to get food," Zaraiella mumbled.

"It's because I I mean, he wants you to learn. No more butterflies and sunshine, time to learn more about reality."

"M, you ready?!"

"Be right there! Wait for me downstairs! Come on, Zaraiella."

It was like pulling teeth to get this girl out of that room. She and her salon friend needs a life.

"Okay, how long will we be gone?" Zaraiella asks as the wet mud stuck to our shoes.

"Not long, we'll be just getting a few fish and be heading back. Are you coming with us, Janice?"

"Um, no, I have to go and clean up."

"Suit yourself. Don't worry, Zaraiella, you will get back to the salon once we're done, I promise."

If we weren't out here in the middle of nowhere, Janice could be in the salon getting paid instead of just doing work for free. I need to really consider her joining us once we leave. There's more than this here, and they could be living their best life regardless of the conditions in this world. There must be another way for peace with longevity.

"Now, I want you all to wait. Zaraiella is going too?"

"Yes, Mr. Wilson, she is, as you can see. We're going to have some fun, aren't we, sis?"

"I need you all to be back in no more than an hour. Sara isn't too cheerful about you all going out without me."

"We got this, Dad."

"Be careful you here. I'm going to get more of that application to put on. This bite is starting to itch a little."

It looks like a good afternoon to hang out. I could only imagine being on a mountaintop with the breeze flowing like this. "What the hell?!"

"What happened, M? Don't tell me you can't stand the mud."

"Mom's car, the window is broken."

"Oh yea, that's the windshield, actually," Jason said.

"Smart guy, it doesn't matter. Somebody must have come and did this."

"Maybe the wind blew something on it, and it caused it. Lucky it didn't shatter. Don't worry about it. The crack isn't that bad," Jason says tapping the glass.

"We can't get it fixed, huh?" I asked. "That's the real problem."

"I mean, if it still drives as it should, Dad will take it to get a new one put it. They shouldn't bother him for that."

"I'm pretty sure it's not cheap. Tsk, let's just go so we can get back."

How can Mr. Wilson get that fixed if they must have an ID to do anything in the city? Unless he knows someone like, Kenneth who barely comes.

"Your sister is so quiet."

"I'm okay," Zaraiella says as she straddles along behind us.

"If you're not with Janice then you're just as quiet as a mouse. Let me stop before your big sister beats me up."

"Zaraiella is observing the forest. That's what she tells me all the time. What are you observing now, little sis?"

"Just looking at how dark the trees are."

"Remember what that old woman called it?" Jason says. "The Black Forest, and I can see why. No matter what time of the day it is, these tall trees keep light from within. That is why the trail never really looks like sunshine comes through."

Since we were out here, I wonder if we could go and see her. Something told me I should. "You think if we get close to where the old lady is we could stop by, Jason? I want to go and thank her."

"She's not this way we're headed."

"I thought she was by the lake we're going to."

"Oh no, that small pond near her has dirty water. We could go on our way back if we make good time."

"How long are we going fishing?" Zaraiella asked.

"There you go, Zaraiella, no need to be so muted. We won't be out here for long. Mr. Wilson said"

"One hour. I heard him."

"See, you already know," I said. "I knew you heard him. What are you looking at now? Your head turned pretty fast."

"Uh, nothing. Um, you all might take longer."

"Why the rush, Zaraiella?" Jason asked. "You have something to do?"

"You already know why. I disturbed their appointment, so she has to get back," I rolled my eyes as Zaraiella continued looking at her surroundings.

I knew and felt, it was more than nature her eyes witnessed.

"I want to write poetry, not just talk to her."

"You write poetry? I didn't know that."

"She's pretty good with it, actually. But poetry only feeds the brain, not our stomachs."

Better stop before she started making fat jokes.

"I already know she's smart. Everybody has their own God gifted talents."

"I don't have any, at least that I know of," I said.

"It takes some time for each person. Maybe you would like to draw or paint."

"Tried it, suck at it."

"Likewise. If it makes you feel better, I believe my only special talent is working," Jason said, cracking his hands. "I take real pride in my handwork and come to love it."

"Your mom told me you think it's the end of the world if your chores don't go in your favor."

"She's right about that. When my craft looks crappy, I'm ashamed of it. Like, Dad is teaching me to weld now. If I do plan to move from the area, I will definitely need it."

They always said that everyone has their own special gift. What if you never find it in this lifetime?

"Finally, we're here," Jason says, placing his hand in the calm quiet lake. "Feels like the water is being generous today."

"Last time we were here, we sat for about an hour. Then we caught something just as small as, Zaraeilla's hand. I don't see the point of this. If we catch something that small, were not throwing him anywhere but the frying pan."

"If, Dad sees we brought back a baby bass, he'll make us retrace our steps and throw it right back in."

"Your dad is awful sometimes," I frowned. "No, really, he is."

"Well, how would you like it if someone took your baby son or daughter out of the house and didn't let them see the world?" Jason says while putting his rod together.

"First, that's different because they're cannibals if they plan to eat people. Second, didn't God make fish so we can eat it? Ba by fish too."

Jason chuckles. "You're a tough cookie, M."

"I know. Want to go first, Zaraiella? I'll watch you."

"Go for it, Zaraiella, pull us in a ten pounder. Maybe a juicy bullhead would be nice."

"Bullhead?" Zaraiella grimaced.

"Not an actual bullhead sis. It's a fish."

"Munisha the fisherman, I mean woman."

"…Just make sure you tell me if it's pulling too hard Zaraiella or Jason will have to pull you out of the water."

The lake was so nice and peaceful, even more beautiful when it's misty. It was to the point I wanted to take my dry clothes and let them sit somewhere while I go for a dive. If the water weren't so cold, I would have jumped in.

"There you go, see, I already got one," Jason says, reeling in his rod.

"It better be enough for us to eat tonight."

"Oooh, look at the fishyy!" Zaraiella said, with finally a smile.

"This one…he's too small"

"Wait! Don't throw him back in!"

"I told you, M. They won't let us eat something that size. Give it time to grow and let it multiply will ya?"

"Hmph. Give it to me next time. I'll eat it myself. Throwing our dinner away. Crazy, isn't he, sis?"

"Alright, you'll be the one that walks back here. Nothing yet, Zaraiella?"

"Nothing…I don't like this."

I can tell my sister was ready to get back. Probably get her hair done in another style. "It's boring isn't it?"

"Yea…no, not really."

"Give it time, Zaraiella," Jason says. "It's coming."

"Have you ever taken a swim in this lake before?" I said, kneeling near the water. "I really feel like going in."

"You're crazy, and no mam. There are snakes in there, just so you know. Dad told us not to anyways."

"It doesn't look like snakes are in here. I thought they mainly be on land anyways."

"Trust me, snakes swim; but you don't want to come across that. A nightmare would be if an anaconda just pokes his ugly head right out."

"What are, andaconas?" Zaraiella asked.

"They are fifty foot long snakes. As crazy as M is, she wouldn't care if there were in here. She would still jump in."

"You know, I don't think I would be scared of snakes. Their color has always been pretty to me."

"We will see, but about that, there's a place where I saw a red one. The colors on that thing, it had to be poisonous."

"We need to get a pet. I just thought of that. Maybe your dad can get us"

"Help, HELP! EYGH!"

"Oh shoot!" Jason said, dropping his rod. "She has something. Come on, Zaraiella! Reel it in! You got this!"

"Don't fall sis! I got you!"

If she falls, I'm throwing the crazy boy in too.

"It's, strong! I don't want to drop it!"

"You won't, Zaraiella. Just hold your left hand on the pole and reel in with your right."

"I got you sister. Tsk, that boy is going to get you to fall right in. Can't you see she needs help?"

"I think…think I have it now," Zaraiella says as she reels in faster.

"You see M, she has it."

"What, wait…what happened?" Zaraiella asked.

"What is it, sis? Keep reeling! Don't stop until it's in front of you. I'm so hungry, I can already taste him out the frying pan."

"It's…" Zaraiella says with a questioned look. "It's gone."

"Jason, what's so funny? The fish got away."

"You girls, oh man, that needed to be on camera right there. The look on your two faces are priceless."

"What happened to the hook? Jason?" I frowned.

"It's in the fishy's mouth along with the worm," Jason and his annoying laughter continued.

"How did it pop the string, Jason? You meant to put it on like that you idiot."

"Silly rabbit. You must use the drag properly or you'll lose the catch."

"I have no idea what you are talking about. I just want to know why the fish took off. We need food."

"You two aren't about that life, I forgot. That's a real fisher men skill to catch anything. It is time to get back anyways," Jason says as he stretches. "That was fun. At least we got to go out. Cheer up, Zaraiella. There is always next time."

"He's just a jerk, sis. Don't worry about it. Still with barely anything to eat when we get back. Don't even think I'm giving up this little bit we have here. Mr. Wilson will have to fight me for it."

That small fish was only for one person and looked like you could only get about three bites off of it. The lake sure was generous.

"Remember you told me that lake leads to the ocean, Jason? I am still waiting."

Jason grins. "I know, M. Just give me some time. I will think of a way to take you there."

"Uh huh. By that time, the water will be dry."

"Y'know, back then, Mom and Dad used to go down to the beach. There were islands I remember briefly. It was beautiful. The sand was a golden color, and Dad told me it's now a dark one."

"I wonder what's causing that. Me and Zaraiella have never really been to a beach before."

"I remember, kind of going to the beach. It, it was a small bridge and water everywhere. It was so pretty."

"Zaraiella, Mom never took us to the beach. Unless it was a field trip you went on. So yea, we never been."

"Really?" Jason said. "There are so many around. Not a big public one, but the ocean is yours to visit whenever you are ready. I don't think, Janice ever seen the ocean either."

"That's why you only need to take us all one day or Mr. Wilson. I'll tell him when we get back."

"Dad isn't going way out there. He used to love the beach. I don't know what happened. I once try to convince him to take us. Unfortunately, it never happened."

"He's boring, all he does is work," I said. "How can he just live like that?"

"That's, Dad, work, sleep, eat, repeat. Trust me. I'm not going to be like that."

As the family lifestyle, he had no choice but to become like his father. Isolated from civilization and unable to meet new people unless they invite them to the household. People don't live forever so I hope he keeps that in mind.

"There goes your friendly spiderwebs, M."

"You see that, Zaraiella. You can't tell me that doesn't look creepy."

"No, it's just webs."

"We're not in the area where it was everywhere, that's why," I said as I continued to look up at the fading daylight. "If you were to see that, sis, that would have been it there. What's that smell?" I grimaced.

"I smell something, and you guys hear that?" Jason said, stopping in front of us.

"Sounds like something is eating. We don't need to see what it is. Let's go back, Jason. Stay behind me, Zaraiella."

"You said you wanted more to eat, didn't you?"

"I have what I need. It may be enough just for me and Zaraiella though."

"Exactly, I may want to have some meat too along with, Janice."

"We don't have anything to kill it with. Where did you get that?"

"Dad gave it to me before we left," Jason says as he spins the bullets in the cylinder. "Looks like he finally trusts me. Even though it's a little pea shooter, it'll get the job…what in the world. What the hell is that?"

"Zaraiella, Jason, let's get out of here."

"Wait…I have…never seen something like this."

"What is that, Munisha? It's nasty!"

"Oh my god sis! Run…Jason, RUN!"

BANG BANG…BANG BANG BANG

That thing was so indescribable. It's not from here. Maybe we were just hallucinating. A man, with scales? "Oh no, here it comes now. Oh god."

"Hey."

"Ey, mmhm!"

"It's me it's me," Jason whispered as he covered my mouth. "You're not hurt, are you?"

"That thing…it's revolting. Where's, Zaraiella?"

"I don't know, we'll find her. She couldn't have gone too far."

"Jason, what, I mean, was that real? That thing couldn't have been."

"It was, and something we've never seen before. We both know where it came from."

The looks of it was enough to make me so sick. S.I.L.O made the monstrosity, and now it's in our beautiful forest.

"Zaraiella!"

"Ssshh. We can't let that thing find us."

"I don't care about that, thing," I said, pushing Jason's hand. "Zaraiella, where are you?!"

"I'm telling you, M. We can't be so loud."

"Where could that girl run to so far? There are only so many places here. We didn't run miles."

"Don't start panicking. That's the first way you lose it," Jason says, grabbing my arm.

"Shut up, Jason! Please!"

"Look, tracks! See, we'll find her"

"What the hell are you two doing out here so late?! You all should have been back thirty minutes ago. Where's your sister?"

"I…I don't know, she ran. We're looking for her. Oh my gosh."

"Dad, we got caught up with"

"Tim Wilson! Enough games. What is going on?" Mrs. Wilson said, pushing the hanging moss from her face.

"You followed me out here? I thought I told you stay at home with, Janice."

"Missy, what my eyes tell me, your sister went missing, no?"

"Sara, we have this under control. How about you go back and begin to prepare dinner? Zaraiella probably wondered off while they were walking back. I know you don't want to hear this now. Come on, it's getting dark. We'll see you when we're back. Promise."

"You all get back. Please, Tim, keep them safe."

"Now, which direction do you think she ran off to?" Mr. Wilson asked. "Munisha, you crying over there? Munisha?"

"How can I be so stupid to let her run off like that?"

"Don't blame yourself. It was a mistake, M."

"I heard the yelling, it pointed me right to you all location. What were you all fleeing from, bear? Don't tell me another feline."

"Dad, this thing wasn't even close. It was something…I don't know how to describe it."

"The damn thing was hideous, and it had us running to the point we got, freaking separated! Now it's probably after my sister."

"Calm down, Munisha. You both said it was what?"

"Remember when you told me, Dad, something was running in the streets? No doubt what, that…I don't know what it was. It walked like a person. Only thing, we got front row seats and it's couldn't be nothing; but from S.I.L.O."

"I can believe that," Mr. Wilson says nodding his head and looking up to the trees. "Now, from that, we need to find that girl. So, don't be overwhelmed about anything, Munisha. We'll find her."

It has been more than an hour and there's nothing. She won't even yell back to us. Why won't she just make a sound? I feel she's still out here. Something would have told me she wasn't; don't want to contemplate it.

"This thing you both saw, was it coming at you all fast?"

"Sort of, I just didn't get a chance to see where it went. Zaraiella and, M went in the same direction, so I thought. She must have turned another way."

"What did you get to see of it, Munisha?"

"I told you already, the thing was hideous, it scared us to death, and now it has my sister lost out here," I rolled my eyes. "Where in this ridiculous forest can she be?"

"It's dark. Can barely see a thing. Sara is going to come out and give us all a whole lecture. I can already sense that's coming," Mr.

Wilson said, shaking his head then looking at me. "I'm sorry, Munisha. We"

"You can go back; I have to find my sister."

Mr. Wilson frowned. "You know we're not leaving you out by yourself."

"Yea, M, we'll find her. It's not reasonable for you to be out here. You have to stay calm, okay?"

"I'm not losing my sister. We were trying to help your dad and now my sister just a while ago. Why is this happening? Why is my life like this?"

"Cool out, will you? You, coming for my aid along with Jason, you went out and did what you had to save my life. Things go around, and they most certainly will come around. She will be okay. We cannot get down and out when the bad days come. There's always a storm, but will you weather through them?"

"This is not normal. My sister is lost because of me. Is it all my fault?"

"Munisha, Munisha, stop this right now!" Mr. Wilson growled, shaking my shoulders.

"I'm the one who lied to her and brought her out here. It's my fault."

"We both know why you wanted her to come out here, you want her to learn and there is nothing wrong with that. When I brought you out here with Jason, my accident happened. It could have been any one of you instead of me. Life happens. Regardless, you never give up hope.”

“That thing probably got her, Mr. Wilson, and it’s all my fault.”

My mind racing, I didn’t know what to do or what to think. Succumb to the fact she was gone? Maybe she went home.

CHAPTER 13

Mind Affliction

Don't be so mad at yourself, Munisha. We will find her tomorrow," Janice says.

"It's not that easy."

"Zaraiella is my bestfriend. She will be okay."

"You don't understand," I said, shaking my head. "Tsk, there are so many things going on in my mind. I don't know what to think or what to do."

"Can you please, stop crying? We will find her."

"If we never went out. If I never lied and told her to come, she would have been here now."

"Or me doing her hair. Sorry."

"Don't worry about it. Please, just let me be alone."

"You girls alright?" Mr. Wilson asked, peeking into my room. "Keep positive, Munisha. First thing in the morning, we're heading out. We'll find her."

"Daddy, she's still crying."

"Everyone's upset. Sara isn't doing too well either. Tomorrow morning, daughter. We will have light and good news. If we can't see a thing out there, neither can it. Much love to you, and good night."

"Hey, Munisha, I'm sorry. Can I get a hug? Goodnight."

"Janice, you should. I mean…if you want, you can sleep in Zaraiella's bed. If you want."

"I don't mind."

"Thanks, and yes, we'll find her tomorrow," I said, as I tried my best to smile.

I didn't know what was worse. Having to think about my sister missing and having no family left. There was something that always seemed to slither its way into stealing my happiness. I am not a person that believes in curses, but sure enough feels as a hex is over me.

"Good morning, you two. Time to roll, time to roll!"

"Can you give me one more hour, Mr. Wilson. I barely got any sleep at all."

"Fine, one hour," Mr. Wilson says, looking at his watch. "Or unless you would like to stay in while me and Jason go out searching."

"No, I'm definitely coming. Just, give me a few minutes."

"Very well then, because we need many ears and eyes. Janice, I see, is still knocked out. Tell her breakfast is ready whenever she is. I'm going to grab something before our big day starts."

The funny thing, when you're asleep, you kind of seem to forget all your miseries and heartaches. Unless a nightmare educes a thought, that is where there is no escape. I used to believe that you only have good dreams, that swiftly subsided.

"Sleepyhead, it's time to go. Don't act like you don't hear, M. I even brought you something. Oh yea, I knew you would turn around then."

"Breakfast in bed, how sweet," I said with my first smile on from the hours spent.

Jason looks as though he didn't rest either with his low eyes.

"Yea, um, Dad wants us to go as soon as possible I"

"I told him I was going to get up. It's been…two hours."

"Yup, and it's going on seven. The earlier we get out there and search, the better. We need as much light as possible."

"Tsk, you're right. Tell him that I will be ready after my shower. Give me about thirty minutes."

"Thirty minutes, I'll insinuate that's an hour. Gotcha, take your time, and M…nothing."

I frowned. "What a weirdo."

Please sister, wherever you are, come to me. "Good morning, Mrs. Wilson."

"Good morning, darling. I hear you didn't rest as pleasant. Are you sure you're ready for the outdoors?"

"Yes, mam, I'm okay. Just my head is a little foggy."

"You were snoring, which meant you were really tired," Janice said.

"Oh gosh, I was snoring? Now I know I need to work out harder," I said. "My life is so miserable! I hate it so much."

"Munisha!" Mrs. Wilson spat, frowning and coming to me swiftly. "Stop it! We do not speak negative thoughts out of our mouths and place them in the atmosphere. You will find your sister. I just think she got separated, that's all."

I didn't know how to be positive. It was like one thing after the other.

"Don't mind that, Munisha. They're waiting for you outside."

"Mrs. Wilson," I said, looking back into the kitchen. "Are you still upset with me?"

"Being happy or furious with you would not make a difference, child. It happened. When my husband needed help, you and my son went out and came back to aid him. This family are people of faith, and when something comes to us, we pray and conquer. Speaking the negative only attracts it. This world has become so much of it, don't let it consume you as well."

"Yes…I understand."

"So then, you go out there and find your sister. She's waiting for you, you hear me?"

"Be careful, Munisha," Janice says.

"See you all later."

I wondered if they thought last night I would pull another knife stunt. Zaraiella is somewhere out here. I know she is. If not, my feelings would have been worse. Like a guardian angel telling me she is.

"About time you come," Mr. Wilson said. "It's bright today, so we shouldn't have any problems finding anything from her that could give us a lead. How are you feeling? You look a little drained."

"I'm okay, Mr. Wilson," I said, taking a deep breath. "Let's find her."

"You sure you want to tag along? Me and Jason pretty much have this under control."

"When she starts moving, Dad, she'll be more alive."

"I told you both, let's go. I can already sense that hideous thing is out there looking for her, if it already hasn't. Tsk, oh my gosh."

"Now, don't be thinking like that. Everyone is coming back home today. Jason, you have it locked-n-loaded?"

"Yes sir."

"Wait, were not taking the horse?"

"No mam. Best for us to keep on foot. S.I.L.O could be infiltrating these woods looking for that creature and if it is, it's better to approach it silently and take it out."

"I don't know, Dad. I think I hit it, but it kept coming for us."

Mr. Wilson chuckles. "That little piece I gave you probably couldn't hurt that squirrel right there."

"Huh? So why would you give it to me? I trusted that thing with my life yesterday."

"You must still learn to respect a weapon, or it definitely won't respect you."

Looking at how there was no ending to the trees and bushes of the jungle, Zaraiella could be anywhere. From where we first saw her, she could be there. You would think she would at least try to find her way back, but she will only find herself deeper in the woods.

"You all fished here?"

"Yup, this is the spot," Jason says. "Pretty much where we always fished old man."

"Don't call me that. It is not a soul out here. The water is nice."

"Maybe she went swimming to the other side," Jason says, smiling at me.

"My sister can't swim."

If Zaraiella was able to even cross the other side, she would've been a fool to do so.

"Hey, you never know. She probably hoped in thinking she couldn't, then she did. Can't people do it like that, Dad?"

"Tracks, tracks are leading in and out of here. Assuming it was you all."

"Dad, I just remembered you forgot the walkie-talkies."

"We don't need em'. I actually forgot it on purpose this time, so Sara doesn't radio in on me every five minutes."

"These tracks are definitely ours; I can see Zaraiella's shoe print here and M's own. Where we kept walking, that's where we ran into that thing."

"We follow them," Mr. Wilson says, as his eyes stayed glued to the ground. "Maybe we can track her footprints if they show up well. Not too much soft dirt out here. Her feet are the smallest, so that will give us some leeway."

"This is where we saw it, Dad. Right here eating this, dear."

"It didn't clean its plate either. Now these maggots are doing their job. Check around and see if there are any small footprints. That's our lead."

"I see the hideous thing footprints here. No sign of my sisters."

"Those prints, they're not symmetrically proportioned," Mr. Wilson frowned while placing his foot in the print.

"We told you that it was something out here out of a horror movie, Dad."

"I believe you, Jason. If we have something like this running around, our home is in much more need of shielding and more providence. That damn S.I.L.O, excuse me. It's them making our world more polluted than it already is. Nothing but them."

Of course, they are. It will only worsen because they will only take and take until nothing is left. "Hey, you all, I see some small footprints here. Thank god!"

"Great job, M. She ran the whole opposite direction, I kind of figured that happened."

"You didn't get a glimpse of her when we ran, Jason?"

"Remember I was trying to shoot the thing with that pea shooter. Didn't see where anybody went until I ran into you. The creature kept creeping up, and after that, it was gone."

"No time to waste you two, we could probably catch up. She will not move too far since she's lost out here. Let's just hope she's running around in circles and not noticing it."

It has been hours, and nothing but the tall trees, birds chirping, and the animals staring at us as we strolled pass. Looking at them made me want to look silly and ask, have any of you seen my sister? Maybe one of those flying squirrels could lead us straight to her. "This place looks familiar, doesn't it, M?"

"This is the lady place where we, there it is right there! Let's go ask if she seen her! Maybe she's in there!"

"Wait up, M!"

"Maybe she's inside. I know she must be here. Hello, hello! Anybody here? Zaraiella! Are you in there!"

Knock Knock Knock

"This place looks much more friendly than when it was pitch black."

"Helloooo!" I shouted, slapping the door. "Mam, we need your help! Why won't she come to the door?"

KNOCK KNOCK KNOCK

"This is where you two brought me the medicine from? I'll be damned."

"You should see it at night, Dad. I'm surprised you haven't ever noticed this place before."

"Not so much noise, Munisha. Whoever it is must not be home at the moment. I usually never go this way towards the city; this goes east from the lake. However, it seems to be between us and the city a few miles out."

"Maybe we can just wait until she comes back," I said. "Maybe she found, Zaraiella, and she's bringing her back to our home. There must be something the lady can tell us."

"We can't wait here, Munisha. It's a good, hopeful idea, and all. We can't just sit here hoping. We have to keep moving."

"What if she has her?" I said, as I continued to slap the door.

"You don't know that," Mr. Wilson frowned.

"Listen to Dad, M, please."

"You all can go. I'll."

"EEEYYYGGHHHhhh!"

The world became so quiet for a few seconds. "You heard that?!"

"Let's go, M!"

That scream echoed throughout the mid dark woods. The only thing is that, Zaraiella voice sounded a bit awkward. Her voice is soft. I would never think she could yell that loud. I hope it was her. It's hard to think properly when negative thoughts always invade your mind.

"Well, looky here," Mr. Wilson said, kneeling down.

"That's her necklace! Thank goodness, she's still around then. You have good eyes because I probably wouldn't even have noticed it. Where are you, Zaraiella?"

"It's silver, and with that reflective wing helped signal it. "

"Dad, her footprints are here. And looks like some other prints are here too."

"It's that damn thing chasing her probably. My poor little sister lost with that thing in the woods."

"Calm down, Munisha," Mr. Wilson comforted, looking around the area. "We're a step closer here. No need to lose it. If she keeps moving along with whatever it is out here, we'll find them both, perhaps even find us. Keep your eyes sharp, you two."

"Aw, crap! Gosh, I hate it out here sometimes. Jason, is it anything on my back?"

"Um, no, what's wrong with you?"

"Stupid, spiderweb went right into my face!"

Jason grins. "Oh lord, miss spider girl here."

"That's her phobia, Jason. Once she walks into ten more, she will be cleared of it."

"Hmph, I wish it were that easy," I said, checking my shirt. "You know something. That smell, that was the same scent I smelt when that thing was eating, whatever. You didn't notice it, Jason? It had a odor of a rotten egg."

"I don't know," Jason shrugs. "I smell many things out here, and some animals just die, and I smell it."

"It could have been the dead animal it was eating, Munisha. But hey, anything is possible."

My patience was growing impatient in this forest. Too many obstacles.

"What we should have done, Dad. Leave a note at the lake saying we came back looking for her. She probably would have saw it and waited there."

"She's a twelve year old girl, not even a full blown teenager. She would still move around regardless of, if we left one or not. My main concern, we're losing daylight fast. Plus, this forest makes it harder to see, that's why our, what you called her? Spider Girl here ran into a web. Once the sun say says goodnight, you can't see anything, and it's the worse out here."

"I don't get why she isn't over here, no more tracks," Jason says. "We did hear her screams coming from this way, didn't we? It's just her voice isn't that loud. She could scream, but it always been so low."

"I was thinking the same thing earlier. I know my sister, and that scream just didn't match hers if she did."

"Possibly, they're two girls we don't know about out here. Sorry, three."

"Crazy boy, I know what you meant."

Night made this place look like, Mr. Wilson said, just a black maze. At least in daylight, you can decipher which way you have already searched. Everybody just seemed tired and they were about done and ready to give up hope. Whatever possessed me to make that decision, I hate it with every bone in my body. It wasn't supposed to happen.

"Well, my children. We will try again tomorrow. Not enough light out here, and I know Sara is losing it right now."

"You should have taken the radios. Mom is going to get both of us now."

"I'll take the hits for the team and take the walkies tomorrow. Ready to go, Munisha? Munisha, we have to go now. Aren't you hungry?"

"I am," I whimpered.

"So, let's get back. We haven't eaten all day but some apples. We will try again tomor"

"I can't eat, Mr. Wilson…I can't go back."

"Oh, come on now," Mr. Wilson says, walking towards me. "Don't be ridiculous. It's night, and you need to get home along with some food down ya'. I understand you're in distress, but you must make the right decisions, for you and your sisters' sake."

"I…sniff, can't go back."

"Listen, staying out here is not safe. Temperature is dropping fast and there are creatures that hunt specifically at night. We need to get back"

"THEN LEAVE! I JUST TOLD YOU TO GO. CAN'T YOU HEAR?"

"Alrighty then missy. I don't have time for this. I'm not your father and not going to pretend I am."

"Dad! Give us a minute. We'll meet up with you."

"Hmph…alright. You know the way back, fine? It's about fifteen minutes to the house. It's dark out here, and I don't need my wife on my tail all night. You're in charge."

"Yes sir, I understand. This is our normal trail anyways, and M needs some time. I got this, Dad, trust me."

"Don't disappoint me, and please not your mother. I won't stop hearing her cries for as long as I live then. Remember, you're in charge."

"Don't worry about us, Dad. We'll be there."

All I want to do is just stay out here. I can't go back not knowing where she is. Going back will just be another restless night.

"M, we can't stay out here. Why are you not thinking?"

"Jason…Jason. I'm not going anywhere until I know Zaraiella's okay."

"So, you will stay out here all night sitting on a rock waiting? Answer me!"

"Get away from me! Go home, your family is home! Sniff…the only one I have is out here. Tsk, sniff, in this stupid forest."

"That's not true," Jason says as he stands in front of me. "If you weren't family, then Mom wouldn't be looking for you also to come back home. Don't think like this, M."

"Just go home, Jason. Please. I don't want you taking the blame for me. Please."

"Well, if you're going to stay out here, then that means I will have to as well. I'm left in charge and you heard the man."

All the tears that seemed to freeze up on my face didn't matter. I did everything right, at least, I thought I did.

"Here," Jason said, as I looked the other way. "It must be at least fifty degrees out here."

"No, you need it. I have one on already."

"That thin thing. Double it up. You'll feel better."

"Sniff…thank you."

"Wish I had a wash rag. Your face needs some WD-40 or something, for that matter."

"Shut up. You're always making some stupid joke."

"I see a smile, and that's all what matters."

Even though his jacket was scruffy, it did help me to relax in the frosty temperature. Wish Zaraiella could just come out to us. I will not succumb to the thought something happened to her.

"M, M, sleepy head. Whew girl, you need a rag bad now. I would take some fresh saliva and give you a nice cleanup."

"And you would have a black eye by the afternoon. Time went by fast; dawn already began."

"That's right. You owe one big time if I catch a cold."

"You're the idiot who wouldn't keep your jacket on. You know, your dad and Mrs. Wilson is going to kill you. You stayed out here all night."

"Just like you, so we tell them we spent all night looking."

"And didn't find anything, oh yea, this useless necklace," I muttered, tossing it into the air.

"Aw, come on, M. Look, now it's dirty."

"Need to just bury it, at least we would know where that is."

"Stop it, stop it! We will find her today. You understand me?"

Looking into his eyes, I felt the warmth greater than his jacket. "Now I see the man side off of you. Or you're just trying to be like Mr. Wilson?"

Jason chuckles. "Yea, uh huh. So, your ready to find, Zaraiella? Get up and let's go you ashy face woman! We have a family member to bring back."

The misty morning forest makes me feel a side of a relief, then again lost in the midst. The weird thing, I was not as hungry as I thought I would be. Once we get back, my first thoughts are just packing up and leaving. They should respect my decision. I've caused enough damage. "Jason, we looked enough. This mist isn't making it any better either. I want to go back now."

"Give it another hour. We're getting closer."

"Then you'll say another hour. If anything, I'll come back once this fog cleared and search. Also, bring back some food too. She'll be cold and starving out by the time we or I find her."

"Patience, Munisha, patience. I can"

"EEEYYGHHHhh!"

"It came from the stream. Hurry up, M!" Jason shouts along with his body being swallowed by the gray dimension.

"I'm right with you! I hope you're going the right way! Can't see a thing!"

"It came from here. I know it."

"Where, you said, the stream? I don't see, wait"

"Look, over there!" Jason said, pointing.

"Zaraiella?! ZARAIELLAAA! We're here! Oh my gosh! Are you okay? Zaraiella? Answer me?"

My little sister, starring down at the steamy lake like she was in trance.

"Is she alright? What the hell? Looks like a cougar."

"Zaraiella? What happened? Sister, did it hurt you?"

"The lady, she killed the big cat," Zaraiella said, still hypnotized by the calm lake.

I grimaced. "Lady? Are you okay? Did it scratch you or anything?"

"No, it just kept following me. Then she killed it."

"Check this out, M. This knife looks from medieval times."

"Yea, this is something that looks…never mind that. Let's all get home. Thank god we found you. I was beginning to think we wouldn't."

"Got to keep the faith like I always tell you, M. Gots to keep the faith."

Zaraiella eyes spoke to us, witnessing something she shouldn't have. Even though the animal was killed, she seemed mesmerized by something far worse.

"Everything looks calm. Hope Dad, and Mom aren't too upset."

"They shouldn't be. We found her. Now Zaraiella, we can get a nice hot bath. I smell like you know who," I whispered.

"Hey, all of us need one," Jason says, smelling his underarm.

"Thank God! Thank God!" Mrs. Wilson cried out, sprinting from the porch. "I don't know what my husband has been thinking lately. You all get right inside. Now, I mean it!"

"Mom, we're okay. We needed to find her, so we did."

"I see," Mrs. Wilson said, hugging us all tight. "Now you all will never go out again. That is final!"

"Where's Dad anyways?"

"He said he went out early for you two. I guess he didn't find you all. Little seed, are you doing alright?"

"…Yes," Zaraiella mumbled.

"You look so sad," Janice says. "Did you see a ghost or something? What's wrong?"

"She's been through a lot. Me and my sister are hungry like no other. I hope you have something. Yes, I don't care about my weight today."

Mrs. Wilson grinned. "Of course, you three make yourselves decent. I will give Tim a piece of my mind soon enough."

Now that Mr. Wilson is out there, I hope he does not think we are still searching. This place was getting a little too hectic.

"I don't understand why she had to kill it," Zaraiella said.

"I'm still trying to understand why you think whoever did it shouldn't have."

"It didn't hurt me."

"Oh, you still have a lot to learn, sis. Be grateful that she helped you, whoever she was. Can't wait to finish drying this hair. It was a long day yesterday."

"Why did you keep the knife?"

"It's…I don't know," I said, observing the silver and red handle. "Let's just say I will keep it to remind me of the person who, practically saved your life? Yea."

"Girls, brunch is most certainly ready when you all are," Mrs. Wilson said.

My stomach feels as empty as mom's car. It's been over twelve hours. "It's the same thing we always eat, eggs, greens, and pork. I get it. Breakfast and lunch combined does not sound bad right now. Did Mr. Wilson come back?"

"Believe it or not, he did. He is afraid to come inside. He came back and started plowing. He is a funny man. Be a dear Jason and get your father in here. I'm not upset as I was."

"Ma, I'm almost done eating."

"And you will have more chores for not obeying me," Mrs. Wilson smirked. "Men, they can be a bit of a push at times. My, Zaraiella, you've hardly touched your plate."

"Zaraiella, Mrs. Wilson is talking to you."

"Oh, sorry. I'm okay."

"You keep staring off. Are you okay?" Janice asked.

"You noticed it too, Janice? Tell Mrs. Wilson what's going on, sis."

"Absolutely. You can tell me in our circle here. This is girl talk. Hurry before the men come back."

"Tell, Mrs. Wilson why you stare off like that."

"Well Munisha, she's probably still in the sense of trauma for her being outside the way she was."

"Maybe, but Mr. Wilson said she has something called shrez…so…phenia, or however you pronounce it. Is that real?"

"I heard of it. Like that ailment, I believe things come to you when they're not really there and other variations. It will blow over. That's mainly a child's phase, such as when they have an imaginary friend. You'll be fine dear."

"Don't look at me like that!"

My eyes stretched. "Zaraiella? Zaraiella, I'm"

"I don't like when people look at me like that!"

"What's all this yelling in my house? Good to see you both, Munisha, and most certainly you, Zaraiella. It's a blessing really. Can't forget my princess and, my queen."

"Your meal is getting cold, Tim," Mrs. Wilson says, avoiding her husband's kiss to the lips but to her cheek.

"I'm sorry, baby, they just"

"I told you, it was alright. Please, just take more precautions next time. Remember what I told you about that slick try with the radios? I don't want that ever happening again."

"You hear that, ladies and gent?" Mr. Wilson smiles. "We all have to be more cautious now. Are you happy now, baby? Apologies twenty times, plus ten."

"You two should get a room," Jason says as his parents just give kisses in front of us.

"What?! Get your son, Mr. Tim."

"Need to be looking into that plate because that shovel is waiting for him."

CHAPTER 14

Anima

You've been great Munisha, however, you shouldn't be so harebrained to what's going on.

"Harebrained? What do you mean? I'm doing well. Me and Zaraiella are moving out of here as soon as we can."

"You still have a lot to learn. Your hot heat mentality that will drive you into dust. I can promise you that."

"I'm no hothead either."

"Whenever you're out there, and things don't go your way, you're not yourself."

"I don't even know what you are talking about right now. Who are you anyways? You came around this place, and you needed help. Now you're trying to judge me?"

"Nobody's judging you. You want life to be exaggerated, you know it. I just wish those things that happened to you never did. It happened for a reason; everything happens for a reason. Don't worry about it. You will see them again."

"Who are you?"

"The real question is, what are you going to do to make, you happy? I don't matter. I'm just strolling by. Lost my way. None theless, I'll find it. I hope."

"Well, let me ask the person in charge of the house. He will know how to help you."

"No time, I will be on my way. Remember what we conversed. Take care and find me one day."

"Hey! You might get lost again! What's your name?"

Who was she, in and out of my dreams? What was she trying to tell me?

"Ha, I miss this thing."

"Zaraiella, what are you doing? Early in the morning with the shenanigans?"

That girl loves that crazy camera.

Zaraiella grins. "You were snoring and talking."

"I was? What was I saying then? You are the one who has the full convos with herself in her sleep, not me. Really, Zaraiella? Delete it right now!"

"No! This is too funny."

"Get back here! I will find that camera, Zaraiella! Should have just left you out there for one more day."

Still wondering what that dream was about. That was an odd one. She said, she strolled by. "Hey, so that means someone is coming here."

"Oh wow, she's talking to herself too," Janice says standing with Zaraiella by the door.

"Why did you show her that sis? Is this payback for telling them about your imaginary friend? Didn't like that, huh," I smirked.

"Look again, Janice!"

"That's fine. Just know sis, I'll take that camera and throw it up a tree. I went out searching for you to bring you back, and now you're joking me as soon as you're all jolly again?"

"Aw, I see you're up," Mr. Wilson says, smiling at us. "Don't forget your leaves outside. The rake is waiting for you, don't let it get too dark. Your chores, too, Zaraiella. There are no off days around here. Come on, Janice."

"See there, karma is real, sis."

"You have to do it too."

"Right, but I won't be as tired. My nap gave me a little more energy from being out there all day and night. You look like you've been running around the whole time I've been sleeping."

"I did fall asleep when I was lost."

"What, Zaraiella? You weren't scared of the things out there? I find that hard to believe, my little sis just went to sleep in that jungle?"

"I did. It was a tree that had a hole in it. I went there, hiding. Just was so cold."

"Like the one we first went inside of? I don't know if you'll remember that. It's been years."

"Kind of. Um…there is something I didn't tell anybody," Zaraiella murmured, as she gave me no eye contact. "That lady, who helped me, said your name."

"My name?"

"After she killed the big cat, she said, Munisha is looking for you. Then she just walked away. The way she sounded was scary. That's why I ran from them. He wouldn't stop chasing me."

"He?"

"Oh, I meant, the big cat and her."

"Hmph, okay," I said, nodding my head. Now I definitely know who it was. "I wonder why she said my name to you."

"Maybe, it's because…she knows you? I don't know."

"Nah, I don't think that's it. After she killed the cougar, where did she go after, Zaraiella? If you remember."

"I don't really know. That old lady was so scary, scarier than the cat."

"I'll go one day to find her. I need to thank her for so much."

"You all coming?" Mr. Wilson says as he peeks in. "Night will come soon. Then there will be double the chores for tomorrow."

"We're coming. Keep your panties on," I chuckled. "You can tell me more sis soon okay."

It could have only been that lady. She even called out my name. I wonder what she wants with me. I could sneak out and try to meet her if there is time. She could have some answers to get out of this place.

"I can't believe we're almost done. We just need to bag those last piles up and be finished, Zaraiella."

"He must have known there wasn't a lot, so we didn't have to be out all night."

"It would have been impossible to finish it by night. What is going to be for dinner you think? My tummy hurts. What is your squirrely face laughing at sis? Yes, I get hungry too, and I did put on weight. It's called growing up. Hmph, what now?"

"Jason is staring at you again, and I'm thinking about what, Mrs. Wilson said."

"He could look at me or us all he wants, better yet. HEY! COME HELP US FINISH BAGGING!"

"I'm not done with mine!" Jason grimaces. "You have someone helping you anyways!"

I can insinuate Jason will be seventy five percent like his father. "Yea, see, he's no man. A real man would have come and helped."

"I've been thinking about mommy a lot lately."

"Me too. Especially our oldest sister. Every day that goes by, they never leave my mind. Like yesterday too, my heart was beating out of my chest. Just the thought of losing you out there was so traumatic for me. I would have been alone."

"You will still have Jason, Janice, and their parents," Zaraiella says as she rakes.

"Wouldn't matter. They're not blood. Imagine losing your favorite…I don't know, pet. Then you will have to replace it with one that's not given to you by Mom. I know it's not as severe using that as an example. Trust me, it's the worst feeling having no family. Thank goodness for that lady. I think I will go tomorrow to thank her."

"Mrs. Wilson said"

"I know what she said," I smirked. "Munisha can take of herself."

Especially for the past couple of adventures I've been on in these woods, I definitely felt I can handle myself.

"What about Daddy?"

"Your, Dad? I'm not sure. When I last saw him, I think I told you this. It was so long ago. He had a suit on. Mom was trying to hold back tears when she returned to the house. I wish I could tell you more; but there is only what I can explain to you. Look who it is."

"You girls are pretty much done; you were yelling like it was way more."

"Oh no! The bag ripped!" Zaraiella frowns. "Tsk, this is too much work."

"See, having me and my sister work like a man. This is too much. Don't worry about it sis. We'll clean it up. I need to talk to you alone, mister."

"You sure, Munisha? I'm the one that did it."

"Yea, go and help prepare dinner or something."

Zaraiella didn't need to be in my business any longer. Now it was just about us. "What are you looking at? Get these leaves!"

"Affirmative general. How are you feeling, general?"

"Better, just recuperating, you know."

"Well, I'm fine too. Thanks for asking, general."

"Sorry, how are you servant?"

"Servant? Whoever you marry M, they will have a ride with you."

"I know, my husband will be tall, built strong, basically the sexiest man ever."

"You said everything you want in a man, but you forgot one important thing."

"Yea, I did, long curly hair. I will give you that. Unfortunately, you're not over six feet, are you?"

Jason grins. "You do know I'm not fully grown yet. There's about two feet more for me and then that's it."

"And that's not that bad. My husband must be over six feet tall, hopefully. Taller than those famous basketball players my mom used to watch. Gosh, imagine if he's over seven feet."

"Control yourself M, control yourself."

Now that was someone I have never witnessed seeing before ever in my life. Only the lucky girls get to marry men like that. Who's tall, built, and of course, have major credits. I guess it wasn't meant for everyone.

"What did you have to talk to me about anyways?" Jason asked, as he continued bagging.

"First of all, I wanted to say thanks again. Last night…I never felt that way before. You stayed out there when you didn't have to. Thank you so much and for helping me find her."

"You're surely welcome," Jason smiles.

"I hope you won't catch a cold from you lending me your jacket."

"Believe it or not, my nose began to run. I don't mind it at all. And ouch! What was that for?"

"For you not getting close enough to me yesterday, you should've had your arms around me."

"Wait, what?"

"And this is for being there for me when no one else was."

"You're a bit violent along with feisty, you know," Jason blushed. "A slap to the face, then a kiss?"

"You know me by now. Finally done here and I've worked up an appetite."

I hope that wasn't a mistake. That boy could go and tell everyone that he finally got to me. What was I thinking? He could tell Zaraiella, then she will be extra annoying now, along with her little friend. He better not or he will get an even harder slap next time.

"Thanks for the food Mrs. Wilson. Always great now since I have gotten use to it."

"No problem, dear. Long ago, you complained, now are grateful for much I presume. Hope your sister is alright. Leaving the table the way she did, I am anticipating she has a upset stomach from all the busyness that has been happening around here."

"Maybe so," I said.

Situations has been so traumatic. I wondered what was really going on in her head.

"Have a goodnight, M. See you in the morning."

"Right, yea. Um, goodnight."

Oh my gosh, this is so awkward. My first time kissing a boy now. Why does it feel this way? "Ah, gosh, why is it so cold in here? Of course, we left the window open." This girl isn't even covered up.

"Sleeping good, huh sis?"

Now look whose whispering. Time to play the same game. Where did you put that camera? "Here we go."

"He's...he's behind us. I...we, we have to leave. The twister...he's in it."

"Zaraiella," I whispered. "Are you okay?"

You could hear a drop of a needle hit this noisy wooden floor now.

"Aw, the battery is dying; she uses this twenty four seven; no wonder. Goodnight sister."

Don't know why I drift away to sleep. It's been a few hours since I said goodnight. Soon it'll be time to do chores again. Maybe if I do some exercises, it could help me. The handstand I was so good at needs work. "Let me just, come on…I can do it. One more try. Eygh!"

"What the? Are you okay, Munisha? How did you fall out of bed?" Zaraiella says, squinting her eyes.

"Long story. Sorry. Emph, go back to sleep."

"You rolled out the bed? Bad dream."

"To tell you the truth, I can't fall asleep. I meant to talk to you about something earlier when you went berserk out of nowhere at, Mrs. Wilson. What is going on with you?"

"Did you touch my camera?"

"Answer me, Zaraiella."

"I didn't mean to. I just hate when everyone's looking at me funny," Zaraiella mumbled, looking down at her camera.

"We were just trying to help; you do know that? Never mind it then. Yes, I touched your camera. Why?"

"I left it on the other side of the dresser."

"You got me. When I finished dinner, I looked over at you and noticed how much you love talking to yourself."

"What?"

"That's right. Even a little drool I caught. Right back at you."

"That's okay," Zaraiella says, taking her pillow.

"Where are you going? Let it dry outside on its own. The weather is cold. Keep that window closed, trust me. Oh yea, I almost forgot. Your necklace. Mrs. Wilson would have destroyed it in the laundry."

I need to get her a new one. This one popped and looked so dirty.

"…Mommy gave me this. Thanks, but it's broken."

"Hey, at least we found it on the ground while searching for you. No need to cry, Zaraiella."

"That…"

"You can tell me sis. Speak up."

"It, she…the lady grabbed me. Then when she wouldn't let me go, she was the one that popped it."

"That's how it happened? I thought you put it on the ground to let us know you were in the area."

"Are you really going to go look for her tomorrow?"

"You mean later today? No, I don't think so. You know they don't want us to go around out there alone anymore. I don't want them to think I'm being all the time. It sucks we can't go out freely, but it's understandable. There are all types of things out there you can come across. Now that, monstrocity is running around out."

"What if it was to come here?".

"That's what everyone's thinking. We'll have to get Moms car and run it over, if that works. A gun couldn't even stop it, I don't know what will. Mr. Wilson needs to make this place more secure. That is why I think when next year comes around, we're more than likely will be gone. What do you see?"

"Him," Zaraiella whispers with a blank stare.

"Sis, I don't see anything. You're pointing at nothing but a closed door. Okay, this is creeping me out."

Her eyes and head turning slowly while I couldn't make out if it was really a fly or a annoying mosquito.

"…Zara"

"Why doesn't anyone see it?!"

"Zaraiella, don't cry. It won't hurt you; I won't let anyone, for that matter."

Holding my little sister and gazing at the mysterious door. If she was telling the truth, who was this man, and why was he after her?

"I'm scared."

"What is it, Zaraiella? The, boogie man, the devil or something?"

"It's…a man. He just looks at me. He won't say anything."

"Is he still there?"

"…No," Zaraiella whimpers, wiping her face.

"See, he's not going to do anything to you, especially as long as I'm here. Move over. I'm sleeping in this bed with you tonight."

"You don't have to, Munisha."

"This bed is better. Mines have lumps, and I need to rest my bum on something soft. That floor hurts."

"So, you did fall out."

"You can say that. Landed right on the thing you like to laugh at."

Zaraiella grins. "You're funny, Munisha, but you're the best sister ever."

"You too, let's sleep. I have a surprise for you later."

"Okay, can't wait."

Whatever was haunting her can only be in her head. Something she made up, and it attacks her. I just hope it does blow over or maybe even take her to the old woman to cure it possibly.

* * * *

"Morning sis, time to start another day of boredom. Zaraiella? I'm talking to myself. She's not even here."

"What's up, M? I mean good morning," Jason said, waving.

"Hey, have you seen my sister?"

"You two are strange. You know that?"

"She took pictures of me and showed them to you, didn't she?"

"She said you snore too loud."

"So, she slept downstairs? Wow, she has the nerve. I'm definitely killing it today."

"You're in luck. Dad said nothing for you, Zaraiella, and Janice today. He said let the ladies have the day off."

"Aww, that means you'll have to do everything today," I smiled.

"It's not as bad out there as you think. Should be done probably in two hours."

"Well, good luck to you then."

"No kiss good morning or good luck for the day? Alrighty then," Jason smirks.

"It's too early for your shenanigans, lover boy."

"This girl must be really tired laying up the way she is. Zaraaaiielllaaa."

"She got up around five a.m, Munisha," Mrs. Wilson says from behind me.

"Morning, Mrs. Wilson. I heard she ran from me because I was snoring. How rude, isn't she?"

"That snoring could cause someone to run out the house. That Tim, you do not know what snoring is until you discerned by him. Years and years of that made me immune to it thankfully."

"To be honest with you, Mrs. Wilson, I couldn't do it myself. When something disturbs my sleep, that's a no no and you will have to go."

"Wait till you have children, principally babies. They will change your world along with your sleeping patterns."

"I know, I can imagine how babies cry all, night, long. That is the duty of mothers."

"Fathers have their duties as well. We took turns doing it when Jason and Janice's pampers needed to be changed."

"Did you breastfeed?"

Being a mother was never something my mind grasped on.

"I did, not for long though. When I first started doing it, he made me sore. So then, Tim decided to start giving him solid foods, soon enough he wanted that more than anything."

I see now why he was such a mommas boy. "He grew fast then."

"Too fast. I told Tim not to start giving him such foods as peas and green beans too early. He may not want me then. We as women have our days, which is why we do the majority of work as we nurture. Thank goodness I pretty much stayed, a stay at home mom. You will understand once your time comes."

"From what you told me; it makes me skeptical for having one early."

"Most certainly, don't rush it. Go see the world with the one you love. It will be an extraordinary experience that will stick to you forever. Never be anxious or rush anything. That's the biggest mistake you can make in life."

That is something I felt like I tend to do the most. Everything should happen in its time. "If I ever have a kid early, then it will be with the person I will want to be with for the rest of my life."

"That's it honey, be fruitful and multiply. Just take your time. Life is not a race."

"Right. Looks like little sis is still knocked out. I'm going to go work out. Cut down on some of the calories my poor body consumed."

"Don't forget your schooling, Munisha when you get done. You will need it one day, trust me."

"Don't worry. My book is almost done. Going to need a new one soon."

"Glad you mention it then. My husband just got you a new one. He picked it up right on time then. If you ever decide to go back to the inside atmosphere, you will need to have the brains and they can give you something from there. Look at it this way, S.I.L.O may not be here forever. Go on, I don't want to take more of your time."

Why did we have to learn all this stuff if it seems we will never need it? Then, getting a job does not even seem possible if we can't live in the city. Not even an ID we have. If S.I.L.O finds out, we'll be slaves to them or sent off somewhere else. It's bad enough she also says go and see the world with the one you love when that is a little farfetched as it is. "What a life."

"No wonder I haven't seen you all morning. I thought Jason said the women aren't working today."

"This isn't work. Milking cows is fun to me. Want to try?" Janice says with her bare hands, pressuring the cow udders.

"Um, no thanks. Mrs. Wilson just got through talking to me about the same thing, basically."

"Whaaat?!"

"Nothing, sorry," I grinned.

"Come on, it's fun. Just pull, squeeze, then do the others. It's easy."

"Your right, it is, and I'll leave that fun for you and my sister. I came here to work out, but before I do that, need to say good morning to Betsy."

I don't believe I thanked her for the help. She did phenomenal out there that day. I wish I could get her something good other than wheat grass and hay.

"You want to ride her, don't you?" Janice asked.

"Of course! We're under strict guidelines now, we can't go anywhere."

"Hmm, too bad then. What are you trying to do? Stand on your hands?"

"I almost had it. Last night I bust my behind trying this."

"That is what Zaraiella was saying. She came downstairs and then told us you woke her up."

"I told her that because she makes fun of me when I'm working out, and of course, you know that," I said, then trying to push harder to keep a balance.

"Mommy should make something that won't make you fat then."

"Nah, it's just my genes. See, I have no stomach," I said, lifting my shirt. "Just a little pudge. So, if anything, I gain weight in my lower body. My thighs have taken a beating. That's why these jumping jacks and squats will help me get rid of the…meat."

Maybe if I sprinted around the area I would be fit in no time. "What are you doing in here, boy? You can't be done already."

"Told you this morning it would only take me about an hour. Dad knew it would be too easy for me."

"When Mr. Wilson comes, he's going to put you back to work."

"If you say so," Jason says as he stares at me.

"Again, Janice! Hold me up straight!"

"Wo wo wo. What do you have my sister doing?"

"What does…it look like?"

"She needs me to help her handstand, duh!"

"Okay, you can, let go now, Janice."

The feeling of blood rushing to my head felt so weird yet so relaxing.

"You're doing it, Munisha!" Janice claps. "See, you're not fat!"

"I think that was a good ten seconds."

"That's called cheating, just to let you know, mam," Jason says as he strolls past me. "Cheaters never win."

"Yea, I want you to do me a favor, chicken legs."

"I'm not flipping you like we're in cheerleading, M."

"No boy, help me up on top of, Betsy."

"If you think you're going for a ride, you have another thing coming, M."

"Just help me up on her."

"…Certainly, your majesty."

Mrs. Wilson was right. "Men can be so stubborn sometimes ouch! You don't have to be so rough."

"Yea yea. Okay, now what are you going to do? Just sit there and look straight?"

I chuckled. "Come on, girl, yah!"

Betsy and I have affixed souls. I felt it, similar to Zaraiella's energy.

"Munisha, stop!" Jason said as he chased us with Janice following.

"I'm not going anywhere with her. Just circles in the middle of the farm. You are so goody two shoes."

"She can ride a horse, oh wow."

"Until she takes off with it, Janice. Come back in before…too late."

"Hey, Mr. Wilsoooon!"

"I see you, Munisha! Put her back now, kindly!"

"Okay, no problem. Wo, wo."

"Jason, look!" Janice said, pointing.

"Yea, A drone, it's just flying there."

"I see it too. Wo girl. It's probably looking straight at us."

"Jason, Janice, go inside," Mr. Wilson says. "You missy, I told you to return Betsy to her stable and get inside right now."

CHAPTER 15

Forced Aura's

You're cheating. I should have never asked you to play. This man just seems to know my every move.

"How am I cheating? Is it because you cannot get a jump? Or are my three kings intimidating you?"

"None of that, Mr. Wilson. There's no way I can do this."

"Good to see someone else show her how it's done in her own game. She's afraid to play me in mine, Dad," Jason said.

"Never afraid, sweetie, just not interested."

"Focus, Munisha, focus. I don't want to this match to be over kill now."

"You have two kings and are more about to be one. This game is over with my one king and three pieces left."

"Seems like you gave up your faith. Not so soon, I hope."

"Come on, sister, you can do it," Zaraiella says, standing behind me.

"Let's cheer for her, Zaraiella."

"Munisha Munisha Munisha!"

"Alright, sis, you both are so loud. I can't concentrate."

"You should have taken your jump, daughter," Mr. Wilson smirks.

"Aw man, I didn't even notice."

"No, you made your move, no redo's."

"Looks like somebody will be cleaning up the horse crap. I'll go get the shovel for you, M."

I already had a feeling I was going to lose. "It's whatever, Mr. Wilson. You won the deal."

I feel like getting some exercise in again anyways. I needed a new skill or hobby.

"You're not going to finish?" Mr. Wilson asked, with his fist on his cheek smiling. "You still have a few dead men left."

"Exactly my point. You can go sis. Don't be scared of Mr. Wilson. He's just a cheater like his son. Let me know how many times you've won, Zaraiella."

Haven't played checkers in decades. When you don't keep doing something, you will lose your touch. "Geez, it's colder today. Almost need my jacket."

"Munishaaaa!" Jason says, twirling a shovel like his staff in the air. "Your instrument awaits."

"You are so annoying sometimes, you know that?"

"And you are so beautiful always, do you know that?"

I frowned. "You still kiss like a little kid would."

"Hey, it's not my fault you're my first," Jason grins.

"What does that mean? Who else have I kissed? Stop making excuses boy. You're just…weird. I don't see anything, but I smell it."

"You don't see all that feces on the side there?"

"Oh my gosh. Do I have on my raggedy boots? If I were to step into this, it would never come out. Good lord, what did you eat, Betsy? The cow didn't poop as much as you did."

"It's like having a baby, M. Have you ever thought about having kids one day? Pamper changing is just like this."

"Of course. I think about it now and then. Though, I'm having my kids later in life. Your mom told me how it is, so I'm taking my time."

"Likewise. If I do have a kid, I would want it to be a boy."

"What if it's a girl? Tsk, this is so gross, Betsy."

"You're doing a good job, M. Anyways, then I'll have two headaches instead of one. What about you? I can already guess you want a boy too."

"Not going to lie, I want to have, hmmm…ten plus kids," I said, trying to smile carrying the rotten smell outside the barn.

"Good luck with that. Imagine a house full of babies crying all over. That's enough to make a person grow a full head of grays by the time their thirty," Jason says as he watches me pick up more of Betsy's mess.

"That's why my husband will want the same thing as I do. He will have me picked in his arms with all my kids on his back and not, having me pick up, horse crap! Why is your silly self always chuckling?"

"Nothing, what you said reminds me of an opossum with all those babies on its back."

"Ha ha ha, very funny. That is why you look just like one."

Jason holds out his arms. "That's why you love me, baby."

It would be crazy if I wind up with Jason and having children with him. Then I will be stuck here for sure. "That should be it."

"What about the chicken droppings?" Jason frowns.

"Chicken droppings? Who the hell picks up that? Mr. Wilson must have told you to do that, not me. Tsk, chicken droppings, yea right."

"Calm down. It's just a joke. You just wanted to get back to that staff and spin it. Only if you were in a tournament, you would have been the real deal."

"You think so?" I smirked. "You know what's been on my mind lately."

"Moving away, trust me, I know," Jason says, rolling his eyes.

"Ew, don't do that. Makes you look, funny. Well, what do you call those things? That drone that was in the sky a few weeks ago. You're still not worried?"

"You think they're coming here, huh?"

"Most definitely. That thing was looking right at us. What, you don't think so?"

"Using my hypothesis and educated guess, no."

"Really?" I grimaced. "Why not? Someone flew that over here to eavesdrop on us. Oh, come on, you know that's what happened."

"It could have been a random person flying it, just to look around, you know. Better yet, if it were S.I.L.O, don't you think it's a little late for them to show up? It has been some time now, and they haven't shown up yet. Usually, when the law is looking for someone, they send out units to the area the same day or definitely the next. I'm not worried about it."

"Hmph, I hope you're right. It's a lot to think about. Just trying to survive isn't easy."

Jason nods his head. "It never is."

It's hard just doing the little chores around here. I don't know if we can keep in hiding in this forever, even if we wanted to. "That's it for today. I don't see anything else. Zaraiella? What's wrong?"

"So, who won?" Jason asked, folding his arms.

"She did, I know it. I know you got him sis."

"Mr. Wilson is good. He won fair and square."

"Looks like you're in third place now, M. Tell you what, I'll let you be number one in uno."

"No thanks, I'll be number one at staff spinning. Then, my sister, Zaraiella will be number two, or just call her my little sidekick. Come here sis. Time for you to spar with me finally."

"Spar with you?" Zaraiella says with her apprehensive eyes.

"It's not like I'm going to hurt you or anything."

"You want to fight me? Why…why would you want to do that?"

"You've been doing a lot better; I've seen you swing this thing as if you know what you're doing."

"I don't know how to fight with it. It's not in me."

"Well, you will learn today. Haven't you seen her improve, Jason?"

"She…um, has, but"

"Exactly! Here's mine. Don't go too fierce with it. Then I will have to use Jason's own, maybe his leg. Feels like if I hit hard enough against something, it will break."

"And if you break it, you're crafting me a new one," Jason frowns.

My sister needs to get out of her fearful habit. She must learn how to get mean and malicious. Just like this world that took Mom and Lakia from us. "You look ready, sis. You got this. Remember, this is just sparing. We're not going to kill each other. Okay, referee. Be sure this fight is fair."

"It already isn't."

"What, Mr. Chicken Legs?"

"Nothing, nothing."

"Munisha, I eygh!"

"See, you blocked it. You know what you're doing."

"She may be better than you in staffing, M. Watch out now."

Zaraiella might try to run in circles, trying to dodge me. She is older now.

"I don't want to fight! I don't like it!"

"Try to hit me. Go ahead. Oh, shut your giggling, Jason. Don't mind him, Zaraiella. Chicken legs is just a distraction. Now, try again. Swing it like you want to hit me this time."

"I can't! Munisha!" Zaraiella whimpered, trying to wipe her eyes holding the staff. "We're not supposed to be hurting each other."

"Oh my gosh, you know what?!"

This girl will not try to do anything. She has to stop being so weak. Maybe a couple of hits to her side will provoke her.

"Munisha chill out," Jason says, approaching us.

"She's fine, Jason."

"Munisha, please, I don't want to do this. Ow, ouch."

"Stop your tears. It's not going to get you anywhere. Put your staff in front of you, or I'll hit your leg again!"

"Eygh! Munisha, please stop!"

"Move, Jason! Let go of the stick before I hit you with it!"

"M, what is wrong with you?! Can't you see she had enough?!"

"Hey, I'm not letting my sister stay weak. I need her to fight when S.I.L.O comes. Nope, we just talked about how bad it is out here, and we must learn to survive."

"What's going on out here?!" Mr. Wilson growled. "Speak up when I'm talking to any of you. What's the matter with you, Zaraiella?"

"Zaraiella, come back here!" I shouted.

"Munisha, please don't tell me you're trying to brawl with your little sister."

"Mr. Wilson," I chuckled. "She needs to learn. I'm doing what I'm supposed to do."

"Okaaay, you do know she is much smaller and weaker than you?"

"I knew you would say that. That's why she needs me to help her become stronger. Zaraiella!"

"Listen to me right now, young lady!" Mr. Wilson scowled. "This is not how it's done. If she is not ready for this, then she is not. You can't force things on people. Do you want your sister hurt? I see her walking away with a limp."

"That doesn't matter. When she was out there by herself, anything could have happened, you know that."

"I agree with you, but to a certain extent. However, you"

"So why are you telling me to stop?! She will always be like that if she doesn't learn!"

"Don't force things on your sister. That is all I am saying. Do you understand me? I said do you understand me?!"

"Get your freaking hands off of me! You're not my damn dad, you can't tell me what to do!"

"I'm not trying to tell you what to do. Listen here. If I catch you or even anticipate you're trying to spar with your sister, you will have to deal with me."

I should have asked him; did he even use the mouth wash he gets us. "And what are you going to do, ground me?" I smirked.

"Far greater than that missy. You keep up with that bad attitude, and you will end up in a bigger hole."

"I wish you would put your hands on me. Tsk, I don't need this."

"Where do you think you're going?" the old man asked as I kept my eyes on the whispering trees. "Munisha, don't turn this into something far greater than it needs to be!"

"M…Munisha!"

"Jason, be still. She will learn."

Who is he to tell me what to do? I'm almost an adult. Then if my sister were to be killed out here, it was because more than likely she couldn't defend herself. "This family must be crazy. I know for a fact those S.I.L.O people are coming, and when they do, we are good as dead. Ugh, and there goes those nasty webs again."

Maybe it was a sign for me to go back. I can only imagine if someone who climbed up the tree and then they fell right into it. Would that be a nightmare of what?

"MUNISHAAAA!"

How did he find me so quickly?

"Munisha! Where are you?! Dad sent me to get you! Quit playing, alright! MUNISHAAA!"

He followed exactly where I was. That tracking Mr. Wilson taught us really worked.

"Munisha, please! It's dangerous out here! That girl is something else."

"Hmph, not that good. Guess nature is your best friend."

Going back to the farm is just like prison itself. It did not feel as though I had a life there. "Oh my gosh. That thing is so pretty. Who left their belteygh, ouch. Tsk, dammit."

I could have sworn that was a belt, it shape shifted into a snake. Now I'm going crazy? "Great…this is all I needed. Tsk, what is going on today? Now I'm bleeding."

What am I going to do? First, the annoying old man, then softy Zaraiella, now poor me. It is like we are cursed. Hope it wasn't poisonous.

"Where the hell is this trail taking me? I know the swamp is this way, and now I'm by the nasty webs again. The only thing close is…her place."

"Hellooo! Is anybody home?"

Knock Knock Knock

It was really starting to drip now. "Hello! Oh thank, god!" I said, hearing those locks shift.

"Dear, greetings once again. How may I help you?"

"Um, hi. I was walking through here. Actually, I came by to thank you. And uh"

"He is doing much better then; I am truly contented. Goodbye, deary," the old woman says as she closes the door slowly.

"No, wait! Can you look at this?"

"What happened? Looks like you have a bite as well," the old woman smiled.

"It was from a snake; I didn't know it was alive."

"Why would you want to affiliate yourself with such a creature?"

"Can you just help me? Then I will be on my way, won't bother you ever again."

"Last time I helped you, child, you, along with your friend, you both fled. Very ill-mannered, wouldn't you agree?"

"We, I mean, he was spooked, I guess. It wasn't nice, you're right, and I am sorry. Can you please help me?" How can she say that wasn't nice, but then close the door in my face? Guess she doesn't want to help. Just my luck.

"Where are you going child?" the old woman asks with her everyday long black robe. "I must unlock my door before I can open it."

"Thanks! Ugh, that smell again," I said as I walked inside the old wooden house.

How could someone eat such a thing with a revolting smell as such?

"You should really try it. The taste is more enjoyable than the scent, my dear."

"Maybe another day. Look, is this bad? I swear to you, that thing looked just like a belt before I picked it up. Am I poisoned? Please tell me it's okay."

The hunchback woman smiled. "You did tell me it came from the slithering serpent, I would not know. Here in this area, there are not many poisonous creatures roaming the land. Ha, if you are that curious, you can suck out the toxins. You will feel much better."

"No way. How is that even possible?"

"It just is my deary. Now I will go to get something to aid it. Do not move from this spot, or your heart will be lingering on your condition."

"Yes, mam. Thanks very much!"

This place was just something you would not think is in a forest or even think people like her exist out here. If she were to live out in the city, they would think she is a weirdo. "That was fast."

"I have already had an ointment for something as such. The wound does not look as if it needs much aid; you are in luck," the old woman says as she immediately applies the ointment.

The old woman seems to have everything in this creepy place. She sure is knowledgeable. "Agh, it stings a little."

"That implies the application is working, my dear. That should be all."

"Thank you."

"Don't go on tampering with any more trouble. You best to heed a old womans wisdom. You and your sister are so similar, yet so different."

"Wait, I almost forgot about that. She told me a woman saved her life. How she described the person made me know it was you."

"The youngling was wandering alone. How could you lose her in such a way? The Black Forest contains many dangers."

"There was a, uh…I don't know how to explain it. It was something I had never seen before. We ran from it, and that is how we got separated. I'm surprised you didn't see anything when you were out or went out, have you?"

"There are many fiends out to devour. These eyes have witnessed many corrupt spirits also, especially within my forest."

Her eyes would be considered blind from how blueish gray they were. If I didn't know who she was and she was peeping through my window at night, I wouldn't know what to do.

"As I was down below the other day. I noticed that someone fiddled with my books. The only lives in my home were you and the boyfriend."

"I guess I should apologize for that too. I got carried away. This place, I have never seen the things you have. It amazed me, along with that weird light down there too. What was that book anyways?"

"Did it interest you?" the old woman asks with a smirk.

"Somewhat. I remember there were a few weird things in it."

"As my spirit told me before, your heart is so adventurous, so undaunted," the old woman smiles. "You want to search for a life; but it seems life never searches for you."

"How do you know these things?"

"They are my ways, child. I would be willing to lend you my studies if you wish. You can take it home and learn a few things from it. Yet, I will need it back in due time."

"Sure. What will I learn from hey? Yea, that is what I was reading."

She must have been just looking through it. "Those colors on the star…it's so beautiful."

"This book is precious. It is more than just it's appearance. Neither, this book for the weak minded."

"Trust me. I'm not weak, like others I know of."

"This book will take you places you wished you have dreamed of, or…you have wished you have never dreamed. If your mind is open to this, you can master it, my dear."

"Sure, I'm always open to learning. Geez, it's, pretty heavy."

"Weight of knowledge, dear."

Carrying this thing home will definitely be a job. "Before I go. What is your name, by the way? I never asked."

"Just call me, Jezebel. And yours? I believe it is, Munisha."

"Yes. Thanks, I'll bring it back!"

She was so nice. Someone like that would be judged for the way how they look, and how they live. Only thing I judge her on are the chitlins I can't bare to inhale. That will always be something that I will pass up. "Forces Of Nature. This thing could literally be three dictionaries in one for how many words and pages it has."

Hopefully, whatever I can learn from it will make life more interesting.

"Home sweet home."

Hopefully, they aren't too mad with me. I don't feel like arguing right now. "Hello, Mrs."

"Have you cooled off, young lady?" Mrs. Wilson says, knitting on the porch. "Tim told me what happened. What has gotten into you lately?"

"I'm sorry. I guess I am a hothead," I said, rolling my eyes.

"Then you need to extinguish that fire in you, or you will most likely wind up in deep trouble. Didn't I lay the rules for no one to wander off like that?"

"You did, and"

"So, you will abide by what I say. Munisha, we are family here. No one is trying to tell you what is wrong. It is to keep you safe."

"I know, Mrs. Wilson. I will do better, I promise. Can I go to my room now?"

"Yes. By the way, I am glad to see you found another book to help you stay occupied. Reading will take you places even if you can't go there."

I chuckled. "I bet."

"Hey, sis. Zaraiella? Fine, you don't have to say anything to me. I'm sorry about earlier, I should have never forced you."

"It's okay," Zaraiella mumbles as she jots swiftly in her small pad.

"As you do your studies, I will do mine."

"Mrs. Wilson left your book on the table. Just telling you."

"I forgot all about it. Doing math right now, nah. I will do it tomorrow or whenever. I have something better to be reading up on."

This book had so many things in the beginning. It was nothing more than common sense rules of daily life. Respect one another. If it doesn't make you happy, find another way. You need to always believe in yourself and control your ego along with mani festing your destiny. Then, there were some things that I just couldn't interpret, seemed to be side notes. The symbols and wording made me realize this book was very much thought of, and it's more than just looks with its intricate styles. Ms. Jezebel didn't lie when she said she wanted it back.

"What is all that glitter on your shirt, Munisha?"

"Oh wow," I said, brushing it off. "That stuff is everywhere. It's probably on my sheets too. I'm about to take a shower anyways. It's all over my chest. Too bad we're not going out."

"Where did you get this book from?"

"Someone gave it to me. Should have hopped in the tub as soon as I got here."

"Who gave it to you? I have never seen it around here before."

"Hey, don't look in there! It's…it's for older people only. Trust me, if you're scared of the boogie man, you will hate this if you see some of the stuff in it."

I need to keep it from her. That is the last thing I need for her to not be able to sleep when she already claims she is seeing things. Besides that, I believe it can show me how to make life more interesting. I need something that can take my mind off what goes on around me.

"The book is so good that you have to bathe with it?"

"Of course I didn't bathe with it," I said, drying my hair. "Just don't need you looking into it. Tsk, and there goes the damn lights," I sighed. "This place, I swear."

"At least I am not afraid of the dark anymore," Zaraiella says as the moonlight only revealed her lower half.

"Once we know where we are going, we are up and gone from this forsaken place. Guess the moon is telling me to read there, so be it."

"You're not going to sleep?"

"Just because lights are out doesn't mean stop what you're doing, sis. These people think we are robots in a factory or something, like they can just shut us off. Hmph, I will see you in the morning, Zaraiella. I want to look into this a little more before I rest."

This book, filled with information and logic. It will take months to a year to finish it. She must want it back to see if I keep it in good hands because it's impossible to read the whole thing.

Bam bam bam.

"What the hell!" I said, getting up swiftly from my sheets.

"If you ever walk off like that again, young lady, you will be in more deep trouble. This isn't a safe place, and I can't have my wife always distressed when one of you disobedient children want to do your own thing. It doesn't work like that, not in my house. Now you're quiet. You are almost old enough to make your own decisions and until that time comes, you will have to"

"Abide by your rules. Gotcha."

"Unfortunately, you haven't done it at least once. Just complete your chores today and settle yourself in with your studies. I hope I am making myself clear, Munisha. You're not a troubled child, you just want to do things your way. In life there are rules and principles. When those two are broken, best believe consequences will happen. When you are ready for the world, we want to send you off with our best knowledge so you can survive and be successful. The world is changing faster than we know it everyday."

He must be crazy to be banging on my door early like that. "I have a question, Mr. Wilson," I said, shaking my head. "If you say that you want me to learn about the world and it is constantly changing, how can any of us learn anything if we are isolated away from everyone?"

"That is simple, hmph look around when you're out there for once. Nature shows us how to live. You start from there with nature. You will find the basic principles of living, life. How to get through tribulations when that strolls yonder and near. Now go on and get to work. I know you're starving since, Sara told me you didn't even grab something last night. Your sister is waiting too, by the way."

He made it seem like I am such a troubled person. How can he tell me how to feel? Especially about my own family. I have never gotten into trouble before, and I should be able to make life how I want it.

"You must be in trouble, really big trouble," Zaraiella says as she pulls weeds from the garden.

"It's whatever. I am sooo, tired. I knew he wasn't going to let us off for today. Should have gone to sleep when I was supposed to."

"You stayed up all night reading?"

"I couldn't help myself. It's interesting, it really is. Hope you weren't looking in it while I finally dosed off."

"You told me not to. It looks old and dusty anyways."

"Exactly, it's not your flavor for something to read, sis. We should take Mom's car and travel somewhere."

"Then you will get in more trouble. Do you like getting in trouble?" Zaraiella asked.

"No, it gets boring around here. You get to play with Janice all day; all I have is Jason."

"Jason, me, and Janice."

I sighed. "I want to be free, to be able to go with people my age. It's nothing wrong with you all. Just, the chemistry with others is important, I believe."

"I felt like that too before. It doesn't bother me as much."

"Well, it bothers me, just…like, pulling these…stupid weeds!"

"He's your boyfriend now, isn't he?"

"What?" I said, tossing the weed to the floor.

"Jason, I saw you both kissing," Zaraiella giggled. "I won't tell anyone."

"When did you see that?"

"When you kissed him that day after you two found me."

"You were supposed to be in the house. I could have sworn you went in."

"The window is right there. That's how we saw you."

"We?" My eyes stretched.

"Everyone saw you."

"What?! Really? Oh gosh, I didn't even notice. How embarrassing."

"It was only me and Mrs. Wilson. She's the one who told me. I think it's cute."

"God, now I know why she looked at me funny. Should have known that wasn't going to be easy to hide."

"Don't worry. We won't tell anybody."

CHAPTER 16

Wistful Aspiration

Some of these words are so hard to pronounce and even have symbols in between them. How does Ms. Jezebel even think I would understand most of this anyways? She wanted me to just read what I could. The letters are so nice and unique. What could be made in this book to create text like that? "Nepesh, Neypesh." Sounds like something that happens when you are dying. "Thine body, mind, and soul are congruent. One must respect thine laws; therefore, thine will be lost in calamity. Guess this means you will lose yourself if you can't respect who you are?"

Why does it have a wolf with a spirit in front of it? This book has everything. You might as well call it philosophy. "Thine shall only content thy self with sober intakes. Clouds will shift to fog if thine intake intoxication is filled. Devour the flesh only from wholesome creatures, therefore, thy shall reap contaminates of its malignancy."

This chapter was not that hard. Basically, it's common sense. I need to start eating more healthy foods anyways like it said. I did lose a few pounds with my new eating habits. Now I can use some abs. "Get,

Zaraiella to help me with my sit-ups once I get in. What the hell! Crazy boy, you scared me. Quit doing that!"

"Well well well. The Munisha I know is never scared. Here you go," Jason says, tossing a fruit to me.

"This is just what I needed. A good fresh apple. Lay off some the meats for a while."

"Don't be trying to starve yourself. Your body looks amazing with the tummy showing. You cut your shirt up, huh?"

"Yup, and your dad can't tell me how to wear my clothes neither."

"I don't get you, women. You can have a stomach as flat as these leaves yet still think you're fat."

"I don't think I'm fat. Just want to tone up a little. Thanks for bringing it to me. Em, this particular one is so sweet and delicious."

"You know, Dad gets these out from the forest. Too bad the winter season is coming soon. I know your goals. How long have you been under this tree reading that book?"

"I've lost track. Once those lesson books were done, I took my book and came out with my favorite tree that gives me shade and relax."

"I didn't know you were a reader. You always seemed more of a fighter."

"Sweetie, I'm both. Do not think since a girl likes to read, she's a nerd or whatever. I will pick up my staff in a heartbeat."

"Look."

"Eygh! What is wrong with you, crazy boy?! Why do you have to always be so ew and pick up bugs?"

"M, come on. It's harmless."

"It's a bug, and that is all I need to know. Looks like the main bug I can't stand in your hand right now. Get back, Jason! I am not playing with you!"

"Do you trust me?" Jason says as he continues to follow me.

"What?!"

"I asked, do you trust me? If you do, then stop backing away."

"Jason, that thing could be poisonous. Why would you pick it up? Just put it back where you found it. Stop playing before I slap some sense into you!"

"If it were, do you think I would be holding it?" Jason smirks. "Just trust me, okay?"

"What do you want me to do? If you're trying to put it anywhere on me, not only will I kill it, but you'll be lying on the ground too."

"Don't be so cruel. I want you to break the fear. This here, is a jumping spider. They are the most harmless of the species. I used to play with them a lot before I met you."

"Ever since I have known you, not once have I ever seen you holding one of those things. Eygh, Jason you weirdo! Get away from me!"

Jason chuckles. "Come here. It won't bite you; I promise."

"Jason! Quit your foolery! I'm so serious right now!"

"You know I could have just let it crawl on you while sitting down over there. You probably would not even have noticed it. Hold one hand out, and I promise I will take it back if it bothers you too much."

No matter what I did, he kept getting closer to me. Though, it did look harmless. "What if it bites me?"

"Then you have my permission to knock the hell out of me. Come on, hold out your hand."

"What will this solve?" I frowned.

"I told you already. It will break your fear, just a little."

"I can't believe I'm doing this," I said slowly, holding my hand out and eyes shut tight.

"Hold your hand steady. This little guy is petrified already, and you are shaking more than him. Better yet, put this darn, oof this book is heavy."

"You bet not drop my stuff in that dirt. Making me hold a spider, this boy."

"Okay, ready? Hold both of your hands out now, don't drop em'."

"And if I do?"

"You failed the test, friend," Jason smirks. "Glad I didn't squish him, trying to hold your cinder block. Now keep those eyes closed. How does it feel?"

It felt so itchy. "Oh my gosh, oh my god, oh my gaawwdd. What does this silly boy have me doooinnng!"

"Open your eyes. See not so bad, is it?"

What was I doing? "I am holding a spider. You actually have me, holding a spider..."

"He's your friend. His name is, Lucky," Jason says, holding my hand beneath the terrifying hairy insect.

"And I don't feel that right now."

"All he wants you to do is trust me, and then trust him of course."

It looks like he was looking straight into my eyes. "I have never seen one with eyes as his. It's eyelashes are just like Zaraiella's."

"Oh shoot, it kind of does. Spider version of, Zaraiella. Now, you have just broken your fear of step one. The next one we move to will be something bigger."

"I will only go this far. This took every bone in my body to adjust to."

"You probably like him for his eyelashes. It's cute to you, huh?"

"Matter of fact, he is cuter than you, and he would eygh!"

That thing was literally a jumping spider. Good thing it was tiny.

"See you talk too much."

"Now I am afraid of it again, so your teaching privilege is no longer valid."

"It's a jumping spider. He should have been jumped, guess he liked you, then decided to head out once you said he was cute. Anyways, it's late. You did a good job, M," Jason says, then gets close to me.

"I don't want to kiss your spider lips. Your hair feels like the spiders' legs. I'm just playing."

"I know. That is why Lucky is on your shirt!"

"…Stupid boy."

"You are the lucky one M, remember that. Hey, I think that's Mr. Kenneth, and Mark. Maybe get a game or two in basketball. You in?"

"Um, no thanks. I'm going inside. That son of his always acts weird. Like someone is telling him not to talk or something."

"Oh, you know he's one of the shy types," Jason says, waving as the truck stops in front of us. "I used to be like that. That's just who he is."

"Yea, but he's been like that forever. Thank god you grew out of it, or I would have been bored out of my mind with you."

"Hey, Mr. Kenneth! What's up, Mark?!"

"Howdy. Didn't mean to disturb you two. You young ones grow up so fast. Where's your father? Got some supplies here for em."

"I'm going inside, Jason. I will let you and him have your fun while I have so much reading to do."

"What's your book about?"

I grinned. "You barely talk but ask me about a book?"

"Chillout, M. He's just curious. It's a book about Life. Come on, let's get this game in B ball. M passed on me."

I kind of like what Jason did. Never thought I would ever hold a spider. When the book said, respect the creatures as they respect you, it is right in a way. If you can use things to break your fear, you can also be fearless. "Carrying all this weight of knowledge should make me understand more and more. I need more time with it."

"Smells good in here, Mrs. Wilson. Must be something new tonight."

"Mommy is making meatloaf."

"Don't go on spoiling the surprise, Janice," Mr. Wilson says as he walks back and forth in the house.

Great, when she knows I am trying to keep the weight off. "Meatloaf, that's something new. I know you all are not meat lovers. Hope it tastes good."

"Child, it most certainly will. Tim better tell you this is my alltime favorite mix."

"Only reason I picked it up is that the clerk was not offering to trade as much," Mr. Wilson says, sitting in his favorite dining chair with his arms folded. "If it wasn't for my guy Kenneth, getting granola bars, we wouldn't have those. The real healthy products are difficult to come by anyways."

"How come? They don't want people healthy or something?" I asked.

"Survival of the fittest," Mr. Kenneth said. "It is a dog eat dog world out there, especially with S.I.L.O. The whole world is being corrupted by selfishness and greed."

"I told Janice earlier it's why we don't have as much food in the fridge. We may need to start just owning more farm livestock here. Tim, I don't feel comfortable as you know. Times are changing rapidly, and it's only getting worse."

"What do you expect me to do then, Sara? We need more than just here. Livestock would not make it. It's an inadequate amount of land."

"It's about that time. Time changed again, and it's getting dark early. Thanks for the tea, Madam. Your wife aced it."

"That's her. My family stands supreme," Mr. Wilson says, shaking Kenneth's hands. "Take care old friend, and thanks again!"

Sometimes I do wish I could go with him. When they leave, it always makes me think of returning to an ordinary and simpler civilization. "We all need to move."

Mr. Wilson grins. "We all know that is what you want. This family is safe here. There are not too many places where we all can be safe. It is my job to protect my family and that is all that matters along with being grateful for what we have in the present. Life will never grant you more if you are ungrateful. Why did you bring that enormous book to the table? You could read it all night once settled in your room."

"That is the thing. There is no light while I'm trying to read after the lights go out."

"Grab yourself a candle. Just don't make a fire."

"Don't tell her that Dad, I will just lend her my flashlight," Jason says as he walks in behind me. "The last thing we need is to lose everything, and we will have to stay in the city."

"I'll be fine; don't really trust candles either. The moonlight shines a little in my room. I just cannot understand what is going on. Why is this world falling apart?"

"This was inevitably going to happen. That is why we must remain steady on how we do things and when we are out to survive out there. Every day will be something new. This meatloaf hasn't changed, dear. Mm, simply delicious."

Tap tap tap

"Another friend for you at the window, M."

"It should come in and grab your plate," I said. "What is wrong with you, Mrs. Wilson? You two are looking at each other like you hate that bird."

Mr. and Mrs. Wilson must not like things flying in windows. Their shining faces shifted to somber ones quickly. Besides that, there was no actual point of living in the city at all if they are becoming that strict. You barely can use cash nowadays and then they are making food just as hard to obtain. It seems as though they wanted this world to become like hell.

"You were quiet while we were having dinner, Zaraiella. I mean extra quiet this time. What is on your mind? Having those sightings again? Don't lie to me. I wanted to say something while we were having dinner. I didn't want to put you on the spot. I know how much you hate it when everyone is staring at you."

"I just had a feeling," Zaraiella says, laying down with her eyes to the ceiling.

"And what was that feeling this time?"

"It feels…like, Mommy…came here. In spirit."

"Wow. You don't know that, Zaraiella. I came to a conclusion; she is in S.I.L.O, along with Lakia. One day we will get them out. I just need to find some others that can help us. Grandpa Mr. Wilson looks like he wouldn't hurt a fly. Then he couldn't kill anybody with that stone age gun. Yea, we need to find new people."

"What if you get taken or get killed?"

"That is the thing. We would have to find others as I said. Some people hate them just as much as we do. I know it for a fact. They are destroying the world along with making life harder. We can barely even get food now. You heard what Mr. Wilson said. It's terrifying to say the least. Imagine if they shut down the city again, and only allow those with certain qualifications to buy food. Then how are we supposed to live?"

"…I don't know."

No one really knows what to do and surely, I didn't. Just me wanting to remain optimistic is enough, I hope. "Read me what you are writing, sis. Let me hear it," I said. This girl stays in that notebook.

"It's not finish."

"I don't care. Go on, read it to me."

"My heart is big. My heart is big, just like the world. The world should have one, too. It only swirls. When you look at the birds, they fly over. They see everything. We only see what we want. Is that really caring? Maybe it will change…That's it."

"Not bad, you're definitely improving. You want to write poetry for the rest of your life that is good. Hopefully, you will see why I am hard on you one day."

Zaraiella nods. "That book you're reading is going to take forever."

"I know. I won't even have it for long either. It opened my eyes to many things already. Dammit! Now I can't see. I am beginning to hate this place with a passion."

"At least I'm not afraid anymore."

I chuckled. "I remember, Zaraiella, you would holler, then over the month you did improve. Finally sis!"

When the room went black, I did feel something with her in the darkness. As long as it doesn't touch us, we we're fine.

"I want to train with you tomorrow. I want to try again," Zaraiella murmured.

"Really? Good. Let me get in my little corner again. I will see you in the morning then. I'm so proud of you."

It's about time, now she is beginning to think about what I have beaten into her head.

"Hold me, Jason! Your sister, does a better job almost."

"I already told you, this is cheating," Jason says.

"Okay, let me go!"

"See, you got it without me. Just focus."

"Whew, wish your dad had a gym around here. I would have been had abs."

"You look good, M. Hey, I wish I could handstand. Let's get a one on one in basketball, shall we? We haven't played and I want to see you perform. I'm definitely tired of playing with these sticks."

"Maybe later," I said, stretching. "Besides that, all I see you do is push ups. You must have everything right to actually handstand."

"You're right. Then let's have a round then? I want to see something."

"You already know you're going to win. You are so eager to compete with me today," I hissed.

"Na, you have gotten a lot better. We haven't spared in a month, seems like now, that I think about it."

"Unfortunately, I will have to say no to that too. Zaraiella is supposed to come out in a few, after she is done with her so called schoolwork."

"Oh, well we can try tomorrow."

I have a surprise for the big mouth.

"Oh crap! You almost got me," Jason chuckles. "You're good, but not that good. Trying to come for me while I'm not looking is the worst thing you can do. This M, is called a reverse headlock. Mmmh, your hair smells like cherries."

"Alright, alright," I grinned. "You can let me go now. Curly girly hair."

"Give me a kiss."

"I am all sweaty, oh my gosh," I said, trying to break free. "You are so gross."

"What does that have to do with anything? I just want to help you with the sweat."

"Help! He has me in a headlock! Jason, no no no, don't do that. What are you, a vampire?"

"Ewww, you two are nasty. Should I leave?"

"You see, crazy boy. Sorry about that, sis. Jason is…always playing!" I said as I couldn't stop myself from blushing. "Ready?"

"Would you like me to referee again?"

"A matter of fact, yes. You better not have left a hicky," I whispered. "Here you go, Zaraiella. Remember, don't hold anything back."

"I am here to watch too!" Janice says, walking in with Zaraiella's camera. "Zaraiella told me she was going to fight you."

"She looks ready, M. More confident than the last time, for sure."

"That is what I want, be sure to get a good shot of us, Janice. Quickly sis, I want you to try and hit my leg. Pretend like there is, like a fly or something, and hit it. Go!"

"See, that's it, harder, harder, harder!"

"She is going to break your staff, M."

"She won't," I smirked. "Now it's my turn. You see the way I was blocking? Do the same thing. I need you to focus even harder, okay? Go!"

"Eygh!"

Sister continued running back. Thought she said she was ready.

"Come on, sis. You are not afraid. Again! Don't run back. You will trip yourself."

"See, it's not in me," Zaraiella says, dropping the staff.

"If you keep telling yourself that, then it never will be. Believe in yourself."

"Zaraiella, you can do it!" Janice cheered. "You can write poetry, and you can do this too!"

"And how will that save her life, Janice? One day, never mind. It will come to you. Pick it back up sister."

"I am done for the today," Zaraiella sighed, wiping her eyes. "It's not my thing. I'm sorry, I did try."

"Maybe one day we could get, Zaraiella and Janice to spar together," Jason says. "Wouldn't that be something?"

"No way, I don't fight. Hair is my thing and the only thing I will do."

"You should let Janice braid your hair, Jason. Get it pretty, just like, Zaraiella's."

"You're not funny, M."

"Let me do it, Jason. Pleeease, at least let me braid it."

"Go back in the house and braid your yarn. I wish I would catch you, or even you, M trying to play in my hair. Take dads razor and clippers then show you both a real makeover."

"Aww, don't be mad. Who knows, it will probably make you cuter," I said, squeezing Jason's cheek.

"Janice! I knew you were all in here. No fighting, sparing or whatever you all call it. That Tim, I tell you. I need you, Janice, give me a hand with cutting the greens, please. We have a good amount to cut for tonight."

"Don't give up on yourself, sis."

"I won't," Zaraiella asserted, looking back with a smile.

"So, what are you going to do now? No basketball?" Jason asked.

"Hmph, yea right. I'm tired."

"Looking in your eyes, hey, they look a little…lighter today."

"Really? I never noticed."

"Being up all night with your book is the cause I'm assuming. I need to see what is so interesting about it."

"Nothing exciting. I don't want to lie to you. It is, but it is something for you to understand about life. That book has over a thousand pages, and I think I am only on page two fifty or somewhere near."

"Wow, so you have really been into it then. That's good, keeps you from being bored all the time."

"Something just pulls me into it every time I begin reading. She was right."

"Who, who was right?"

"Oh, nothing," I smirked.

"All I can say is M, just be careful with things you read or let come across that are…not good. They can take your mind out of reality. Remember what Dad did to my phone? Hmph, are you happy?"

I frowned. "What? Why do ask so many off the wall questions?"

"Just asking. You know me, I am always curious."

"Hmm, semi happy, if that is a way you can put it. Some days are okay. Other days I am bored out of this world. Makes me want to take Betsy and ride off without anyone knowing."

"Your time is coming. I am going to go and have some fun playing uno, or something. Just have to keep yourself occupied."

Me, and Zaraiella are getting out of here next month. I can feel it approaching. Something is going to come and be so much better, I know it.

"What are you looking for, Mr. Wilson? Mr. Wilson, are you"

"There is a rodent in here. Most likely from the air being cooler inside. We rarely get them, heck, that sucker made his way in. They tend to migrate into people homes and cause even more problems, which we don't need either."

"I can help you find him."

"Hmph, afraid of spiders, not scared of rats?"

"Long time ago, we had one in a cage in school. Every now and then, the teacher used to have me feed it. Cuter than a creepy spider. Just to let you know, Jason did the most."

"What is that?" Mr. Wilson questioned, turning his head quickly at me and with one eyebrow raised. "Hope there is no fooling around in this house."

"No, nothing like that. He had one of those jumping spiders in his hands, then he placed it in mine."

"You actually held it? That's hard to believe."

"I did until it jumped off and my fear for them clung right back to me."

Mr. Wilson chuckled. "He tried using the no fear method I taught him."

"It gave me confidence once the spider was calm in my hands, then it just went away just like that."

"We all have that one thing we are afraid of. Mine is losing my lovely wife. That isn't a phobia, just something I would hate to witness."

"Very understandable. You know, I have learned a lot from living here. I want to apologize for the times I've acted a bit…silly."

"Nah, don't worry. We all have been children before"

"Eygh! He's under the grandfather clock!"

"Don't let him move. I don't know how he managed to squeeze up under there. I have something for em'. Thought you weren't scared of rats."

I don't care. That was the last thing we needed to try to keep the peace at night. Rats running around through the walls. "Wait! What are you doing? I thought you were going to kill it."

"I believe we taught you all life is precious," Mr. Wilson asserted as he carried the rodent with a cloth. "Must have forgotten to inform you, or you haven't really learned much."

"So, what if they eat the metal, wood, or…y'know? Isn't that what they do? That is what one of the books we learned taught us."

"That is true. Still, all life is precious."

"That is crazy. Mrs. Wilson would have killed it. Then you throw it outside like it was someone's dirty shoe."

Mr. Wilson chuckles. "I should have surprised her with it. Sara hates them."

"I believe all women do, I just don't really care for them and would not want it in my own house either."

"That is when you have one, you will understand a little more. Think of it this way. One the smallest of all is the fly and it disgust people the most. What is the purpose of its life?"

"To eat people's food when they're not looking, aannnd fly on people who smell bad?"

Mr. Wilson shook his head, smiling. "You called out all of the negative. Fly's take care of waste, as your poop, the livestock own and all. Their job is a little repulsive; it is. It's just the way nature attended it to be. The circle of life."

"This book talks about respecting all creatures, so in some way, I could understand that."

"You carry that thing like it's your child, must love it dearly."

"It is pretty interesting. I learned a lot from it just as I learn from you all. About to read up on it some more and then take a nap."

"I hear you, might just do the same. Thanks for help by the way. You would make a good help mate someday."

My studies acknowledged that if something constantly bothers you, and continues to do so, execute it. However, it said to always respect everyone and all nature, as what you give, you will receive.

* * * *

Knock Knock Knock

"Why do people always disturb me while I am sleeping well? Zaraiella, can you get it please? I don't even know why the door is shut."

"Zaraiella, M," Jason said. "Dad and Mother needs us downstairs. It's important."

"What happened? Tsk, I hope it isn't a lecture about a mouse."

"Mouse? Don't know what you're talking about M, but they need us all downstairs."

"Great. I dreamed of being on a beach and flying away over the ocean. It felt so good to be free."

"I can tell, you were you sleeping with your arm over the book," Zaraiella said.

"Wow, didn't even notice when I dosed off. This book lets me sleep like a baby, I guess."

"Doesn't that mean it's boring?" Jason grins.

"You're an idiot. Let's go before they start yelling our names."

The weird thing is I haven't seen a beach in so long. My mind gave the illusion of the golden sand with the rich blue colored water. Then something just lifted me up and took me across the skies, with its purplish pink color shifting into the night. Life is so much beyond this.

"Don't bring your ten pound bible, Munisha," Mr. Wilson exclaimed as we stepped downstairs. "You won't need it right now."

"She carries that thing everywhere, Dad, even sleeps with it."

"Family, me and my wife have decided, and it has been difficult. We are going to go out to the city where we all can get a authentic view of, S.I.L.O. You all have not seen what is really out there. How life has changed. Letting you all see it with your own eyes is the only way. The only issue we will have to gamble with is the use of time."

"Isn't it getting late?" I queried. "It's curfew time, isn't it?"

"We know this, Munisha. That is why we are leaving before the night, and once we have observed everything, we head back out. You have the keys, Sara? Bracelet and whatever with it?"

"Are you sure we are doing this, Tim? It's risky."

"I am aware. Though, this has to be done."

In a way, going out to see this city once again. I could not really think of being excited of going out or us being caught and never returning. At least being optimistic to what is to come, drives me to see anything that has changed.

"The sun already looks as if it's going down," Mrs. Wilson said. "My heart never tells me to go out once the sun sets."

"We will make it, Sara. If the car does not have enough to get us there and back, we won't go at all. Where are you going, Munisha?"

"To check on Betsy. For some reason, I feel something…weird. See, you left the padlock unlocked!"

"Good. You see, that is my stepdaughter there! Be quick and lock it up for me."

It would be crazy if S.I.L.O was to follow us back here. "Hey, girl. Do you feel like going out tonight? We may need you. I believe you could do it. I wish we could go out by ourselves."

"We're taking the car, M," Jason implied, holding the stable door open. "Come on before you get left."

"Now we will be all crammed up in there. Thought about that? I really wanted to bring my book too."

"Bummer. You really have to bring that thing everywhere? You are truly addicted."

"Hey, it is like my new best…what the?"

"What is it?" Jason asked, turning around behind him.

"I could have sworn I saw something in the bushes over there."

"You're looking so hard in the book; it's making your eyes bad. Come on, their waiting."

"Maybe it was a fox or something."

"You two love birds ready?" Mr. Wilson sighed, tapping on the car. "We have little time peoples."

Even though it was a fox or some sort of creature. Why was it staring at me directly into my eyes? Crystal eyes. Never seen an animal stare with eyes the color of the moon then run off like that. A matter of fact, I have, just can't recall when.

"Oh gosh, Jason, you can go in the middle. Let me have the window. Told you we would be smooshed in here."

"It's amazing that this vehicle still keeps its new car scent, No matter when I drive it, it seems so refreshing."

"That is how I am going to have mine. Prefer a truck like yours back then, Dad."

"Your time is coming, son," Mr. Wilson says. "It is coming."

How could Mr. Wilson see with half the windshield being cracked? "Your chicken legs, Jason! Move those pointy things. Just that you have hair all over. Get your chicken legs off of mine."

"What do you want me to do? There are four people back here. Zaraiella, can you scoot over a little? Your whiney sister is always complaining. You two are laughing kind of hard over here."

"That is because they do look like chicken legs. Sorry about that, brother. It is funny, chicken legs."

"How about you just sit on my lap, M?"

I grinned. "Sitting on your leg is like me sitting on a broom."

"Be nice to my son, Munisha," Mrs. Wilson frowned.

"Sorry, chicken legs," I whispered.

"Ma, she said it again."

"Look at our city, you all. Hope all of you can take in how different society is now."

"Doesn't look like many people are out at all. So, it isn't like this at this time, Tim? Could be curfew schedule in effect."

"Dunno. The population is getting smaller and smaller, I realize now, especially at night. Curfew couldn't have start at this time. Bangor has always been small, not as small as Ellsworth but now it just darn near empty. Hmph, S.I.L.O."

"There is no one at the fun land, Daddy," Janice said.

"That has been that way I bet for a long time. Even Munisha and Zaraiella's hometown, the small fair was closed and stayed that way since. Everything's changed."

"So, this place is becoming a ghost town then," Mrs. Wilson asks as her head turned left to right. "The radio never speaks on this. This is madness."

"They don't want those to know what is happening in the world, Sara. It's actually worse than it looks. Maybe curfew has changed. There should be more people than this, it has to be."

"Right, if the car time is still correct, it is only six o'clock. They can't possibly lower curfew hours any more than that. That is absurd too. Drive slow, Tim."

"Did they ever mention on the radio anything?" Mr. Wilson asked. "I didn't catch an update."

"No," Mrs. Wilson replied. "This is a bit terrifying to see. Please drive slowly, what are you on the pedal so hard?"

"Trying to make this quick baby, that's all. There they are. They have upgraded their trucks and look more…pernicious."

Those S.I.L.O trucks always look to me like something out of the military. Nothing like how the police cars were if they were actually any left. "Can we stop by Mom's house, Mr. Wilson on our way back."

"Negative on that. That's a forty minute ride back and this car needs fuel. Plus, residential areas are more under surveillance. Then, it is a gated community. The code changed a long time ago, I'm sure."

"What's the matter, Zaraiella?" Jason asked.

"Zaraiella, what's wrong now, sis?"

"I looked over my shoulder and she was watering down. She was just laughing at my legs a while ago."

"Zaraiella, if you're upset about us not being able go there then I am sorry," Mr. Wilson says. "It is futile."

"She misses home, Tim."

"Wipe your face, sis. Everything is fine."

"Last stop we all are making is a gamble. Sara and I wanted you all to see how bad it has gotten. S.I.L.O will really open your eyes. This is why I tell all of you, you must know how to think for yourselves in this new world. These people are ruthless to the core."

Wasn't upset at Mr. Wilson for not accepting my request. Only that it persuades me one day to just go and find out on my own. Need to see what is there and what is left. Possibly, Mom some how returned and left a letter like we did for her. Tears rising in my eyes will not stop, either. Why did these people make life so hideous? Ever since the breakout. Life has been different for everyone. There is no need for making life hell. It is like the world is manifesting chaos on purpose. If life continues this way, what will it be like twenty years from now?

"The funny thing is, have you seen police cruisers around?" Mr. Wilson asked.

"I definitely haven't seen any. Are you saying that they have removed law enforcement, Tim?"

"S.I.L.O is the new law enforcement. They were planning this all along once the outbreak happened. Full of fabricated words. If you cannot judge on how to live, you are bound to fall for whatever they say."

"Is that it, Dad?" Jason says, leaning up from the seat.

The glass building fused with darkness only made it look like it was another dimension. "They built it, much bigger from what I remember," I murmured. "See it, Zaraiella?"

"Also, the thing with you all back then when you and Zaraiella were smaller. The facility since then has doubled since the accident. They are sucking the life out of the earth every day."

"Get closer, Dad."

"This is as far as we go, and sit back. Crap!"

"What, what is it,Tim?"

"Behind us," Mr. Wilson whispered. "A S.I.L.O cruiser is pulling up with siren lights on."

"Go, Mr. Wilson, get us out of here!" I shouted.

"Calm down! We can't. This car has no potential of outrunning those. Just, stay calm. Pretend like we chose the wrong street. If this god forsaken light missed us, we would have strolled on by. He's coming behind us now."

The big black truck looked like it would turn us over with one hit. I wish someone would just distract him. This was most likely it.

"Oh my God, thank goodness," Mrs. Wilson grinned, placing her hand on her heart. "I thought we were in trouble."

Mr. Wilson chuckled. "Me too. My hands are sweaty on the wheel."

"Wait, look!" Jason says. "They have people coming out of that same truck."

"These people Jason, most likely were caught out without having their regulations in check," Mr. Wilsons says. "They pretty much have authority over everything now. We have seen enough for this evening."

"Are you okay now, Zaraiella?" I asked. "We are going back home in a few. Well, back to their place, okay?"

"I'm...okay."

"Hold my hand, Zaraiella," Janice comforted.

"True good friends," Mrs. Wilsons smiles. "Nothing like good friendship."

"I know, Mrs. Wilson. I have said that numerous times."

"What the hell?" Mr. Wilson says. "We didn't need a check before we came in. Everybody, stay calm. Good evening officer. How ya' doing?"

"Are you aware sir that curfew is in effect?"

"Really? It is only about seven o' clock basically."

"It is the weekend. Only weekdays it stays at nine p.m."

"That's right, apologize about that," Mr. Wilson chuckled. "When you have a family, you have a lot to think about, you know."

"I see. Where is your sticker?"

"Sticker, the sticker must have been scraped off while I was trying to fix this cracked glass, see?"

"What happened to the windshield?"

Why wouldn't he just let us go?

"Damn tree from the storm cracked it. Checked with auto glass place and they told me to come back tomorrow."

"Hmm, you don't say? They usually take care of that in no time. No problem, I will issue you a temporary sticker. Digital cache last only a day or two. That is one thing that you must have to enter certain parts of the city. Clearance is important. Give me a second."

"Yes sir…jackass."

"I don't get why people need all of this, Tim. All of this is really necessary?"

"That is why we have moved from the inside world, Sara. This is ridiculous. I never was issued one, but since I have been up early out here, they don't check for it as much. Betsy in my opinion is superior to any car for sure. The fool isn't done yet? Anyways, back at that building. S.I.L.O I did hear from, Kenneth that they found someone some time back that they we're interested in. A group of people they call the, Figure Eights. Supposedly having better genes and immune to certain diseases, so they say. They had the person but they broke free once the accident happened that day."

"So this is what it is all about?" Jason said. "Finding who, like you call, Betsy, superior to nature."

"Something like that son. I guess those who are not valuable in that sense is expendable and obsolete."

"I will place it right here. Once you receive a new windshield, be sure to reapply it unless you use your own. Have a goodnight."

"I thought he was going to ask for license, oh thank God," Mrs. Wilson said. "Tim, not a great idea."

"We made it, Sara, and gave the children a little insight into what is happening here. Did you all understand what is going on? Your eyes did not lie. This is only the beginning of the works of all depraved."

CHAPTER 17

Ember Within

Can you help me with this math problem, Munisha? It's too hard.

"Algebra, I think I can do it. It is better than the geometry Mrs. Wilson has me doing. Okay, remember variable X' is always what you're looking for. So, you have to think what twentyfour equals is to by three, that's it."

"What you mean is, divide twentyfour by three?"

"You can do it like that. It's that you are solving for X'."

"Is it eight?" Zaraiella asked with her pen to her lip.

"I don't know, is it?"

"Got it."

"Why?" I asked.

"Because, when you put three times eight, it equals twentyfour. Right?"

"A round of applause for sis. Only wish you could understand geometry. Tsk, I never understood why I need this."

"Can't Jason help you?"

"He has problems with it too. Hey, scoot over a little. This tire swing is comfortable. Mr. Wilson knows what his crafts better than anything, I will give him that."

"Ever since he built it. I have always used it. Do you really think Mommy and Lakia is in there?"

"We have been over this already, Zaraiella. I believe so. It has been a month since we all rode to the city and saw what happened. The world is just not the same at all. It sucks big time. Hey, don't feel bad. We have each other. Plus, I promised you both that my hair is all yours if I lost the bet."

"I can't believe he actually beat you in checkers," Zaraiella grins.

"That's fine. The only reason he was able to win was that I have not really been focusing on it as much. How many times have you seen me play? Checkers is almost not my thing anymore."

"You're focusing on your book a lot, that's why. Almost every night I see you reading it."

"Have you ever thought about life? What your destiny will be? In my case, it never is how it seems in your head. You sometimes need someone or something to take your mind where you could believe you are actually there."

"Like...heaven?"

"Heaven, no one really knows about that. Almost pretty much like a forbidden land, I don't know too much about that. Only what I see, taste, hear, and touch goes by me. But hey, if that is where your mind takes you, go there. When I think of illumination everywhere, there is no night, only day."

"That is pretty, just by me thinking it."

"Too bad no one doesn't know. If we could ask…never mind. My book is far from finished. So far, it has taught me so much. Unfortunately, I will have to return it. I've held it long enough."

"So, you did get it from someone," Zaraiella says as she turns her eye to look at it.

"The woman who saved you, it's hers. Remember, I had to go and thank her for all her help. She gave me this book and said it's basically strenuous on the mind. No lie, it is."

"That's why you didn't want me reading it?"

"You do not want to look into things like this yet. Look."

Zaraiella grimaced. "What is that? It's scary."

"That is all you need to see. Question, why do you think the skeleton looked all meaty? What was it interpreting?"

"I don't know, because it shows you what is inside our bodies?"

"Not quite, men and women are two different creatures. Life allows us as beings to honor our body with only what is…you can say desirable for it. As you can see, or I don't know if you noticed my skin is clearer. When I turned thirteen that was when acne was not my best friend. It is because of one. Puberty sat in. Two, not eating right."

"Oh, that is why you only try to eat fruits and veggies now. How come I don't have bumps on me?"

"That is the thing, everyone bodies are different. It may come later, who knows. Hold this here, will you? Now I can do this," I said as I got up and placed my hands on the ground.

"Wow! You can do it way better now!"

"Not only that."

"Show off!" Zaraiella grins. "It's like your hand standing with push ups."

"Whew, but it takes a lot out of me. Jason wishes he could do that, but he is too weak."

"How do you get low then go back up like that?"

I can see she was so interested. I may just teach her one day. "I do not know. To tell you the truth, suddenly my handstands have been on point then one day I closed my eyes and felt so, energized and did push ups while doing it. I never seen anyone do that before."

"Can you teach me to do it?"

"Sure, tomorrow if you want, when we're training. That stance still takes my whole body strength to do. Just need to get rid of this minor, flab, then I'll be able to do them longer. Here comes trouble," I sighed.

"I'm ready, Munisha. Sorry, I took long. Mommy wouldn't let me leave."

"Hmph, was hoping you forgot. I kind of like my hair the way it is already."

"I am just going to braid it."

"Come on, Munisha," Zaraiella says pulling me back from the swing. "You will look so pretty."

"Zaraiella, please, I already am."

One day this book will have to go back. Maybe she will let me review it for a few more weeks. There should be about four hundred more pages left and that will take me at least another month to read and comprehend it entirely.

"Where did you get that gel from?" I asked as Janice rubbed her hands together.

"Mommy tells Daddy to get it for me while he is out there. It is good for your hair. Blueberry gel."

"It smells good. Just hope you two know what you're doing, and this stuff doesn't damage my hair. I never had it cut and don't plan to."

"We know what we are doing. The gel just makes the hair easier to braid. Like, makes it softer."

"Zaraiella, please don't have one braid bigger than the others. Then I will get all the jokes from you already know who."

"She knows what she is doing," Janice smiles. "Trust us Munisha, you will love it."

It's been so long since I had my hair done. The pulling and twisting felt so peculiar from how long it has been. Mom would never have time to do it herself, but I do recall a time a girl came and did it just once and Mom got mad at her for braiding it since I was only about four or five maybe. It has been a while, but vague memories come to me now and then.

"I was thinking, we should go out for girl's night," Janice says.

"Where?" I asked. "Because your dad, especially Mrs. Wilson, are not going to let all of us go out there alone."

"We can just have a campfire by the tree. Tell stories and only us. Mommy can come too, no boys. What's the matter, Munisha? You are just starring away like how Zaraiella does."

"No, just kind of had a flashback. Do you remember, Zaraiella? No, you would not remember. You were too young. There was another girl in the house. She did my hair just like this with, Lakia. I remember that for sure now."

"Who was it?" Zaraiella asked.

"I am not sure; she was always in and out of the house. Maybe it was Lakia's friend."

"Was she better than me doing hair? Your sister, Lakia, I mean."

"I wouldn't remember. That other girl was always kind of rough doing my hair too. Telling me to hold still. Then, Lakia would always wash it for me. I do remember someone, but who, who could it be?"

"Did we have any brothers?"

"Doubt it. If we do, I have no idea who they are. It would have been nice to have an older brother. Let me say, maybe."

"My brother is annoying, sometimes funny. Especially when you two are together."

"You girls, dinner is ready when you all are," Mrs. Wilson says. "Now, look at you! The style suits your face very nicely."

"We are almost done, Mommy."

"Thank god! My head feels as if it isn't on my body."

"Mommy, before you go. I wanted to ask you."

"No, mam. I will leave the hairdressing to you all. As you can see, my hair stays in one straight down style by brush and comb."

"I wanted to ask you; um…can we have girl's night?"

"Sure you all can, get nice and cozy in here if you want."

"We wanted it to be outside," Janice murmured.

I did not want to go out there, especially at night.

"You all want a party outside?" Mrs. Wilson raised her eye-brow. "With the danger and the cold out there? Absolutely not."

"We will be by the tree where the swing is. We aren't going to go out in the actual forest."

"Hmm, do you all tend to stay out there for the night? If so, that is already out of the question."

"Not all night," Janice replies. "Maybe till midnight. I want all of us to just do something different. It gets…boring."

"How about this? Once the lights go out, then you all return inside. Non negotiable."

"She means you can't argue with that, Janice," I asserted.

"Okay, um…I guess we can do it that way."

I did not know what was so special about going out there. Especially with everything going on. I insisted on staying inside and reading more of my book. Me not going out there labels me a party pooper. Then again, I did not want to leave my sister out there alone.

"How does it look?" Janice asks, holding a mirror out.

"Wow, just wow. Then, Zaraiella…not a bad job either. I love it!"

"Told you we could do it. High five, Zaraiella!"

"Now, my friend will not stop staring at me for sure now. Besides that, if we are going to go out, then we need to do it now. It is already getting dark. Oh gosh, my legs are numb. Thanks sis. Just got my hair done by the two best hair stylists in the world. I feel honored. Thank you both. You two did a fantastic job. Wonder where you got the idea."

"No problem," Janice says, moving quickly. "I will get the blankets for us."

"Oh no, I don't plan on laying on the ground too long. Bugs and all type of foolery is out there, and they come out at night. Then again, I just had my hair done. That is your best friend, sis. Better help her out. I am just coming along to just relax with you all."

"Love the hair! Very nice…nice," Jason says with his funny smirk.

"They really did it. I was surprised myself. They took a good five to six hours with it. My head is still tender, so don't give me a headache, please."

"Where are you going with blankets, Janice?" Jason asked.

"We are going to have girl's night outside!"

"That is right, and guess what?" I smirked, pulling Jason's pig tail hair. "No curly head boys."

"Sorry son, no boys. Sara told me what you all wanted to do. I am surprised she is okay with it."

"It was Janice idea for the most part," I said. "We won't be out for long."

"That's right. Lights are out at eight, so doors will be secured and locked tight."

"Here are your dinner plates," Mrs. Wilson says. "Do not drop them."

"Thanks. Wait, almost forgot my book. Be right back."

Walking around with a new do made me feel like a new person. Jason's eyes would not leave me for one second. Only if we could go out with it. "Gosh, isn't it cold out here, Janice?"

"Yea, but it is not that bad."

"It feels almost like it's mid fifties. Are you not cold, Zaraiella?"

"A little. Uh, I don't mind."

"This here looks like a nice area. Hopefully there aren't a lot of ants," Janice says as she whips the blanket onto the dirt floor.

"Your crazy brother had me holding that spider. Lucky was his name and he could be anywhere."

"That is still hard to believe, you hate them. I feel like you and my brother are going to get married."

I grinned. "Why do you think that? You told her more about us, didn't you, Zaraiella?"

"No, everyone could see you two, I told you. You both don't try to hide it."

"I thought we did. Zaraiella you look like a little eskimo with that big hood over your head."

I hate when everyone knows my business. I guess it is our fault.

"Let's play this game called truth or dare," Janice says, smiling both ways at us. "You first, Zaraiella."

"Get her good, Janice."

I was not reading tonight for sure. The only light was coming from the faithful moon, yet the swift winds kept turning the pages.

"Truth or dare?"

"Dare. Don't make me do something bad, or stupid."

"I dare you to…throw this bean into your mouth. Try to actually catch it in your mouth."

"Ouch."

Janice chuckled. "I said your mouth."

"Told you not to make me do something stupid, Janice."

"Guess it's my turn then. I am automatically going with the truth."

"Good. I was hoping you would say that," Janice says with a stretched smirk.

"Oh no, go easy on me."

"Is it true…that…you…and Jason, did it?"

"Really?" I hissed, barely spitting out my juice.

"Did what?" Zaraiella asked, with clueless written all over her face.

Janice chuckles. "You look so funny, Zaraiella, with one eye like a pirate. Did your sister, Munisha"

"That is too personal, okay. Next question."

"Come on, Munisha. It's just a game, answer it. Me and Zaraiella won't tell."

"If you want the truth then the answer is, no."

"No? Hmmm," Janice grimaces. "Are you lying?"

"I am telling you, Janice, no. Where would we do it? That is nasty, making love in a forest? There are bugs, dirt, and all that. Maybe when you two have someone, you can be all out there getting busy."

"I could imagine you with a big belly, then Jason holding it," Janice grins.

"Gosh, please. I am not ready for a baby. Being pregnant and pushing a baby out is a bit…horrifying."

"So, what about you…best friend, who made me hit myself in the eye. Truth or dare?"

"Truth, I don't do dares."

"I have one for her, sis. Tell us what the main truth you never ever told anyone."

"What? I don't get it," Janice said, scratching her head.

"Tell us what you won't tell anybody. That is a dare, but I wanted to ask that question and need the answer with your nosey self."

"That sounds better. Here it goes. I was born with half a heart."

"Oh no," Zaraiella gasped with her hands over her mouth. "Why, how?"

"It's nothing wrong with me. Just when I was a baby, my heart was acting weird. Mommy, and Daddy took me to the doctor, and they told us what it was. That is why they don't let me do the hard chores."

"Oh, tsk, that sucks," I said. "I mean, you didn't have to go and tell that. Zaraiella had a similar problem, I remember."

"My heart is bad too?"

"No, you were rushed to the hospital because you had bad pneumonia. Mom cried and Lakia calmed her down. Weird thing is, I never could remember us as babies playing together. Only us going to school together and being home talking. My brain is so foggy from that time."

"So, you never were sick, Munisha?" Janice asked.

"Definitely, not pneumonia like, Zaraiella. My heart is broken from not seeing my family. It is similar to a sickness that rarely heals, and no medications could cure it."

"Like my family always say, you can't give up hope."

"Sometimes you feel as though you do, and then you don't want to from that little speck of hope in your head somewhere. Anyways, you two can talk. I have some studying to do. I will try, I mean."

There is nothing to be ashamed of about Janice's condition. Everyone has their own problems along with born misfortunes. My life has not been slowed down or tampered from an illness. However, my thoughts are that I still have complete control of what haunts me and implants an ailment in my soul. As this book tells me about life. It informs us that we all have complete control, physically and mentally. We are our own masters in life.

"Morning, morning!"

"What? Huh?"

It could only be Mr. Wilson waking me while I rest soundly.

"You all fell asleep and still in one peace."

"I didn't even notice I fell asleep," I said, looking up at the dim stars. "What time is it?"

"Almost about five thirty. Me and Sara came out looking right when the lights went out. You all were talking, having a good time. Sara said give you all a few more minutes then bring you all inside."

"You should have told us. I could have had that…Lucky the spider crawl on me."

"After seeing how you all stayed up conversing with one another. I nodded off right there on the porch myself. Glad you all are alright. I don't even expect, Sara to be upset her husband never came to bed. I"

"Wait wait. Have to pee!"

"Hey, where you going?! Go inside the house!"

"Won't make it!" I drank all that darn pineapple juice last night. I am so surprised my mind just drifted off like that. Not one cricket didn't even make a sound. "Almost didn't make it, whew! Can't believe I slept with the bugs."

Wonder when it will start snowing. It feels even cooler this morning. Last night was fun too. Maybe we should all do it and have a fire next time. Get to know everyone better that way. "Wo, I didn't make those. Mr. Wilson's footprints must be. Geez, Zaraiella, almost gave me a heart attack. You okay?"

"Mr. Wilson told me that you had an emergency, and I ran."

I grinned. "Not that type of emergency. Just had to use the little girl's bush. Good thing I finished before you came."

"Why didn't you"

"Hello there!"

"Who said that?" I said, looking around the misty forest.

"Over here!"

"Who is that, Munisha?" Zaraiella whispered.

"I don't know. This is private property! You can't come here!"

"It's okay It's okay. I am just a man strolling through these quiet woods. You two are sisters?"

"Who are you?" I asked, standing in front of Zaraiella.

"I am a mercenary. Looking for citizens who may need some help. Where are your parents? Hey there, you're a pretty one."

"Go get, Mr. Wilson, Zaraiella."

"…Munisha."

"Just go."

Just by how he had his shirt tucked in, I knew he didn't belong here. How did he find where we live? "You cannot be here. I just told you this is a private area."

"Yes mam, but I am not a threat," the man implied as he held his hands up.

He has a gun.

"You look smart. Yes, I carry a weapon. That is important out here, especially when you do not know what is lurking to bite you in the ass. How about"

"Don't touch me!"

"Okay, okay. Where is your family?"

"They're coming," I spat.

"How many are there?"

"Why do you need to know? Just leave already. Leave us alone!"

He's dressed like someone who would be selling cars, gray shirt and black slacks, with combat boots. "That's the S.I.L.O logo. MR. WIL"

"You're not going anywhere!"

"Okay, please don't shoot me! What do you want from us?!"

"Just my job. Believe me, this is for your family own good once they come. My partner is late. Speaking of the devil."

"These woods are ridiculous," another man says with the same exact uniform. "What is the info on this one? Any others?"

"Her family is coming, but they are taking a mighty long time."

"She is a mean one, isn't she? What is your name, sweetheart?"

"None of your business. You all need to leave people alone. We are here, living our lives without harming anyone. Why do you have to bother us?"

"Told you already, it's our job."

"That's right. Let's go, the family should be near by. Damn mosquitoes."

"Show me where they are. Your little sister pretty much led the way. Hmm, you smell good. How do you"

BANG

"SHIT, CHRIS! COME OUT, OR SHE'S DEAD! I'M SERIOUS."

"I don't want to die. Help me!"

"Alright, let her go!" Mr. Wilson shouts. "What do you want?!"

"You killed my partner! I oughta' take your life too!"

"Whatever you want, we will give it. Do not, harm, the girl."

"Drop your weapon! I will put one in her head and two in yours once you miss with that rust shooter!"

"I am putting it on the floor. Do, not, shoot."

BANG

"AGH!"

Birds flew as the man voice echoed through the atmosphere.

"You alright, Munisha?" Mr. Wilson asked, helping me up.

"This stupid man!" I said, with tears building up. "Freaking asshole! Serves you right!"

"Go, Munisha. We'll take care of this. Nice shot son. Talk, who sent you here? Aw, you belong to S.I.L.O."

"He's from those pigs!" I said, watching the man in agony. "Kill him! Kill him now!"

"Calm down, Munisha. Help me take him to the stable, Jason."

"What?! Kill him! He tried to kill me and take us all!"

"Jason, help me with him, please."

From all of that, they want to keep him alive? All because I had to use the restroom in the bushes, S.I.L.O came for me. We need to get out of here as soon as possible. They know where we are.

"Are you alright, Munisha?" Mrs. Wilson asked. "Thank God nothing happened."

"This place, Mrs. Wilson. They know where we are!"

"Do not worry about it. Go inside and cool off."

"They put him in the barn. Can you believe that?! That is so stupid! Don't you think so?!"

Mrs. Wilson shook her head. "They must be asking him questions."

"He should have killed him. He could have killed me."

"Everything will be okay. Just…take it easy and cool off, as I said."

This family does the most idiotic things at times. I would have thought that, Mrs. Wilson understood where I was coming from. She needs to tell her husband what needs to be done.

"I heard what happened. I am sorry, Munisha."

"It is not your fault, Janice. This is unbelievable. I don't understand them. Thank you, Zaraiella. At least you did something right."

"What did, Daddy and Jason do?"

"They killed one of the guys; but they kept the other one alive. That doesn't make any sense."

"You are not supposed to kill anybody," Zaraiella murmured, looking down.

"So they could kill you, Zaraiella?! Didn't mean to yell. Just leave it alone. I have reading to do."

"We should just go downstairs, Zaraiella. She's upset."

What page was I? What page? "Oh yes. Azazel's Dust." I cannot even understand at all what these symbols are. "Thee substance of thine Earth grants plentiful talc. One must grant thine mind along with spirit to manipulate such a source. So that's the black powder that keeps getting on me."

So, this stuff does something, I suppose. She left a note that is not even legible. She must use it often. Maybe it was in the application she gave to help, Mr. Wilson. I want to give her this book back, however when I get deeper, it mesmerizes me to the point of not to.

"You two are done playing already?" I asked as the best friends entered the room, gazing at me.

"We are worried."

"I am glad you're okay, Munisha. I was so scared when you told me to get, Mr. Wilson. I didn't know what to do."

"You did what you were supposed to. The thing is, I am starting to lose patience with this place. Did they ever come back out?"

"No, I think they have him tied up in there. They closed the barn, and Janice almost got caught trying to look."

"I wanted to see what happened."

"That is what I am going to do."

"What?" Zaraiella said. "Don't go. You're going to get in trouble."

"I'll be fine sis. Just do a little eavesdropping and see what is really going on."

I know I wasn't crazy. Keeping him alive can only give him time to get away. Then S.I.L.O will be surely looking for the two. I must be still dreaming.

"Where are you going, Munisha?" Mrs. Wilson asks with a frown. "There is nothing to see. Tim is handling the issue."

"Just going out to ask your husband something. I am not going to start anything, I promise."

"Do not be led by hate, Munisha. I understand your frustration."

"Uh huh, thanks."

The thing we need to think of is really leaving here. Who knows when more will show up? They are pretending like these people won't raid our home.

"You think you all are safe here? You're not!" the soldier spat as his arms pulled from the barn pole connected to the roof. "You all are dead once they find out me and my partner are missing. Just you wait. You and those girls are under, System In Lives Omni. There is no hiding!"

"Dad. I think we shouldn't tie him to this. He might try to pull the whole thing down."

"Don't worry about it son. I still want to know; how did you find us?"

"Take another guess then, pops. It really doesn't matter. We know where you and your family are, we will always know!"

"We will be back later. We have to figure out what to do with that body. Pass me that sack, over there, Jason."

"You can't keep me in here, old man! You are only making things harder!"

"There, he will be good like this now."

"You sure he won't get away?" Jason queried. "I think we should tie him with a chain."

"If the horse cannot break these ropes, neither can he."

I just don't understand why they are keeping him alive. "Oh no. This can only mean they will send more here then."

"Hey!" Jason yells.

I didn't think he would look over to the other side of the barn.

"Are you okay, Munisha? Dad doesn't want us out here."

"Your dad…" I shook my head. "What is wrong with him?"

"We're taking care of it, M. Don't worry about it. You were lucky earlier. Hey, why do you always have to be so grouchy? Can't you be content with anything?"

"Jason, I am worried, okay? Something about keeping him alive just…bothers me."

Jason sighs. "I know what you mean. We can't kill him. He is"

"One of them? Tsk, those people are evil, and you know it."

"We know that, but you have to understand we need to play our cards right or we won't be able to know what they are up to. Think about it. If we kill him, we take away the ability to know what S.I.L.O next moves are. Then suppose if more do come. We need something to bribe them with, if that is possible. Dad went out and took the body of the other soldier and disposed of it."

"This is bad," I said, shaking my head in frustration. "I don't know what to say or what to do right now."

"You're going to leave?"

"Don't know yet. The idea of me staying, I used to be skeptical. Now time is already running out. You know they are coming, and it is like you all don't care."

"The thing about it is, we can't do anything about it. Where will we go? Where, Munisha? This is the best for now. You have seen with your own eyes as you made fun of my legs in the car that whole night. The world is changing, and it is doing so, so fast. Be patient. That is all I can say. How about you come inside? There is nothing to look at out here."

"I'm looking at the sky. It's a beautiful sight how we can see the moon, even in the daylight. It's always up there alone peacefully. I admire it."

"Y'know…when he had you hostage. My heart felt like someone stuck their hand and squeezed it. I was lucky enough to get him in his leg. You don't know how I felt. Imagine losing your best friend with whom you always enjoy playing uno or checkers. Better yet, training your heart out with. That could lead you to insanity like how I lost, Hercules."

"Aww," I blushed. "Did you cry for me?"

"If anything had happened to you, I would have. My eyes didn't even gaze upon your new hairstyle fully. Janice did a better job than I thought."

"Zaraiella too. Wait, what do you mean better than you thought?"

"I told her to give you a certain style. I told her you would look amazing with it, and I was two hundred percent correct. They gave my Pocahontas the style which is the most beautiful of all," Jason said, caressing my cheek.

He always knew how to get to me. To make me smile even when I was mad at the world. "You're nothing but a sweet talker, you know that? How did you figure out the style? I know she's not on that particular level to do something like this yet or to come up with it. Are you serious?! How long have you had this?"

"When we went to the strip mall," Jason says as he smirks and rubs his hair. "That model I saw caught my eye and she looked like you. I told Janice to give you this to make you even more perfect."

"…You are weird are weird, but I like it. Just never, ever let me catch you looking at any other female."

"M, we're in the middle of nowhere, where the hell will I find anyone? Hmph, now go upstairs and get some sleep. Everything will be fine. I promise."

He is something else. I guess we have one more thing in common. "By the way, Jason. You have good taste."

Boys are so dangerous. He clearly took my mind off what happened by his flirts and handsome smile. Long time ago, Mrs. Wilson did give me that lesson and told me to be so careful. They will do things to get your mind off something, then on them. I never really understood it, till now. Stay focused is what I need. Love will come at its time. I am afraid of giving my heart so easily when it already has holes that need patching.

"Still up, sis? Who gave you the candle? I thought they said they didn't want us with one."

"Mrs. Wilson gave it to me, and then she said blow it out once I'm done," Zaraiella says as she continues writing. "Are you feeling better?"

"Actually, my head hurts from reading this thing on and off all day."

"Your head is going to be so big. That is what happens when you read a lot."

"Ha, according to Jason, my head is already big."

"…He really loves you."

"You think so? He likes my new style a lot, I can say that. Just don't be talking to Janice about us having sex or anything. I won't give myself up that easily. Remember, Mrs. Wilson taught us, women should wait for the right man, or we can gain unwanted sexual ties. I do want my first to be my last."

Zaraiella grins. "You two are going to get married. Jut watch."

"Is that something you have envisioned or you're just being funny?"

"Just a thought," Zaraiella smirked. "I hope to find someone and get married one day."

"You will, sis. Just make sure he is an amazing guy. Be sure he takes care of you too. Like for instance, closing these windows. I don't understand how you're not..."

"What is it? Munisha?"

"Be right back, sis. Stay here."

That has to be the same one I saw before we left that night to the city. I felt it that is why it drew me to the window. It wanted something.

"Gosh, it is dark out here. Where did it go? Could have sworn, oh shoot. Hey, um…I saw you that day. Now you're staring at me through the window?"

This wasn't an ordinary creature, was it actually a wolf? If my eyes weren't playing tricks on me, the creature had black smoke flowing from it's body. Then those sapphire eyes I can see miles away. "Sooo, guess you want food? You know it's cold out here. If you're hungry, I can bring you some food. Okay, I am going back in. We have something for you."

"GRrrr."

"Guess not. What do you want me to do? You growl when I walk away. Wow," I chuckled. "I am having a convo with a wolf. You want me to follow you? Is that it? Okay, just don't get me killed."

I can feel it's energy even though the temperature out here was near freezing. This wolf really persuaded me to walk through a dark forest. "Where are we going? Like you could understand what I'm saying. Crap! Spider web went right into my face. Hope where you're taking me is for a good reason. Then hopefully"

"GRRrrr."

"Okay, sorry. I'll shut up."

Should have known this wasn't a good idea. What in the world was I thinking? We have been walking for a good twenty minutes probably. "I see. Why did you bring me here?" I murmured, starring at the small light coming from the old miniature house.

"GRR ruff."

This sure wasn't an ordinary creature. "Okay, okay, I'll go inside. Hello?"

"Deary, Munisha," Ms. Jezebel says with a huge smile. "So lovely to see you once more. Come in, come in. How is your soul feeling?"

So funny she didn't have one lock secured. Also noticed her hair never seemed to grow. Maybe Janice can make a wig for her. "Up and down. This is so weird."

"What is, as you call weird, child? You attending this late is abnormal? You still attended with great energy."

"Something like that," I sighed. "My mind can be so tricky at times. I literally followed a wolf. What was I thinking?"

"You followed your instinct, that is all," Ms. Jezebel says as she pours hot liquid inside a cup for her.

"He's not even outside. How did he manage to bring me here like this?"

"That creature there is a dear friend of mine. He kindly guards over the area for me. If bad energy comes around, he wards it off. So intelligent, so spectacular, can you agree?"

"Sure. I see you are not making that smelly stuff. That would keep me in the restroom. Sorry, didn't mean to insult your food."

"It is well, deary. Come, have a seat."

"Wait, so you mean to tell me you sent that, I guess it's a wolf, to get me? That's"

"Abnormal? Tell me, Munisha. What is strange to you? A creature along with a beast, has its own mind and feelings, just as we do."

"Conscious. Everything has a conscious, so thy shall respect thine abilities."

"Swell," Ms. Jezebel lightly claps. "You have been dissecting my lessons thoroughly."

"You know I forgot the book. If I knew that, I mean…the wolf was bringing me here, I would have brought it back to you."

"That is completely fine. You just do not have it just to stare at the outside as you spoke of before. You are comprehending what is on the inside, which contains the normal."

"The book has given me a lot of understanding of what life is, how you can make things work for you. I am on the chapter where it speaks of that powder stuff."

"I believe you are speaking of Azazel's dust," Ms. Jezebels nods her head. "Very powerful. It takes more than the mind to channel it suitably. Let me set this spoon down, seems I have stirred it long enough. Let you enjoy a taste shortly. Now, where is it? There should be some in this cabinet. I keep plenty of my variables around as you have witnessed. Hold out your hand, deary."

"Agh, It's hot! Oh shoot! It disappeared. Did that stuff just catch fire in my hands? How did you do that?"

"This substance in my hand harvests itself along with a mixture of herbs. As you continue your studies, it will show you how it is made. How it can be manipulated."

"If I learn to use it properly, can I teach my sister too?"

"Take into consideration, deary. Those without an open mind will have difficulty understanding foreign forces."

"That's right. She's too young to understand anyways. I keep her away from looking inside."

"That is good. Let me help you hasten your knowledge. Hold your hands out, please," Ms. Jezebel smiles. "I will not scorch you, deary. Close your eyes. Think of something you love, then something your emotions despises, swiftly."

"Zaraiella, my sister."

"Despise…hate?" Ms. Jezebel whispered.

"…S.I.L.O. Oh my god! That is amazing! How did it glow like that?"

"Your emotions altered swiftly child. You will learn as you proceed."

The dust colors shifting from bronze to golden, then turning into flames. I have to learn this. "Hey, this is kind of what was on the wolfs body. I should have noticed how the glittering colors levitated from it's body. It's like the dust. What can I use this stuff for again?"

Ms. Jezebel just smirked, seeing and believing I was interested in her ways. "Feed your mind with my knowledge and my studies will grant you everything. It will explain all that is needed. Be cautious as well, as you witnessed it has ways to be destructive."

"I saw. Wish I could use it on S.I.L.O, every single last one of them," I hissed. "Can you believe my people keeps one in the stable? I think that is so stupid."

"Truly? Their army are devouring everything in their path. They are evil at its finest. Your face tells me you're disgusted by them. As you should be."

She knows so much, but yet she stays in the isolated woods. "Do you think…my Mom, is still alive?"

"Close your eyes once again, child. Let my mind affix to yours. Hold still. My spirit tells me…she is home."

"Crap," I said as the powder sparked. "I am so sorry. Didn't know I still had some on my hands. This stuff is no joke."

"That is your first lesson on using Azazel's dust properly. Control your thoughts along with emotions, and you will master it with a swift of a finger," Ms. Jezebel says, snapping a flame from her thumb.

All of this I have learned from one place. I learned nothing from Mr. Wilson's place, but to eat healthy and be isolated. There must be a way for me to get this knowledge down quicker. Now a long walk back with my good friend, Mr. Mystic Wolf.

CHAPTER 18

Take Me Away

You know you might take off spinning it so fast like that, M. "I've gotten that good, huh? Do you really think you can kill someone using one of these?"

"Y'know, Dad always claims this is one of the best weapons for self-defense, yet offense too. This is not just a thing we do when we're out here training. Why do you keep cut up your shirt like that?"

"Because I like to feel the cool air on my body. You have a problem with it? I didn't get a chance to get enough crop tops from the store, so I managed to make my own. Anyways, that day when you and Mr. Wilson got those soldiers. You guys didn't use these."

"Come one, M," Jason chuckles. "This is worse than a knife to a gun fight. Though, if my training was up to part, I probably could have whacked him from behind with it."

"I feel so unsafe with him here. I just don't know how you all are sleeping well when that he's alive in there."

"Hmph, M. We have to start cutting wood soon. It's that time of the year," Jason says.

"I will leave that to the man. Women, we nurture while you men work."

"Guess that means you don't feed the baby. That is work, is it not?"

"Nurturing is caring for something, not necessarily doing labor. Boy, you all are so naïve at times."

"And you women, if not all the time, are gullible. You didn't like that, did you?"

"Chicken legs... Hey, what are you two dong?"

"We have to bring him food. Mr. Wilson told us to."

"No way! He has my little sister and yours feeding him now. Isn't this ridiculous, Jason?!" I grimaced.

"They just throw him his plate, M. He eats from the ground technically. Dad I guess let them do it because Janice is in there with the cows all the time, and he's not cutting that rope. Your sister is in there too, so they shouldn't have any issues. Dad wants us all to learn and become more mature. You should see that by now."

I was wondering when he was going to stop making up excuses. "You see, I just don't get you all. It has been three days since he's been here. What are we going to do? Keep him here and feed him till he is fat, sitting on the ground tied up? Surprised his friends didn't come for him yet."

"Like I said. It is up to, Dad. We do not make the rules."

I rolled my eyes and spun my staff. "That is why the time is coming, and we are getting out of here."

"You say that all the time. You don't make a move because you are still skeptical about whether to go. Why are you so grouchy today? My mistake. You are always grouchy, Pocahontas."

"Maybe, because I don't see any sense of this. Or maybe because my hair is kind of tight. Janice and Zaraiella did a good job, but these braids are kind of irritating."

"I love them on you, it brings out the true Munisha in my opinion."

"You two took long enough," I said.

"We had to feed him, Munisha. He is kind of funny. Isn't he, Zaraiella?"

"What is funny about him? He is a apart of S.I.L.O. Why would you two even feed him?"

"Me and Zaraiella just put the plate on the ground, and he eats it on his stomach."

I just needed to know for myself, not just take Jason's word. "He put too much trust in people, I see."

"Daddy watches us. Just this time he told us to go do it. He's trusting us. He told Zaraiella she is very pretty and looks like a princess."

I shook my head. "That isn't funny, especially with my own sister."

"That is not all," Janice giggled.

I saw nothing funny about any of this. "Then what was he saying, Janice?"

"Don't tell her, Janice. It's mean."

"He said, why is your belly out and it's cold? He said you're squishy."

Jason chuckles, looking the other way. "Damn..."

"Shut up, Jason! One day we will see who's laughing. That is another reason we need him out of here. Then he's flirting with my little sister."

All those two did is jump around as if there was not worry in the world. I didn't like any of this.

"Dad will do something soon. Think about it, M. Dad knows he has to go. I guarantee you it's on his mind every second. Give it some time, and when we do it, it will be for the best. I will train for a few more minutes, then I have some, other things to attend to."

In the back of my mind lately. I have wanted to go back to the mall. Been wanting some new clothes lately. "I wish I could slap the hell out of him for looking at my sister and criticizing me. I lost weight so I don't know what he's talking about."

"Oh come on, you're perfect the way you are, M. Stop focusing on that, or even irrelevant people. You don't see me losing sleep over my legs when you ridicule them."

"Jason, women are more entuned about their bodies and features. Try to understand how I feel."

Jason chuckles as he puts his arms around me. "You are beautiful, no matter what anyone says. I will show it to you one day, and it won't be from a mirror."

"From what, your words?"

"You will see it one day. Just wait, be patient and trust me."

Only once in school, someone antagonized me from how chinky my eyes were. Did not pay him attention at all. However, my body is something I feel so delicate with. Besides Zaraiella, never have someone spoken on how my body or features till now. He needs to go. "What else did you all hear from that peasant? I know he told you all more things."

"He just said something that he wanted to leave. Oh yea, he told me and Zaraiella, that he will get ice cream for us if we let him go."

"Tsk, this is so stupid. He needs to be six feet under or I'll do it myself."

Janice's eyes said that she knew from my demeanor it would happen.

"Hey, um…found this you might want," Janice says, handing me a scroll.

"A map? Guess this could be of some use. What made you get this for me?"

"Zaraiella told me that you all would leave soon. Daddy always had it in one of the drawers, he doesn't need it."

"Thanks, Janice. This should help more since I kind of have it planned out already. You see here, this is where we will go. Just north to Canada. It will be so much better there, I know it."

"Those people are everywhere," Janice shrugs. "That's what Mommy said."

"Maybe not. How would they know? All respect to her, but Mrs. Wilson nor Mr. Wilson knows about anything out there. Unless they have actually seen it before. Jason told me the same thing before. The world is so big. Then we are living here away from people. I still don't think, if there is any, people living like we do. It's too hard." I sighed. "My conscious is clear, and it tells me that life is out there. Wish you all could see that too."

"Zaraiella doesn't want to go. I can see it in her face all the time."

"Remember in the geography book. It shows how beautiful Niagara Falls is. Freedom, Janice."

"That would mean you and Jason would have to separate. He isn't going to like that, and he's my brother, so I know."

"It is not much with how we feel about it. He is an amazing guy and all; he will find someone. Just as I will once in a new place."

Janice shrugs, "Well, I'm going to go see if Mommy needs help with anything."

I will find life one day. Even if I have to remove someone from it, physically or mentally.

"What are you reading now, Munisha? You're stuck in it."

"Wouldn't you like to know, sis?" I said, turning the page.

"You stay in your book and won't say a word for hours. Why? You never really talk about it. Just showed me a few pictures."

"It is saying to…as a matter of fact, it is saying to use fury on those who try to manipulate or destroy you. One day I hope your mind will be open to this so you can understand it. I haven't seen a flaw yet in this book."

"What is it? I don't understand. Destroy people…that isn't good. People should"

"Your mind is not ready, Zaraiella, trust me. The things I am learning from this book is extravagant. My spirit is telling me just to go out there and end it right now."

"End what?"

"Nothing, sis. You just stay doing what you are doing."

"Your eyes…they are, funny colored."

"Really?" I asked. "That is weird. Maybe I need some more carrots in my diet. Be right back."

What is she talking about? "Oh my gosh," I murmured. "It is…different. Looks almost purple, both of them."

Something with that book is tampering with my eyes. I know it has to be. I have to worry about it later. Right now, for business.

"Hey, why are you going in there?"

Crap, why does he have to be so nosey? "Let me go talk to him, Jason. You watched me when I had put my staff back. I am not going to do anything."

Jason frowns. "Talk? Hmph, okay. Hurry up. Hold up!"

"What's wrong with you? Oh…"

I almost forgot about my new lenses.

"Your eyes are different."

"My sister was just saying the same thing. Don't really know why it's like that, just getting older I guess."

"Don't mind it. Just ask him what you will ask him, and then we are out of here. Dad will lock up soon."

"Whose there?" the S.I.L.O soldier asked, squirming on the dirt floor.

"Shut up!"

"Oh, it's you son. How are you?"

"Better than you are," Jason says with a serious face and arms folded. "We're here to ask you some questions."

"Have I not answered your questions? What is it now? You cannot take any more info if I do not have it. Can you take this stink crap off of my face? Your pappy is a real one," the soldier chuckled.

"Never mind all of that. I want to be clear about something. Do not ever look at my sister in an unmannered way again. I will cut your balls off, I swear to god. Second, don't ever ridicule me. I am not the one."

"Yes, mam. Oh, I get it. She told you what I said. It was just a joke, sweetheart"

"Shut up! Enough about my sister you pervert. Now, what is S.I.L.O trying to do? Why are they doing this to everyone?"

"S.I.L.O is the new world regime; we are the future. We are omniscient. I told you degenerates this five times already. Let me go and I probably will give good feedback about this smelly ass place."

He doesn't know his life is about to end. Maybe I should take the bag off for him. "Why are they doing this to people just trying to make a living? People are just trying to live, and you all are taking life away."

"That is just the way it is. We are not living in the early two thousands, sweetheart. This day and age is to make life superb, just wait until we find the dominant lifeform. I doubt it is you all. Your lives are…"

"Lives are what?" I asked.

"I am guessing your brother saved you and got me in the leg. I didn't want to pull the trigger on a helpless girl, but I can't wait to look you in the eye and get you back the same way my friend."

"You're not going to do anything," I snapped. "Now answer the question. You are already a dead man. It's been a while, and no one has come and found you yet. Or haven't you noticed? So, I would be careful about what I say if I were you."

"M, that's enough. We have to"

"Tsk, move Jason. Better yet."

"Oh…you look angry. I can tell you're a feisty one! I love that. I'm not scared of no little girl or some old man with his little punk son! AGH! SHIT!"

I grinned. "Yea, that wound still hurts, I see."

"M, don't do that," Jason says, pulling my arm. "We're not supposed to be in here in the first place."

"Call your dog off of me son! Get er'!"

"Tell us what you mean about people lives," I said.

"You idiots! Use your damn heads. Living in this world where S.I.L.O is universal, you have to be living at least on the mid side of the pyramid. No minorities, like you all, as pest hiding out. You all deserve to either be vassals or dead. If they find you, possibly use your blood, then you may be lucky to be tested on."

"What are you talking about? Testing on people?" Jason asked, as though he doesn't already know.

"Where have you…oh wait. You all are isolated out here; you would not know what's going on. You all will figure it out soon enough. I promise you that. Those two little girls probably have more sense. Hey, whose the light skin one with the hair almost tot the floor? She's damn sure a pretty one and has more such a cute AGH, shit," the soldier grinned.

"Keep my sister from out of your mouth! You know what?! That's why I wanted to look you in the eye. You're pathetic! Tsk, we're wasting time here! Move, Jason! He has to die! I'm going to slit his freaking throat!"

"Keep your doggy on a leash, son!" the soldier chuckled.

"What the hell?! What the hell you all doing?!"

"Crap!" Jason frowns, then looks me. "Nothing, Dad. We just wanted to ask him something."

"Get out of here, both of you!" Mr. Wilson says, holding the barn door open.

"HEY, DAD! LET ME OUT OF HERE, WILL YA?! I'M WILLING TO PUT A GOOD WORD IN FOR YOU ALL! WELL, THE HELL WITH YOU ALL THEN!"

"I don't need anyone playing games with him!" Mr. Wilson says, placing on the padlock.

"Mr. Wilson, that guy is a pervert! Why are you letting him live?"

"Because."

"Because of what?! Then you have my little sister giving him food! He should be dead! What's wrong with you?!"

"Munisha! Enough!" Mr. Wilson growls.

I knew they had to be doing something bizarre in that building. Those people that went crazy right in front of the actual soldiers had an exceptional reason. Loved ones are being tested on, and just hand picking people as though they are flowers. Definitely a sick world.

* * * *

"I got one! Hope it's something good. This really isn't my thing."

"It is, M. You just need more patience. It will always come to you. Great, a salmon!"

"Whoopty do," I said, rolling my eyes. "We have been out here for an hour. Let's go back."

"A little bit more time, then we will leave. You still need to get yours," Jason says, trying to unhook our dinner.

"I am kind of cutting down on the meat, you know. I am transitioning more into a plant based diet."

"I don't think my taste buds are as strong as yours just to eat greens all day. Fish are everything to me. This hook will not come out of your mouth, won't it?"

"From what I have learned. You should not eat fish without scales."

"Who told you that?" Jason frowns.

"Something I've read. It said they are unclean. For instance, like shrimp, it's bad to eat because they are like roaches of the sea."

"Only place where you get that info from is that silly book you keep reading. Couldn't even understand what that stuff was saying."

"Who told you, you had permission to look inside?"

"One day, you fell asleep on the porch, and you had that ridiculous heavy thing lying on you. I picked it up aaaaand, took a little peek to see what was so special about it. You should return it to wherever you got it from and I already know who."

"Tsk. Whatever. You didn't comprehend it, that's why. Those who are not open minded to something, they will not understand it. That is why my poor sister who goes to feed a complete stranger, a monstrosity, isn't ready for it."

"They don't do it often. Only when they are going inside to do their chores. I don't think Dad wants them speaking to him anyways."

"That is so crazy to me. Feeding someone who wants to kill us. Just yesterday he told us what they are doing. Those people deserve to be six feet under, not six pounds heavier."

"You have a point. They are crazy."

"Of course, I have a point they oh shoot! It's a big one!"

"Reel em on in Pocahontas!" Jason claps.

If it is one of those sweet tasting fish, I may just have a bite or two.

"Aww, that is cute. Looks like a baby Blue Gill."

"You might as well take it off and toss it back. I don't really care for it as much anyways."

"Yea, we will be back when he is three years older! This is what he meant."

"Who meant?"

"When Dad said to you that you don't get it. He was basically saying that all life is worth living. No matter who, what, or what they have done."

"Oh gosh, not with the foolery right now, Jason."

"No, listen," Jason said, casting back out. "Life is precious. That is Dad's motto. We haven't witnessed much life yet. We may not see it because we are, you know, young. Only surrounding us in this forest. That man in there, laying on his back or stomach tied to a rail has a life right now. That is the least we can give him."

"I still don't get it. Just let him live with us? Is that what you are saying?"

Jason sides eye me. "Not necessarily. That guy belongs to an organization that has corrupted the world, yes. He can be used in different ways as such."

"Like feeding him like a cow?" I frowned.

"See, once again, only thinking of the negatives, M. That will not help to see what you need. Dad had to think about this hard. Me, him, and Mom. We decided to keep him alive just in case we need to use him for bribery, as I told you before."

"Bribery? Bribe S.I.L.O with him so they won't take us?"

Jason sighs. "Yes. That is basically what it boils down to. He is a part of S.I.L.O, a soldier at that. He probably has the chip in him."

"Chip? Oh my gosh. It's been so long. It kind of slipped my mind."

"If he has that chip in him. Hmph, Dad told me to keep this within the circle. If he has that implanted in his body, those people already know exactly where we are."

"What?! Are you kidding me?" I sighed. "It's only a matter of time."

"M, calm down"

"I told you we needed to get rid of him when he first came."

"M! It wouldn't do any justice. Where he is marked last, that satellite or whatever they have will pinpoint him exactly where the house is. That is why we need to play it safe and play our cards right. Trust me, I know this is crazy, but it's really the only way right now. Get me?"

"No…not really. So many issues are going on, it's hard to figure things out."

"I know exactly what you mean," Jason says, pointing his finger at me. "Just know we will be ready for anything if we think ahead. Dad always taught me that. Also, they haven't come and it's been almost a week. Probably forgot about the bastard. Welp, time to end this outing. Nothing didn't hit the line yet. Your eyes are back to the same color, by the way."

"Thanks, I didn't know why it did that before."

"Age, but you age uniquely, Pocahontas. I just…hey you!"

"Who is it?" I muttered, looking behind me.

"I just saw a boy. He ran that way over there towards the swamp."

"I don't see anyone. Your dad wanted us to bring back three fish, we have two."

"That is okay, I am more concerned of who that was."

"Maybe we will find him on our way back. It looks like it is about to rain, so we need to be heading back now. My braids cannot get soaked, or I am for sure taking them out then."

"Don't you have to take it out soon?"

"Maybe in a month or so wo, you see. Told you I saw a little kid."

"Hey," I said, squatting in front of the little boy. "Why are you out here alone? Are you lost?"

"Is he okay?"

The young boy, younger than my sister looked like he was not from around here at all. His clothes similar to the dark ages, yet his eyes, they were like mine in a sense.

אותך צריכה שלך המשפחה, הביתה לך

"What what? Can you understand that? Jason?"

"He's speaking…something. I have no clue. Wait, that's He brew."

הביתה לך

"Wait! Catch him, Jason! He could get killed out here."

"Tsk, I am not running after a kid. He said something about, family."

"He could probably get lost. Never knew you knew another language. What other secrets are you hiding, Mister?" I said, tapping Jason's shoulder.

"I don't know much, just the basics. Mom is half Jewish so I know a little. Still, something to tell everyone once we're back. It is always something we run into when we are out here the majority of the time, I'll say. Reckon that even Mom knows she can't keep us in. We need to learn to survive out here. Regardless of getting into trouble, we are almost adults."

"Technically, you are. You are seventeen now, right? How does it feel to be an old man?"

Jason taps his curly hair. "Hmmm, feels great! My mental state is tough as steel, much stronger, wiser, and with Pocahontas at my side."

"What does that mean?"

"With you…it takes a lot, M…it takes a lot."

I grinned. "Oh, shut up."

It is weird that the boy came and just ran back through the forest. He must know where he was going even though he looked ten years old. He didn't seem like a average kid, he just looked at me then ran away. The forest summons so many things.

"I am glad we have some good fish to eat for tonight."

"That is on you all. I will ask Mrs. Wilson to make me some of that good vegetable soup. Back then, my cravings were only for mac n cheese with nuggets."

"How do you feel eating actual real foods? Not that garbage what society provides for you?"

"Well…when you are smaller, you tend to not really care. As you grow, it dawns on you that the effects of what you consume have consequences on your body, even down the line."

"When you leave, you will have learned a lot from here," Jason says, looking into my eyes.

"It would be a dead lie if you haven't. Trust me, I am very satisfied for what you all given my sister and me. She is still a little upset about it, she will get over it soon. We all have to grow up sooner or later."

"Hey, Dad! We didn't do as bad the last time. What's wrong with the generator?"

"It is always something," Mr. Wilson says, frowning. "I cannot figure out what it is. At a time like this, we need it for the cold tonight. It is always something when you need your equipment the most. It just somehow wants to break on its own. Darn it!"

"Looks like we will be freezing out here then. Tsk, help me mother nature!" I said lifting my hands to the sky.

"Just give it time, Munisha. I will have it up and running before dark, hopefully."

"Hope so. I have so much reading to do. Guess I better take care of it now."

From how long we have been living here, the generator just now giving out on us, makes sense. Things and especially life gives out when you least expect it, especially when it's out of date. This place, it is another reason for us to move on.

"Mrs. Wilson. I'm already anticipating you already heard the bad news."

"Did not hear it. I saw it when the toaster kept the bread inside."

"It was on my mind while me and Jason were on our way back. Could you make some of that vegetable soup for me? That is my alltime favorite around here."

"If my husband can get that forsaken machinery working, I certainly will."

"I have forgotten that I need to learn a few things about cooking. I have no skills whatsoever," I grinned.

"There is always time to learn," Mrs. Wilson smirked.

"Don't know how much. We are leaving very soon, I believe."

"Have you made your mind up on where to?"

"Going up north to Canada. There is where our life will begin again. I know how I do not have any license, but me and Zaraiella will figure it out."

"Whatever your heart desires. Just make sure it is just as I always tell you."

"I will always remember that. Whatever sent us to you all long ago really knew what it was doing. Never would have believed we would grow up living on a…you know, a farm."

Mrs. Wilson smiles. "That is favor, Munisha. The creator always watches over those who are young. That is why when you two relocate, all things will come into place in your favor. Those are my prayers for you all."

"Thanks. Janice and Zaraiella must be doing their hair salon thing again."

"You do not plan to take out those braids anytime soon, do you?"

"Not really. I love the style."

"So does my son," Mrs. Wilson says, folding her arms with a frown led with a smirk. "He will not stop looking at you. What did you do to my son? Huh?"

"Stop making me blush, Mrs. Wilson."

"It is true, you know it. Just, remember if you two ever come to marry, you will take care of him, as he will for you."

I will definitely miss, Mrs. Wilson. Mom will never be replaced; Mrs. Wilson was definitely her substitute. How do these girls do their hair all day, every day? Zaraiella probably is in her poetry. I should get her to learn to cook as well, so I won't be the only one doing the catering in our own place. "Janice, what are you doing?"

"Looking for the camera. The one, Zaraiella always have."

"She doesn't keep in the drawer. It's in the closet. Where is she anyways?"

"She's outside. She told me to go upstairs and get the camera while she milked the cow. She wanted me to take a picture of her doing it since you all are planning to leave. I just couldn't find"

"Hold on. She's in the stable?"

"Yes, silly," Janice giggles. "The Cow is in the barn."

"Oh my god..."

"What's wrong!"

Why would she leave her in there by herself?

"Munisha!" Mrs. Wilson snapped, grabbing my arm. "You're running like there's a fire."

"How long has she been out there?!"

"Calm down...now who?"

"Zaraiella! I thought Janice and her were inside."

"Not sure. What's the matter?"

"What the hell!" I said, pushing the door open. "There better not be anything going on. I swear to god!"

"Munisha…Munisha! Where are you going young lady?"

Why don't he just mind his own business?

"I said no one can go inside the stable without my permission! I am trying to work out here and you're being disobedient!"

"I'll see what's wrong with her Dad. Yo, M!"

"What the hell! EYGH! GET OFF OF HER! GET OFF OF MY SISTER! ZARAIELLA!"

"Help me, Munisha! Mmmhh."

"Nobody move! I will slit her throat faster than a heartbeat."

"Help me, Munisha mhmmh!"

"Let her go," I mumbled, raising my hands. "Just…let my little sister go. Please."

"Your little sister, she is a unique one. Check this out. I am going to walk out of this barn, and I'm getting the hell out of this place."

"Don't hurt her, please," I said, as the water began to surface eyelids. "She is all I have."

"If everything goes smoothly, you have my word. Be a good girl, okay? Walk back, both of you…walk back."

There was nothing I can do. That knife almost piercing her little throat as they both slowly stepped.

"You can't get away with this. Me and my father will hunt you down," Jason says as he held me from behind. "Better for you to let her go."

"Trust me, son, I am getting out of here as we speak. Just a few more steps, and I'm back to civilization. I was about to say I'm taking the horse. Ha, where did you all get the car from? I know you all can't afford that. We're taking the wheels."

"Jason, Munisha, get back," Mr. Wilson whispered. "Let her go. We'll handle this another way. Take the car and let her go."

"Pops, I want the keys! Pretty little, Zarale here, is riding shotgun."

"No deal!" Mr. Wilson replied. "You are not taking the girl."

"Do not play with me, old man!"

"Alright alright, take it easy. That is a child. I will get what you want."

"No games. Last time I was too lenient. Not this time."

"Agheyh," Zaraiella cried out.

"JUST LET HER GO!" I shouted.

"I'll go get the keys, Dad. I know where they are. I know where they are, M," Jason winked.

I couldn't stand to see my sister in so much distress. If I saw blood, then I am coming for him.

"Make a move, any of you and she's dead, I promise you. I am ready to get back to decency. Had me sitting in that stink barn with chickens jumping on my damn head at night. I oughta' cut you first old man! Where the hell is that punk little son of yours?! I'M READY TO GO RIGHT NOW!"

"Why can't you just leave us all alone?!" I wailed. "My sister is only thirteen years old. How could you be so disgusting?!"

"Really?" the soldier said, sniffing on Zaraiella's hair. "She's a ripe one too."

"I'M GOING TO KILL YOU! I SWEAR TO GOD I AM! Mr. Wilson…no."

"Hold on to er' now, her sister will have it! I know you don't want that for pretty little thing here. She is still…in once piece. Pretty little thing, Jesus," the soldier said, as he popped a kiss to Zaraiella's head.

"Here, now take the car and leave." Jason said, throwing the small hoop.

The soldier chuckled. "Now I know you all stole it. Poor degenerate leaches. Get in through my side and in the passenger seat, pretty little thing. This baby should get me back in no time. You all will be having a visit soon. Just know that."

"Dad, here," Jason whispered.

"Nice work. Wait on my go, Jason. Do what he says, Zaraiella! Everything will be okay!"

"See you all soon."

"Now!"

BANG BANG BANG

Gunshots tearing up the left side of Mom's car. I couldn't believe this. "Zaraiella!"

"Hey! You alright you alright?!" Mr. Wilson shouted.

"Oh my god, Zaraiella! Get out! I just can't believe this."

"She's alright, Munisha. Jason, give me a hand with this one. Have to dispose of him quickly.

"How could I be so stupid? Come on, sis! I am so sorry. I should have never gone out. I'm so sorry, Zaraiella."

"M…".

"Don't touch me! You all are so stupid! I swear! Come on, Zaraiella, we are leaving. This is too much."

My mind cannot wrap around what just happened. Why did Janice leave her out there by herself? They were always together, now the moment they're separated this happened?

"Zaraiella, get cleaned up. It is going to be okay. I will be waiting outside. He didn't hurt you? Did he?"

"Sniff…no. Just, my neck hurts a little. I"

"Get cleaned up so we can leave."

Just hearing her small voice whimper, elevated me to another level. This place has to be the most oblivious and selfish place ever. How can they not know she was still in there? I hate this place; I hate this world. I hate even sometimes living. My head is throbbing as if a thousand horses are stampeding around it. What have I done to deserve a life like this? Nothing goes right. Looking at myself in the mirror, I see uncertainty, wonder, and most of all, pain. "Take out these stupid braids. That is the first thing I will do."

Knock Knock Knock

"Zaraiella…Munisha?" Janice murmured.

"What is it? We are busy."

"Is…Zaraiella okay? I am sorry, I didn't know."

"You are sorry," I said, opening the door. "Along with everyone else here. It could have been more severe than it was but thank god it wasn't. Tsk, pathetic people."

"But…I didn't know," Janice whimpered, wiping her eyes. "What did he do to her? She wasn't hurt when I saw her."

"Just go, Janice. Me and Zaraiella are leaving in the morning. Maybe even earlier than your stupid father when he is up."

"Hey, sniff…that isn't nice!"

"Go away, Janice. Just go!"

"Zaraiella? I'm…"

"Why are you yelling at, Janice?" Zaraiella says, frowning. "I said I am okay."

"Don't worry about it. We are leaving tomorrow. I don't even care if people see that the glass is broken and with bullet holes to the side. People will mind their business as we move on to a much safer place. Tired of this crap. Find your bookbag or anything you could put clothes in. I will do us the favor right after I get my hair fixed back to my true style. Should have left this place a long time ago. Procrastinating hurts people."

Years we have been here, the only thing that will be memorable to me here is Betsy, Ms. Jezebel, and of course, that mystic wolf. The creatures in the forest probably have more sense than these people. Even the way Betsy was whinnying out there. She knew it was something wrong. "That should be it. Too bad I will not be able to put this bed in the car. This was as good as the one Mom had me sleeping in, Zaraiella. It is okay. No need for tears sis. I love you, and you are going to be alright. When we leave tomorrow morning. You will see there are places cleaner, friend lier and more moral and cultivated people."

"Why did he do that to me?" Zaraiella mumbled. "We gave him food."

"He is a part of that corrupted group, sis. Don't you see that? They are nasty. He did not care if you were giving him food or not. He wanted to break out and got what he deserved. How did he even get free? That is what needs to be answered."

"After Janice and me fed him. I went to go milk the cow. After that…he put his hand over my mouth."

"The bastard is dead. He thought he would get away with it, but he got exactly what he deserved. I wish all of S.I.L.O would just…die."

My heart continued pounding fast. Every time there is a massive rush, it just might as well beat out of my chest. My poor little sister doesn't even know anything about sex, and the bastard took something special. Something that she could have given to someone she loved. I hate people so much; they are so nasty. They only think of themselves. Just like the ones in this house.

"Munisha, come in. Please eat something."

I liked it better outside to concentrate. "I'm okay, Mrs. Wilson. My stomach isn't really open to anything from anyone right now."

"When the kitchen is closed, you know what that means."

"I do. I am glad since I can see my book a little longer tonight."

"Suit yourself," Mrs. Wilson says as she walks in front of me, while I kept my eyes in my illusion. "I will leave this here once you feel like getting some food down you."

"Told you, I'm okay."

"We are all sorry about what happened. It is totally unacceptable. Before you leave, I will give you two some things to assist on the road. I pray for your strength, Munisha. Have a good night."

Don't want none of that foolishness. I have my studies anyways to keep my mind off of food. "Thine dust of Azazel's gains potent as thee manifest its abilities further. One shall use thine dust to rehabilitate or demolish one's soul."

So, you can do things with this stuff to harm people. She was not lying; this stuff is powerful. Never knew things like this could actually be real. "I might use some to practice with it later tonight. Hmph, could have done it to that bastard."

Maybe one day I will be strong enough to do something about these true devils of the world.

"How are you feeling, M?" Jason asks coming outside slowly.

"Just here."

"I see. How are you feeling? Better…worse? You are reading, hopefully that is a sign you're doing better. Janice is a little upset too."

"For what?"

"Besides the issue with your sister, I didn't know you yelled at her; but she is definitely quiet tonight. Hmph, everyone's quiet."

"You should eat that food before it gets cold. I told your Mom I am not feeling for it right now. I just have some fruit before we go in the morning. I am just so ready to leave. You just don't know."

"I know," Jason says as he leans against the wall behind me. "You talk about it every day and it's not my place to stop you. Things happen…I can't tell you how to feel or what to do."

"The thing is, how did he get free? My mind still cannot come to that conclusion. It's getting in the way of my studies. Tsk, I don't think my sister unleashed him. Hmph, you all probably think so."

"None of us thinks that at all, M. Dad thinks he didn't tie the rope tight enough, but then he actually did not notice the real issue lying on the floor in your moms car."

"What was it then?" I said, closing my book and standing to Jason.

"He had this to Zaraiella's neck. You saw it."

"How…how did he get this?

"I am afraid to say…you don't remember?"

"Say it! Where?!"

"M…the rope wasn't untied. It was cut."

"Cut? He…I didn't…oh no. Oh god…no," I said, covering my mouth.

"It was a mistake, Munisha. Calm down calm down."

"I dropped the blade, I dropped it right in front of him. I am so dumb. I caused it! Oh my god! What have I done?!"

"It was a mistake, M. We were both wrong. Hell, all of us. I should not have let you in there. Dad shouldn't have let them go and feed him, even let them be in the barn alone. We both agreed to that. Though, it was an accident waiting to happen. Come on I got you. Get up."

"I hate my life! Sniff…Zaraiella got raped because of me!"

"Stop, M! Stop it! Blaming yourself for everything won't change a damn thing!"

"Let me go, Jason. Let me leave…I've caused this to my own sister."

"Munisha, I need you to calm yourself. Everyone makes mistakes. You are not alone in this, alright?"

"I just need to be alone, Jason," I said, walking towards the dark whispering trees.

"No, I am not going anywhere. I need you to listen to me for once. Before you leave us tomorrow, I need to show you something. A place where I can help you take those burdens off your mind. I need you to trust me, just once. Dad gave me the green light to let me take the horse and for me and you to go out for one night. I need you to trust me right now."

"There is nothing left. Okay, Jason."

Nothing mattered anymore, nothing I can do to fix what insolence I've caused to the family and what basically possessed me to get my little sister, my own blood, in her position. Just thinking of it is killing me right now. How can I look her in the eye and tell her what really happened? How could she ever forgive me? Will she ever? I tried my best to protect her. I wish a lightning bolt would strike me on the back of this horse but spare Jason and Betsy's life.

"M, try not to dwell on it so much. It hurts, I know; it will make things only worse. We will get through this together. Your tears have my back as if I've been working."

"Sniff…I'm sorry."

Jason grins. "Don't worry about it. We are almost there. Hopefully, it will give you an insight into how beautiful life is. For today and tomorrow."

I wonder where he is taking me. I wonder where the wolf is. "It better not be your favorite fishing spot."

"It is good to hear you are being at least sarcastic. Better yet, a smile would be even better to go along with it. It isn't a fishing spot. Once we are there, we have a little walking to do. Rest, I will let you know when we get there."

Resting is far from my mind now. My body cannot recognize the actual temperature out here. I must have been chilly from the bumps risen on my arm. I can't feel anything anymore.

"This is the place," Jason says.

"This…this looks like where a bear lives."

"Stay here, Betsy," Jason says, tying the rope to a tree. "That is a good girl. No, there are no bears, not that I know of."

"It's a tunnel for trains. I see the tracks."

"Not quite. More like a mining cart track. I know how much you like to explore, so I know you would love this, M. Let's move along, shall we?"

I wondered what tricks he had up his sleeves. Why bring me here? "I'm not going to lie. It looks creepy."

"I'm with you," Jason says, taking my hand. "I won't let anything happen to you. I promise."

"Sniff…did you bring any radios with you?"

"I didn't want to. I just wanted us to be out and alone."

"Look at you. Now you want to be a bad boy?"

Jason grins. "When I was out here about two weeks ago, I got lost while looking for meat. I wanted something instead of fish and show Dad my hunting skills. I took the wrong turn, and I didn't have the radio to ask Dad for any help. Then I ended up here. C'mon, M. This will help you."

"This better not be a trick, Jason. I am not up for one."

"I know that. Just…trust me."

It was getting colder and colder as we strolled in the dark echoing atmosphere. We needed a lantern, not a flashlight. "Now I am really starting to feel the cold."

"That is part of the surprise causing the temperature in here to drop significantly. The coolness isn't so bad when the sun is up."

"How far are we going in this weird place, Jason? It even has a weird smell to it too."

"Down there, then you are in for it," Jason says, looking down and his face glowing from the light.

His face was giving me all types of emotions. Someone caring and loving and who will break their back for anyone.

"Watch your step, M. I can't carry you back up this."

"If I get hurt, then that is all your fault," I said, stepping down the steep rocks.

"There you go. This is what you have been waiting for. Mind if you close your eyes?"

"Jason, what is this place? Lights are going straight through my eyelids?"

"Almost there, Pocahontas. Keep those eyes closed. I should have brought a blindfold; we all know you don't like to wait."

"Only when I wait too long," I grinned.

Never have thought a smile would cross my face anytime soon. The bright, purplishblue and yellow lights glared through through me. I felt the exhilarating energy. I just had to open them.

"You can open them now. Tsk, you already"

"Oh my gosh," I said with my jaw dropping. "This is so…"

"Beautiful, I know."

"How can something be down here? Be down here for so long without anyone knowing about it?"

"The world made this place just for us, M. Told you I was going to show you how beautiful you are. Let's take a closer look together."

"Jason…"

This is like heaven to me. I have never seen something so radiant. Peaceful, full of energy, and rare.

"Aw now, don't start with the waterworks again…not yet, at least."

"I am not a good person. This place…it is so beautiful, not like me."

"Naa baby, turn around and look at me. Then how come the creator along with the world, made this place just for you? They both knew I would bring you here. That is why I needed to wait for the right time to show you. Today was the perfect opportunity to prove to you how beautiful you are inside and out."

My eyes just had to witness again without a blink towards the crystal illuminated stones, along with the crystalclear water that mirrored it's ripples on the walls. This place had to be a fantasy.

"I have something I need to ask you," Jason whispers behind my ear.

"I am doing better, if that is what it is. If that is not it, I am definitely not getting in that cold water with you. I…"

"Will you marry me? I hope this is the proper way you kneel. Only seen it done in books."

"Jason, what are you doing?" I grinned.

"Will you marry me? It is a simple question."

My heart, again racing, and it felt much more enlightened. "Oh my gosh, this is too much," I muttered, wiping a tear.

The beautiful underground cave, the sparkling water, now a dazzling stone. This can't be real. "Yes, Jason…yes."

"I know this is not a ring, that will come later."

"What kind of stone is this? Never seen anything like this before."

"Black opal, I think. I managed to make a necklace out of it. The rope is strong. It should be durable, hope it doesn't bother you. Euof!"

"It is perfect," I said, holding Jason tightly. "I love it! More glamorous than these crystal walls. This whole cave, to be honest. Thank you, baby."

"I love you."

Blushing with the lights nearly blinding me. "I love you too."

"Let me have you then?" Jason says as he wipes my teary eyes.

"What if…I become pregnant?"

"Then we will become amazing parents, don't you think?"

CHAPTER 19

Rectifying Decisions

Hey, Remember me?

"You again. Yes, I remember, You ran off."

"Only to lead you to more of an adventure, that is all. You look weary. Spending too much time reading that book may just create insomnia."

"The book gives me insight on what is real in this world. It helps me to decipher what I should or should not do."

"Your life is led by words? You best to be careful with things like that. It can take you places you may not want to go. You should have some discernment while reading that despicable book."

"Why do you always say something to me as if I am doing something wrong? You are still anonymous. You speak recklessly then flee. Are you a demon or something?"

"Ha, ha. Let us just say your…inner peace."

"What do you want from me? You should tell me if you are me, so I could be the best of myself."

"Notice that when your soul touched, I appear. Can you guess why this time?"

"Me and my boyfriend had sex, is that a bad thing?"

"Not at all. In your heart, you desire to leave him. You want to go on to make a living in a new place. Would you like to be a single mother?"

"Of course not. I will just have to adapt to a new situation. That is how life goes."

"Your book that informs of being your own master tells you that you have to have complete control over your destiny."

"Right."

"You are guessing your destiny; both cannot be correct."

"Whatever, I am human. We make mistakes."

"Control your thoughts, feelings, desires. Each one has a door that could lead to rapture or damnation. Got to go."

"M, Munisha. Whoever you are talking to better be me or someone in the family."

"Gosh, I was sleep talking?" I smiled, covering my eyes. "Need to find a way how to fix that before I become like, Zaraiella."

"I could not really understand what you were mumbling. It must have been a nightmare."

"Na, just something that likes to come and go in my dreams. This stone feels so cold on my chest. I can't believe you found something like this, then this place."

"It is extraordinary," Jason says as he looks around. "I don't think anyone else knows this place is down here. We have it all to ourselves. If you want that of course."

"You never told, Mr. Wilson or your mom?"

"Nope, they could have spoiled the surprise for you. Everything has it's time."

I don't know if I can keep this a secret. This is beyond unique. "The color on the crystals, how do you think they are made?"

"All I know is they cool and harden after years. In school, I remember doing a volcano project, right. They say most crystals and diamonds are formed inside there because of rocks cooling. What are you trying to do?"

"I want to take a piece with me to show, Zaraiella."

"You could just bring her here. Wouldn't that be better?"

"My sister doesn't need to know about our spot. I don't believe I should be bringing her anywhere where she could be in danger."

"That is fair enough. Let me see if I can get a piece."

Just thinking of her, that atrocious feeling toyed me. "Thank you for everything, Jason. I can truly say you are one of a kind."

"I try to be. To be the best version of myself."

"What a coincidence."

"What?" Jason asks while struggling to break the rock free.

"Just, I was talking to myself about that earlier."

"Here you go."

"This is smaller than a coin. It's fine, maybe in the future, she and I will come back and see it together. This place is amazing, just like this necklace."

"Don't sweat it. I am hungry now and have no idea of the time."

"Hmm, a fruit salad would be amazing right about now. Ew, don't drink that!"

"Mh mh, mh…fresh!" Jason says, wiping his mouth. "Come have a sip."

"That is cave water you idiot. You want to kill me after you propose?"

"The water is purified by the rocks surrounding it. It's clean. You don't see any algae, do you? Give it a try, my love."

The water did have its sign of purities with its glittering ripples. Just the thought it's hugging the walls, it may taste a bit bitter.

"See. From one to ten, give me a taste rate."

"Seven. It does taste pure like it has many minerals in it."

"Only thing about it is, I get hungry once I start drinking. Ready to go, wifey?"

"Carry me, hubby. At least carry me on your back. Isn't that what the new husband has to do once they're married? Eygh! Do not drop me!"

"I should, right in the water, Pocahontas."

"That is when I knock some sense into you. Hey, I didn't tell you to put me down."

This will always be a place I will come to. Zaraiella needs to see this, and Lakia and Mom too. I wanted them all to witness my wedding. The feeling and title of being married to someone you truly love is enough for me. I could not ask for someone better. "There is still no light outside. It has to be at least three in the morning."

"We could have stayed in the cave the," Jason says.

"You are by yourself on that one. I am finally starting to feel the cold. No, not this time, keep your jacket. I will be fine."

"Betsy girl! You are still here in one piece, I see."

"I wonder what she was saying when we left her out here," I said as I rubbed her cold nose.

"You two left me outside, don't forget about me, you crazy kids!"

"Help me up, hubby."

"You should be able to do a front flip onto her. You're the one always exercising."

"I know, you're the man. So I want you to do most of the work. Just kidding."

"We work as a team," Jason says, frowning as he pulls me up. "Not a one man, woman show. The greatest couple rulers of the world were always working together to dominate."

"Bonnie and Clyde, basically."

"Right, but they were killed. I am not trying to go that route. Let us be our own self but rule the world someday."

"Sounds crazy, but I like it! Wouldn't that be romantic? We then get caught and taken by, S.I.L.O. Maybe we may get caught robbing a clothing store like we did before. We need to go back by the way. I want some new things."

"Not a chance, my love. They're most likely S.I.L.O infantry patrolling, and then there should actually be people shopping. That leads me to ask you as far for this question. Will you stay for a little longer?"

He did take my mind away. "I am not sure yet. Time will decide for me. You persuaded me to add to the hourglass."

"Good then. We will find something when the time is right. I truly believe we are destined to be where we need to be."

I thought about a lot of things. My first day seeing, S.I.L.O take my family away. Having a new family, then starting one. Bringing a child into this corrupted world is a big decision. What would make a parent want to see their child suffer? If I were to be pregnant, life will have to be very similar to how Mrs. Wilson and her husband live. Starting a family on an isolated farm is not a bad idea. Maybe even on an island.

"Home sweet home!" Jason says patting my leg. "The sun should be rising once we settle down. Hope Dad left and didn't leave the barn locked. You can get off here."

"Thanks for everything. What if they see this? Will it be too unveiling?"

"You should be good," Jason says, smiling at me. "It glows with your eyes, you know."

"So you're going to make a flirt out of everything? Okay, mister."

"It is good to see you smile. When you are frowning, you make me think of those mean looking cats that knock things over, then stare at you."

"You are too much sometimes," I grinned. "I will not be able to sleep once I go in. I already know, Zaraiella stayed up looking for me to come back all night."

"Go to her. Let her know you're alright. I will see you at dawn. The bummer is, we may have chores."

"Tsk, I guess you're right."

"One last kiss for the morning? Need to start fresh, Pocahontas."

He is an amazing guy. He truly is. Other than that, what a time. I know there is another beautiful place beyond that, just by what I've witnessed. The book even says the Earth always will provide everything we need. Nothing that man can make, the Earth cannot destroy. Mother nature retaliates on those who take advantage of her world. She sends the high winds, floods, and earthquakes to punish them every time. I do not blame her for their irrationality. "Sister. Are you awake?" I whispered.

Her mouth moves every night. Talking to or fighting whatever. "Sleep tight. Hope you have been sleeping well and are not worrying about me. I love you so much, and everything will be okay. One day we will be living in paradise. There is so much out there that I cannot wait for you to see. Our destiny will be bright."

This necklace is so beautiful. I have a black outfit that would look so elegant with it. How did he manage to put it in this socket so perfectly? Who cares? I will definitely take me some pictures with Zaraiella's camera later on. "Oh my gosh, that thing looks so creepy out there. What does it want? I am definitely not going back out there to go anywhere with that wolf. Guess it just wanted to say goodnight, perhaps good morning. Let me get some reading done with a little light from the gorgeous morning sunrise.

"Good morning! Your finally up, sis."

"What happened to you, Munisha? Why did you run away?"

"I"

"Because of what happened to me?"

"Of course not," I said, gazing into my studies. "So much was on mind."

"I thought you and Jason left. Nobody didn't see where you two went. Janice was here sleeping with me, then she must have left."

"I wonder why. But…my mind was in so many different places. I thought I was going to lose it. Me and Jason took a walk where he showed me some new ways of thinking, you could say."

"Where did you get the necklace? It's pretty."

"Crap…um," I smirked, tucking it into my shirt. "Jason gave it to me. This is a gift to me since we never really celebrated a birthday around here. I can't fool you, can I? Okay, I will be honest with you. You cannot tell anyone, okay? Not even your best friend, Janice."

"You stole it didn't you?" Zaraiella asks, shaking her head.

"No, nothing like that. He took me to a place that we both would not believe existed, even if someone told us about it."

"Heaven?"

"Hm, it does come close to it. This place had lights as though it was illuminated; but I guess you could say these crystals gave its reflection color. The most beautiful atmosphere I've seen. Then I looked at something that shined brighter than the sun itself. He asked me to marry him. This is my, ring for now."

"I told you!" Zaraiella grins. "I told you, you two were going to get married! I wish I were there to see it."

"One day you will, sis. I want to take you, but for now, it remains secluded from the world. Maybe I will decide to have a real wedding there."

"You two are finally in," Mr. Wilson smiles. "How are you both feeling?"

"I am…better, Mr. Wilson," I said, semi smiling. "Thanks."

"Long night, I am sure. How about you, Zaraiella? Your face seems to glow this morning."

"I am…yes, I'm okay."

"Are we doing chores today?"

"Since I thought you all were leaving, I had nothing planned for you. I gassed you up and everything."

"I have a change of plans, Mr. Wilson. When the time is right, I will know the day, and we will know exactly where we are going."

"Hmph, sounds like a wise choice to me. Well, it would be nice if you both could help out. I will see you two downstairs. Also, Munisha, keep strong and positive! You too, Zaraiella."

Last night pretty much fed my mind some ease and leeway to new ways. Even though what happened was somewhat of my doing, I forgave myself and will be better and more careful. Jason, thank goodness for someone with his spirit and energy.

"Thanks for breakfast, Mrs. Wilson. It was amazing," I said, the milk stain from my lips.

"You are truly welcome, dear. I am very glad that you have made a better decision. My thoughts on you all going out there alone is the last thing I wanted. How come you changed your mind so quickly?"

"Just my perspective on life has changed. I thought about some things. Jason gave me some good advice too. Situations happen, and sometimes it's not in our control."

"Precisely. Zaraiella will be fine. I prayed diligently, more than ever before. How is she doing?"

"As you can see, still a magnet towards, Janice. I want to apologize for being so upset at you when it could have been worse. My anger issues need some working on."

"Do not stress about it. We all have our days," Mrs. Wilson smiles. "Especially you were not wrong. I can put myself in your shoes and understand exactly what you felt. Remember, I didn't really know my family. It is not easy being alone."

"That is true. I am still hoping that one day, I will find my other sister. Something still tells me she is out there, somewhere. That would be something if I find her; then we all could be united again. S.I.L.O caused this; it is only them. Hopefully, oneday, people will stand up and wipe them from existence."

"Tim tells me basically only those who are wealthy, will survive in the new world order. Unfortunately, Munisha, it is very difficult."

"How rich do you need to be to live?" I asked. "Nothing but selfish mindless people. They do not know that they are just making life harder every time."

"We see it already happening. Life was peaceful; however, it was never fair for the minority. It was always a tough decision to come out here to make a living. You all made a living, so I guess it works."

"Sometimes, I miss when we all go to the movies, dining, ice skating, some things you cannot have once you're isolated from society."

"That is the other thing that bothers me. Thanks again for the pep talk. Going to see what is out here today."

I haven't been to a movie since I was twelve. Not once will I have the opportunity to go out with Jason to experience those nice things.

"Munisha, I need your help!" Zaraiella shouts, kneeling in the soft dirt. "There is a weed that won't come out."

"Go ahead and help your sister. Tim should have given you all the light work today. In my opinion, I would have given you all a day off."

"It's okay. The air outside feels amazing. I would rather work in the overcast weather than the sun beating down on me."

"You see, it won't come out."

"I got it…it…just…won't come out! Dammit!" "

"You swore."

"So what? Okay, it's stuck for sure. Just leave or better yet, where is Jason when you need him? I didn't know weeds play tug of war."

"Get some scissors and cut it," Zaraiella says.

"I am about to say forget it."

"Let me try again."

"No, I got it. Oh my gosh. Damn, S.I.L.O!"

Boof

"Crap! What the hell?!"

Never have I seen anything catch fire without the dust.

"What happened?! Are you okay, Munisha?! It's smoking!"

"I…I have no idea. Well, you're welcome. Just go and get my work done now."

She told me I must have the dust in my hands in order to channel it. How on earth did I manage to ignite a plant on its own like that?

"Hey, Munisha," Janice says but makes no eye contact. "Daddy wanted to let you know that he doesn't need you to help with the garden. He said to take a break."

"That is good. Wait, I know you are probably still mad at me. I want to say sorry for yelling at you. It wasn't your fault. I am okay, not upset like I was. What happened to Zaraiella was, unfortunate. She told me she is okay now."

"Yes, I am counting on her to be okay. I thought you two were leaving."

"That is what I wanted; I need more time. Once the time is right, then we will leave."

"Why are your eyes that color? They look violent black or something, especially when the sun hits it."

"That is what everyone is saying. One day I will go and get them checked. How about one day, we have another picnic? Would you like that? It would be nice to have everyone this time come along."

"We should huh?" Janice asked, finally smiling. "I will ask Mommy if we could do it again soon."

"You do that. I have a surprise for everyone, by the way."

"That you and Zaraiella are going to stay?" Janice blurted with her hands folded.

"Maybe. You will find out soon enough. I want the whole family to be there once we, I mean, I announce it. Oh and thanks again for the braids. I just like my natural."

"It's okay, I figured that," Janice smiled.

I needed to find out why this stuff reacted when I didn't have any of it in my hands. What if a bad dream comes one day, and my bed is ignited without me knowing? She was supposed to tell me everything if the book did not. The way she snapped her fingers and created a flame was a bit inconceivable. I do not even recall her getting any on her hand. Need to go and pay her visit to find more answers.

"Hey, beautiful!"

"Hello lover boy. Are you okay?"

"I see you rushing your way upstairs. Where's the fire?"

"Need to go to do my studies," I smirked. "You know me."

"That book will have to battle me in tug of war one day, I swear."

"Na, those weeds do though. Anyways, when I am done, I will be all yours. Hey, what are you doing?"

This boy never stops getting me in my neck; he knows that's my weakness. "Stop before your parents see us you idiot."

"Your stomach is so soft yet toned. I forgot to mention that to you. I wonder what else is inside."

"Jason! You are such a jinx. I am not ready for that."

"Yea, me too. Just fooling around. Perhaps one day, when we both are ready, we can go take pictures somewhere, maybe even the cave with that baby bump."

"You and this baby fever today," I blushed. "Now stop!"

"Nevveeerr. Don't want to hold you up. See you at dinner."

At least we're on the same page. Hope he's not looking for me to be pregnant. The way he held my stomach was more like he wanted a life in there.

"Achoo!"

"Bless you! Geez, that was the fifth sneeze. Are you okay? Your head gets bigger each time," Zaraiella giggles.

"Oh, shut up, sis! Help me put this necklace on."

"I thought you wanted to hide it."

"I am. About to take some selfies with it on. Get all fabulous, you know."

"The outfit is pretty with it."

"Thanks. Where is your camera? If I fill it up, please don't be mad sis. I never made myself perked up before."

I really want Jason to take me out in the car tonight. His Dad did admit he put gas in it.

"I can help."

"No thanks. You can see them once I am done."

"This girl has forgotten to charge the battery. Just my luck. Forget it, then. Wait…maybe. Think of something that I love…and hate…Oh my god, it worked!" I blurted, witnessing my eyes in the mirror transition from one color to another.

"What did you say, Munisha?"

"Nothing, sis…nothing. This is just phenomenal!"

CHAPTER 20

Persevering Notions

I think it's about time you cut your hair, Munisha. What do you think Mrs. Wilson? It's grown rapidly since the braids. "I've notice and it's truly up to you. I recall you saying your mother was a firm believer of a womans hair being divine or as such.

"Yea, but it fits me. I believe it's my signature hairstyle. Zaraiella can keep the long hair."

"Suit yourself. Have you been putting aloe in it?"

"Nothing. It's just has been growing on it's on. Hmph, I think I know why and it's working its magic."

Hair growing rapidly, eyes shifting colors, even my nails that I would have to snip every now and then. "I needed to ask you something, Mrs. Wilson. It has been on my mind for a few days now."

"Speak your mind, child. It is just me here, and you know we can socialize about anything. I sense concern."

"Something like that. My um…cycle, it hasn't come on yet."

"Really," Mrs. Wilson frowns, throwing her towel around her shoulder, then folding her arms. "How come?"

"It is a few days late; I always keep track of it. You think it could be stress that is causing it?"

"I see. So"

"Please don't be upset with me."

"Now now. This is girl talk. You and Jason has been a bit…busy, I presume."

"Um…tsk, we only did it…once. I didn't know what I was thinking. I just felt any type of way. He comforted me, and that was that."

"Well, Munisha. It is in human nature to have these, feelings. Child, well…you should have been more careful. I do not believe you missed your period because of stress, but anything is possible. On the other hand, if it is a fertilized egg. You do realize that it is yours and his responsibility? Don't you?"

"Oh yea, certainly. We need our own space soon enough, I know."

"That is not the issue, dear. The issue is, Tim and I already take care of you all. A new born is an extra job for us. It will need formula, care, and most of all credits."

"I know. That only means we will have to fetch it all ourselves."

"No need to be in a rut about it," Mrs. Wilson says, rubbing my back and smiling. "We make decisions, and for you to be a young adult, your decisions will force you to become more mature. Does he know?"

"The crazy thing, not at all. You would think he would be the first person to find out. I am scared to even say. You told me about this situation before, I figured you would know what to do."

"Only advice, my new daughter-in-law. Have the child, be the best parents you possibly can, period."

"Geez, thanks a lot," I sighed. "Well, I am going to do some reading. That tree out there always provides shade no matter which direction."

"That tree has always been like that. Funny thing is, I have never sat under it long enough to enjoy it. My eyes always glance over at you while you're reading your anonymous book."

"It takes my mind away along with the nice breeze. One day I will read to my child under it. Oh, and please do not say anything to anyone. I will make the move once I am ready."

Mrs. Wilson smirks. "Cross my heart, child."

I don't see how I have so many pages left. Not that bad. Only about one hundred left. The way how I can manipulate energy is one of the best things I have learned from this. By skimming through some of those texts, a person can make objects shift. Azazel's Telekinesis. I will be on that chapter in a few days. "Need to master more of the dust magic."

"Sweet cheeks! You look lovely today," Jason says, poking his head from behind the tree.

"You know you love to come here while I am studying. That is so rude, isn't it?"

"I am not here to bother you, just need to ask you if you want any fish tonight. I may go out and grab some with Dad."

"No thanks. Hmm, maybe one. I feel like I should have some meat every now and then."

"Good, you need your omega three's any way, my love."

I wanted to tell him, but not just yet. I needed to be more sure. "By the way, mister..."

"What, uno?"

"No, sir! I needed to talk to you about something. How come your mom called me daughter-in-law? You opened your mouth to her, didn't you?"

"I do not think so. Unless she figured something out."

"Zaraiella or Janice probably…who knows," I shrugged.

"You told them?"

"Not at all. Well, Zaraiella found out about the necklace as soon as she woke up. I had to tell her, but she promised she wouldn't say anything."

"Look at you, about to blame me," Jason chuckles. "You are the one who got busted. It is not a big deal anyways. They were going to find out sooner or later."

"You know who?"

"Mom is a spiritual person, probably more than Dad."

"What do you mean? She asked God if we got married?"

"What her spirituality teaches, when a couple has sex, they bond as one. It basically makes two people, in other words, become married."

"I guess."

In that case, people making love all over, are married and don't even know it. "One more thing before you go. Remember when I told you I need more clothes."

"Oh no, not this again," Jason frowns, then stares me up and down. "What's wrong with the ones you have? They still fit; I know they do. Don't go on telling me anything about you gaining weight either!"

"Pleeease, just this last time. Come on, Jason. I am your wife. A woman's husband does his duty as one. You are supposed to take care of me. I want to get a few things, and then we're gone."

"We don't even have credits, silly rabbit."

"I know, trust me."

"Stealing clothes. Okay then, uno. We will place our bets on that."

"No…hell no," I said, rolling my eyes. "Why can't you just take me?!"

"Staff fighting or one on one in basketball. Take it or leave it."

"You are so unfair, Jason. Are you my husband or competitor?"

"Hey, this is how to decide fate. I win. I do what I must. You win, we do what you want to do, deal?"

"Whatever, as long as we go back to the strip mall with all those different stores. I will be satisfied. Basketball, you damn cheat."

Jason knows darn well that we aren't going anywhere, and I shouldn't even try to play. Some way, I need to go and get a test. "Let's do this then. I swear if you do some crazy acrobatic stuff, I am quitting."

Jason grins. "You're the wifey. I have to take it easy on you. There is no easy choice but to be smooth and fair with you."

"You say that now, and you seem as though you will bully me through this. I never get how you bounce the ball in the dirt anyways."

"Since I have a slight home advantage of a B ball player, I will grant that you can travel."

"Um, what's that?"

"Y'know, you need to bounce the ball in order enough to run with it. Just hold the ball and go to the basket, M. Gosh, you never played basketball before?"

"I was going to do that anyways, you jerk. Your dad should see this."

"You want him to be the referee?"

"Matter of fact, I do."

"We won't need him," Jason smirked. "Take your shot, M."

There was no way I can beat this boy. "Eygh, oh my gosh!"

"See, very nice," Jason claps. "All you need to do is believe in yourself."

"You let me do that."

"You're the one who shot it. Now I am going to play for real."

"EYGH! YOU JERK!"

"Look at you. You are better than that," Jason teases.

"I should have bet on staffing. My chances would have been higher, tsk."

"Think so, my empress? I don't think so."

This boy really just jumped over my face and slammed the ball through the hoop. He isn't getting a kiss from me all week, that is for sure. "Hey! See, I don't want to play anymore."

"That's how the game is played, baby. You can't leave the ball open like that for someone to steal and then get dunked on."

"I tried to shoot it, jerk. Chicken legs self. Try me in volleyball or tennis you show off! Tsk, you're not right, Jason."

"That is how it's done, son! Don't maul her up too bad!" Mr. Wilson shouts.

"Will do, old man!"

"You and your father are something else. He should have given you a few words for what you just did."

"Come on, nine to four. Show me what you are really about," Jason says with a serious face, getting in front of me.

"Move, Jason! You are taller…you won't let me shoot it. Oh my gosh, Jason! Stop touching my stomach like that. You want something to be in there, I believe."

"Hmm, maybe…"

"I am so sweaty too. You always love to put your wet self on me."

"Give me a kiss for game point, yes?"

He is nothing but a sweettalking jerk. "You see, I'm done."

"Ten to four. That is how it's done, Dad! He's not even out here."

"Yea, because no one wanted to see that. Let me go, you idiot! You are a jerk, for sure! I will remember this day for as long as I live!"

I'm sorry, baby, but looks like we are going to the store."

"What?"

"You know darn well I was not going to disappoint you. I just wanted to see some athleticism, and see you work those hips. You get what I am saying?" Jason says with an awkward smile. "Then again, if you listened clearly, I said do what I must. As a husband."

"You are so weird, but so sweet of you. I need to go the bathroom; I feel a bit nauseous."

"You do, how come?"

"Yea…I um…I must have eaten something bad."

"Take your time, my queen. I'm going to get ready myself."

This cannot be happening. What was I thinking that day? Truly my mind nor my body is ready for a child. Why does it feel like I need to throw up but can't? This is the strangest feeling my body has ever felt.

"Why are you behind the door, nosey?"

Zaraiella's eyes quickly looked elsewhere, though I felt her presence.

"Are you okay, Munisha? You were in there a long time. I didn't hear anything so that is why…yea."

"I just felt a little sick, I'm okay now. Hack hack. Um…how is your poetry coming along?"

"Good. I am trying to write a whole page now."

"You can do it. Takes time for everything."

Zaraiella grins. "I saw those pictures. You looked pretty."

"I knew we were going to be all inside of that camera. Did you show your friend?"

"No, I know you wouldn't like it. How did you charge it so fast? It was dead when I tried to use it?"

My observant and naïve sister, she was so cute at times. "Don't know, just…don't know."

"You, okay? You look sleepy."

"A little," I said, yawning. "I'm just going to rest for a while."

* * * *

"He is so adorable, Munisha. He has your eyes and Jason's head."

"He should have had my head. Jason could have kept that peanut head of his. He mainly has your complexion."

"Let me hold him, Munisha. My baby is so cute."

"Just do not make him cry, please. I don't want to hear all that crying the entire night."

"Hi there, you're so cute, Magic."

"You like, Magic, sis?"

"It's okay. I can't wait to get clothes for him."

"That is why we need to go to that mall. However, changing the diaper nightmare has begun."

"You should have told me having a baby was this fun, Munisha. Me and Janice never knew it would be."

"How is the little fella doing?"

"You have a better name for Magic, Jason? Zaraiella likes it."

"Magic is not bad at all. I was thinking, Zack, Zachariah or something."

"Noo, not that name. Only you chicken legs would think of that."

"Yea, I always like to have the first letter similar to the parent."

"Ew. Oh my gosh, Munisha..."

"He got you all over sis. Sorry about that. Imagine months of getting bathed on like that."

"Especially for you, Zaraiella. Gosh, eighteen years. You're only what? Eleven, twelve?"

"Twelve. I'll just love him forever and ever."

"You need to take care of him because once M and I have ours one day, we'll be in the same vote."

"Munisha, Munisha. Let's go, sleepy head. Dad said go but be right back. Why are you so tired all of a sudden? I was expecting you to be reading your book."

"We have to go to the store."

"Chill out, we're going," Jason says, then stops smiling. "You alright?"

That dream. That dream was a sign. "Let me get my necklace."

"You do not need all that, Pocahontas. It's not a party to remind you."

"What's wrong? You scared another man will see how gorgeous your wife is out there?"

"Typical…"

I need to end up swiping two tests from all that has been happening. Zaraiella needing one almost slipped my mind. That bastard, if you were able kill someone twice, he would be my first candidate. Everything will be okay. Just need to think positive.

"Where are you going, Munisha?" Zaraiella asked.

"Stay here, sis. We'll be right back."

"Tim told me you all were heading out for something. Keep these radios close to you no matter what, understand?"

"We will be fine, Ma. I have driven before."

"Really? When was this?"

"Got to go, Ma. Love you!"

"I want to hear about your interesting driving experience once you return," Mrs. Wilson says as Jason slowly drives and his parents near his side.

"See, you talk too much."

"Remember, Jason. You two be back here in an hour. I mean that. We need to test you all out there on your own. Do not disappoint me or your mother."

"We got this, don't we, M? We are just driving around as I told you. We will be fine."

"Okay. Good luck out there, you two."

"I am very surprised of how your parents let you do this. Taking the horse is one thing but letting us go where S.I.L.O may take us and they have no clue. If it were my mom, she wouldn't have let us drive off the lot."

"Maybe she would have. More and more you can see they're letting us become more free and flexible. It would have been funny if they saw you wearing that big jewel. Probably anticipate we were going out to a club or something."

"You know I wanted to experience that one day. You know, get drunk…see what it's like."

"Yea, until you do something stupid with yourself and end up walking outside naked."

"Goody two shoes. It's just having fun."

At least we are away and on our own. That feeling what I used to have about my biological home, soon became the nowhere land.

"I am surprised you didn't bring that book that is always glued to you. Finally finished?"

"Not yet, but I like to look and see what's happening out in the inside world. I like nature also you know. When we all went out that time to the city, my eyes could not stop viewing how things changed so drastically."

"And it will keep doing so. There is no stopping this. I am sorry, I hate to sound so…out of luck about it. Calling it how I see it, that's all."

"It's understandable. Accepting the truth is the only way to understand things after. As my book told me, knowing oneself is the first step to comprehending the truth."

Cars swarming the streets as a regular day would. Then again, S.I.L.O seems to be growing in numbers. These bastards we're everywhere, making those who are strong, lives harder.

"What was your father like? As long as I have known you, I don't think I have ever asked you about him."

"My Dad…I do not have many memories of him," I sighed. "Last time I saw him was when our mom talked to him, then that was it. He's probably dead."

"Hmph, what a thought."

"He was some doctor like, Mom. That is what me and my older sister Lakia were told."

"Same mom, different father?"

"That's right. Zaraiella doesn't have the same father. Hers is…actually have no clue."

"I believe Zaraiella's dad, she doesn't even know who he is I think. You will have to give me a pass. I have bad memory from that point of time."

"Your good, M. I just cannot understand how men do things like that. It makes them soft. Running from their responsibilities."

"I know that is the truth but you have to move on and understand how to deal with it, I guess."

Jason's mindset, truly ravishing on the topic. That is beautiful for a man to love his wife and then his family. He sees it all the time and I truly believe that is why so many homes are broken for the lack of love for one another. It is more than looks in a marriage but a bond and understanding for each other. I am truly lucky. If my test comes out positive, I would rather that than Zaraiella's.

"We're here. A lot more people this time and seems to be getting back to normal. Hope these clothes you want to steal are worth us getting prosecuted, M."

"Nobody is getting in trouble, scary boy. We are just going to go inside and look around. You could go inside another store while I do my own thing, if you want."

"Sure, but I think we should stick together. Don't know how you will swipe something while there're people going in and out of the store. Then scan drones are up and down isles."

"Just look around with me and act normal," I said as we both exited Mom's car.

"Damn, there is a S.I.L.O officer in the gun store."

"Go inside and say hello. What can they tell us, Jason? Everyone looks the same."

"Hmph, you're right."

"Gosh, haven't felt air conditions like this in a while."

From all the years, it is like a different atmosphere, especially the new clothing styles people perceive as nice. I must have been living on that farm for too long. I need to get back with the trends.

"Why are we in the pharmacy? You're sick, or you want to get some new threads?"

"Why not go and grab some things for good use later on? I'm looking for something," I muttered, quickly skimming through shelves.

"We do need some antibiotics. Dad would not mind if we got some for the house."

"Exactly. Grab useful items, and I will get some for personal use."

"How are we going to steal with that thing up there?" Jason says, pointing. "Guess they don't want anyone stealing even if they thought about it."

"The way it's flying up and down the aisles like that, someone ought to knock it down. I'm not worried about it."

"Just look at him. Why won't he just go about his business?"

"Aw, someone is jealous," I smirked. "That's cute, hubby."

"Maybe he thinks you are stealing other than you bending over looking for what to take."

"Oh, stop being so je"

BANG BANG BANG

"What the hell!" we both said looking at each other, then towards the entrance.

"Let's get out of here, M. Sounds like someone was shooting."

"Give me a…second. Alright…found it!"

Luckily, the shooting helped me to keep my privacy.

"Everybody, stay calm. Are you two alright?" the store clerk asked as we stood in front of the exit.

"Yes sir, me and my girlfriend are spooked. We're getting out of here."

"Sorry about that, and everything is okay. You can still purchase anything if you like."

"No thanks," Jason says. "But we will surely"

"Hey, may I check your bag, mam? Mam?!"

BOOM

"EYGH!" I yelled.

"What the hell is going on out there?" the clerk says, ducking behind the counter.

"Come on, M! Damn…that's a S.I.L.O truck."

The black smoke and flames coming from it along people running around like our chickens at home, was more than enough. Just when his parents let us out on our own.

"For crying out loud!" Jason says as we continued to look back at the incident. "That was a close one."

"I wonder who did it. We are definitely not the only one who doesn't like"

"YOU TWO, HOLD IT! STOP!"

"Open the door, Jason!"

"You have the bracelet! Just open it!"

"This has to be the craziest thing I have ever seen."

"You two get out now!" The store clerk demanded, pulling the door handle.

"Hurry up, Jason before he breaks the window!"

SSKKRRrrrr

"Gaaawwddammmitt, M!" Jason frowned. "Stealing from someone is the worst you can do out here! That was the perfect example right back there! Haven't you learned anything?"

"Oh, hush. I needed my stuff, and that is how it will be. They need to blame the ones responsible."

The owner needs to tell those S.I.L.O people who just had their car blown up to reimburse him.

"You get everything you need?"

"Something like that. I just hope and pray it works."

"I know you wanted to go to the store to get some new threads, sorry."

"I am fine. I got something I really needed. One thing I do have a problem with. I did not like how you told him I am your girlfriend."

"Really?" Jason grins. "We look too young to be married."

"That isn't what you said in the cave that day."

"Next time when someone asks, then it will be wife. Happy, Pocahontas?"

"Hmm, words are words, actions speak louder. One more favor from you. This would really make my day and make me love you like never before."

"Let me guess. Go back to the store?"

"Nope, It will reveal how much you truly love me. I need to see you to do this for me."

Jason sighs. "Really, M? What could this request be?"

"Hmm…take me to my house. It's not that far from here, Jason. I"

"No, M. Jesus…did you not see what just happened back there? We should be on our way back, plus we have…twenty minutes left."

"Oh, come on! We can just make an excuse, like how we just saw what happened. Then it will be fun while we are out here on our way back. Let's at least see how it is. As your wife, that is a special request. Don't look at me like that."

"Hey, you can't use that wife stuff on me."

"Please, hubby, I just want to go look. I know you have always heard of the term, happy wife, happy life," I chuckled.

"Youuu are a peace of work, madam."

"Kiss me, my love. Thank you so much. I will never forget this."

"Hmph, better not."

Everything happened in a matter of minutes. Things have definitely changed to the point they are manipulating humans as though they're robots. What kind of life with so many restrictions? Jason couldn't even go fishing if he wanted to. Something you love you could not do because of the new world system.

"That was crazy back there, wasn't it? I always knew people would start to retaliate sooner or later."

"Wish we could have seen who did it. When that clerk asked for my bookbag. I thought for sure we were going to just have to make a run for it."

"We probably wouldn't have made it. S.I.L.O was down two stores, and they would have likely shot at us. In their law, I believe it is to shoot first, ask questions later. Surrender and die."

"It makes you want to get at them yourself," I frowned. "Just every thought I have of them makes me hate them more and more."

"It's not worth it. There are too many of them. What if you do what they did and then get caught in the process? Exactly, that will be it for you. You have to think about your future, my love."

"Okay, Mr. Wilson."

"Hey, got to get the wisdom from somewhere. No wisdom, no sense of direction. So, where is this place of yours? Hold up, do you even know where your old home is?"

"You think I would tell you to come way to Ellsworth and get lost? Of course, I do. It's on Albers Avenue."

"Like I know where that is," Jason grinned, shaking his head.

"Just follow my directions, and we'll be there in no time."

Even though it's been a while, my home is still clear in my head. Just a few streets I may not recall. It would be something if S.I.L.O came chasing us over these pregnancy tests.

"Jason, Jason, come in."

"He's driving, Mr. Wilson. Hiiee."

"No fooling around, Munisha. It is ten minutes to the hour. You two on your way back?"

"Um, kinda'."

"Kinda? Well, enough sightseeing around. I need you all back. I just heard on the news something happened nearby. I need you all back here."

"There was a bad accident we saw, Dad. We will tell you about it once we get back."

"Alright, drive safely, Jason. Get back as soon as possible. Your mother is getting in a bunch here."

"Bye," I grinned. "Moma and poppa's boy."

Jason frowns. "Hmph, good to sightsee. We need to see more things in life. It's a shame the world is so big, and we haven't seen half of it."

"Maine is like the smallest state, I think. Zaraiella thinks this is one of the biggest places in the world."

"She hasn't been anywhere, of course. Now, where to?"

"I see the lake there. Go all the way around it, and then the front entrance will be three blocks down if I remember correctly."

Everything seemed to look fine. I wondered who was living there now.

"You think S.I.L.O will be in the community?"

"Probably. Didn't your dad tell us how they basically are all over the place?"

"That means there are no security guards anymore. They have taken jobs for no reason either."

"Just like how they're all in airports, Dad told me. You have to be stupid to walk in there without your chip," Jason sighed. "What a world."

It is still how my mind reminisced. A lake that stood still in the middle of the community. Too bad we never could go out for a swim. At least get our feet wet if we were allowed. Nothing really seemed to change, only the color of the fence used to be blue and white but now plain black. They want to make things charming to the eye but destroy those who create it. Something is just so backwards.

"It is beautiful, M. This is the upper class area, isn't it?" Jason says as he gazes at how graceful I once lived.

"You see my mom's car you're driving. I wouldn't say we were rich, but she made good funds."

"Yea, then you see the new things out there. They really upgraded with luxury cars. They must run on special hydro or just plain electricity like this one."

"This takes gas too."

"I know that. The new cars have only electric ports I've noticed. Fuel pumps are at the bare minimal now, mainly electric stations. Only thing I noticed that hasn't changed, you still can place coins to use air for the tires."

"Yea yea. Look, we're in luck; the gate is open! Actually, I remember they have it open on the weekends."

"I was wondering how we were going to get in too. Most communities like this one have gates shut tight."

"Now you can take me to my house. Turn on century lane once you get down to the lake part."

"Sorry about this, M."

"What are you sorry for? We made it in, didn't we?"

"I am sorry for S.I.L.O destroying how beautiful things were. This place is beyond. The sun shining on the water like that makes you wonder how life can be taken. Just so beautiful, just as you."

"Aww, so sweet chicken legs. It's alright. I have learned to move on. You know hey turn here, turn! Geez, almost rammed us into the stop sign."

"My fault," Jason chuckles. "Sightseeing a little too much."

"There's my house there! Still in one piece."

I can feel the tears roaring up as my house still stood the same. "Still the same color. The trees in front are gone though."

"Don't worry, you still have your favorite tree at home," Jason says as he wraps his hand around mine.

My heart skipping a beat, thinking they were someone inside looking from the drapes. I had to see if someone was inside, maybe they left something. Whoever lived here will tell what happened. "Let's stop and look around, Jason."

"I thought you said we were just going to take a look, M. C'mon now."

"This will be the last thing, I promise."

Jason growls. "Five minutes, M, five minutes and we are getting out of here!"

"Jason, Munisha! Come in. Where are you all?"

"Jesus, now here we go. Great. Dad, we're"

"On our way!"

"It has been more than thirty minutes, you two. You all need to get back here now!"

"We will be right there, Dad. Over. You see, M."

"Oh, stop whining. We won't be long."

Not much of a difference from when I last seen this place. Mr. Wilson said it was abandoned for a while. I hope whoever lived here did not take anything Mom left hiding. The real problem was, they taken all our pictures. There was only one picture of Mom in the car.

"How on earth are we going to get in?" Jason says with his hands on top of his head. "This place is locked up tight."

"There's a back window. Come."

"You think any of your old neighbors are still around?"

"Who knows? That grumpy old lady probably still lives next door."

"You still should go say hello before we leave. Hey, maybe she knows something."

"Yea right. She probably won't even recognize me with that one funny looking eye she has. This is it here. Yup, they have this shut tight too. Mom showed us a way how we could open this from the outside. The new people noticed it and…jammed it, crap! You think you could help me up on the roof? I could probably get in from the upper room window."

"Why didn't you just break this window right here? You know you have a history of it."

"I already thought of that. More than likely this house still has an alarm. The windows upstairs should not be as sensitive, I think."

"Let's get this over with. If that alarm goes off, we're out of here."

"Momma's boy. I can almost…reach it!"

Felt like there was something in here that surely belongs to me still. "Alright, throw me the rock."

"If that alarm goes off in there, you better hurry and get out!"

"Got you. Be right back!"

Wow, a lot different from what I recalled. Looks like they left the floor rugs and walls the same. "Home sweet home."

How come they left and didn't take the beds and dressers? Maybe they left things. "Nothingnothing and nothing. Under the bed, nada."

Knock Knock Knock

"M! Helllooo!"

"Oh, almost forgot."

They haven't really changed much. I just don't see any pics of us anywhere.

"Welcome to my home," I smiled. "I would tell you take your shoes off but there's a new owner."

"You just started searching for things, and forgot all about me, didn't you?"

"Not really. I just checked my mom's room. Have my old room and the guest room to check, and then we are out of here."

"Was this, how would you say?" Jason says, looking up at the vacant ceiling with a hanging chain.

"A chandelier, yes. I didn't even notice that it was missing from up there. Quinsa, hello?"

"Whose that?"

"Our home AI. Mom said she was our babysitter at times when she went out. I guess they removed her. Seems like they confiscated everything but the furniture. We had a seventy inch tv on the living room wall. It's gone along with a lot of things of course. The weird thing is, I saw no clothes in the dressers. Like there's no one living here."

"Too bad, this couch is surely comfy. If my people were not rushing us to get back, we could have taken a good nap. Better yet, let's try and put this in the trunk."

"You are crazy," I grinned. "I am going to finish looking around."

"Remember, five minutes," Jason says as he observes around. "We should have left by now but I'll start it back."

The kitchen was clean still, actually spotless. The pans are like they haven't been used for a while. That is strange. "No way!"

"What happened, M?!"

"Come look at this!"

This is more than odd. Nobody didn't seem to live here until now.

"What in the world? It's almost full. How could that be?"

"Someone still lives here," I said, smelling the fresh milk. "Could be my family."

"Maybe…or just someone else."

"I'm going to check upstairs. Look through the other rooms, we might find out who it is."

"It is a shame how they left the milk open like that. This chick en is still fresh too."

I frowned. "Help yourself!"

Ownership to this house should belong to me. If someone else was living here. If it is Mom and Lakia, then me and Zaraiella have been wasting years not trying to reunite with them. Jason family teaches about faith, and we truly manifested the mindset. Then it dawned on me that they would have looked for the car. "I thought you were going to stay on the sofa. You seem so tired."

"Can't leave my wife alone in this place. Could be some mani ac hiding in here."

"Good man. Anyways, this is Mom's room here. I am going to finish going through it."

"Does it look like she would still be living in here?"

"Kind of. Her favorite mirror still sits in the same spot as I remembered," I sighed. "Doesn't mean anything. Go and check the other rooms. The guest room should be empty."

Just so strange about what was going. This drawer should have had something in it. Another strange thing, there are no clothes in the dressers; but the fridge is full. Yup, still nothing. "Not even a garment in the closet."

"I didn't see anything valuable," Jason says, leaning against the door frame. "Two beds and nothing in them."

"You should look a little harder. There has to be something."

"There is another room. I saw on the other side."

"Oh yea, Mom's study room. Go and check it, and I will go look in my old one."

Mom, I know you have something in here for us. But where do you have it? Where? "Hmm, your favorite mirror? Geez, girl, look at you, flawless as always."

Then this view from the window has always been something with the lake. "Hey, what do you know? This looks like the girl again from the car."

Why does Mom have a picture with her behind the mirror? Wherever they are, it looks like a facility.

"M, COME LOOK! This will blow your mind!"

"What is it? I found something too. Oh my gosh! What happened?"

Jason grins. "We should have looked around the other side. Surprised we didn't see it on the side at least."

"Who could have done this?"

"Looks like someone shot a canon into your wall. These are the type of neighbors you have?"

"Shut up, Jason. You're always joking. This is serious."

"Let me go see something"

"Stop," I said holding Jason's hand. "You hear that?"

"Yea, someone is coming upstairs, and fast."

RRRrrrr

"What the hell, Jason? What the hell is that?!"

"I don't know, but I got something for it!"

"Bricks aren't stopping it. Jason!"

"Forget this!"

"What the hell! Jason…HELP!"

"MUNISHA, YOU HAVE TO JUMP!"

"No, Jason, IT'S TOO HIGH!"

"M, JUMP! THERE'S NO OTHER WAY!"

RRrr.

"Oh my god oh my god. EYYGH!"

"Gotcha! You alright?!" Jason says, lifting me up.

"Kind of. Ahh…landed pretty hard on my ankle."

"Come on. We're almost to the car. Where the hell are your neighbors?"

"Where could that thing have come from? Is it behind us?"

"Keep looking forward, M. Get in, get in. I got you."

"Damn…my ankle. Jason! Hurry up. It's coming! Get us out of here, man!"

"I'm trying."

"It's shaking the freaking car! Get away from us! Oh my gosh, it's nasty!"

"Alright we're out of here," Jason grumbled as he inhaled deeply.

All I wanted was to see my Mom's house once more. Why was it always something persisting to break me?

"What's so funny?"

"This is crazy. What in the world is going on? Tsk, my ankle."

"We will get something for it once we get back. Luckily it was just that. You'll be alright."

"That thing was similar to what we saw in the woods."

"It did, more like a boar version. Those S.I.L.O scientist are experimenting with anyone and everything."

"It could have been that old man from the store."

"Look who's making jokes."

CHAPTER 21

Greater Fortune

I am telling you, Dad. That is the only reason we took so long. "You told us you two would drive around and then come right back. You did not have permission to go out to the city. You saw what is out there."

"Your father is right," Mrs. Wilson says. "I think you took a sightseeing trip and then went to the store as well."

"We arrived back safely, didn't we, Ma?"

"Don't be smart with your mother! I gave you my trust, Jason. You didn't screw up, but things could have gone bad quickly."

"The only way we can live, Dad, as you said. We must become more experienced, as you said. Yes, we have seen the way the world is. That is why we must learn to adapt."

"Okay, sir. Just know your privileges of taking the car are revoked."

"Mr. Wilson, he is right," I mumbled.

"Oh really? You both are not understanding the gravity of the situation. Seems you two are miles away from what I am trying to say. Better start putting on that thinking cap. I don't want to even think you all are becoming insubordinate."

"We are okay! I don't get it. That is all that matters, Dad."

"Right. Then again, you said she hurt her ankle when I don't get in the laws of physics how that happened in the car without an accident. What about the gunfire and explosion? One of you could have been in the mix. What am I saying? I do not need to explain myself to anyone. Go upstairs, both of you."

"Don't worry about it, Jason," I whispered as we walked upstairs together. "Thanks for everything."

"Hmph, you're welcome. Hope you are satisfied now."

He should have anticipated the noise from his parents. It did not bother me. I do not think they understand how bad the world is becoming. If they witnessed how that S.I.L.O truck exploded in the middle of a shopping center and no one knows who did it, they would understand a little more. There is a war going on out there, and it will only get worse. "I saw you two peeking your little heads from upstairs."

"We had to; everyone was yelling. Zaraiella said that you were coming right back."

"You did say that," Zaraiella says. "I was worried because Mr. and Mrs. Wilson were yelling on that walkie-talkie thingies."

"They were boiling way before we got back then."

"What happened to your leg?" Janice asked.

"Long story. We have much to talk about, especially me and you, sis."

"Do you want me to get some ice?"

"That would be nice, Janice. It isn't that bad, I think."

"Tell me what you saw at our house," Zaraiella says as she comes and sits on my bed.

"You sure are smart. It was…the same. Not too much of a difference. When me and Jason arrived there, I felt I needed to find answers and only was able to pick up one thing."

"They were not there?"

"Unfortunately, no. Me and, Jason checked every room. Someone does live there, but whoever it is, they left in a hurry. Left the fridge full and cleaned drawers."

"That is weird. Shouldn't they have taken the food?"

"Not if they were in a hurry. Then right when we went into Mom's study room. A hole as big as that door was made into the wall."

"No ice. Sorry, Munisha," Janice says as she sits on my bed.

"I don't know who could have caused it hole in the wall. Only that thing that I have not mentioned yet. There was another one. However, this thing was more of a giant pig. That tells me S.I.L.O is making these things and letting them go around," I shook my head. "Free as a bird."

Zaraiella sighs. "…Wow, just, wow."

"We have so many problems right now. It only shows what people are up against. The explosion was enough, but when I saw our old house, that was enough."

"Janice! Come down here and help me with dinner, please!"

"I am glad you and my brother are okay. Hope your ankle feels better. Did he get hurt too? My brother didn't want to talk."

"Don't think so. Maybe I drove him too hard. Go downstairs before Mrs. Wilson gets upset with you too."

"Munisha. They are gone forever, aren't they?"

"I do not know, sis. Though, I have this."

"Who is this?"

"This person sits on the dashboard. The strange thing is, why are there two pictures of her?"

"Maybe she is a person who Mommy saw at the hospital. That is what people wear in there, isn't it?"

"That's it. She could have had a deep connection with her patient. That is a little too deep. Anyways, that was the last picture I could find of Mom. Two are better than one, right? Put this in my bookbag so I know where to find it."

"Nothing with, Lakia?"

"Sorry, Zaraiella. Hey, we will find something relating to them. I promise."

Mom never spoke of her. Could it be that Mom worked with her, and she was a patient and did not have a family? Mom had a heart like that. Always so generous, she would welcome a stranger into the home and give that person a life. Guess that is what people have lost. To be generous and kind to one another as Jason's family did for us.

* * * *

"So, how about today, M?" Jason says to me while we pass each other in the hallway.

"It was spectacular, I would say. You know, I thought you were still mad at me."

"Why would you think that?"

"You did not really talk to me once we arrived back. Maybe you were frustrated with your people. I don't know."

"That is what it was, not you. I grow exhausted with them from time to time along with them degrading my intelligence."

"You let them," I frowned. "I have no idea why they still think you're five years old."

"Parents will be parents. In their eyes, I will always be their baby, just as Janice. Your parents, too, sorry."

"Stop saying sorry," I said, squeezing together Jason cheeks. "They treat you like that because you act too...yea."

"It's all good, M. I know who I am."

"You are Jason, aka, chicken legs. That's right, smile, that is what you told me. Do you think if we leave, you will come with us?"

"I still haven't decided on what to do. So much going on, M."

"You can come with, Zaraiella and me to somewhere more sheltered. Janice can come too."

"I do not know, Munisha," Jason scratches his head. "There are things that holds me here, you know that."

"Think of it this way, you can't stay here forever, and your family will not be here forever. One thing I learned for sure. Sometimes…you just have to let things go. My mother, Lakia, they are gone. I avoid telling, Zaraiella the ultimate truth because sometimes you can live with it for a while. Ha, she already knows anyways. Just wish I didn't have to believe it. I think…once you lie to yourself for a long time, the truth…it hits you harder than running into a wall."

Jason grins. "Hmph, sure enough right about that one. Though, it is the nostalgia that I hold on to along with it."

"Just like me. That first night we arrived here, the moon looked just how it is now. Thinking if my family are not here, maybe they're looking at us up there."

"Give me more time, M."

How much time does he need? The time is near. "Oh no, now what."

"What are you staring at?"

"Nothing," I said, drinking down my juice quickly. "Yea, you will have to figure it out soon. You're done with your food? I'm done with mine, here."

"You could have helped take most of it in, M!"

"Thank you, hubby. Have a goodnight! I'm going to check on the stable lock. I have a feeling it wasn't locked."

"Sounds good. Still glad we did it, M. Maybe we can do it again soon. Don't go out with, Betsy. I trust you."

"Nighty night, chicken legs," I said, looking back and blowing a kiss.

"Where is that creature? I know. I just saw it staring at me."

One thing I love is the calm breeze along with the trees whispering to me. "There you are. To Ms. Jezebel, right? Lead the way. Do you have a name? You don't have to look at me like I'm crazy. Maybe I am. I'm talking to a mystical wolf again..."

Walking through the dark forest didn't give me the chills as much anymore. Only thing I hated were the spiderwebs that you cannot see, only by the sunlight that pervades the area. From that, the moon could not be more gorgeous. Life creations are so complex and intricate. How can people destroy it? They can be so heartless and destroy everything but cannot touch what is up there. When they do, that is when calamity falls.

"Someday, I will be free from this, don't you think, friend? I can't believe I just walked away from my place without letting anyone know. They're going to begin to think I just want to be insubordinate for no reason. Then again, I forgot to bring the darn book. I need, Ms. Jezebel to help me with that dust problem. Wish you could say something back; it would make it easier."

RRRrrrrr ruff!

"Wo, what's wrong, boy? Eyyygh! Where the hell did they come from?! Eygh! Why did those bats just fly out like that? Yea, I am okay. How did you manage to get one in your mouth? Ouch, my ankle. I'm alright…I can make it."

As long as I have been through this forest, have I ever seen a bat? It places a picture in my mind of what we all saw that day and had to run for our lives. Sometimes it feels as though all of this is, is nothing but a dream. If it is, will I wake up?

"Thanks for the help, friend," I said while I caressed the wolf's cold wet nose. "You are physical, not just an illusion. Wish you could stay with me back home. That is a good boy, see you in a minute. Oh wow, you scared me!"

"So startled," Ms. Jezebel smirks. "Are you not aware of me by now?"

"Of course. Just did not think you would have been outside at this time. I have never seen you in your garden. What are these plants called? They are beautiful, and they have my favorite color."

"Sundial lupine, I believe they are called deary. They take forever to grow. However, once their fully developed, they are extremely resilient. I feel this plant and you have mutual aspects."

"Think so? I can tell you my studies have improved a lot. Just one problem I am having."

"You can explain once we are settled inside, deary. It is becoming a bit nippy. Let me finish up with these," Ms. Jezebel says, watering with a watering can.

That is something I have never seen ever in my lifetime. Only made her appear older.

"Question. How come you're doing garden work at night? I thought that was not good for plants."

"What fool apprised you with such dense information?"

"No one, just that when we always water plants, we do it in the sun."

"That is fine also. The sun is not so much my ally deary. The heat is one thing, though watering my babies for the sunrise gives the early morning vitality."

"I almost forgot that you are more of an earth person. You would know."

"Most certainly, Munisha. Now, how about going inside, shall we? I also have some tea brewing."

The air seemed fresher. Something probably with those plants she was watering made a nice scent in the air. It would be a bit uncanny to move out and live here. That won't happen. Those chitlin's again, ugh.

"What is the trouble with your leg, child?"

"I have a long story for you. Can you believe I actually went to my old home? There was no one there but a hole in the wall," I grinned. "Well, I jumped out of a two story building which resulted in this. It is just a little sore, no big deal. Then one of those creatures that most likely came from S.I.L.O came inside."

"Goodness, the power those devils have."

"I know, right? They even had their car destroyed at a store my husband and I went to too."

"Husband?" Ms. Jezebel eyebrow raised, then smiled pouring her tea.

"Oh right, I haven't told anyone else. Somewhere in this forest, your forest, is an underground cave. A place I would not believe it were true if I have just seen a picture. The colors are beyond this world."

"Really? That is something. Never have I witnessed such a place."

"When we settled down, he shocked me…with this."

"My…that, wait a second. My eyes are not so good from afar objects."

"I had to put it in my pocket since we are keeping it a secret from his parents. Just for now. Beautiful, isn't it?"

"Mm, hm. Now, hold still," Ms. Jezebel says while applying that ointment similar to what help aid Mr. Wilson. "This has even felt a bit abnormal once applied to my skin."

"It was not as bad, Ms. Jezebel. Thank you. Hope it heals quickly because I have some ways back."

"Now, let me take a look at thee necklace. That is beautiful…most fascinating. Turn it around for me. Yes, black opal. A very extraordinary, rare stone. Hmmm, where did he find it?"

"Somewhere he said. He proposed to me with this. In my opinion, this is far better than a ring."

"I have seen some unique stones, this one extremely rare with its energy on the inside. Though, it is not required to wed with a ring, this will certainly do. Did you two mate?"

"We did," I blushed. "Um, pretty much right there in the cave."

"That is the real marriage. Once two souls mate as one, they unite."

"Funny you say that, his mother believes in that too."

"It is the truth, deary. Life binds, then the souls give to the world. In time, the souls wither and the cycle continue. It is only nature, deary. Nothing to be fearful of."

"I am kind of afraid of being pregnant, Ms. Jezebel," I said as she turned from me.

"Why? Life is still an excitement."

"Yea; but I don't think I am ready for that lifestyle yet. Maybe a few years from now, being sixteen and a mother is not easy."

"Hmm, child. When actions as such happen, life is produced. Any symptoms of expecting?"

"Every now and then, I feel nauseous, and I get a headache. Every now and then, as I said. The real issue, I haven't oh wow, this stuff you put on is burning."

"Only means it is working, child," Ms. Jezebel smirked.

"I missed my period for a few days. One day it felt like it was trying to come on, but it didn't…"

Ms. Jezebel smiled. "Hmm, nausea and late menses. However, such a thing is rare."

"What? Am I just sick?"

"Not necessarily. The Azazel's dust. Have you so happened to inhale any?"

"…I don't really remember."

"It is a great possibility you did and not notice. Azazel's dust reacts as your eyes have seen. If it invades your system, the body reacts to the substance."

"Hopefully, that is what happened then. Better than dealing with something that will keep you up all night."

That is weird. However, that stuff lays in the bed with me while I am sleeping, so hopefully that is why. Taking the pregnancy test only gave me goosebumps.

"How is the ankle feeling now?"

"Cool, just like the water inside that cave that day. Speaking of the dust, it was giving me problems."

"I see," Ms. Jezebel said, sipping her tea.

"When I was pulling weeds, that stuff ignited. That never happened before. Maybe the dust was on my hands?"

"Possibly. You must learn to use the substance wisely. Have some tea deary."

"Oh no, Ms. Jezebel! It is far past being late. I have to get back and my people will have a bigger fit. Thanks for helping me with my ankle."

"Anytime my young apprentice," Ms. Jezebel says, stretching her wrinkled smile. "My friend will help aid you home safely. Blessings be upon you."

With such a friend, I wanted to give him something, all friends should have. "Does he have a name?"

"No, I do not believe so. Futile in his eyes," Ms. Jezebel smirked.

"I will just call him…Magic."

"It is your choice, deary. Just remember to be receptive of my words."

It kind of made me wonder if I should have done what I did in that cave that day. It can cause so many other problems. I did not care, Jason made me feel like nothing mattered, only that I was happy. Perhaps it was just the dust. I wish she would have warned me about it so I would have known before. More importantly, Zaraiella needs to be checked. Oh gosh, the feeling is so daunting.

"Here he is."

"That is so amazing! He just comes out nowhere made of supernatural forces."

Ms. Jezebel smirks. "Supernatural abilities my dear."

"Ready to go, Magic? That name suits you, doesn't it? Only if he can speak."

"Oh yes, he already has he tells me. To you, he did."

"Really? I never heard him. When was that?"

"Go home deary. Travel safe, and goodnight" Ms. Jezebel muttered, closing her door slowly with locks turning.

Now I have three things to guess on. Should I be learning so much of what is, supernatural? Hoping that the stuff in my system is causing this and being ill from it for who knows how long, or just being pregnant and having to have other responsibilities? In a way, I have never even thought of it.

"Thanks for bringing me back, Magic," I said, as my hand disappeared through his mystical black fur. "You would be a great watch dog I mean would wolf. Goodnight to you too."

The house looked so deserted. Everyone's asleep and of course, the door is locked. Great, the only way is up. "Damn, it is grimy up here. Now my pants are dirty."

Tap tap tap

"Zaraiella," I whispered. "That girl is sleeping hard, and she would turn the opposite direction. Can't bust another window, Mr. Wilson will kill me. Sister, come on. Oh, thank god," I murmured, witnessing a miracle step inside the room.

"M, where the hell"

"Ssshh, don't be so loud you idiot."

"Where the hell were you? Do you know how I had to tell my folks you were just outside? Don't tell me that you went off to that hunchback woman's house again."

"There was something I had to do. Sorry, I hope you didn't get in trouble because of me."

"Had to tell them you were in the barn practicing then you were in the bathroom. The girls didn't say anything. You just ran off without telling anyone."

"Sorry about that. Okay, I'm here, you should be happy."

"How did you even manage to get on the roof?"

"Just used your dads' water can thingies, or whatever. Common sense, hubby. Now go to bed before we wake her up."

"You are such a unique person, M. I will give you that. I would not have given you this if I thought you weren't."

He wants something. That is why he isn't leaving but I will play his game. "Soon, everyone will notice it, and I am tired of hiding it. It even glows at night. That is my favorite feature."

"You're surely welcome. Goodn"

"Wait," I said, grasping Jason's hand. "What's wrong with you? Don't ever turn your back on me without a kiss, understand me?"

"Yes, mam."

"Alright alright, Jason," I chuckled, pushing Jason from my neck. "We are not going this far. Crazy boy, my sister could wake up and see everything."

Even with all of that, she managed to stay asleep. Tomorrow we will have the moment of truth. "Please, whoever you are, God or mother nature. Please don't let us have anything we don't want, especially my little sister. Please…"

"Good morning, sis! Slept well?"

"I did. I felt a little weird last night. Maybe I'm catching a cold," Zaraiella says.

"Almost every night, you manage to open the window, now you had it to the point I could not lift it."

"But I didn't close the window last night," Zaraiella said.

"Really? I wonder who, then? Never mind that. There is something I need you to do for me. Where is my bookbag?"

"You had it when you came inside yesterday."

"That's right, I placed it under the bed."

"I think I know who closed the window," Zaraiella murmured.

"Here, I just need you to go to the bathroom and pee on this stick. Give it back to me when you are done. Don't drop it okay? Trust me sis, it isn't anything wrong. Go on ahead. Please, God…please."

"Good morning, Munsiha," Mr. Wilson says as he knocks.

"Hey, morning. Mr. Wilson. Tsk, what did I do now?"

"Hay…Hay are for horses. I believe telling you this long ago. I took a drive and noticed that there was a big gap of fuel used. You and Jason really did go out traveling. I will not condemn you both. As I said, driving is revoked until further notice. You two must become wiser."

"I hear you, Mr. Wilson."

"Munisha, I'm done."

Now why would she hold it out like that? "Tsk, damn."

"I am not finished speaking to you, young lady! Don't you ever close a door in my face like that again. What in God's name is going on with you younglings? Go on ahead downstairs Zaraiella. This isn't about you. For you young lady, I let you have a little freedom and"

"Have to go the bathroom! Be right out! I heard someone knocking. Go and see who it is," I said, closing the door behind me. "And leave me alone."

Why was the old man being so aggravating in the early morning? "Okay, this thing should be done in a few. Moment of truth in a matter of minutes."

Gosh, my heart felt so weird, like it senses despair arriving. Then the cold walls are not making it any better. What will happen if this test comes out positive? It won't be. I am the one that must stay positive. Still nothing. This thing better work. I only had a chance to grab one.

"Everything okay, Munisha?" Zaraiella asked.

"Yes, um did you do what I told you correctly? Tsk, I don't know why it's taking so long."

"I came back because I'm worried. Am I sick, what is that thing?"

"First of all, no you're not sick. Just…" I sighed. "Just need to check something."

"Come on down here, you two!" Mrs. Wilson shouts. "There has been a bad spill!"

"Be down there in a few, Mrs. Wilson!" I shouted. "Let me check this, and…still nothing."

"Am I sick, Munisha?"

"I told you no. It's nothing like that. Hopefully, Mrs. Wilson doesn't have all of us picking up grains of rice. You know they have weird ways of punishing us."

Why the hell was that test taking so long? My crazy sister probably ran water over it.

"Oh gosh! How did this happen?!" I asked, looking at the floor filled with mushy white stuff.

"Jason dropped it," Janice frowns. "Brothers, ugh..."

"Thanks a lot. Boys never do anything right."

"Quiet, M! I lost my balance."

"This porridge stuff is sticky," Zaraiella grumbled, teasing with Janice.

First, she had to pee on a weird stick, and now she is back to her normal jolly self. Her spirit energy just like Ms. Jezebel said, Well balanced and phenomenal.

"You got to be kidding me! Leaving town?! We need you and your help around man, and you know that!"

"Forgive me. The state is shapeshifting each day rapidly. I believe it's because of a S.I.L.O headquarters is near. Me and my son have to find another way."

Wow. Now I knew, Mr. Wilson was really mad.

"Ken, the whole world is like this," Mr. Wilson voiced, from the entrance room. "We must make the best of what we have, as a friendship and a team. We need you around here. At least in Maine."

"I know. I thought about it. Howdy, Sara. I"

"I heard the news next door," Mrs. Wilson says, giving Kenneth no eye contact.

"Kenneth, please. You have to reconsider this. We can make"

"My home is already on the site for auction. I wanted to tell you this sooner but didn't know how. Perhaps, maybe I can just put in a good word for you. Ya' know, tell the new shopkeeper you need some aid with you and your family. You know me, Tim. I'm a man of my word."

"And so am I. We need to stick together as we planned. Hmph, I'm not begging a man for a damn thing. Get out of my house, Kenneth. This isn't right."

"Tim"

"No, Sara. I need this disloyal guy out of here. I don't want that bad energy near me or my family. O, u, t, out, my friend!"

"Geez, I've never seen, Mr. Wilson angry like this before," I whispered, looking at the stunned family. "His eyes are about to pop out of his head."

"M, where are you going?"

"Oh, shut up."

"I'm sorry about all of this, Tim. I really am," Kenneth says as he opens his umbrella and looks back at us. "I am truly sorry you all."

"Yea, yea, I know you are! Get the hell off my porch. You're nothing but another weak citizen. Giving up when times get rough. We make ways around here, not giving in when it gets difficult. Feel sorry for your son. Ass."

"Tim, that just isn't fair. He came and apologized when he didn't have to."

"Sara...just. Really?! Aren't you kids supposed to be cleaning up?!"

He looks like he's about to lose it. "Boys always do things to make our lives harder. Clean up your side, Jason. Don't leave your pile for us!"

"What am I doing, M? They had nothing to do with it, Ma. I'll clean it up."

"When one person fail, we all fail in this house, son," Mr. Wilson chuckled. "For miss, walk away while I am speaking to you. Rules will be followed; this is my house, my kingdom."

"Tsk, some kingdom."

"Just for you, smart mouth. You can do the honors first and take out the garbage in the rain. Thank you. See Sara, we will have our authority back even if you decided to leave today. This is my kingdom and you will abide by my rules!"

"It's alright, Jason," I shook my head. "I got it."

Mr. Wilson must have stolen my period, that's why it's not coming on. Gosh, it's cold out here with this rain. People change, and I know I have over the years. It's nothing you can do about it. "Magic, Magic, are you out here?"

The trees were still whispering to me with the soft rain. I love it so much here with the peace but I cannot live stay with the an noyance and aggravation too much longer. "Why does it look like…what…the? I could have sworn. Oh no! That has to be them."

How did they find us? "Hey, hey! They're here! We have to leave!"

"Whose here?" Janice asked, looking out the window. "Mr. Kenneth?"

"S.I.L.O, it has to be them! They have some, some type of…I don't know. I saw them!"

"What?! No way, M."

"Zaraiella! Go upstairs and get your stuff. We have to go!"

"Now, young lady, what do you think you are doing?" Mr. Wilson asks with a frown then smirks.

"They're outside in the woods! Okay, go and look! Gather what you need, sis! Hurry up!"

"So, you two are leaving now?"

"Mr. Wilson, they're"

"What is this negative test about?" Mr. Wilson smirked, then frowned. "You can be rude with me, but fool around in my house?!"

"What the hell is wrong with you, man!" I said, pushing Mr. Wilson off of me.

"You hold your horses, missy. Do not ever raise your voice at me or touch me!"

"Dad, she's not lying! They're outside, coming from the main way out of here!"

"I saw them too, Daddy! Mommy is looking."

"What? What the hell is you all"

"EYYYGHHH!"

BANG

"Dad, don't go…Dad!"

The silence and despair feeling. My eyes widened and heart racing. "Zaraiella, go to the room."

"What are we going to do, Munisha?"

"Jason, your dad is not going to make it. Jason, come back!"

"YOU ALL KILLED MY WIFE!"

"DROP YOUR WEAPON!"

BANG BANG BANG

"Jesus. Dammit…Dad! No," Jason says with eyes tearing up. "We have to get out of here."

"How Jason? They're everywhere," I said holding on to Zaraiella from behind.

"The bathroom. We can get out from there."

"It's too high, Jason," I said, looking down and hoping there was a roof to the side.

"Look, we can use the shower curtain. We're getting out of here."

"Sniff…they killed, Mommy and Daddy."

"Janice, stop it," Jason mumbled. "We need to get out of here. Okay, go go. You first, Munisha."

"What about you?" I said while holding on to the side of the window.

"I will be down there. Go, hurry!"

"Oh gosh…"

"Jump down, M. Hurry!"

"Eygh…Okay okay. I'm fine. Zaraiella! Come on. I got you, sis. Come on! Run to the forest, I'll catch up. Come on, you two."

"I don't want to leave, Janice. I have to wait for them," Zaraiel la said.

Looking from both sides from behind the house, I don't know where they could pop up next. "Oh no. Janice…Jason. Hey, leave them alone!"

"Catch her!"

"Are you okay," I said. "Jason, come on! Jason?!"

"He said go. They were at the door." Janice says, rubbing the tears from her eyes and misty rain.

I didn't know if they took him. He knew we needed him more than anything. "I can't believe this. He will catch up with us."

S.I.L.O sending what it looked to be a truckload of men. How did they end up finding us again? Oh God, Mrs. Wilson, Mr. Wilson. What have these people done? Why could they not leave us in peace? We could only have peace when we are out in the woods. Early in the morning, with death on your mind, not knowing where to go nor even knowing if the parent of your child is alive, the ultimate heartache. "Janice, we have to go. We can't stay here."

"Daddy, Momma…."

"Please, Janice. We can't stay right here. They'll figure where we are. Come on, get up! Zaraiella, help her. I have to figure something out."

"Where do we go?" Zaraiella mumbled.

"Working on it. From this way, I have no idea to get to Ms. Jezebel's house. This rain isn't making it easy."

"We should try and get the car," Zaraiella said.

"No way. You didn't see how many people came out of the woods? At least five, I think. I am so sorry, Janice."

"Stop crying, Janice, please," Zaraiella says, hugging her best friend.

The cold rain falling from the trees felt extremely cold on my arms. As they always felt like bullets, hoping not from real ones. What a morning. It did not dawn on me that I pretty much left everything I had. The only thing in this sack I was able to take was my book, and a little dust. Can't even recall where I left the bracelet. Those people just take and take more. Please, Jason, don't allow me to believe they have taken you too.

"Munisha,"

"What is it, Zaraiella? Oh, just what I needed. It's about time sis you woke up." I smirked, with the utensil that help save my sister. I will claim another life with it, if I have to. "Okay, this path leads to the swamp. I want to try and go to Ms. Jezebel place."

"Who is that?" Janice whimpered.

"A good friend of mine. Only me and your brother have met her. She could probably give us some help get down, go go go."

"Is it them?" Zaraiella asked , putting her head against the wet dirt.

"Shoosh, sis."

"Centipede! Mmmhmm."

My sister is about to give us away. "Zaraiella. I told you," I said, holding Zaraiella's mouth shut.

"I heard something over here."

"Stay quiet," I whispered.

I couldn't tell where any one of the could me. They appeared invisible, though a weird reflection behind them gives them away, a little. With Ms. Jezebels weapon, I will spill as much blood as I must.

"Come on. Maybe it was a dumb animal."

I gasped. "Thank god, I"

"Halt! Come from under there!"

This is it. The freighting feeling from the soldier's energy and his rifle pointing at the last of my running days. At least Zaraiella and Janice could possibly still get away.

"You thought you could get away, didn't you? DROP THE KNIFE! Where are the others?!"

"I don't know…they're at the house," I said, holding up my hands as the soldier stepped closer.

"Don't play dumb with me! Where are the rest of your family?!"

"Go to hell!"

"Sweet talker. Get moving. We'll find em'."

"Just leave us alone. We have nothing."

"Whose we? Ah, they are out there. It's more than just you and this big ass dagger. Crap! What the hell?!"

A rock banging the soldiers' chrome black helmet left him spinning around to find where it came from.

"Oh, hello there. This your little sister? You look angry."

"Leave her alone!" Zaraiella shouted.

"ZARAIELLA JANICE, RUN! RUN!

BANG BANG BANG

"Let go, you stupid girl! Let go!"

"EYGH."

"Munisha!" Zaraiella cried out.

"Keep your damn face in the dirt until I say otherwise. Come here, little ones."

The wet dirt barely entering my mouth, I felt so weak. "Run! Get out of here!"

The detrimental feeling, being low as dirt and seeing my family in fear and in tears was tearing my soul apart.

"Now, I want you little girls to come with me. Be good, and I'll give you a nice treat later on. Now, come here."

"Don't do it…Zaraiella. Go…before"

"Shut up before you get them both AGHH.!"

"Don't ever touch her!" Jason says, stabbing the soldier from behind. "Zaraiella, Janice you alright?"

I should pour dust all in his eyes, may he never see again.

"AGHH!"

"What are you doing, M?! We have to get a move on!"

"I wanted to give him a taste of what they all deserve. "Jason, thank goodness!" I said, constricting my knight and shining armor.

"Come on, I got his assault. Let's go!" Jason said, grabbing my arm and forcing us to run through the rainy forest. "What did you blow in his face?"

"Can't explain now. I just wanted him to suffer."

"You all right?"

"Where is Mommy and Daddy?" Janice asked.

"Mom…Dad, I believe they have taken him. It's alright, Janice, we'll find him."

"You all, halt!" Another soldier says right when we thought we made it free.

BANG…BANG BANG BANG

"Where the hell do we go, Jason?!"

"I don't know, M! "Just keep moving!"

"Hold on, wait!"

The shooting pain. "Oh my gosh."

"What's wrong, M?"

"…My ankle"

Jason grimaces. "Here, come on," Jason says as he picks me up.

"HALT! YOU TWO, OR WE WILL OPEN FIRE!"

"Jason put me down. It's alright…it's alright."

What was the point? Us being killed or us being captured, then having our lives lived alternatively. I could not let them kill my husband or hurt, Zaraiella or Janice. At least they had gotten away. We tried.

"What's so funny, M?"

"It's just like the beginning. How the rainforest made me find you."

"I love you," Jason says, holding my left hand.

"I love you too, husband…" I smirked. "You did great."

"Get your hands up, both of you!"

BANG BANG BANG

BANG BANG…BANG BANG

Gunfire came from out of nowhere. The illusion that the trees opened fire on the soldiers and the lightning gave the idea of a guardian angel.

"Hey! Come on, hurry!" A man and woman holding guns said, along with Janice and Zaraiella, standing by the trees.

"You all alright? The man asked with a bandana over his face.

"We're alright," Jason replied. "Who are you?"

"Peter, and this here is my partner, Shadrine. "We heard the gunfire, and we knew someone needed some help. Shadrine, watch our six."

These saviors looked to be pure professionals. I am glad I could shoot off some rounds first, so it can help us be located. We would have been walking the opposite way.

"Munsiha, we made it," Jason comforted, smiling down at me.

I can feel his pain, hiding behind that smile. "I was beginning to believe I lost you."

"Not even close. I almost got caught, but they were going from room to room. Dad kept an underfloor hidden in the bathroom, I had to fit in quickly."

"Ooooh, so that what was in there. That squeak I kept hearing."

"You all were traced, most likely." Peter said.

"How?" Jason asked. "We didn't get the chip."

"That's good to know. However, they probably put something in your clothes you bought."

Finally making it out of the woods and seeing that they came with a jeep. One of the ones I always wanted, a pretty red or green one.

"You all hop on in quickly," Peter said, holding the door for us and rifle pointed towards the trees.

"Did they ever place a stamp on your car or any vehicle you all may have?" Shadrine asked, closing the door behind her.

"A matter of fact, yes," I said. "When we all went to the city, Jason, remember?"

"Yea, that's right. They put something on the windshield but that took it off."

"See, I knew it, Pete. That is what they are doing now. A sticker that is a no brainer, but they are fooling some independents with it."

"Hmph, if they are out here with any modernday car, they were already being traced."

"My Mom, it was her car," I said, looking at Jason. "We had it the whole time. We had it for years."

"That's right. They never came and bothered us, even right after the sticker. Also when me and M drove out to the city by ourselves. They just…I"

"As I said. S.I.L.O knew you all were in there the day you all had that car. It doesn't matter where you all bought it from. If it is a new modern car, or if the tracking system wasn't removed, you all were tracked since day one."

I placed my hands over my mouth, looking at Jason with his watery eyes. The years we lived in peace, no one ever came to bother us. Why now? Why not when we first came to Mr. and Mrs. Wilson place and lived? "I'm sorry. I am so sorry."

"M…M," Jason said, holding me close. "What are you two doing out here anyways? We are um…more than grateful."

"We're scouts. Technically we try and help those who need our help. Even those who are trying to succumb to S.I.L.O orders, we try to help those who refuse to be under their jurisdiction. There are many like us. You all will see soon. I see you all are shocked about the car," Peter said, looking at me through his rearview mirror. "If you all are curious. This is not rigged up with any type of tracker. We stay in the shadows from the system. Have you all seen any, weird things other than S.I.L.O around?"

"Not, really," Jason muttered. "Just these creatures that look like they came from them. Seen it twice."

"Exaclty! See that, Shadrine. The system of the beasts."

"What?" Jason asked. "Those creatures are meant to attack people?"

Peter sighs. "Not only that, but there are also made to feed on nature. With you all living out here, I believe that they place them to study how they will react on human nature itself. S.I.L.O, hmph, they don't care about anything. That is why we must do what we need to make a living. There are ways but it is difficult."

"We tried that. They…let's just say they taken everything. Now it is just me…my wife," Jason says, trying to smile. "And those two back there."

"Zaraiella, the one with all the hair, is my sister, and Janice is my husband's sister."

"What is wrong her?" Shadrine asked.

"We lost everything. Our mom and dad. They're…"

"Goodness," Shadrine muttered, looking back at us as she seemed to get teary eyed herself. "This is just a mess. Peter, we have to take them all the way."

"I know. That is the plan."

There is always a way. Jason and his parents constantly reminded me of that. "Where are we going?"

"There is a place not far from here where Shadrine and I keep to ourselves. We are limited on the people who can know about our camp. Just as we found you from S.I.L.O, we would have let you all go after. In favor, you all definitely need some help. The place isn't the best, but it will give you what you need for the time being. A new chance, for a new beginning."